WILDERS

Also by Brenda Cooper

Edge of Dark
Spear of Light

The Creative Fire
The Diamond Deep

Project Earth | Book One

WILDERS

BRENDA COOPER

an imprint of Prometheus Books
Amherst, NY

Published 2017 by Pyr®, an imprint of Prometheus Books

Cover illustration © Stephan Martiniere
Cover design by Nicole Sommer-Lecht
Cover design © Prometheus Books

This is a work of fiction. Characters, organizations, products, locales, and events portrayed in this novel are either products of the author's imagination or used fictitiously.

Inquiries should be addressed to

Pyr
59 John Glenn Drive
Amherst, New York 14228
VOICE: 716–691–0133
FAX: 716–691–0137
WWW.PYRSF.COM

21 20 19 18 17   5 4 3 2 1

Library of Congress Cataloging-in-Publication Data

Names: Cooper, Brenda, 1960- author.
Title: Wilders / by Brenda Cooper.
Description: Amherst, NY : Pyr, an imprint of Prometheus Books, 2017. | Series: Project earth ; book 1
Identifiers: LCCN 2017003389 (print) | LCCN 2017009268 (ebook) | ISBN 9781633882652 (paperback) | ISBN 9781633882669 (ebook)
Subjects: | GSAFD: Science fiction.
Classification: LCC PS3603.O5825 W55 2017 (print) | LCC PS3603.O5825 (ebook) | DDC 813/.6—dc23
LC record available at https://lccn.loc.gov/2017003389

Printed in the United States of America

To all those fighting for vibrant, healthy cities and sustainable wild lands.
In particular to E. O. Wilson and to Forterra.

PROLOGUE

The city sang a song of humanity. People and their companions sat in rounded robotic cars and talked together as they sped through the city on smart streets. Others rode a nearly infinite variety of wheeled devices on paths that ran by or between roads and through parks. These they variously pedaled and pushed or simply stood or sat upon. Singles and families alike walked through greenbelts stained orange and red with fall. Many delighted at the controlled chill that pinked their cheeks and the chance to show off their fall wardrobes. Most chose golds and greens and scintillating browns, but others fought the fall with pastel pinks and snowy whites. Some people chatted with other people, while others talked with their companion robots, with their dogs, or with their virtual coaches.

Many people moved less. They dove deep into the wells of themselves, painting and writing and searching for the next great idea, for the key to happiness, for the perfect body, the perfect fashion. Still others traversed the city's data and pulled out threads of information, suggesting ways to make it even better.

Some walked alone and unhappy. These were left to their own devices as long as they followed the city's simple rules and did not steal choices from anyone else.

Under the melody of humanity, the heartbeat systems of the city pumped water and waste, created oxygen, and ate extra carbon. The bones and structure started miles away, reporting and then damping extreme weather, controlling wind and rain and gloomy clouds from the snow-streaked Cascade Mountains to the wild Puget Sound. Automated decision makers in the city filled the air, danced between sensors, and raced through a tangled mesh of fiber optics that infused every street and building.

News packed the city, a glorious cacophony of conversation and facts. The people who owned property or businesses voted on ideas in their neighborhoods, and made change upon change, sometimes to fix problems and sometimes just for fun. This same social experiment filtered through everyone for votes on city leaders and laws.

Greens and blues imbued the city with a natural brightness. Grass lawns covered roofs, some bounded by community orchards of miniature trees no more than five feet tall and festooned with ripening yellow lemons, red apples, and sun-colored apprines. Veins of blue water crisscrossed the city almost like the roads.

A seldom-visible dome of managed air met the ground all around the city; Outside stayed Outside.

People could leave. They could take high-speed sleek hyperloops between cities, which meant never really leaving the protected Inside at all. They could kayak away, walk away, drive away, and even fly away. Even though they could do so, very few people did.

Most who did so never returned.

The very old remembered the times when the barriers between Inside and Outside were naturally permeable, when humans maneuvered cars by themselves, when the great preserves were ripped into being by force as nations everywhere started the great rewilding. But to everyone else, those times were no more than stories, tales of another year, easily dismissed and forgotten.

Those not born to the city had to prove their worth to get in. The tests had become quite difficult to pass as the world inside the cities became more interconnected and quick, more dependent on skills that could only be learned by living them.

Cities held most of the world's population. Human computing systems, blood and gut bacteria, vitamins and medicines, workouts, and infinite streams of data and entertainment flowed through the city like the milk of a mother's teat. Objects customized themselves to meet every whim and need of the city's many inhabitants.

Outside, the great wilding continued like a wrecking ball, encountering resistance from those who had been displaced, stalling in the still-wild weather, or failing, as human and machine alike struggled to comprehend the complexities of biological design and redesign. A dance of chaos and success, of tears and death and rebirth, orchestrated by a combination of NGOs, law enforcement, scientists, and human workers. Assistance came from robots designed to enforce the rules of wild places, to do the heavy work, the destroying work, and the building work. All of these together culled invasive species and managed native ones, counted bears and cougars and bobcats and coyotes. The loosely federated North American cities funded this effort, in hopes of long-term survival.

As fall prepared to give way to winter, the city appeared to be infinitely stable.

CHAPTER ONE

On the last morning of the easy part of her childhood, fifteen-year old Coryn Williams stood on the top of the Bridge of Stars and watched Puget Sound shiver with winter. From the fenced observation deck, the seawall below looked thin and foreshortened. Whitecaps punctuated the waves, whipped up by a wind Coryn couldn't detect. She knew what a breeze felt like, but not what wind that could whip creamed froth out of water might feel like. She imagined that it would pull at her skin and blow her hair around her face and try to force her to move with it.

Paula stood beside her, taller by far, dressed formally in a black uniform with white piping and her sea-blue scarf. She squinted as she took in the view, her smile slight but genuine. Her unblemished skin and perfect features could belong to a model, but instead they showed that she was Coryn's companion. In spite of her nature, she seemed be genuinely interested in the horizon, the white ferries that plied the choppy water, and the pleasure of standing on top of the highest spot in Seacouver.

Coryn had finished her last assignment of the year this morning and sent it off to be graded. It was good, and better yet it was *done*. She had written about the great restoration with the help of her older sister, Lou, who had her own rather strong ideas. Coryn had compromised with her on the paper, accepting that the rewilding wasn't even halfway done but not that progress had stopped and perhaps even fallen backward. Standing here on this bridge, with the vast sound to look out over and, beyond all that water, the white-capped mountains of the peninsula, she was even more sure she had been right: the city would be okay.

The bridge under them had stood since before she was born, the tallest bridge in Seacouver, starting just north of historic Pike Place, curving up and over the city in graceful loops, and landing in West Seattle. Three midspan spiral ramps joined the bridge deck to significant old-Seattle neighborhoods, like ribbons falling onto the city. An artist had designed the Bridge of Stars, a scenic skyway designed for walkers and cyclists and runners.

Lou couldn't be right. Surely Seacouver would continue forever, or at least for years and years into the future, more years than Coryn would ever see.

Up here, she felt like she could touch the roof of the world. She'd earned this perch; only the fit could get here on their own. Coryn's thighs still trembled a little from the long climb up on bicycles.

Paula, as always, seemed to understand her unspoken feelings. "You are conflicted. Does it feel good to be finished?"

"Oh, yes!" It did feel good. The paper had been a fight—they'd moved in the middle of it, and all the packing and unpacking, while familiar, took time. Her mother begged her father to move them regularly, as if the next house would be just right.

Coryn had stayed up every night for the last two weeks to finish on time. "I thought it would feel entirely different to be in high school."

Paula raised an only slightly too-perfect dark eyebrow. "Does it feel different at all?"

"Not really. Now I have two weeks off, and that feels good, but every other year I've had two weeks off after finishing up. Maybe they should give us a longer break. After all, high school's a big deal."

"Don't get too full of yourself," Paula replied. She leaned over the bridge as if contemplating the idea of freedom from gravity. The wind plucked stray strands of dark hair and blew them around while Paula tried in vain to tuck them back into her bun. "Did you know that you always come to where you can see out of the city when a big thing happens in your life?"

"Do I?"

"You went to the edge of the seawall when you passed elementary school, you rode your bike all the way to the edge and back when Lou went to summer camp in Tacoma, and now you're way up here, where you can see over and past the entire downtown. Where are you going to go when you finish high school? Space?"

"Silly robot. That would take years of school." And money they didn't have. She squinted, wondering if a largish black thing she saw might be a boat. "I'd like to see a whale."

"They would appear very small from way up here."

"There was a baby orca born last week. A girl, no less." Coryn had printed a picture and pasted it on her bathroom wall beside a pic of wild horses running free in eastern Washington, and another one of a twenty-foot-long great white shark off of Guadalupe Island in Baja, California.

"You're going to be late for your own graduation party."

Coryn didn't respond. It would drive Paula slightly nuts—it always annoyed her when Coryn refused to do what was expected. But this was her day, not Lou's. Besides, she wanted to burn the horizon into her memory.

Her mother hated the city, and so Coryn did most of her exploring with Paula. This particular bridge cost credits to access and she couldn't just come up here any day she wanted. Her mom had given her the money for the trip, bending over her with a sweet smile. "Your first junior-high graduation present," she'd called it. She had smelled of soap and medicine and unhappiness. But then, Mom always seemed to be unhappy these days. Dad, too. Coryn often felt like she lived in a different world than the one her parents inhabited. What was there to be afraid of, after all? The city was full of fascinating things, and if she got bored of real life, there were a million virtual worlds. More.

She didn't really want to go home, not even for a special graduation dinner. Her parents would find some way to ruin the evening.

While Coryn counted ten long, slow breaths, she stared at the joining of sea and sky, at the wind-torn waves, at the far land where Hurricane Ridge had been slammed by its first snowstorm a few days ago. Bits of white still sparkled in the sun, matching the whitecaps, and a pale sky hung over the entire scene. "I want to watch this forever."

"We have to go," Paula insisted. "Your mother will be upset with you."

Coryn turned to her, a slight spark of anger infusing her voice. "That's not my fault."

"Which has nothing to do with anything."

Coryn stared out over the water, determined to remember the sharp ridges of the Olympic Mountains, the rippling white-caps, and the fascinating, unexpected gardens and pools on top of the biggest buildings. "I can't wait until I'm eighteen and you can't tell me what to do any more."

Paula eyed her with the infinite patience of a companion robot. "Lou will be worried."

Yes. And Lou would make her party fun. Even though she couldn't depend on her parents to be in a good mood, she could depend on Lou.

She reluctantly turned away and pulled her AR glasses on. They were required for transportation, even biking. The city saw more clearly through her glasses than she did, always ready to keep her safe. Lines of travel and traffic began to paint themselves in a light wash over the real world, showing the foot and bike traffic on the bridge and, far below, the heavier city traffic. Green for cars, blue for bikes, yellow for peds, red for trains and other mass-transit. She swung her leg over her bike, settled her hands on the grips, and blinked twice to tell the city she was ready to go.

Maybe Lou would be home by now.

She pushed off into an opening in the bike traffic to glide down the long, gentle slope toward the South Seattle streets. The overlays on her vision sparked and changed as she moved, traffic control directing the complex dance of transportation. A blue light blinked to show her Paula had started down as well.

Wheels thrummed and wind pulled her hair back and whipped it against her cheeks. As she neared the bottom, the ramp plunged into the city, housing and stores rising around her as she powered down through skyscrapers.

At the bottom of the bridge she slowed precipitously, barely managing to stay on her bike, cutting it close enough for traffic control to scream in her ear. She frowned, slid right, and almost fell, then headed home at a more dignified pace. Down here in the crowds, the city would notice and record safety risks, and she hated drawing attention.

Fifteen minutes later, she turned onto her family's current street, Paula right behind her.

Blue and red circles of light stunned her eyes, the primary-school colors of ambulances and police cars. Warnings flashed in her peripheral vision. She squinted and rode forward. The city allowed her through while it detoured others right and left.

As she drew closer to home, a deep dread made her want to stop. She didn't, but her thighs felt as if she wore stones on her feet instead of neon yellow sports shoes with purple laces.

Cars had chosen to park at odd angles, blocking the street. Men and women and robots in uniforms padded in and out of her house.

Maybe it was just an AR hack.

She ripped the glasses off her face.

Blue and red light washed across her face, forcing her to squint.

Someone spotted her. Lou.

She stood on the sidewalk, shaking, fists balled at her side, her hair wilder than usual, some of it falling over her thin face. Her blue eyes looked bright and wide. Red handprints smeared her shirt.

Coryn's bike clattered on the street as she raced into her sister's arms. Lou smelled of blood and fear. She felt like metal in Coryn's arms, like the unyielding bridge, even though tears ran down her face and fell onto Coryn's cheeks. Coryn's breath came fast and she shivered, rooted on the street, nothing existing in that moment except her sister.

Paula grabbed both of their shoulders and hissed, "Stay here." She marched straight into the house.

"What happened?" Coryn whispered.

"They . . . they died. Someone killed them, I think. I don't know. I couldn't stay. I came into the house and there was blood everywhere and blood on Mom's face." Her words stopped as she heaved for breath and clutched Coryn even closer. "Blood on her shirt and everywhere, everywhere, oh Coryn, it was everywhere. I've got it on me." She pushed Coryn a little away and looked down. "And now you've got it on you, on your shirt; we're stained with it."

Lou was still seventeen. In a few months she would be an adult. Lou's head rested on top of Coryn's and Coryn's arms circled her lower waist, her fingers running along Lou's backbone.

Coryn watched the crowd seethe with uniforms and onlookers. When Paula finally came back outside, she wore one of her strict robotic expressions. It was the same one she used when she was furious with Coryn or Lou. "You can't go in. I'll take you up on the roof, and we'll get some food, and we'll wait together. The police will come find us as soon as they can."

Coryn didn't want to see whatever Lou had seen. Lou never came undone like this, never lost it, never cried. As frightened as she was about her parents, seeing Lou cracked into pieces was . . . impossible.

Lou always led. Always. Except now Lou trudged behind Paula with her head down, shoulders drooping, one hand holding Coryn's loosely.

Paula drove them slowly and inexorably through the gathering crowd and away from the sirens. She took them into the apartment building next door to theirs and up the elevators to the roof. She had them move like they had when the girls were little, all in a line: Lou in front, then Coryn, then Paula watching over them both.

Lou sobbed and sobbed, blowing her nose. Still, she led them carefully through the patio tables. Coryn tripped on a table-leg and Paula caught her halfway down, a graceful arm appearing for Coryn to grasp onto before she landed in a flowerbed. A short bridge joined two rooftops. As they crossed it, Coryn looked down to where the revolving colored lights illuminated the gathering crowds and saw her bicycle on the ground, unlocked and orphaned. She had a sudden urge to turn around and put it away.

A few of their neighbors had come up onto the roof as well, people Coryn recognized but didn't know well. One couple got up as if planning to speak to them, but Paula blocked them, murmuring soothing words.

The robot directed the girls to a table in the middle of the roof and they sat silently.

A faraway look came over Paula, her eyes fastening on the horizon, or maybe on the thin ribbon of bridge far above them. Coryn knew the look; Paula was getting a lot of information and processing it. She'd notice if her charges left, or any kind of danger approached, but she probably wouldn't demand anything from Coryn and Lou for a few minutes.

Lou looked even more lost in thought than the robot. A cat worked its way over to the girls, rubbing up against them both and head-butting Lou until Lou dropped her death-grip on Paula's hand and touched the cat's cheek. The cat stayed near them for a long time, circling and then stopping for pets and then circling them again. Its wide, golden eyes matched the brown and gold stripes on its tail and forelegs and contrasted with the brown fur that felt like silk under Coryn's fingers.

"Be careful," Paula admonished them. "That's got to be someone's pet gene mod."

"Why?" Lou asked.

"It's too perfect," Paula said.

"Like you?" Coryn shot back, immediately regretting it.

"Of course."

She didn't call for an apology the way she usually did, but Coryn gave her one anyway. "I'm sorry, silly robot." She had to work hard to get the word through her thick throat.

Paula smiled in approval and watched the girls entertain themselves with the cat until it appeared to get bored and walked off.

Even though she hadn't known the cat, she felt bereft as it walked away and left them alone. They were lost. Alone. Everything had just changed.

Eventually, two policewomen made their way carefully through the crowded rooftop, one for each girl. The youngest one knelt by Coryn, a beautiful woman with the dark eyes and the old-amber complexion of an East Indian. "Hello," she said in a honey-soft voice, a sad voice, "I'm Mara." She knelt down so her eyes were even with Coryn's. "You know that something happened to your parents?"

"They're dead," Coryn saw no reason to pretend she didn't know. She'd known since she saw the blood on Lou's shirt.

The policewoman's eyes softened, and she bent her head and made notes on her slate.

"Why did they die?" Coryn asked.

"Do you mean how?" Mara asked.

She already knew that. Lou had told her they were killed. But they were just normal people, and that shouldn't have happened. "No. I want to know why."

Mara shook her lovely head; her thick, dark hair swished back and forth across her navy-blue uniform. She took Coryn's hands in hers. Her long nails were painted a bright pink, and the little finger and the thumb on her right hand had started chipping.

Everything Coryn could see looked like that, colorful and crisp. The street lights shone unusually bright, with pale haloes around them. The cat stood on the edge of the roof, flicking its long tail back and forth. The beer in a nearby glass glowed yellow-orange.

Her parents were dead.

Mara reached for her, but Coryn turned away. Paula stood right behind her, opening her arms. Coryn leapt up into them. She gave the robot her weight as if she were still a small child, clutching Paula as if her life depended on it. She buried her head in the robot's soft shoulder and squeezed her eyes shut.

If only they were back on top of the bridge, with the wind blowing beyond them and the possibility of a whale.

CHAPTER TWO

Coryn stood at the single small window in the room she and Lou shared in the orphanage, leaning on the silvery sill and looking down at a ragged community garden three stories below her. Two or three of the raised beds were bright with flowers, but the rest looked ragged and thin. One held only brown bushes too far gone for recovery but not yet weeded out. It bugged her; weeding was one of the city's assigned chores she had chosen when she was ten, and she had loved to weed for years, making up silly songs as she cleaned and straightened beds. The orphanage's chore list was all internal, like bathroom cleaning and neatening the pantry, but weeds still demanded to be pulled.

The room smelled of antiseptic and something flowery, and the cold glass and metal reminded her of a doctor's office instead of a home.

She was alone. Lou and Paula had gone together to find them something to drink besides water.

An orphanage. Who would have thought they could end up someplace so cold? It all seemed surreal.

If her parents were still alive, if this was one of their homes, the room would be full of color. Her mother liked browns and off-whites, with teal accents and soft lighting.

Coryn still couldn't remember the last thing she'd said to her parents.

Old, good memories surfaced over and over. Her mom reading to her on her fifth birthday. Her dad feeding them juice and fresh bread from the corner bakery for breakfast.

The hole where her parents had been ran deep. Even though she'd managed to sleep last night, it was digging at her consciousness again right now, making her think silly little things, like how her father would have taken some of the garden, even just a row, and cleaned it up. He would have done that even if they weren't staying. But what did it matter now? He would never garden again.

She glanced at her wristlet. No messages. Nothing. No one came to see them. People Coryn had thought of as friends had messaged them a few times, awkward little messages that soon stopped.

She cringed as she heard the high whine of a small drone through the half-closed doorway. It belonged to one of the other orphans. Ghit. He was such a deep Autie the city had assigned him a keeper drone, and apparently it had tried to find the noisiest one possible. One of the other girls, one of the mean ones, named Justina, told her and Lou that he'd been beaten so often as a child that his parents had given him up and moved away.

Ghit poked his head into the doorway. A deep red scar marred his left cheek and his gaze always looked wary. "Killed parents."

He meant, "Did you find out who killed your parents?" but he never spoke in full sentences. Lou was always after the answer to that particular question, but Coryn was always the one Ghit asked. He asked her a few times every week. She sighed. "I don't know. When I find out, I'll kill them."

He looked fascinated, as if he'd never heard her say that before. "Could you?"

"Of course not."

Thankfully, Ghit withdrew and pulled the door closed behind him.

She had no idea what she'd do when she found out. She just wanted to be busy and get past the grief that nagged at her. Lou had turned it to anger, and the anger to nervous action, but try as she might, Coryn couldn't really get angry about it. Just sad.

Surely anger would be easier.

She returned to staring down at the entry street, willing her sister and her protector to come home soon.

Paula came back in half an hour, carrying ginger-flavored drinks from a corner store and sweet plums from one of the nearby roof orchards. Lou didn't follow until long after dark. As soon as she came in, she grabbed Coryn by the hand and walked her outside. The orphanage's back porch jutted onto a small lawn beside a thin street that hardly ever saw any car traffic. As they stepped through the door, a long ribbon of bicycles spun by, flashing spandex and spinning blue and sparkling gold wheel lights. In their wake, it grew quiet, windless, and hot.

Lou led Coryn past the chairs and sat on the railing, looking up at the pale, fuzzy stars in the night sky. "Do you still want to know how Mom and Dad died?" she asked in a low whisper. "Really want to know?"

Coryn suddenly felt as cold as if she'd just inhaled a whole scoop of frozen cream. She stuttered. "If we know, maybe Ghit will stop asking."

Lou didn't even crack a smile. She seemed infused with sadness, her face still and shocked. She brushed a strand of hair away from Coryn's eyes and, finally, looked directly at her. "Do you?"

"Yes." Her voice sounded small so she said it again, a little louder. "Yes!"

"You're not going to like it."

"So tell me anyway. I can take it. I can tell you hate it. I can see it in your eyes and I can smell it on your breath. Whiskey?"

"I only had a little." Lou looked down at her feet. "I needed courage to say this to you."

Coryn chewed on her lower lip. "All right."

"Remember how much Mom hated the city?"

Coryn sighed. "Yes." Lou hated it too, but Coryn didn't bother to say so. They both knew. "Mostly she didn't hate the city itself, but she hated living with so many people."

Lou raised an eyebrow. "I think that too, but I didn't know you picked it up."

"I'm not stupid."

Lou laughed a little, and exhaled; her breath smelled like stale beer. Coryn wrinkled her nose.

"The coroner ruled on it last night."

And clearly Lou knew what they had said and had swallowed the secret until now. Coryn played along. "So how did you find out what they said?"

"I have a new friend—he's wicked good with city morgue data."

"Yuck."

"There's a lot of reasons to know about dead people. Like why they died, and if they died of a disease or if old age got them . . ."

"You're procrastinating," Coryn said. "I told you I can take it." She stood up, pacing back and forth on the uneven surface, angry at Lou for holding out on her.

Lou drew herself up to her full height—still a head taller than Coryn—and stopped looking at the stars long enough to meet Coryn's eyes. The low light turned her blue eyes colorless as glass. Her lips thinned to lines; she looked more like a grownup than she usually did. "They said . . ." Lou hesitated. Her face screwed up and the next words came out more slurred than any of the others had. "They wrote in the report that . . . Mom and

Dad killed themselves. Or more precisely, they killed each other. A mutual suicide pact kind of thing."

"On my graduation day?" Coryn blurted.

Lou had the grace not to comment. She clasped her hands and rested her chin on her raised index fingers.

Coryn sank down into one of the chairs. The weight that had followed her around since that awful day drew her down so far she felt as if she might sink through the chair and through the painted concrete floor of the porch and into the earth and worms below, and on through to the very center of the earth.

Above her, as if speaking from far away, Lou said, "I didn't know she hated the city more than she loved us."

Unbidden, Coryn's arms and legs curled inward; she sank to the porch, a small compact ball, heavy with grief, protecting a hole in the very center of herself. This was worse than the pain the day they died. Deeper. That had been incomprehensible, and this she understood. Of course this was what they had done.

Lou stared down at her, expressionless.

Coryn couldn't move.

Lou extended a hand, which looked outsized through the haze of Coryn's tears. She reached up and took it. Lou's hand felt strong, warm, sweaty, and alive.

Lou pulled, but she couldn't budge Coryn, still curled tightly except for the one arm extending up toward Lou.

"Stretch your legs," Lou almost yelled. "Open your shoulders."

Coryn tried.

"Get up!" Lou took in a deep breath. "Let it go."

And then, as if following Lou's commands, all of the weight and all the grief fell away from her. In its place, anger pulled her up to standing, made her stomach sour and her fists clench.

Anger felt good. She's been hungry for the heat of it, for the life that came with it.

She wanted to hit something.

Her mother had left her for no good reason at all.

Depression. Her mother had even said the word a few times.

Depression. Depression. Depression.

Coryn had thought it was like a cold. Her mom took medicine for it, and shouldn't that have made it all better?

She stood in the warm city night under the stars and she was mad as hell. She stood there for a lot of breaths. Sweat ran down her shoulder blades and the dried streaks of her tears cracked on her cheeks. Her balance began to come back, and she smelled the clean, oily air and heard the hum on traffic a few streets away. She turned to Lou, and quite carefully stated, "Fuck."

Lou listed to the right.

Coryn took her in her arms and rocked her. It felt like holding a tree while it tried to fall, but then Lou found her feet. Coryn rocked her back and forth, rocking her bigger, older sister like a baby.

Lou had always been the strong one, but right now—in this minute—Coryn was stronger. She could feel the shift, big as an earthquake. She felt herself giving to Lou and Lou taking.

CHAPTER THREE

Coryn woke up in a cold sweat, unable to sleep. She stood up and stared out at the empty, dark street. Lou was about to graduate. Coryn had three years left here, and those would be alone. Surely Lou wouldn't stay here after her finals. She hardly ever stayed now—she wasn't in her bed yet, and it must be after midnight.

What if she didn't even stay close?

Every graduating student had to declare what they were doing next by the time they graduated. They could pick a job, a year of approved travel, more school. An infinite number of choices, nearly. But they had to choose something. The city provided a basic stipend for everyone. The lowest was basic-basic, and the city added to it for risky or difficult careers, or subtracted as people made money working for corporations or in their own businesses.

No one with an able body and mind was allowed to do *nothing* before they were old. Sloth had been experimented with right after the basic program started, and nothing had turned out to be a lousy thing to pay people for.

So Lou had to choose something.

Light came on slowly, brightening the tiny room a little. Lou's bed was still neatly made, ready for morning inspection. Paula stood in the corner, watching the doorway. "Were you dreaming?" she asked.

"No. Worrying. What will Lou do?"

"She hasn't told me anything."

Which meant Paula might know something, but if so, she wasn't saying. "Damned robot."

Every time Coryn had asked Lou, Lou had turned the question around on her. Since she had no idea what she wanted to do, and two years to decide in, she refused to answer, so neither of them had an opening for the very real conversation Coryn felt sure they needed to have. She glared at Lou's empty bed before she fell back down into her own and pulled the covers over her head.

The very next morning, Lou asked Coryn out to breakfast. She treated

Coryn to Sirella's, one of the best breakfast places within three miles of the orphanage. Lou wore new-printed jeans and a simple long-sleeved shirt and an old denim jacket she'd loved for years. She had pulled her red hair up in braids and piled it on her head. She didn't dress up often; it worried Coryn. When she suggested, "Coryn, have the French toast and fresh blueberries," Coryn shuddered, even more sure this breakfast wouldn't end well.

It wasn't that Coryn minded the comfort food. Dependent students were paid far less than workers, and she hadn't had such rich food for at least a week. But surely this breakfast was about Lou's choice, and it would change things. It mattered.

When Lou hadn't revealed anything by the time they were halfway through breakfast, Coryn's food began to taste like paper. She took a deep breath and asked, "So what are you going to do?"

Lou put her fork down. "You know I hate it here."

"Lots of people don't like the city, but they stay."

"You love it."

Coryn swallowed. "It's not as easy to love as it used be."

She didn't love Kent at all, not really. Not like Seattle itself. The girls her age here were meaner and harder. They teased her. But she hadn't talked about that to Lou, and she wasn't going to start now. "What are you going to do?" she whispered.

"I'm going to work for the Lucken Foundation."

"Which one is that?"

"It's one of the conglomerates. I think it's owned by four of the philanthropist families. Maybe five. I'll probably get all of that at orientation. They've taken on wilding one of the biggest unbroken reclaimed spots in the country. It used to be part of three states."

"Is it nearby?"

Lou leaned forward, steepling her hands. "Yes."

Coryn thought for a moment. She did know her geography. "The Palouse Reservation, which includes parts of Promise, Oregon, and Idaho. It used to be Indian country, and then it was farm country, part of Breakaway Promise, and then it was all taken back, right?"

Lou smiled at her. "It's all NGO now. The wilding center is on RiversEnd Ranch."

Coryn closed her eyes to block out the excitement on Lou's face. "That's all the way across the state." The Palouse region was huge. Miles of rolling hills with three thousand foot passes, few roads, and fewer people. The Snake River ran through part of it, and the Columbia bordered it, and maybe another river, but she couldn't remember the name. So much space. She picked a few leftover blueberries up from around the bits of French toast on her plate, trying to imagine what so much space might look like. Maybe it would be like standing on top of the Bridge of Stars or something. "What will you do?"

"They'll train me, and then I'll protect the land."

Even though she couldn't tell what that much open space would feel like, she could picture Lou in a uniform, all formal and maybe even with a knife and a canteen, and with her hair slicked back in a red ponytail.

Lou looked guarded, her face tightly controlled and her eyes hard. "I won't be able to come back for a long time. It's a basic-basic job. I'll get some of my living expenses for free. If I save half of the rest, I can come back and be here when you graduate."

The words battered her like physical blows. Coryn stuck a fork in a piece of French toast and pushed it around on her plate, getting the syrup and butter to ride ahead of it like a brown wave. She took a bite, chewing slowly, unable to think of what to say.

She couldn't fight Lou. Lou had always been unhappy. She'd always been obsessed with Outside, and she'd always planned to travel. If their parents were still alive, Coryn wouldn't even be thinking twice about it. Well, she would. She'd be happy for Lou.

"Look," Lou said, "you have Paula. I even checked again. You own her. Mom and Dad owned her outright and you got her. You remember that, don't you?"

"Yes." It had been a serious meeting somewhere in the unhappy and lost time between being sent to the orphanage and finding out her parents were suicides. Adults in suits had told them both about the few things they had left. Lou got stuff like small kitchen appliances, which she sold as soon as she could, and their dad's leather coat, which she kept. Coryn got Paula, but she'd had Paula for years so it didn't feel like an inheritance. If she had even thought for a minute she might lose Paula she would have been frantic, but she didn't imagine that until after they told her it wouldn't happen.

They each got to pick a pair of their mother's earrings. Lou sold her pair right away, while Coryn tucked hers into an old purse. Everything else went to the city for a variety of reasons Coryn didn't understand, perhaps because she really didn't care to.

Lou worried at her lower lip. "You'll be all right."

Coryn tried to find a smile to put onto her face. She managed to hold her features still long enough to agree. "I'll be all right."

"Of course you will," Lou snapped, and looked away.

She wouldn't. "What made you go now?"

Lou lost some of her serious face. "I can't stay. That's all."

"You can stay for me."

Lou looked away. "I hate this place. I really, really hate it. If I stay, maybe I'll do what Mom and Dad did. I don't want to do that to you."

That stopped Coryn, but only for a second. Her voice rose. "You wouldn't! I know you would never leave me alone like that." Just the idea froze her from the inside out. "You would never do that. You couldn't. Not ever. Promise?"

Lou put a hand on her arm. "Shhhh . . . calm down."

Coryn bit her lip, struggling to stay calm. Already, the couple next to them was peering their way, faces drawn in curious frustration.

"I have to go," Lou whispered. "I have to get out of here."

"You can't," Coryn replied.

"You'll be okay. This is a really good opportunity. They only take ten new people a year. I had to apply, and I got in." She leaned forward. "I got in. They want me."

Coryn sat back, watching her sister closely. Lou had always wanted to be a Wilder, had always wanted to be on her own and away from their parents, but Coryn had always thought they'd leave together, after she grew up.

Lou smiled. "I get to ride horses."

That stopped Coryn. Horses. She couldn't compete with horses.

"If you wait a few years, do something else, I could go with you." She sounded pathetic, so she shut up, waiting.

Lou clamped her mouth shut. Her eyes brightened, and a tear formed in one of them but didn't fall.

They watched each other. Lou's gaze was steady and sad and she held herself so still she could almost be a robot.

Coryn heard her own breath, started counting.

Maybe Lou would relent.

Instead, before Coryn got to twenty breaths, she smiled the saddest smile that Coryn had ever seen on her, and then she went back to eating.

Coryn watched her, wishing she knew what to say. She tried some small talk, but every phrase seemed like the words of a stranger.

Lou looked up, her eyes red but her cheeks dry and her jaw tight with resolve. "I would take you if I could."

It didn't matter. She couldn't leave now. Without her high school diploma she wouldn't even get basic-basic. She'd starve or get kicked out of the city. "Really?"

Lou touched the back of Coryn's hand with the tip of her index finger. "Really. I'll write to you. But you know I don't belong here, and that you do. You know I can't stay with you and you can't stay with me. So I might as well go. I'll think of you every day, little sis. I will."

Coryn bit her lip and took a deep trembling breath. "I'll think of you, too." Lou looked away, and Coryn knew there was more. "When are you going?"

"Tomorrow. I finished my classes early, and they want me to start work."

"Really? You can do that? Just leave?"

Lou looked miserable. Her voice shook. "Take care of Paula and let Paula take care of you."

Coryn's throat clogged with words she didn't want to say.

Lou lifted her hand. "I swear I will be here if you really need anything. Just call me. I'll come."

Coryn managed to break the logjam in her throat. "Okay. I'll come for you if you need me. I'll find you."

Lou shook her head. "It's way too dangerous Outside."

"And you think the city is safe?"

The people at the table next to them stared. The waitress came over and practically snatched at their plates. "Are you finished?"

Lou said, "Yes," and the last bite of Coryn's French toast disappeared.

Lou stood up and offered her a hand, which Coryn refused. On the way out, Lou leaned over and said, "I'll send you messages."

"Okay." She wanted Lou gone. "Have fun," she whispered. "Save the world."

Lou laughed. "I don't know if that's possible anymore."

They stood outside the restaurant, the late morning sun painting warmth on Coryn's back. Purple globes of great allium flowers bigger than her fists lined the walkway, and beyond them a whole garden of fruit trees bore green apples, oranges, and avocados. "Sure it is. It's getting better."

"If you say so."

This was the same argument they'd had about her last junior high school paper. "We're not doomed. Things are *better* than they used to be. All the news says so."

"And the naive little girls believe it."

Before Coryn could respond, Lou turned and walked away. She didn't turn around even once, but then Lou almost never let her feelings show. Coryn watched her disappear down the street and fade into the crowd. She wasn't even going toward the orphanage, so who knew when she'd be home.

A small part of Coryn wanted to die right then, so she wouldn't have to wake up alone in the city. The only family she'd have left would be Paula, and for all that Paula was, she wasn't alive.

She allowed herself three dry sobs and wiped her eyes. She would be okay. She would be okay. She would not turn out like her mom, crazy and depressed and self-obsessed enough to die on her daughter's graduation day.

Right in that moment, she felt more alone than ever, more alone than the day her parents died. Damn Lou. Damn her mom and dad.

She drew a deep breath. She had Paula. Her dad had always told her to use her resources. He had given her Paula. She would use Paula to train her to be strong. For one, Paula could help Coryn keep moving.

Maybe she should start riding her bicycle again.

Or run.

Or something.

She would be all right. She would.

She slid her VR glasses on and tuned them to mirrors, putting on some of her favorite music and trying to walk on the beat. The familiar, friendly, distant city surrounded her, and she fell into its data streams and walked, and walked, and walked.

CHAPTER FOUR

Coryn's feet pounded on the pale blue running surface on the north side of Queen Anne Hill. Her arms pumped, her hair whipped back from her face. Tree branches arched above her, providing shade. Virtual fairies and elves hung from them, clapping and singing and sometimes dropping down and chasing her. They were real enough that she heard the patter of their feet and the slightly off-key notes in their songs. But if she reached for one it faded into a smear of color as her hand passed through it.

Since it was summer she had a week free of the orphanage for vacation, and Paula had chosen the central city core for a training location. Not quite a real vacation, but it fit in her budget if they found temporary housing. Besides, she could see the Bridge of Stars from here, and of course everything was brighter and newer and bigger than Kent. After two years of running, Coryn's body moved easily, her muscles fluid and lean, her joints limber. Running made her feel like a bird, free and open and far away from the orphanage and the faceless social workers and the dotty old minder robot that manned the door. Running felt like fire and happiness, like purpose.

Nothing like hours and hours of endorphins to stave off the darkness of being alone. She'd gotten good at it, too. She'd become fast. Whenever she ran on safe enough paths, she used an enhanced AR world to hype her adrenaline.

Anything to give her more strength to make the decisions that were threatening to paralyze her. This would be her last summer as a child. Senior year would be hard. Then, next spring, her own time to choose would come up.

She reached up for bright yellow butterfly and batted at it, surprised when it turned out to be real and flew up and way.

Paula ran about twenty strides behind Coryn, her dark hair up in a bobbed ponytail and her robotic feet bare. At the moment, she played protector and trainer but not friend. Also, goad. Coryn ran until Paula's voice, linked into her earpieces, called out. "Time for a breather."

"Yes'm. I can go farther."

"If you rest, you'll go even farther."

"I hate it when you tell me what to do."

"I know. But you do want to stop."

"You know everything?"

"No."

Coryn smiled and slowed to a fast walk, pulled off her glasses, and the world returned to a mundane state with no particular visual surprises. Her breath came fast but not quite gasping; her muscles felt oiled and ropy.

Paula came up beside her, her steps light and easy even though she was almost twice Coryn's weight. She wore the smile she chose when she thought Coryn should be pleased. "You have a message from Lou."

"About time. Did you read it?"

"Are you giving me permission?"

"Sure. It's all roses, right?"

"Let me see." Paula paused, obviously reading, and then summarized. "She's got a new horse she likes. A pinto, like an Indian pony. A brown and white one. She sent a picture. She's been assigned to work on wolves this summer, and of course, you know that makes her happy. The wilding—that's what she calls it now instead of rewilding—the wilding is going well, even though they are a little behind. She says there's a lot of work to do. She met some people from Portland at a campout last weekend."

"At least she wrote." At first, Lou had written once a week, then she'd gone to once a month, and this one came three months after the last one. "Nice to know she's alive." In truth, she had been worried.

"Be glad she wrote."

"I am. I just wish she'd come back for a visit."

"I know."

Paula wasn't even breathing hard. She breathed—all companion robots breathed, since it was part of their cover as almost-human. Some even breathed harder with exertion. But Paula might as well have been walking for the last three hours. She sounded calm. "Are you going to write back?"

"In a few months."

Paula's facial expression showed what she thought of that answer.

"Hey—I always write back to Lou right away. She doesn't write me so fast."

"You might have more free time."

"I might. Maybe I'll answer her tonight. I don't have anything as cool as pinto horses and wolves to tell her about." Coryn reached into the small pouch attached to her running belt and pulled out an energy gel. She squeezed it into her mouth, puckering her lips at the sour taste. Paula handed her water, which she sipped on slowly, three times. Her own little ceremony. "All right. Let's go."

"Fifteen more kilometers."

"Ten."

"Seventeen."

"Fourteen."

"The course ends in fifteen. Go."

Coryn fit her headset back on, dialed in jungle animals, and set the AR so a black leopard with golden eyes would leap at her from behind any time she slowed below her target pace. She grinned and took off.

About three minutes later, just as she felt the energy gel's sweet heat give her a boost, a small figure passed her. The woman's gray-braided head came no higher than Coryn's shoulder, but her legs were almost a blur. Surprised, Coryn leaned into her own run and picked up the pace. Even though she worked as hard as she could, it took five long minutes to catch the old woman, who didn't bother to slow down at all. She moved so smoothly that the Coryn almost cursed her for being a robot. But robots didn't sweat, and they also generally didn't have long dripping braids of gray hair.

Coryn put her head down and drove her breathing low into her belly. She found a painful, but faster, pace.

Her breath burned too hot for her to talk, so she finished the training course just behind the older runner with not a word exchanged, and not one virtual leopard encountered. Any virtual leopards-in-waiting were probably two kilometers back.

When they finally slowed to walk at the end of the ped-only path and encountered crowds and cars, the woman moved and looked almost completely unspent. Her gray hair and a web of fine wrinkles around her eyes showed her age, but little else did. Her eyes were a bright blue that demanded attention even if they hadn't been turned on Coryn in open appraisal.

Coryn held her hand out. "I'm Coryn. I'm impressed."

The old woman laughed and took Coryn's hand. "Don't be. I've run every day for thirty years. After some time, you get used to it."

"This is my friend Paula."

"Your minder," she snapped. "I'm not stupid."

Coryn blinked, taken aback. "I didn't say you were. But Paula's all the family I have, except a sister who's out with the Wilders. I don't think of her as a minder."

"I'm sorry."

She didn't really look sorry. Maybe her run had been fueled with sarcasm as well as energy gels. Coryn felt awkward and a little small around her, and she wished she hadn't run with her. And why wasn't the woman offering her name? She could feel a wall between them. "I've been running every day this summer except four. That's twenty-five days since school let out. I finished three full marathons. Came in tenth in my class in one of them, even though it was a small one." She was babbling. What made her nervous about this little old woman? "But I can't imagine running for decades."

The woman smiled. "I never could either—imagine it. It just happened. Sometimes you do things you don't *imagine* you're going to. Now I can't picture a day I don't run."

"No rest days. In all that time? Don't you get sick or anything?"

The woman shook her head. Something in the gesture and the shape of her smile made her look familiar, although Coryn couldn't place where she'd seen her. She said, "Good run today," and started to walk off.

Coryn didn't want her to go. "Will you stay and talk to me for a few minutes?"

"I don't give interviews."

"Interviews?"

The woman stopped, and the look on her face shifted from closed to curious. "What do you want to talk about?"

For a moment, Coryn was lost for words. "Running, I guess." Anything, she almost said. But that would have sounded desperate. Lonely. And it wasn't that, it was just . . . the woman intrigued her, teasing her with that sense of near-familiarity. Who was she?

The woman looked like the word "no" was stuck just behind her lips, but then she snapped to a different decision, speaking with power. "You need dinner. I need dinner. Let's go. I'll even buy. I like to meet new people, sometimes. Find out how they live."

"I'm still a student. I don't do much. I run."

"I'll still buy you dinner."

Coryn glanced at Paula, who offered an almost imperceptible nod. So she saw it as safe. She smiled at the woman. "That would be great."

"Follow me." She led them across two streets and up some wide, fancy wooden stairs to a brightly lit restaurant with rose-colored walls and white tablecloths. It was full, with a line out the door. Nearly everyone was dressed in business clothing. At the landing, the still-nameless woman leaned over to her. "Leave your companion outside."

The surprised Coryn. "She usually sits with me."

A slightly perturbed look crossed the woman's face. "Well, I'm going to *eat* with you. She doesn't need food. She can stay out with my guards."

Coryn blinked. Paula's job was to keep her safe. But if she said that the woman would think she was afraid of her. She looked around. Somehow she hadn't even noticed that there were three other robots near them, two of them designed to look like a couple, and another one a female styled at about twenty-five, kind of like Paula except blond and a little shorter.

Coryn nodded at Paula, and Paula nodded back, smiling, apparently trying to reassure her. It felt strange to leave her companion outside, but this was becoming an adventure, and she didn't want to miss it.

The woman led them past the line, and, just inside, the gracious smells of pan-Asian spicing and hot green tea greeted them. A human waiter looked up from the podium, walked past a long line of patrons waiting to be seated, and took them immediately up a spiral staircase to a private room with a single table for six. At first she thought they were being hidden from the other patrons since they were both still in their running clothes and smelled like exercise. But the cut yellow and white flowers in bright blue vases and the ceramic water fountain in the corner grew on her, and she slowly realized they were in a truly opulent place, the kind of room she'd seen on videos but never been inside.

She glanced through the windows that surrounded the table, including above them. The room showed the city off. Flowers draped from ledges and bridges above them, a running path spiraled up from the ground and touched three of the larger buildings, and a new sky bike path ran directly above them, so high that it looked like a ribbon. She yearned to ride on it.

A huge indoor food garden rose behind them to the left. The Seattle Central Grow. Coryn squinted through the clear building, trying to figure out how this one vertical farm supplied the vegetables for a hundred thousand people. Bots and people both moved through the structure, and machine arms ran along tracks. "I've never seen the inside of the Grow," Coryn mused. "It's pretty fascinating from this angle."

The woman looked poised to comment when the waiter came up with water. "Good afternoon, Ms. Lake, would you like wine?"

Coryn barely managed to keep her mouth from dropping open. She should have recognized the woman as soon as she saw her face, even if it had aged. Julianna Lake had once been the mayor of Seattle, and she and the then mayor of Vancouver, Jake Erlich, had bridged the national border. They'd done it with a grassroots campaign and a surprise vote that barely passed both cities, and then built up Seacouver's defenses enough to make the central governments of both the United States and Canada hesitate long enough to lose any advantage they had once had. After all, the cities were vibrant technology hubs.

She was sitting with a legend.

Julianna and the waiter spoke in low tones, while Coryn's mind spun through what she remembered about Julianna and Jake.

There were rumors of an affair between them, but if it had happened they never made it a formal relationship. But they had moved together to secure power for the city they created.

Julianna smiled at her, a slightly amused look on her face. "Do you have any strong food preferences? Is there anything you don't like or don't eat?"

Coryn managed to shake her head and stammer out, "Anything is fine."

They had been called the Jake and Lake show by everyone, whether they hated them or loved them. It had been a huge historic fight, called either the death of the nations or the rise of the cities. The United States and Canada both still existed, and both flags flew over every neighborhood hall in Seacouver. Other megacities had followed suit, mostly in the Far East and on the East Coast.

As the waitress left Julianna's side, Coryn tried to remember if Jake was still alive. If anyone had asked her, she might have thought them both dead. After all, there had been a whole chapter on Julianna in Coryn's last history class. Now that she understood what to look for, Coryn could see the hard, fighting features of the much younger woman who had moved history forward.

"Miss?"

A waiter appeared from somewhere. She hadn't even heard him. "Would you like anything to drink?" he asked, his voice silky and overly helpful.

"Sure. Yes. Coffee, please."

Julianna Lake smiled genuinely at Coryn, the first smile that hadn't looked at least a little guarded. After the waiter left, she leaned over and took Coryn's hand. Her grip felt strong and warm. "You ran well. Not many people can keep up with me."

"Likewise." She started babbling. "*You* run? Every day? How do find time? What else do you do?"

Julianna leaned back and smiled. "I don't have any formal power, not anymore. But tell me about yourself first. How did you end up with a companion robot as your only family?"

The coffee had appeared, a rich black pool in a lightweight porcelain teacup. Coryn blew on the top of the coffee to cool it. She blurted out, "I'm an orphan," and then wished she'd started anywhere else. It was true, and it defined her, but surely it wasn't what this woman wanted to know.

Julianna didn't look surprised, but merely curious. "What happened?"

If she got it all out of the way she could go back to what she had said she wanted to talk about—running. She took a deep breath. "My parents committed suicide."

Julianna leaned forward. "Why?" Then she leaned back, taking a piece of bread. "Sorry. Are you willing to tell me?"

The pain still had sharp edges. "They couldn't handle the city. Mom never could."

Julianna stared at the harvester robots in the Grow, looking a little pained. "When we created this city, we made a lot of good things. But we made bad things, too."

Coryn hadn't expected any understanding at all. She found herself out of words. She reached for some bread, surprised when it felt warm in her fingers. "I love it, most days. I love the bridges and the tracks and the crowds. But Mom hated it so much she cried almost every day. She stayed inside most of the time, as if it would hurt her to go out. I didn't understand, but maybe I do now. I don't think she had any friends." She put the bread in her mouth. It melted against her tongue, a light sourdough with a touch of cinnamon that tasted finer than anything she could remember.

The "friends" thing. She hadn't really thought about it before. But she felt lonely as hell these days. Maybe loneliness killed her parents. And they had it better than she did; they had each other.

Julianna stared at Coryn as a waitress brought a red beet salad topped with walnuts.

The conversation fell off as they worked on the salad, which had flavors she'd never tasted. Now that the shock of meeting Julianna had ebbed into dreamy disbelief, she felt sore, a little jolted awake from the coffee, and replete. She felt good. Feeling good made her realize she hadn't really felt good in a long time.

After the water whisked away their empty salad plates, a woman put down plates of sashimi and sticky rice. Coryn managed to get her tongue into some kind of order. "What do you do now? I don't remember hearing any news about you for a long time."

Julianna smiled. "I keep it that way. Once you leave power, it's best not to compete too boldly with those you leave behind. It's like letting a child grow up."

"So the city is your child?"

"Mine and Jake's. Except now it has become its own thing."

As she finished her rice, Coryn's mind raced through possible responses, settling on, "Are you happy with how it grew up?"

Julianna smiled, a polite smile that hid things behind it. "Mostly. Who is completely happy with any creation?" Then she shrugged. "At least it is beyond us now, and we only have a little to do with it."

Coryn wanted to ask another question, but Julianna changed the subject. "I do run every day. I swore I wouldn't grow old too fast, that I wouldn't die too young. I wanted to see what would happen." She hesitated a moment, her fork poised unmoving over her plate. "I also run to stay in emotional shape. It keeps me even, like a meditation." She picked up a forkful of dark red salmon. "What does running do for you?"

"It helps me forget."

"Maybe you should run for the future."

"Maybe I should." Coryn couldn't quite figure out what that might mean, so she simply said, "I hope I run for years, like you."

"That's up to you," Julianna replied, smiling up at the waiter, who pulled dirty dishes from the table and gave them clean ones.

Coryn was already almost full, so she was pleased to see the last plate had a pile of nuts and two small chocolates on it, the nuts and sweets linked together with thin lines of some kind of brown syrup.

"That's pretty," she said, admiring the presentation. She wasn't used to food being a work of art.

"It's my training diet. I thought you might not mind."

Coryn almost laughed, catching herself, staying polite. "Of course not."

Just before they finished the dessert course, Coryn asked, "Will you run with me again?"

Julianna said, "Someday. But not tomorrow. Some of my meetings happen with other runners, and I've got an appointment for tomorrow's training session. Perhaps I'll message you. Another time."

It felt like a brush-off, and Coryn blinked. "An appointment? But you don't still work for the government, do you?"

Julianna laughed. "Never again. But I still have friends. Old women have things to talk about with other old women."

"If you have time again, I'd love to join you."

"Thanks for sharing your story," Julianna replied. "It's time for me to go to bed."

"Me too." Paula was probably already fuming since her training schedule left Coryn an hour for dinner and she'd spent two. Or maybe Paula had recognized Julianna? "Can you answer a question?"

Julianna hesitated.

"Sorry, I'm intruding. I know. Thank you for dinner again. I know you run, but are you happy? Does running make you happy?"

Julianna glanced away, toward the distant water. Her voice lost its brisk tone. "Running keeps me sane. I suspect that's what it is doing for you, as well. It's a better choice than many others." She looked back at Coryn, staring directly at her. "I hope you keep running. I'm going to go now, but I probably will see you sometime. On the road."

"On the road, then."

To Coryn's utter surprise, Julianna gave her a hug before they parted at the door.

As she walked home with Paula, she filled her in on the entire evening. When she finished, Paula said, "I suspect she wouldn't want you to tell me about her."

"Did you know who she was?"

"Of course."

"How soon?"

"When she first ran by us. We are skilled in identifying all of the important people in the city."

"I didn't know that."

"Did you know she owns the restaurant?"

Coryn slowed down, thoughtful. "No. But that explains why the waiter knew what to bring us."

"She owns two percent of the city."

Coryn had to think that through. "Two percent of Seacouver or of Seattle?"

"Seacouver."

No wonder she had said almost nothing about herself. "It was a lovely meal." Coryn put her headset back on and turned the fairies app back up on high, setting the level at a hundred visual fairies, which herded her home with the whine of beating wings and slap of tiny feet on pavement.

After Paula had brokered a sleeping cube in a hostel for them, she started to write to Lou, now that she had something to say. Shortly after she started recording, it dawned on her that she couldn't tell Lou a thing. Not if she ever wanted to see Julianna again. Maybe she and Paula would always be the only ones to know about her accidental run with Julianna Lake.

So she didn't have a good story about today, or a pony. Nothing really. She'd write to Lou tomorrow.

CHAPTER FIVE

Coryn jogged in place in a pocket park on First Hill. Toddlers screeched for their mothers to watch them go down a long red slide, and locals walked their dogs. What mattered was a gate on one end of the park, where a guard took tickets from people to let them through. The gate led to Sky Park Way, a partially elevated running track that wound up from the gate and curled through skyscrapers that housed the rich and famous, elite businesses, and expensive hotels. Today, she would be on it.

She felt great warming up, light and ready and bursting with energy.

Rhododendrons and azaleas displayed a few late flowers, and fresh red and yellow tulips splashed color in beds beside the park's entrance sign. It was a day full of clear blue sky and late spring heat. If it wasn't all-too-close to graduation day, it would be perfect.

Maybe Julianna would find her today. She had watched for the older woman during every run. She had only seen her once, at a distance. Julianna had waved at her. The brief encounter had left Coryn pleased that Julianna remembered her, but it had also been a knife of loneliness that kept her up all that night, restless and desperate. It seemed pathetic to hope that someone who had been kind to her once would be kind to her again.

Training to keep up with Julianna had given Coryn enough speed to win two marathons in her age group. One of her prizes had been one-time access to Sky Park Way. It would give her more elevation than she'd ever managed on such a long run, and some of the best views of the city. Her entrance ticket included the Bridge of Stars. She couldn't wait to stand up there again and look out over Puget Sound and maybe find a whale. A simple thing, but she had gotten it stuck in her head, and it would make her happy. Right now, on the cusp of having to make her choices, she wanted something special. A sign, maybe.

Next to her, Paula said, "Pay attention."

She looked over at the guard. This wasn't a race, but runners were let onto this track in small groups. A nod would tell her she could start. "I'll meet you at home," she said.

Paula smiled. "Of course."

Her entrance pass was only for one. To buy Paula a pass would have taken three months of her student stipend. Surely she would be safe here, and, besides, it felt bold to go by herself.

The guard nodded at her. Paula whispered, "Go." She handed her entrance pass to the uniformed man and broke into a light jog, testing the surface. The path felt like heaven, responsive and yet forgiving.

About three miles in, as she pounded at marathon speed along the outer deck of a famous bar on top of the McBride Tower, she heard another runner come up on her. She turned to see Julianna, and grinned. Now the day would go from hard to twice as hard, and maybe this was her sign.

Julianna grinned back, the look assuring Coryn that this was no chance encounter. Julianna had come to find her.

Two runners fell in a distance behind them, probably guards. They looked human, although Coryn couldn't tell how she knew. Something in their gaits, probably.

They ran a long uphill spiral through buildings to the top of Capitol Hill, and from there they sped back down a long bridge built to link Capitol Hill to the University District. To her delight, Julianna stayed with her on the long run down. The older woman almost certainly moderated her pace to stay with Coryn on the steep parts. Even so, only two runners passed them, while they passed at least ten.

At the top of the hill, scenic viewpoints designed for runners or walkers jutted out from the bridge, offering restrooms, glass-bottomed observatory decks to stand on, and free water. Julianna gestured Coryn into one. It wasn't as high as the Bridge of Stars, but they were almost fifty feet up. The waters of the Montlake Cut ran below them. A race seemed to be in progress, oars flashing brightly in the sun as teams pulled boats less than a foot wide through the slender waterway, with barely enough room to pass. The university sprawled across a low hill to their left, and the deep blue of Lake Washington led her eyes toward the shimmering skyscrapers of downtown Bellevue. "It's really pretty," Coryn said, as soon as her breath calmed enough that she could talk. "Nice to see you."

"Especially on a clear day," Julianna replied. "And yes, nice to see you. I came to find you."

Coryn's cheeks grew hot. "I had hoped so."

"Put on your AR glasses and turn to station 565."

Coryn took a long drink of water and sucked an energy gel dry. The command reminded her of the dinner, a burst of activity with no soft introduction. "Okay." She switched her standard wireless headphones for her AR setup and got the right channel tuned in, and then led off without waiting. The AR channel showed Julianna following Coryn, so it must have been pre-programmed for them.

The AR channel looked like a standard exercise world, with mile markers and cheering crowds and selectable music. After a few moments, Coryn stopped expecting it to be anything else and settled into her run.

After they started along Montlake Boulevard toward the Arboretum, Julianna's voice sounded in her ear. "Thanks for running with me today. I thought perhaps you'd be willing to let me ask you a few questions."

"Sure." Then she thought a little better of the open answer and asked, "About what?"

"I'm interested in learning about your life. I remember your story from the last time we met, and how you're pretty much alone and living on basic. I want to ask you a few questions. Do you trust me enough to answer them honestly?"

"You won't report me if I say something the city wouldn't like to hear?"

"You're still allowed to have free speech."

"As an orphan? It doesn't feel like it. One of my teachers complained about me to the principal when I told them that they were being too hard on a girl in class."

"That might have been self-defense on the part of your teacher. The city listens—it has to. But it won't interfere until talk turns to action."

Julianna sounded very sure of that. "Did you make that rule?"

The older woman's laughter peeled in her ears. "The founding fathers ensured freedom of speech. Practical law enforcement means you don't always have the right for that speech to be private, and neither does anyone in power."

Julianna would probably know about that. "Is the city listening to us now? On this private VR channel?"

Julianna didn't seem to have heard the question. To be fair, the noise of a virtual corner band playing loud jazz drowned out their conversation for a moment, and Coryn let it happen rather than turn the AR overlay down.

After they left the corner and the sound in the background, Julianna asked, "Are you happy?"

She hadn't expected such a simple question. "When I run. Now I'm happy. This moment. But otherwise, it's hard. But after what happened to my mom, I try to be happy."

"What about angry? Do you ever get angry?"

"Yes." The question bothered her, although she couldn't say why.

When Coryn didn't say anything else, Julianna prodded her. "What makes you angry?"

She thought about it for almost two miles before she answered. "I shouldn't be. I have everything I need, or at least everything the city says I need." She touched her AR glasses. They were Lucity Lenses, which was one of the better mass-produced brands. "I even saved enough for these. I have Paula, and no one else at the orphanage has a companion. She helps me all the time. But I'm angry about Mom and Dad, and I'm angry that Lou left, and I'm angry that . . . that I'm on the absolute bottom." Three virtual runners and one real runner passed them, all in a close bunch. Coryn ran a little harder. "I was supposed to have a normal life and go to college and live someplace in the middle tiers. That's what they taught me would happen, and then they took my future."

"Who is they? Who are you mad at?"

She'd been through close to a hundred group therapy sessions in her years at the orphanage and knew better than to give an easy answer to that. They passed another screaming AR crowd and then a bunch of kids playing a game in the same channel they were on. For a few moments, virtual bats fluttered over their shoulders. Since they weren't playing, the bats simply flew around them and then through them. Idiot kids should know how to manage their privacy settings. "The city, I guess, but really that's too diffuse. I mean, I can't change it."

"What have you heard from people you know? Are they mad at the city?"

"You mean in the orphanage, or at school? That's really all the people I know. I think we're too busy to do much. We have to earn the ability to make the choices we want."

"Are you a good student?"

"Yes."

"What are you going to do?"

"Everything I think of or test into feels wrong. The best is gardening— I used to like to weed. I have to choose soon, or go Outside, like Lou."

"I don't think many students get to go Outside. Your sister was lucky."

"It wasn't lucky for me. Anyway, anyone can just leave."

"And risk not being able to come back? That would be . . . quite daring."

Coryn hadn't actually said it that way to herself yet—told herself that she might just leave. She fell silent. Julianna didn't say anything as they recrossed the Cut at just above ground level, hundreds of feet below where they had stopped to look around. The race had finished, and the small pleasure boats crowded the narrow waterway. Everyone in Seattle seemed to want to be in the water on a fresh, hot day like this. There hadn't been any days so pretty since just after New Year's, and those had been so cold she'd had to wear long-sleeved running gear and full-length pants. Today felt like a gift, like the city sparkled and greened and flowered all around her. She felt good in spite of her fears about Lou and about the future, happy to be with Julianna and to be here in glittering, green Seacouver.

Surely she wouldn't actually just leave. What would she do without traffic control and AR overlays and beautiful new paths to run on? "There's no AR out there. I really need AR for my runs."

Julianna laughed. "AR will get you killed Outside. You need to pay attention to that world. There's no safe gates to keep the bad things out."

Coryn almost stumbled. "My sister's out there. Is it really that bad?"

"Yes." Julianna waved at two women running past them from the opposite direction. "So, can I ask some more questions? I'm sorry to be intrusive. You see, I get a lot of reports about the hard things here, but I mostly only talk to rich people. That's like living inside half a truth."

Was that why Julianna was interested in her? She didn't like it. "Go ahead."

"What about the people you do know? The other people you live with? Are they going to make it?"

At least she was calling them *people* instead of *kids* or *orphans*. They started up the hill into the Arboretum, and Coryn waited until they'd crested. She stopped at a lovely spot, where the view opened out onto the Seattle skyline: tall buildings and arched bridges and bright colors, and almost all of it green with summer crops. "No."

"None of them?"

"I don't think so. I'll make it, but I have Paula, and somewhere I have Lou. The others? I hope they do okay, but I don't see how. There's six seniors, including me, in the orphanage. Two are addicted to actual drugs—that designer crap that's supposed to make you brilliant and does for about a week. They're both losers. They can only finish their homework if they're high. Two more are addicted to Survival!—you know, the game?"

"I've heard about it. I don't play."

"Of course you don't. I don't either. Survival! is for idiots. Well, no," she amended the thought. "One of them is a high-functioning Autie. He's probably the reason they're still okay."

"I've never even seen the login screen. Can you tell me more?"

"You go through pretend-scary situations, like getting attacked, or almost getting into an accident. If you get out, you go to the next level. If you lose, you die, and you have to wait a week to play again. If you get to the middle levels, the game uses real landmarks and mixes them with AR, and I think it even uses actors. If you pay."

"Actors?"

"People who you pay to pretend to be the bad guy. Anyway, these two can't afford that. It's not supposed to do you any real harm, but two people died last year, in the real world. They were playing together, and the game told them to jump off a building. They did."

"A friend's grandson died in that game."

"These two—I can see them doing that. They almost never have to take a week off."

"Is that everyone?"

"There's one more. Mary Susan. She might make it. At least she's got social skills. She'll probably choose more education. I heard a rumor she inherited funding for it." A small note of jealousy stung her, but she ran it out while she waited for Julianna's next question.

"So that's two out of six that will probably achieve full adulthood. You know the odds are more like seven hundred to one—in the opposite direction—in the places we're running through, in the kind of places where I live."

Coryn smiled at the implication that Julianna expected her to make it. "Yeah, but you're rich."

"That's why I wanted to talk to you. You didn't tell anyone about me, so I decided to trust you. I can still trust you, can't I?"

"Who would I tell?"

"Newsies, for one."

Coryn snorted. "I don't need money *that* bad. I'd rather run with you again." She glanced over in time to see a smile crossing on Julianna's face.

"Maybe we can do that. So you will keep my secrets?"

"I don't have anyone to tell them to anyway." After Julianna fell quiet for a while, she added, "I won't tell anyone about you. I promise."

They finished the next four miles in companionable silence. They ran over the industrial areas on the right side of the old West Seattle Bridge, which had been reclaimed for peds and bikes, but which ran *under* the new rail and car bridge, so the view was flattened and the air smelled of salt and oil. This was one of the few parts of the new track that was actually open and old, and Coryn felt crowded enough that she turned the AR volume down so far it was all a very light overlay on her real senses. She kept glancing over at Julianna, verifying that she was really there, and that she'd really come to find *her*.

The course finished with a trip up and along the entire Bridge of Stars, starting from the West Seattle side. The run up was long and beautiful, and Coryn kept looking for whales. She spotted boats and windsurfers and a small plane. When they made it to the top, Julianna suggested they pause almost exactly where Coryn and Paula has stopped that one day. Coryn's breath was so sharp she had to force out the word, "Please."

At least ten other people stood on top, enjoying the view, so she turned to Julianna, using their secret channel so her whisper would be words in Julianna's ears. "What about you? Are you angry? Is that why you found me?"

"No. I wanted company. I mean, no, anger is not why I found you. I do have anger." She paused. "Don't we all, these days? It's like the whole city is running on the fast button and no one can get off."

Julianna actually sounded a little defensive, which surprised Coryn. She had always seemed so in control. "I never thought the super-rich were angry."

"Why not?"

"Well, they have everything."

"No one is hungry anymore. In some ways we're similar."

"I only have a few choices. You can do anything." She stared down at the building below them, where the rich lived on the top floors. They had walkways between buildings so they didn't have to touch the ground unless they wanted to. That was where Julianna had joined her today, on one of those walkways that had been incorporated into a training plan. For all she knew, Julianna lived like that. She probably did.

Julianna also stared down at the buildings. She didn't respond to Coryn other than to look severe and contemplative. But then, she had never answered questions about herself easily. She liked her secrets.

Still, Coryn was sad to be almost done with her run. She'd be back in school in a few days, and after that she'd have to choose. Whatever she chose, it probably wouldn't earn her much more than basic-basic, at least not for years. She thought briefly of asking Julianna for a job, but that felt so wrong she rejected it. She wanted more from Julianna than that, although she couldn't have said what. She didn't need a mother. Besides, she had Paula for that.

She watched Julianna look down at the city rather than across the water, the anger and confusion now gone from her face, replaced with a simple, thoughtful look. Her body appeared calm, her chest barely heaving, even after the long run up. Wrinkles spread out from her eyes and puckered her lips, but she looked vital in spite of the signs of aging. Coryn tried again. "So what are the rich angry about?"

Julianna shook her head. "Maybe I'll tell you some day."

"Have you ever seen a whale?"

Julianna raised an eyebrow at the change of subject. "Of course I have."

"I haven't. Do you think we could see one from up here?"

Julianna turned around and looked out over the water. "It would be pretty small."

"Still . . ." Coryn squinted at the shiny water, wondering if so much sun would make it harder.

"Is that one?" Julianna pointed a little to the north. "Maybe a whole pod?"

Coryn tried to follow her finger. Black and white half-circles seemed to rise and fall, and she was pretty sure she spotted a tail. "I think so."

"Maybe someday I'll show you some up close."

"That's not allowed anymore."

"Not by whale watching. You can see them pretty well from a small seaplane, and as long as you're high enough it doesn't bother them at all."

Coryn stood watching until she couldn't see the whales at all anymore.

Julianna whispered, "We should go."

"I don't want to leave."

"I can leave you here."

"No."

At the end of the bridge, she turned one way and the older runner turned another, but not until they'd waved at each other and traded smiles.

CHAPTER SIX

Coryn stared at the fifth note she'd gotten from Lou that school year. Less than one a month. This was the shortest, too, easy to see on her wristlet screen.

Everything is going great. We've been working on taking down old farms, which makes the land clean again. Pulling out fences and pulling out barns. I hope you are doing well.

She hadn't even mentioned Coryn's choice. Surely she'd kept track enough to know it was coming. It had only been two years!

And now she only had a few days.

The final semester of school had gone by in a brutal blur. One of the addicted twosome had managed to die in an immersive VR just before Coryn got back. He had been so high he forgot to eat or drink. While she wasn't going to miss him—or any of these people—it made her angry that no one had cared enough to check on him. She'd been out running with Julianna and Paula, the other two—including Ghit—were still making it through levels of Survival!, and Mary Sue had been on college visits.

The old keeper robot had been replaced by a far nastier version, one that she couldn't tease or sneak out past. As a city-registered amateur athlete, the new robot had to allow Coryn out three times a week to exercise. At least she let her take Paula, but three days wasn't enough to keep the walls from closing in.

And then there was Marilyn, the real person who checked in on the orphanage's residents every day; tall and thin with a face like a lemon and the most outdated wardrobe Coryn had ever seen. She often asked the kids to tell her their secrets, which meant no one would say the sky was blue. At least Marilyn turned everyone in the orphanage against herself, creating an awkward truce among the residents, which kept Coryn from being targeted too much.

She reread the letter from Lou. It told her nothing useful. Was Lou happy? Was she safe?

Lou only told her good things. It was one thing to hide stuff that shouldn't be talked about. Coryn hadn't told Lou a thing about Julianna, but she had written about the dotty old minder robot's evil replacement, and the idiots who played games when they should be studying. Lou's letters were too good to be true, like marketing posters or something. In one letter, she'd written that she was working on a fishery. The next letter said that she was still doing that, but now they were wrecking a dam, and the one after that described the winter and the wonder of fresh snow.

Lou's letters and Julianna's words about Outside clashed.

Coryn leaned back in her seat, scowling as she glanced back and forth between the tiny screen on her wrist and the much larger one on the desk before her. She'd recently started getting up before dawn to do research, and what she found mystified her. So far, most of it sounded like just what Lou had been writing. Except that if she pushed hard enough, read enough different articles from different sources, and drew out timelines and lists of data, little things disagreed with one another. Place names seemed to vary. There wasn't very much video—Coryn could pull a video of anyplace in the city for almost any time in the last year and see what had happened. If she discounted pure marketing material, she'd only found about twenty videos of Outside so far. There should have been far more, shouldn't there?

She found some that showed the huge ecobots felling trees and lifting boulders and planting saplings and pulling out old roads to make wildlife corridors. There were videos of birds and frogs and insects and deer.

It wasn't enough. Almost none of the videos were of people.

She hit another link on the screen and found what looked like another news story but turned out to be one she'd read before, except reworded and posted by another source. She closed it and opened another link that turned out to be a list of poems inspired by Outside. Interesting, but not very helpful.

People clearly did work out there. There *were* news stories. Someone had written the poems. Lou was there; she didn't doubt that.

Coryn sighed and considered logging off. *And do what?* She wanted to talk to Julianna, but the older woman had been invisible, even in the news.

She talked about her choices with Paula, which led to logic arguments that Coryn hated and lost.

She stared at the notes again. She would never know what happened to Lou unless she went Outside to find out. There had been no choices like Lou's to go Outside right from high school this year, and even if there had been, she probably wouldn't have won a spot. Coryn was smart and got good grades, but Lou tested brilliantly.

Maybe none of the available choices seemed acceptable because none of them were acceptable. She had family, and that mattered to her. It had to. Every other path seemed to end in the same kind of unhappiness that had killed her parents.

There.

That was the central thing that had been dancing with her, being elusive. Her parents had abandoned her. Lou had abandoned her. She wasn't going to abandon Lou.

CHAPTER SEVEN

On a cool, rainless early-summer day right after she graduated, Coryn toiled up Cherry Valley Road with Paula beside her. They were already far to the west of the main Seattle skyline and near the inside edge of the dome. Partway up, she turned and looked west, toward the glowing megacity she had chosen to leave behind. The sun had fallen past the skyline so she no longer had to squint. Red-gold skies reflected through the windows of tall, silvered buildings, which rose like swords from rivers of green streets.

Coryn had chosen to leave home nearly naked; no AR and no wearables except her wristlet.

She stared at the lights for so long her eyes watered.

The city didn't care what she thought or if she wanted to leave it. Or even if she stayed. It demanded to be full, but it didn't care who it was full of. It kept on shining and moving and being. It was easy to think of it as a living thing from here, as if it breathed.

She was small. It would not miss her.

"Goodbye," she whispered, before turning her back on the lights and continuing up the thin, winding road.

The sun painted their shadows tall and terribly thin on the road before them, so similar at these odd angles she and Paula might have been twins instead of flesh and not. Only their heights showed as different. The six inches between them became a foot or more, as if Coryn would have to tilt her head all the way back to look up into Paula's yellow-green eyes.

It grew completely dark before Coryn stopped again at the top of the ridge, her breath searing her chest and her legs soft and tingly. Why did she feel this way? Didn't she run marathons? The road had wound up and up and up for the last hour, not particularly steep but unrelenting. She stood still and panted for a moment, and then turned to Paula. "This isn't even hard for you, is it?"

"It takes more energy to walk uphill."

Just like a fucking robot. "I hate you."

Paula's voice was silk and laughter, almost as nuanced as a human's. "Of course you do."

"Why did we teach robots to have a sense of irony?"

Paula answered with no irony in her voice at all. "You decided it makes us better companions."

"*I* didn't decide." Still, Coryn laughed. After all, it was true. She smiled at Paula to take any sting from her words.

Trees crowded the road. The soft city wind made the branches rustle and golden-hued streetlights began to shine, leaving pools of light that illuminated the dusky color. The straps of her pack cut into her shoulders as she leaned into the job, working too hard to talk.

They'd spent the better part of the day walking down before toiling up Cherry Valley from Redmond Ridge. They reached the top of the Duvall Ridge. Coryn turned for another glance at the silhouettes of buildings and the gauzy skyways of bridges and transport structures that rose above and beyond Redmond Ridge. The landscape was wilder here than she'd even seen, but still gardened. The trees around her had wild, uneven shapes rather than the neater street and park trees near the city center. A sign hung on gnarled trunk. STAY OUT. REHAB AREA. NO HUMANS. Coryn walked up to it and peered past it into a meadow full of spindly seedlings growing up around blackened stumps. A fire had been through here. In school, she'd learned there had been years of fire. The forests of Washington state had simply burned, one after another. The infernos had been a sort of exclamation point on the great taking, making the land the feds had chased people off useless anyway, at least in the short term. The trees were coming back, but slowly and with a lot of help.

It felt like life struggling through death. Maybe she could do that, too. Find life out here. They weren't Outside yet, but she felt how close to the edge of the city they were, how close she was to beginning the biggest adventure of her life.

They stood above the city of Duvall, or really, neighborhood. It was all Seacouver, after all. Even though it had grown dark, the lights of buildings outlined the waves of civilization that spread below them. First, Duvall's multistory farms and simple housing for farmers and wine stewards. Behind the indoor farms, a few flat river-flood fields. Then the wide Snoqualmie River, full of aquaculture farms. Most of the rest was invisible, but she could see it in her imagination: the busy Bellevue downtown that started just over the ridge and rose high up and fancy for miles, ending on the low hills just above Lake

Washington. Beyond the negative space of the lake, the tallest of the buildings in Seattle proper sprouted beneath the Bridge of Stars.

Tonight she would sleep just inside the dome, and tomorrow she would leave the city. She swallowed, suddenly cold.

Paula looped an arm across Coryn's shoulders. "Are you worried?"

There was no pretending with personal robots. Paula had known her for most of her life. She knew how Coryn smelled when she was afraid, and when she was nervous, and when she was just fine.

"A little." She shook Paula's hand from her shoulder. "How far is the camp?"

"A mile."

"We should hurry."

Paula kept them going straight ahead, and then turned right and right again. She kept her head up and her back stiff, showing the robotic version of disapproval of the whole concept. In this moment, she existed to keep Coryn safe, and this wasn't safe, so she disapproved. But when Coryn turned eighteen, Paula lost her ability to dictate anything. Although she couldn't disobey, she had been coded to influence the behavior of humans, and she was quite capable of using a combination of posture and robotic microexpressions to make sure Coryn remembered her advice.

An automated entry-bot dressed in a City Parks uniform checked them off as they arrived, pointing them toward the path to their site. The small nonmotorized campsite had ten tent spaces. Nine of them were full; they were last in. People sat in small groups, talking and laughing. Many, like Coryn, sat side-by-side with their robots. A few other robots stood a little off the path, conferring among themselves.

Paula found the trail to their site, which was right in the middle, on the side with the best view of the city. Coryn had saved up for this for a month, but now she wished she'd picked a more private site. She felt watched. But then, no one else was alone. Or almost alone.

Paula spoke softly to her. "Will you help me set up the tent?"

Paula needed no help at all, but she always knew what Coryn needed. Right now, that was to be kept busy.

Their site consisted of a square raised platform with two benches that looked toward the city. A small cooking stove and a sink with running water lined the back. The site came with a huge canvas tent that dwarfed Coryn.

Coryn fluffed out the sleeping bag she'd found in the free pile, rolled up a coat for a pillow, and then looked for more work, but there really wasn't anything else to do. She sat, listening to the trees and the low talk around the other campsites and worrying about the next day. After a while she stood back up. "I'm hungry."

"So make food," Paula suggested mildly.

Coryn chose chicken soup from Paula's pack and added hot water to constitute it. While she ate, she sat beside the tent watching the night-dark city. Dull yellow lights glowed inside of windows, a multitude of similar shades. Here and there bluer lights or bright white shone. People would be heading to parties and nightclubs and fancy dinners and plays, or settling in to watch their favorite shows. At the orphanage, most of the younger children she'd spent these last five years with would be laying out games or starting homework or trying to sneak out past the house-bot.

Most of them wouldn't even notice she was gone.

A young man and two girls walked by. One of the two girls looked up at her. "Want to come with us? We're having a fire in the big fire pit." She was dark skinned and dark-haired, with Asian eyes; a real beauty.

It surprised her to be included in anything, especially by strangers. "Sure. I'll be right along."

"We'll wait."

She rinsed her dinner bowl and dropped it in the recycler. "Coming?" she asked Paula.

"Do you want me to?"

"You can choose."

Paula hesitated, but then said, "I'll be along in a minute. There's some research I want to do."

"How robotic of you."

Paula gave her a soft smile and made a shooing motion.

‡ ‡ ‡

The dark-haired girl who'd invited her held her hand out. "I'm Ryu."

Coryn took it. "Coryn."

Her tall, thin companion said, "I'm Luci," and pointed to the stocky, smiling man with them. "And this is Lawrence."

Lawrence's wide smile filled his face, brightening the evening. "Pleased to meet you."

He made it sound a lot less formal than most people would. Returning his smile was easy, too. "Likewise," she said.

An older couple's robot had already started the communal fire pit, which used real wooden logs. Flames flicked and licked and twisted up at the sky, and the wood popped and shivered as it surrendered to the heat.

Coryn stared at it, entranced. She'd never seen a real fire so big.

Ryu sat beside her on a stone bench. "Where are you from?" she asked.

Coryn gestured toward the southwest. "In the middle there. From Kent. It's between Seattle and Tacoma. Kind of the middle of everything, but not in any of the big downtowns."

"What's it like there?"

Coryn shrugged. "It's not the best of Seattle. We have tent camps and temp housing and boarding schools and a lot of farming."

"What's your favorite park?" Luci asked.

It was an odd question, but an easy one. "I like the parks in Seattle the best. I think I like Volunteer Park the most. It has trees with trunks that are almost bent in circles."

Lawrence reached for a log and tossed it on the fire, sending sparks into the sky. "Me too. About Seattle and Volunteer Park. Although I like Discovery Park, too, because of the lighthouse."

"I haven't been there yet," Coryn replied. "But I've seen vids. It looks beautiful. I'm glad they saved it."

"They might have to move it again," he said.

"Will they have to build up the seawall, too?" she asked.

"Probably." He said it with a little sadness, as if the walls would close them in. They would of course. But she was leaving. Another thing not to miss.

Ryu frowned. "Are you eighteen yet?"

Coryn bristled at the tone in Ryu's voice. "Yesterday. How about you?"

"Almost twenty-three. We graduated from Western last week and we start as park designers for Seattle in the fall, so we've seen *all* the Seattle parks. We studied them. We're doing an inner transit, writing an entrance paper on how the rest of the city manages public spaces." Firelight flickered in Ryu's eyes. "Are you doing a transit, too?"

Coryn hesitated, staring at the flames, but then decided not to lie. "I'm going Outside."

Ryu's eyes widened. "Just you and your bot? Who are you working for?"

"No one." Coryn wished she hadn't spoken up.

"You're going feral?"

Coryn had heard the word, but it still startled her. "I don't think of it that way."

Ryu turned toward her, one side of her face lit by the fire and the other in shadow. "What would you call it?"

"I'm looking for someone." Coryn tried for a change of subject. "What's the coolest thing you've seen on your transit?"

For a moment she thought Ryu wasn't going to let go, but she turned back to the fire and whispered. "Deer. We saw three deer this morning, a doe and two tiny fawns." She hesitated, rolling her eyes up in her head for a moment as if deep in thought. "I want to see more animals. Mostly, I want to see a whale. A whole pod of whales. They're back now, you know. There's two families of whales."

Coryn nodded in pleased agreement. "I saw one not long ago. From the top of a bridge."

"I'd love to see one."

Coryn smiled. "Try a bridge. I heard that L pod had another baby yesterday." Strange to realize she'd said this same thing the last day she had parents, when she'd stood beside Paula on the high bridge. There had been five babies since then.

Ryu stood and brushed bark from her pant legs. "Mostly we've seen farms and forests."

"You've gone a long way for three days," Coryn observed.

"We've got bicycles."

"I ride bikes," Coryn said. "But aren't there a lot of hills on a full transit?"

Ryu laughed. "We spent a year planning our route."

A spike of jealousy skewered Coryn, and she shut it down with a clenched breath. "I'd like to see deer."

"Look when you wake up. They come out early in the morning and just before dusk."

The same robot who had built the fire threw three more logs on. Sparks flew into the dark sky.

Ryu called her friends over. "Coryn's going Outside."

Lawrence's eyes widened. "This way? It's a trucking gate."

Luci brushed her blond hair away from her eyebrows. "Do they let people leave just because they want to? I thought they only let a few out a year."

"I think you need to talk to someone," Lawrence repeated, his voice and face full of concern. "You just do."

Like who? But she didn't say that. She regretted telling Ryu in the first place. "I did my research. They won't stop me from going."

Ryu twisted her fingers together, looking seriously worried. "What if they don't let you come back?"

Coryn shrugged, doing her best to look like she didn't care. It didn't matter. She had to find Lou and she had to leave and she'd made up her mind and that was, well, that. She stood up, stretching, relieved when the conversation moved on.

A few people had brought drums. Coryn want to their campsite and brought back both Paula and a small wooden flute she'd had for about a year, and for a while they sat with a good-sized crowd and played music together. One of the men from a group of mountain bikers brought an outside speaker that created a bright, moving light show in reds and golds that changed with the music. It shone so brightly it seemed just like they were in the city instead of out of it, the light and sound beating at Coryn's eardrums.

When she'd had enough, Coryn excused herself, and she and Paula went back to the tent and sat alone together. Paula pointed out the Big Dipper, which Coryn had already spotted, and then went on to name more stars. The party noise and the bonfire grew larger and louder behind them. Paula turned and pointed toward the smoke. "See how it curls way up there? You can see it when the light from that speaker shines . . . it flattens out as the dome bends. The dome will eventually expel it."

Coryn squinted at the sky above the flames and the noisy throng of people. She had to watch the obnoxious light cross the sky three times before she spotted the effect, like a cloud of smoke. "Is that the edge of the weather dome?"

"It must be."

Of course the top of the dome would be closer to them here on the edges. In the city, clouds could be *in* the dome. She leaned back and stared up at the sky, wondering what a foggy morning would look like. Tonight was clear, but the dome fuzzed out stars and space stations alike, so they were all points of pale and diffuse light.

"I'm coming, Lou," she whispered.

CHAPTER EIGHT

Coryn jerked awake, and her eyes flew open. She rolled over and peered outside. Fuzzy stars still decorated the night sky.

Paula spoke from the bench just outside of the tent door. "Trouble sleeping?"

"Maybe."

"We can still turn around."

A brief, sharp anger made her snap, "Don't you think I know that?" She turned on her wrist light and stalked to the communal bathrooms, filled her water flask, sucked it dry, refilled it, drank again, and filled it again. She took three deep breaths, struggling with unexpected anger and fear. When she came back, she said, "I'm sorry, silly robot. It will be okay."

Paula shook her head slowly. "I hope so."

Daylight refused to touch the Olympic Mountains.

She'd been counting down to this moment for months. She'd seen herself crossing with the dawn, stepping into a new world and finally being free of all the things she'd once loved so much.

She waited, breathed, and waited. Finally, she couldn't stand it anymore. "Let's take the tent down," she said.

In five minutes they were ready.

"Is it about fifteen minutes to the border?"

"Maybe twenty."

The edge of the sky glowed gray. She watched until she saw a star fade. "Okay, now."

Paula shouldered her pack, heavier by a factor of five than Coryn's. Coryn pulled hers on and settled the weight across her shoulders before following Paula out of the campground. As they left, Ryu opened a tent flap and whispered, "Good luck."

"Thanks," Coryn responded. "You too."

She'd chosen this exit on purpose; it was still partly unchanged, maybe the last simple border. Roads on this side of the dome connected to roads on the other side. The rewilding preserves didn't run right up to the city's edge here. Small communities hung on, spreading away from the safety and surveillance of Seacouver.

She had stared at this spot through city cameras so often that it felt familiar, so familiar she had a sense of déjà vu as she approached the border between city and not, between Inside and the wild whatever of the Outside, between a place with no family and a place with one family member.

The small hut that marked the border glowed with cheery light as she approached. A uniformed guard sat inside, drinking coffee.

She walked right up and knocked on the window. The occupant startled, looking at her with surprised dark eyes. He might be all of twenty years old; not at all what she expected.

She smiled as widely as she could, in spite of the blood hammering through her veins so loudly she wondered if he could hear it. "Good morning."

His face settled into no expression. "I wasn't expecting anyone."

"I'm heading Outside. I won't be any trouble."

He glanced at a small handheld screen. "Coryn Williams. What brings you here?"

She swallowed. "Family matters. I need to find my sister. She's on RiversEnd Ranch. Working for the Lucken Foundation."

He stared at his screen and sipped his coffee. At least he didn't seem to be able to hear how fast her heart beat. Certainly, his wasn't beating as fast. He seemed to do everything in slow motion. "And your companion robot is all that you have with you. I see you have title to her."

"Yes. She's been mine since I was small."

He stared at her. "You're still small. You'll have to hold onto her pretty hard out there. Are you sure you don't want to leave her here for safekeeping?"

She couldn't tell if he was teasing, trying to scam her out of Paula, or really meant to be helpful. That was the biggest problem with the city— you never could tell. Your best friend might turn on you, your parents might up and kill themselves, anything could turn from golden to black in no time at all. "I won't leave her."

"How long will you be gone?"

Why did he care? "At least until I find my sister."

"Is your sister expecting you?"

She pursed her lips. What answer did he want? "I'm surprising her." She hadn't told Lou. What if Lou told her no? Then what? Besides, it seemed like a good thing to keep as a surprise. That way she wouldn't distract Lou, and if she just showed up, she might learn more about what was actually going on, things Lou hadn't been willing to say in letters.

That was another choice Paula didn't like.

The guard wasn't done with his questions. "Do you have a job on the farm?"

"No."

"Do you intend to get a job out here?"

"I don't know."

"Does anyone know you are leaving?"

Did he have any idea how irritating he sounded? She smiled. "No."

"Then I will mark you a feral exit. You will lose your stipend until you return. If you don't return in thirty days you will have to petition for reentry."

"I know that."

He kept reading whatever was on his screen for a very long time, not looking at her but nevertheless holding her rooted. Dawn had bloomed into hard light.

Just hurry up. She bounced on her toes.

Paula stood silently behind her. Coryn felt her quiet wish that Coryn relent and turn around.

The border guard seemed to be waiting for her to do something.

"I'm going," she said.

He sipped at his coffee, looked down at the desk, and then back at his screen. When he finally looked up at her, his face had a quizzical look on it. "I see you have a difficult family history. You're not going out to commit suicide, are you?"

She'd stopped being worried now and gone all the way to being angry. Still, he could stop her. So she enunciated as slowly and clearly as she could, as if she were talking to a ten-year-old. "I am going to find my sister."

He raised an eyebrow but gave her a hard smile. "Good luck." She could almost hear him calling her a fool. Paula too.

For just a second she froze.

Everyone waited.

She took a step, and then another.

The actual border—the edge of the dome—was invisible. The air felt ever so slightly fuzzy. A message flashed across her wrist. "You are leaving Seacouver. Tap to acknowledge."

She slapped it *yes*.

She took twelve more steps and then stopped to look back. The guard still sat in his booth, sipping his coffee. He watched her curiously.

She turned her back on him, searching the lightening sky to see if it looked any different. Maybe it was a tad brighter. Maybe she wouldn't be able to really tell until the stars came out tonight.

She yelled out, "Goodbye!" at the guard, and turned and walked down the road as fast as she could, not looking back. Paula kept up with her easily, not speaking.

"Lou," Coryn whispered. "You don't know it, but I'm coming. I'll see you soon."

She checked the map she'd created months before on her wristlet. Paula had a copy too, just in case.

They were silent for the first mile. Coryn stared at everything, looking for differences, for change. The neighborhood looked almost urban, almost as if they were still in the city. The streets had some holes in them. Sidewalks were askew and crumbly. Maybe there was more grass, a few more trees, and things looked a little less groomed. Not as planned. It was hard to tell, though.

They passed a few houses, most of them occupied and cared for. One electric truck passed them, and three men on bicycles, all middle-aged and in a hurry. Birds darted and sang in the trees. Here and there, tiny yellow crocus or bigger purplish-blue primrose competed with weeds in flower-beds. They passed three well-kept houses and then a sagging rambler with peeling white paint and glassless windows.

A string of five big trucks passed her, silent except for the spinning of their wheels, surely headed into the city.

"You should eat," Paula said.

She hadn't seen a bench since she passed through the dome-wall. She picked her way over to a rock and sat on it, accepting the bread that Paula handed her and munching quietly on it. Cinnamon.

Something scratched at the ground and rustled the bushes near her.

She stopped. Stilled.

Paula stared at the spot.

A dog nosed through the bushes and gave a soft yip. At least she suspected it was a dog—she'd never seen anything quite so shaggy and unkempt. Hair flopped over its eyes and it favored its back rear leg. She tossed the last bit of her bread at it and the dog took it and backed away.

"Here," she called.

Nothing.

"Hand me some more bread," she asked Paula. "Please."

Paula dug the loaf out. "I don't think it's a good idea to spend your food this way."

"It looks hungry."

"I don't want you to be hungry."

Coryn stiffened. "Stop playing mom."

"There are far fewer stores out here."

"And I won't get any more basic. I *know* that."

Paula's face looked like stone and her eyes had narrowed, but nevertheless she handed Coryn the bread.

Coryn took another bite to make up for the one she'd given away and then called, "Here," again. The little dog pushed back through, taking a piece of the bread from her.

She stood and held out her hand with another piece, taking a few slow steps.

The dog followed, and she rewarded it with a bite of the bread.

She did this two more times before she ran out of bread. She took a few more steps, looking over her shoulder and calling to the dog.

It stared at her for a moment and then turned and raced away.

Coryn looked at Paula, who shook her head. She could demand another slice, but what was the point if all the creature wanted from her was bread?

She had owned a dog once, when she was small, before her parents died. Whisper. She had loved snuggling the dog before bed. Whisper had disappeared long before her parents killed themselves, and Coryn had never known what happened to her. She had simply gone missing in one of the moves. Coryn had begged her father for information, and then for another dog, but he had shaken his head and looked sad but determined.

After they killed each other, she had still wanted another dog, but the orphanage didn't allow pets. A few kids had snuck in hamsters, and one had a fish in the closet, but no one had managed a dog.

She was hardly in any condition to feed another mouth now. She'd saved all of her salary—well almost all—from the last two summers, and it still might not be enough to find Lou. "Come on," she said. "Let's go."

"That wasn't a complete breakfast," Paula remarked.

"I'm too excited to eat."

Even though she tried not to do it, she looked back twice for the dog, both relieved and disappointed when it didn't show up.

CHAPTER NINE

Coryn had planned thirty days for the trip. It was around sixteen marathons of distance to the farm, which was near the Washington/Idaho border, and she'd run over twenty marathons and biked five; she knew the distance like a beat inside of her. She ought to be able to walk one marathon a day, but she'd halved her expectations to be safe.

Her map suggested that this first day would be pretty easy. Shortly after leaving the dog behind, they headed downhill on a wide road, the roadbed sturdy in spite of crumbled edges and grass that grew between cracks here and there. It would get them, eventually, to Interstate 90, which would take them over the Cascade Mountains. Then she'd have a long walk on I-90, and after that a trip up and down some smaller roads to the ranch.

She could do this.

Paula walked quietly just behind her, looking around so often that Coryn finally exclaimed, "What are you so worried about?"

"I'm used to getting much more data."

Coryn fiddled with her wristlet. It worked just fine, but she took in a hundredth or so of the data that Paula was used to. Maybe less. "You're still connected, right?"

"To the net? Sure. But the systems out here aren't very powerful, and they don't talk to each other. For example, if I needed to find a water fountain or a bathroom, I couldn't do it."

She meant for Coryn, of course. "I should be able to do that." She stopped by the side of the road. "Want me to test?"

"Sure."

Coryn spoke to her wristlet, and it told her there was a park in two miles with both water and a bathroom.

"See?" she said. "I can do this."

"I can do *that*," Paula said wryly. "But it's still not real-time. What if the park is broken?"

Coryn shrugged. "It's only a little out of the way. We'll find out."

"Will you eat more breakfast there?"

Coryn faced her, back to the road. She used her most insidious let's-upset-Paula voice. "Are you my mother?"

Paula didn't answer. She stared straight ahead and whispered, "Turn around."

Reflex kicked in; she turned.

Steady movement caught her eye. She identified it instantly. An ecobot. Coming up the hill toward her.

It was real.

She'd never seen one. Well, in the news, in movies, and in virtgames. In the wild, in its own habitat, the sheer size of the ecobot surprised her. Maybe there were many models and this was the biggest. It was easily broad enough for people to ride on, and twenty or maybe more feet long. In spite of its bulk it moved fast and smooth, all six of its legs pulled up beside it as it rolled past them on a set of low wheels that lined its undercarriage. Its forest camouflage color shimmered against the background of trees and unkempt bushes that lined the road. "Could I see it if it weren't moving?" Coryn whispered.

"Not if it didn't want you to," Paula replied.

It didn't seem to be paying them any attention at all. Still, Coryn stepped off of the road and pulled Paula beside her. "Don't they usually travel in packs?"

Paula watched the machine closely. "I didn't know they came this close to the city. They don't seem to be needed here, not really."

"I suppose. Everything looks peaceful here." To be fair, the forest did look ragged. "But nothing in the city is this messy."

Paula's eyes fluttered, a sign that she was busy accessing databases. She might not have as much real-time data out here, but she carried an impressive amount of information inside her. "They don't have wide police powers. They can only act against *people* in rare circumstances. I wouldn't cut a tree down around one, for example. Or kill a wolf."

"But I could rob a person."

"Probably. But you wouldn't."

"That was rhetorical." Coryn drew her arms close around herself to ward off the damp cold. "What else did you learn?"

"They operate inside a narrow band of laws. They were designed to be unhackable."

It was so big. "I hope it's unhackable," Coryn said. But then almost nothing was really safe. Streetlights and entertainment system and ad delivery–bots got broken into regularly, although they never took long to fix. "What if a machine this size got reprogrammed?"

Paula kept staring at the huge robot. "I presume that's a rhetorical question, too."

"Silly robot."

Paula smiled. "They get used in rewilding a lot. There are some on Lou's farm."

"So we'll see more of them?"

"Probably."

The ecobot's primary head rested in a bowl-shaped depression on the top of the machine's body. The head could rise up on a long neck and give the ecobot a camera view to everything. "I like it," Coryn whispered.

Paula only smiled, and for a moment Coryn wondered if she and the machine could communicate on some level Coryn wouldn't see.

She remembered some of the videos she'd seen in her research, "Where's its drone swarm?"

"Inside of it, or parked in the top deck. There might be a few flying so far away we can't see them. They take energy."

"I thought it was solar!"

"It is, and it also generates power by moving. But that doesn't mean it wastes power. It's an ecobot."

"You're always right," Coryn commented.

"Remember that."

They watched the robot pass. It didn't seem to notice them at all, although Coryn had the distinct impression it knew they were there. After it was gone they stared after it for a while before Paula said, "Let's go."

They followed the original plan for the next mile and a half, and then made a turn onto a small side road. She wouldn't have recognized the park except for the sign that said "Russell P. Cooper Park." The grass hadn't been mowed for a while; walking through it soaked her shoes. Crocuses and a few early daffodils bloomed in weed-infested beds.

The bathroom stood near the road, a square black building with moss in the grooves between bricks, and old spider webs in the corners of the roof. Dirt and dried leaves from last autumn had piled in the corners, and the doors needed to be repainted. She cringed, but used it anyway. The sinks and toilets were almost clean, and stocked with paper.

What had she expected? Did she think leaving the city would be like living in the city? If this was as bad as it got, she'd be okay.

In the middle of the park, in the most open spot possible, an older woman sat at a picnic table throwing balls for three dogs. Two were golden retrievers and one was a brown speckled dog that her wristlet couldn't identify, even with a picture. The woman called her dogs back to her before Coryn and Paula reached the table.

Coryn sat down. "Good morning."

The woman looked like she must be seventy or so, with thin gray hair that surrounded a wrinkled face and slightly suspicious gray-green eyes. She wore old jeans with patched knees and a baggy blue work-out shirt. She kept one hand on the brown dog's collar. "You must have just come Out."

Coryn laughed. "Is it that obvious?"

"Yes."

Paula spoke from behind her. "Will you tell us why?"

The woman ticked things off on her fingers, starting with her index finger. "One, your clothes couldn't be bought here, not unless you got them on the black market." Middle finger. "Two, you still have your pet robot." Ring finger, which was two thirds as long as it should be, with the skin sewn shut over the second knuckle. "Three, you walked right up to me as if I couldn't hurt you."

She stared into Coryn's eyes for a long moment, and Coryn saw sadness and a note of warning in her eyes. "You don't look like you want to hurt me," she said.

The woman blinked and looked away. "I don't. But you're a young woman traveling on her own, and if you don't get more careful, you won't get wherever it is you want to go."

"I'm looking for my sister. She's out in the Palouse, near the Snake River, on the RiversEnd Ranch eco-recovery farm."

The woman's lips thinned. "That's a long trip." She held her hand up and touched her pinky finger. "Four. You don't understand weather."

Paula asked, "What should we know?"

Paula had chosen her mom voice again, which made Coryn grimace. She held her tongue and watched the woman, who answered Paula. "What's the barometric pressure doing?"

Paula blinked, and then shook her head. Anything so simple would have been instantly available to her in the city.

The woman offered, "There's weather information from sensors near here."

Enough time passed for Coryn to pet one of the goldens before Paula answered. "It's falling. And the temperature has stopped rising."

The woman let go of the brown dog's collar and gave it a signal. It lay down at her feet, watching Coryn and Paula with a languid, but very attentive, gaze. "What will the wind do?"

"I don't know."

"Dig deeper." She looked over at Coryn. "You should be looking for this, too." She pointed at Paula. "You may not have *her* forever."

Coryn stiffened but obeyed. It took three or four tries to get an accurate forecast, something that would have been easy in the city. "There's a wind advisory."

"Which means?"

Coryn found the right button to push. "Winds up to sixty miles an hour. From the north."

"Are those sustained or is that the highest gust?"

Coryn had to look again. "Sustained. Gusts up to 80."

"Do you know what that means?"

"It's fast."

"It's hard. The city won't block wind from the north. It blocks an east wind. Where are you going to shelter?"

Coryn decided she didn't like this woman. Fast and hard weren't *that* different. "It's not until this afternoon. We'll find a place."

All three dogs looked to the right, and the goldens each gave out soft yips. Two men walked toward them, one the age of the woman and one younger. They'd come from the trees rather than the road. Coryn felt fidgety.

Paula inclined her head. "We should go."

The woman smiled. "Yes, you should go. But first you should pay for my help."

Coryn stood, confused and alert. Should they run? The brown dog growled at her, showing the teeth on one side of its mouth. She tried to be polite. "I appreciate your help very much."

"Show me."

Coryn exchanged a glance with Paula, who had changed her stance to guarding. Artificial muscles coiled under her skin, tense with readiness; she stepped closer to Coryn, weight shifted to the balls of her feet as if she could take off in any direction and any moment.

The men were close enough to see the serious looks on their faces, the hard set of their shoulders. They looked a little more ragged than the woman, a little more determined.

"Do you have any socks?" the woman asked.

"Socks?"

The woman cocked her head. "Socks. One pair will do, since I'm being fair. I've given you a warning you needed, and I told you what to change if you don't want to stick out like an easy mark. I might have saved you from losing your robot right away. I want to have warm feet again. We make socks over here, but ours don't work like yours do."

Was the woman asking for a legitimate trade or trying to steal from them? She'd only brought two extra pairs of socks. "You offered your information freely. I don't think I owe you anything."

The woman smiled, a slightly predatory smile. "Do you want to keep your robot?"

The question was so absurd Coryn didn't even answer it.

"Then you should give me socks."

The men were more than halfway to them.

Paula spoke up. "You can have one pair."

Coryn didn't like it, but she trusted Paula to understand complex situations and calculate risks.

Paula stepped back from the table, where she could watch everyone. She pulled a single pair of running socks out of the bottom of the bigger pack with a deft move, glancing quickly between the woman, the brown dog, and the men. She held the socks up. "We'll be going now. We'll put the socks on the road right there where you can see them. And you won't follow us."

The woman smiled at Coryn. "Maybe you will keep your robot, at least for a few days."

Coryn recovered from her initial surprise at being treated quite so strangely. She started backing away, Paula moving with her.

The woman gestured at the brown dog. "I'll send him after you if you don't drop the socks." Then she smiled at Coryn. "And thank you for the warm feet. A last lesson for you. The small things matter as much as the big ones Outside. Nothing's free out here, and I just helped you more than you know."

Coryn felt more irritated than grateful, but she managed to choke out a thank you.

They had backed almost out of almost out of earshot, so she barely heard the woman say, "Find shelter soon."

The men reached the woman and flanked her.

They watched Coryn and Paula closely. Coryn spoke quietly. "Paula?"

"Yes?"

"Can you turn the camera on the back of your head on?"

"It's been on since we left the dome."

"Then turn around. We don't want to look like we're afraid."

"Are you sure?"

"No."

"Okay."

They turned around. After a few steps, Coryn asked, "Is it okay?"

"They're still watching us, but they haven't moved."

Coryn let out a breath. "Put the socks down as soon as we get to the edge of the parking lot."

She felt the group's eyes on them, as if there were a target on her back.

Paula dropped the socks ceremoniously. They were white with bright yellow toes, and thus easy to see against the greens, grays, and blacks of the edge of the park.

A few moments later, before they turned back onto the road, Paula said, "They picked up the socks."

Coryn's hands started trembling; her breathing shook as it sped up.

Paula's voice remained cool, gentle. "Keep it together until we get around the corner."

Coryn managed, and once they had left the park ten minutes behind, she stopped and stared back behind them. The magnitude of what had almost happened suddenly swamped her. Her voice shook. "What if they had taken you?"

"Then you would go on."

"How?"

Paula didn't answer.

CHAPTER TEN

The wind plucked at Coryn's shirt and hair. At first, it had felt like the winds in the city parks. Now it was more like the ones that sometimes blew between the taller buildings. She clutched her coat to her, shivering.

The city never allowed freezing after February. "I never thought it could change temperature so fast," she said.

"You have another layer."

"I don't want to stop." In truth, the cold felt wondrous and strange. She was used to having to speed and race and work hard for physical challenge, and here simply existing challenged her.

Clouds came in with the wind, rolling down from the north without passing over the city. A wild wind, she thought.

"Look up." Paula pointed toward a stand of tall fir trees on the other side of the road. The tops of the trees swayed alarmingly, the branches whooshing and sighing as they brushed the sky.

The road climbed, slowing them. Paula looked back, her perfect brow creasing in concern. "Maybe we should go back down, find a valley."

"I don't want to go backward," Coryn said.

Paula turned around and stopped, still searching behind them. "We haven't passed any good shelter."

"Maybe we should stand between two trees."

"It's going to rain." Paula fell silent for a time, and then said, "There's a school building that's almost a mile out of the way, but uphill, and another one that's two miles away, and the road looks mostly flat. It's right on the way."

She wanted to get to Lou. But the wind plucked at her coat like a warning. "Any reason to pick one or the other?"

"Not that I can tell. Both buildings are on."

"I thought everything out here was dead?"

"No. Just slow and stupid. I'm used to systems that sing together. The sensors in one of the houses we just passed talked to each other but didn't talk to the street, or to me. At least I could hear the house."

"Are there things you can't hear out here?" Coryn asked.

"How would I know?" Paula stared at her, a patient, waiting look.

Last week, Paula would have made the decision. But now Coryn was a legal adult. "Let's go to the one that's on the way. It didn't turn out to be such a good idea to get off track at the park."

Paula laughed, but she said, "We might have gained more than we lost. You have enough socks."

Coryn shivered again. She thought she'd been so prepared. In the city, no one stole robots, or even socks. There were too many cameras. "Maybe we shouldn't go to a school at all. Won't there be other people there?"

"A crowd is probably safer than one or two people."

"Do you really think so?"

"Yes. They do teach us basic self-defense. How do you think I managed to get you this far?"

Coryn grew quiet after that, listening to the wind in the trees and walking faster. Paula was the only person she could remember from every year of her life. Even after her parents died, Paula was there. After Lou left, Paula was there. Sure, she was a robot, but she knew all of the continuity of Coryn's life, all of the days. She probably knew more than Coryn herself did, since robots remembered more details than people.

The wind left them alone for a while and then came up with vengeance; she nearly stumbled as one gust pushed her from behind. Maybe a hard wind pushed you down and a fast one just blew your hair around.

Dark gray clouds churned directly overhead. Paula said, "I don't hear any more birds."

"Maybe they're all hiding."

"There are people ahead of us," Paula whispered.

They spotted two men and three children heading the same way that they were. Each man carried a child. The third lagged behind; one of the men called back to him in obvious consternation, his words whipped away by the wind. Paula leaned down and whispered to Coryn. "Should I offer to help them?"

Coryn blinked, still unused to being the one to choose things. What would it hurt? Besides, the oldest child—the only one who wasn't being carried—looked seriously frightened. "Sure."

"Hello," Coryn called as they approached. "Are you going to the school?"

The man who had been calling to the child looked up, wind whipping blond hair back from his face, which was creased with worry, his eyes wide. "Yes. Can you carry him?"

"I can," Paula said.

The man squinted at her, clearly just now identifying Paula as a companion-bot. He grimaced, but another gust of wind blew some small branches from the trees and littered the street close to them. The smallest child cried out in fear and buried her face in her father's chest.

Rain started in big cold drops.

"Okay," the man said. "But stay with us. If you don't, I'm armed."

Coryn startled and managed to choke out an "Of course." Guns were illegal in the city, but not Outside. She hadn't expected one. Not with kids and all. She took a deep breath and kept going.

They leaned into cold wind and fat raindrops. Coryn's clothes were soaked through. Her wristlet suggested it was still midday, but the color of the sky convinced her it must be lying through its tiny little teeth.

She swallowed. She had wanted to experience real weather. The wind felt far rawer than she had imaged, more magical and more threatening than she had expected. The city's ability to control it suddenly awed her. She'd never realized what wind could be, so how could she have grasped how much technology it must take to tame it? As this storm reached the city, the wind would be harvested for power, dampened, controlled. The permeable dome would repel it, and, if necessary, the city's lights would brighten to mitigate the darkness.

Coryn craned her neck, looking up and around, watching the wind-bent trees with trepidation. Her hair whipped her face and stung her eyes, and her feet squished in her shoes. She was grateful when the school finally loomed up out of the rainy dark, a long low building with only three stories. "It looks like it's made of brick." Coryn had only seen brick a few times, in squat historic buildings like Town Hall, which had become surrounded by modern nanofabbed giants. "Is that good?"

"Probably," Paula replied. The boy she carried looked about seven, and he clung to the robot with all he had, only occasionally showing his face. When he did, he looked as scared as Coryn. "The heat's on, and it should be dry and pretty safe."

Soon, they were picking through puddles and downed branches in the parking lot. Light shone from a few of the school windows, and a man in a black rain jacket and a soaked red baseball cap stood by the front door. He opened it as the group approached. He greeted the two men warmly, "Hello, Jim, Steve. Good to see you."

The blond appeared to be the regular spokesman. He said, "Hi, Erich. Rough night. There's a few trees might land on the house. Thought it might be safer here."

The man glanced briefly at Coryn and harder at Paula. "These are strangers. Do you vouch for them?" he asked.

"Sure," the blond replied. "They just met us on the road, but she carried Thomas, and she didn't have to."

Paula set the little boy down, and he raced to the darker of the two men, Jim, and stood close enough that no light shone between him and his father's leg.

A long whip of wind ran through the trees in the parking lot, bending them almost in half. "Go on into the gym," Erich said, raising his voice over the roar. "I wouldn't wish this storm on my worst enemy."

Coryn didn't need to be asked twice. She grabbed Paula's hand and hurried past Erich and into the beckoning warmth and light.

CHAPTER ELEVEN

Inside the school, Coryn immediately felt merely cold instead of like ice. The wind sounded both muffled and higher pitched, as if it were licking the outside of the building, searching for weak spots. A short hike through a hall of scratched blue lockers led to the sports gymnasium, a large rectangle of carefully polished wooden floor, freshly painted concrete walls, and metal bleachers. A row of tables lined the far side of the room. Half held food and water and the other half had blankets, coats, and what looked like pillows scrounged from couches or chairs. Groups of people stood talking together around the tables.

Coryn had been expecting chaos. "It looks like they do this all the time."

"They might." Paula surveyed the room, keeping her back toward a wall by the door they had come through. "Storms are common Outside."

"They can't all be this bad!" She shivered at a loud crack, perhaps a tree branch snapping. "Lou used to tell me stories about the weather out here."

"I remember." Paula stood quite still, looking around.

"I thought she was making it up!"

The scents of coffee, grease, and sugar infused the air. A young man with a shock of red hair hanging in his eyes carried two plates of pizza across the gym floor. Apparently the school had an oven somewhere. Well, a school probably had a cafeteria. The pizza drew a smile from Paula, who glanced at Coryn. "Eat."

"Yes, mother." But she was grinning, happy to have walls between her and the wind.

The gray-haired and thin woman at the food table tried to hand Coryn two plates. When she hesitated, the woman squinted at Paula and pulled a plate back, the smile fading from her eyes. Coryn produced an overly cheerful, "Thank you," doing her best not to show she had noticed.

She ended up with a cup of barely warm coffee and a plate with a slice of pizza, an apple, and a cookie. Paula carried the coffee and a glass of water. They climbed to the highest step on the bleachers and leaned against the cinder-block wall. A thin window with metal bars across it ran around the top of the room. Wind-driven rain splattered against it. From time to time a gust improbably hooked under the eaves and rattled the glass.

As she finished off the comfortingly warm pizza, a few young people filled the empty half of the court and started playing a ball game that took three balls and two teams. "You should join them," Paula suggested. "Hand me your coat."

Coryn peeled her wet coat off, pleased that her shirt was dry. Mostly. "They all look like they know each other."

"Go on," Paula said. "Maybe you'll learn something."

Coryn climbed down the steps and dropped her plate in the recycler, then stood at the edge of the game, trying to figure it out. A basketball hoop hung over the court, but for this game it was merely an obstacle. Players threw a dark ball and a light ball at a far larger multicolored ball, trying to knock it out of the air. One team of four controlled the big ball, and there were two on the dark small one and three on the light small one. A tall boy on the dark team waved her in. She grinned. "Sure." As soon as she stepped inbounds the ball came at her. She caught it, surprised at its lightness, and threw it at the big ball, knocking it sideways and earning a grin from the tall boy. Well, young man. Her age, anyway. His brown-blond hair looked uncombed, and his pants had been patched in two places.

The other person on her team was a girl a year or two younger than her, with a long red braid and rather fabulous tats on her cheeks that looked like hundreds of small butterflies in flight. She smiled. "I'm Laurie."

"Coryn."

"Nice to meet you." A ball came toward her and Coryn knocked it just right. It was nearly impossible to play and talk, other than one-word directions like *left* and *right* and short commentary like *good* and *too bad*. She only thought about the storm when a particularly strong wind gust rattled the windows or when the door opened to admit more shivering, wet people.

A few times, she noticed Erich quite near and had the sense he was trying not to look like he was watching them.

After about half an hour, the players were all winded and took a break. They made their way as a group to the water table and drank deeply. The red-haired girl, Laurie, pulled her a little bit aside from the others. "You play all right." The butterflies on her cheeks rippled as she talked.

"Thanks." The compliment warmed her; she didn't often get them from people her own age.

"Where do you come from?" Laurie asked. "Why do you have a robot?"

She hesitated. But there was no way to hide Paula's nature, or to pretend she came from here. "I'm from Seacouver, and I've always had a robot. I've always had *this* one. Her name's Paula."

"I wish we had them," the girl said. "Then we wouldn't have to do all the work."

Coryn managed not to laugh. "They can do work. But usually Paula makes me do work. We all have chores in the city, things we have to do for basic." As she said it, she realized it was almost certainly the wrong thing to say, so she added, "But they could be helpful here. I can see that."

"Does everyone in the city have a robot?"

The conversation felt uncomfortable, even though Laurie seemed genuinely curious. "Many of us do. At least a lot of the kids and the old people, and also some really busy people." And all the rich ones, but she had the presence of mind not to add that out loud.

The other girl grimaced. "I told my dad I wanted one, and he said it would rot my brain."

"It hasn't happened to me yet," Coryn said.

"Maybe it only happens when you're older."

Coryn stiffened, and then smiled. "I haven't seen a lot of people wandering about with rotting brains." She felt really uncomfortable saying more. "How far did you have to walk to get here?"

"Just a mile." Perhaps she sensed Coryn didn't want to talk about Paula anymore since she drifted back toward the water table.

The crowd had almost doubled. Except for a few noticeably unhappy small children, most people seemed to be having nervous, slightly frenetic fun.

A loud snapping sound followed by a crash drew them all toward the door, and when Erich opened it, the entire top of a tree nearly blocked it. Erich and number of others pulled on raincoats and Erich pointed at Paula. "Come on."

There was no way to say no, not politely. Coryn didn't like it, but she pulled her wet coat back on, and they followed Erich and three men into the knife-hard wind. First, they had to force their way through the tangled and broken branches. "Go first," Erich demanded, and Paula leaned into the tree, her arms forward, her head ducked to avoid scratching her delicate face.

"Push," Erich yelled.

Coryn wanted to hit him. Paula wasn't a stupid work-bot you ordered around.

But she did push, leaning in hard. The tree didn't budge.

The robot stood back up, looking contemplatively at the problem. She ripped two or three small branches away and threw them over the tree. She pushed again. It moved a little, and then a little more.

Coryn stepped up beside her and leaned on a branch as wide as her arm, pushing as hard as she could. She wasn't at all sure she made any difference, but it felt good to help.

It took a moment or two before the men stepped in to help, and Coryn felt sure that if she hadn't started pushing none of them would have. They would have let Paula do it all even if it broke things inside her.

Rain beat on them, and the tree moved slowly, a tangled, wet weight.

Her coat dripped water. She had to blink in the rain. Her right foot slipped out from under her and she only stayed upright because of her grip on the tree.

Paula stopped pushing and turned around. "That's enough. There's a path."

Erich stared at Paula. "Maybe we should push it all the way to the parking lot."

"No."

Erich's cheeks turned bright red, and for a moment Coryn though he might challenge them. But he waved them back in to the building without any thank you at all.

Once inside, he barked at the people close to him, "Stay away from the windows."

Commands came easy to him, and people obeyed as easily.

Tree branches slammed into the outside of the building twice, making the walls shake and driving short, complete silences into the crowd.

Families migrated toward the center of the room as if some force pulled them together. Coryn gestured to Paula, and they joined the others on the floor. As people got close to each other, the fact that Paula was the only robot companion stood out. Some of the men and women glanced toward her from time to time with unreadable expressions on their faces. Paula's standard black uniform looked disheveled from her efforts with the tree. It was easy to know what she was with even a short glance. Did they want Paula, or were they were jealous of Coryn for having her? Or were they frightened?

Since the storm was bigger than the robot, for now, it was hard to tell.

With this many people in this place, we're safe, she told herself firmly. *If the wind doesn't blow us away.*

CHAPTER TWELVE

Coryn woke up to an exhausted quiet. Paula's hand rested on her shoulder as a guard against falling down the bleacher steps. Even with her sleeping bag for insulation and the inside of her damp coat for a pillow, the cold steps had been hard to doze on. She stood and stretched, then tiptoed up to the top of the bleachers to peer through the filthy, scratched window. The trees barely moved. Puddles in the soaked ground reflected high, gray clouds.

Paula joined Coryn near the window and looked out. "What a mess!"

In spite of the litter on the ground, most of the trees stood upright and birds flew here and there between branches. Rabbits munched grass contentedly in the open spaces.

"Be quiet," Coryn whispered. The floor was full of sleeping bodies tangled in coats and blankets, heads resting on each other's arms and legs. "We should go."

Paula went silent, probably communing with whatever vestiges of net existed in the school after all that. "The road may be clear, but I can't tell for sure."

"We need to go. These people have been watching you since we came in."

Paula kept her voice low. "I saw."

Coryn rolled her sleeping bag up and tied it to her pack. She started quietly down the bleachers. Jim and Steven were already awake and tending to the youngest of their children. They watched her and Paula quietly, looking almost regretful. Why?

She stopped to fill up her canteen at a water fountain. The water trickling into it sounded like a waterfall in the windless morning.

Erich sat next to the front door, half asleep. One eye opened as they approached.

"Good morning," she said. "Thanks for the hospitality."

He blinked and sat up. "Stay." It was practically an order.

They hadn't even finished half a marathon of distance. "We have someplace to be," she told him, keeping her voice low. "We appreciate your hospitality, but we've got to go."

He stared up at Paula, frowning. "We could use the robot's help with cleanup."

Coryn pursed her lips. Was this like the socks, only now someone wanted time and muscle? She did her best to sound apologetic. "We can't."

He tensed, and his mouth drew into a sharp frown. For a moment Coryn thought he might try to stop them, even though he must know Paula was a match for any one man in hand-to-hand combat. "Surely you can give us a day of help cleaning up. In return for the shelter."

Coryn smiled. "I'm sorry. I do appreciate you letting us stay. But we did help you move the tree, and we have to be somewhere. It's important."

He pushed himself to stand close enough that she smelled his sweat and the sap and cedar on his hands from pulling trees away from the doorway. "If you stay here for a while, you'll be safer. The roads are certainly blocked by trees."

She felt awkward about being rude, but she couldn't be caught here, not so close to the city. She hadn't even seen the real wild yet, much less come any meaningful distance closer to Lou. Besides, she couldn't protect Paula from this many people. If there was a fight, there would be injuries, and she might lose, and Paula might be destroyed . . . She shivered, hating herself for thinking this way but certain that she had to. "We really do have to go."

Erich kept staring, as if the force of his personality could prevent them from leaving.

Coryn gestured for Paula to go, and they passed Erich and went out into a morning washed bright and clean and full of small catastrophes. Wet leaves and stray branches covered the road, and mud from rain-born storm streams ran everywhere. A slight breeze touched her cheek. Coryn drew a deep breath; the air tasted fresh and damp and almost delicious. She grinned at Paula in relief. "Come on."

They picked their way through litter and over downed trees. Twice she and Paula pulled trees off the road. Two of the houses they passed had been crushed by falling trees, and three more had lost some or all of their roofs to the raging wind.

People struggled through cleanup in front of many of the houses. Some stared at them; others waved.

All day, it was slow going. Long before time to stop for lunch, Coryn's feet dragged. Why was it so much harder to walk Outside than to run a marathon in the city? She glanced at Paula. "Maybe I need a virtual band."

"Shall I clap for you?" Paula asked.

"Silly robot. That would draw attention." She shook her head and walked further before saying, "Maybe I should stop calling you that. I've used that nickname as long as I remember, but now it feels childish."

Paula cocked her head to the side. "I consider it a term of endearment."

"Silly robot."

Halfway through the day, Coryn ate an energy bar and one of the few gels they had with them. It helped for about an hour.

The farther they got from the city, the fewer houses they saw. Coryn had imagined they'd be at I-90 by the end of the day, but the little map on her wrist said they were no better than halfway there. Her feet stung, and the long night on the metal bench hadn't done anything for her energy level. And how had her pack gained weight? She sighed in gratitude when Paula finally took it without a word.

When a dusky orange and pink started to tinge the sky, she gave up. "I need to eat. I can't keep going if I don't eat."

"Shelter first," Paula said. She led them into an old barn that had been down to half a roof long before last night's storm. Together, they swept out the worst of the cobwebs with fistfuls of old hay and pulled in downed branches to fashion a pillow for Coryn. After she ate more nuts and two sweet apples, Coryn lay back and looked up at the stars. "I never knew the sky could be so dark or that stars were so bright."

Paula spoke softly. "A windstorm like that clears the dust."

"I thought there wasn't any more pollution."

"Experience suggests that not everything the city has told us is true."

Coryn blinked at that but chose not to talk about it, not yet. Her news sources in the city had lied about a lot. She hadn't decided how angry to be about that. Should she assume it had good reasons?

Paula shifted her position to be a little closer to Coryn. "The brightest stars are planets or stations." She pointed. "The one just north of us? That's from Moscow, and there's almost a thousand people living on it. It's one of the biggest."

"Can we see any of Seacouver's stations?"

"The city doesn't own any. But two Boeing experimental stations should be visible before dawn."

"How many could we see if we stayed up all night?"

Paula went silent for a long while. "Twenty-one, if we were outside. But through this hole in the roof? Three."

"I can't see the moon."

"It will come up in twenty-seven minutes."

"Oh."

"So how do you feel about leaving now?" Paula asked.

"I'm glad," she blurted out. The barn creaked with a light wind, the sound sending shivers up her spine. "I miss weeding."

"You told me you hated weeding."

"Until I couldn't do it anymore. I miss it now." She had weeded rain swales, digging in sandy ground to pull out invasive plants. "I miss making up little songs while I weed."

"Do you remember any of them?"

Coryn snorted. "If I did, I wouldn't sing them right now."

"I bet there are weeds out here," Paula responded.

Coryn let out a long whistle. "I bet there are. Wake me up when the moon is overhead."

"Yes, ma'am."

"Helpful robot." Coryn smiled and closed her eyes. Maybe she *should* have left Paula at home. She might not be a person by any legal standard, but as far as Coryn was concerned Paula had a personality, and Coryn couldn't imagine living without her or seeing her hurt. And there were so many things Paula could do that she couldn't do. Maybe Laurie had been more right than Coryn wanted to admit. Maybe she had become so used to getting help that she didn't even notice all of the myriad things Paula did for her.

Did she have the right to risk Paula's life?

The question kept her from sleep and then followed her into dreams that showed dead Paulas, stolen Paulas, and Paulas that simply needed to be fixed, only there was no place to fix them. She woke once with a deep dread of being even more alone than she'd been in the city. She turned onto her back and caught her breath.

Stars filled the sky through the hole in the roof, a depth of stars she'd never really imagined.

Every edge looked so sharp! If the stars came down and cut her to death out here in the wild woods, no one would ever know. Here, she was tiny and alone and insignificant.

The thought followed her back down into slumber.

‡ ‡ ‡

Something rocked and shook, pulling at her; something else pinned her to the floor. Coryn flailed wildly before she was even awake; someone's feet scuffled against old wood and a strange voice cursed softly. Her eyes flew open; she jerked, lashing out, but couldn't sit up. The gray light of dawn seeped in through a bare, glassless window.

Men knelt on either side of her, grabbing for her arms; she'd no sooner grasped the fact than they caught and held her by her wrists and elbows. They were muscular and young, maybe even her age. Both wore black vests. She had the distinct impression that if she could see the back of the vests there would be something written on them. "Who are you?" she demanded.

They held her so silently she might as well have been captured by police robots. She could barely tell that they breathed. Both looked away from her, as if holding her was a side job, a thing they barely needed to think about.

Fear and fury shot through her; she thrashed from side to side, kicking with renewed vigor. Her feet only met air. Where was Paula? "Paula! Help! Paula!"

"Be quiet," a voice demanded from by the door. She glanced toward it. Erich. He was dressed in the same clothes she'd seen him in at the high school, including the red cap. His small eyes gleamed with triumph.

"You followed us!"

He didn't answer.

Paula! The last time she'd seen her, Paula had been sitting beside her. She turned her head up to where she had been. She surveyed as much of the barn as she could see, and Paula simply wasn't anywhere. She forced herself to take deep breaths and get some control back. "Where is she?"

"She's being reprogrammed."

"No!" The word ripped from Coryn's throat. "No!" She kicked again, hit nothing again, did it again another way. Nothing.

"You might as well calm down," Erich said.

Coryn's gaze darted back and forth between her captors' faces. They remained impassive, uncaring. They might be good-looking men if there was any personality on their faces. They looked like—but weren't—robots.

She gulped air, tried to stay calm and think. Paula had to be nearby or else they'd be gone. The robot was worth ten times anything *she'd* be worth to anyone. Why hadn't she understood that? She had seen the way people asked about her, and the sock woman had told her what to worry about.

Why hadn't she taken her advice?

How could she have been so stupid?

How could she get free?

She wanted the city and its million cameras, its relative and strange safety, its millions of faceless people that didn't say hello to her but didn't accost her either. She wanted its noise and bustle, its music and its safe crowds.

She wanted help.

A hot tear raced down her cheek, and she blinked, hating the tear, not letting any more fall. She couldn't look weak. Whatever was happening, she knew better than to be a victim. Paula always told her that when they were out later than usual or when they passed through the darker parts of the city.

The morning had brightened enough for her to see people's faces. Erich was the only one she recognized.

Why hadn't she been more careful? Why hadn't they hidden?

Each moment that she stayed captive was a moment she wasn't stopping Erich from reprogramming Paula. They'd have to break her security, and there was a lot of that.

Surely it would take them a while.

"Stay still!" Erich commanded. "I'm sure you want this to be easy."

"What?"

"Easy on you. We want the robot. But we can't have you identifying us. So we're going to give you a little something to help you forget about the last few days."

"What?" There were drugs for that. They gave them to rape victims. If they wanted them. It was illegal to give them without consent.

He wouldn't!

Who would catch him here?

Her heart pounded as she stared at the men holding her. They looked serious.

"Marina?" Erich said. "Do it."

A tall redheaded woman dressed in brown leather walked up, her figure strangely elongated as she came close to Coryn and loomed over her. Her black boots smelled like mud and forest. Her hair hung down at her sides in braids, almost like a character of an Indian maiden from history books or from a history game.

She clutched a syringe in one hand.

Coryn kicked at her, but Marina moved easily to avoid the blow, sliding away like a dancer—or a fighter. She stared down at Coryn, a pitiless hard stare, a hungry stare. Her eyes were a wrong-green, some color achievable only with implants or dyes or something.

Coryn spit at her, bucked, screamed.

Marina held up the small automatic syringe. Her other hand darted in to capture the skin on Coryn's upper arm between the hands holding her down.

Coryn sucked in a breath and screamed again. "No!"

Something moved behind Marina, a blur, and then Marina was yanked up and the syringe pulled from her hand and thrown.

Paula?

Coryn kicked again, but her captors yanked her to her feet, facing away so she couldn't see what was happening while one of them looked each direction.

They held her tightly, even while clearly paying attention to whatever was behind them. She tried to turn her head far enough to see and one of them slapped her.

She stomped down on a foot, dug her heel into a calf. The two young men remained immovable.

She struggled.

With shocking suddenness, the men shoved her away. The rough floor peeled skin from her wrists as she caught herself; she barely managed not to hit her head.

She rolled, scrambling to get to her feet, to see what had made them let go of her.

The entire barn door was filled by a set of three ecobots in full enforcement mode, their heads up, twitching back and forth to observe everything in the building. At least two arms held weapons. Swarms of small drones filled the barn.

CHAPTER THIRTEEN

Ecobots jostled forcefully through the open barn door. Coryn backed up against the wall, trying to ignore the ghostly touch of spiderwebs brushing her cheek. The men who had shoved her away were being bombarded by small drones while struggling to get the bolt open on a human-sized door opposite the bots. They kept twitching as the drones slammed into them, over and over and over. One of the ecobots pulled its head down and in. It rumbled forward, filling a good half of the barn, and used two of its hands to pull the two men backward.

As soon as they were grabbed, they stilled, their faces frozen with fear. The ecobot pulled them out of the barn, backing out with precision.

Coryn looked around. The barn was empty. Erich and Marina must have gone the way of the other two men; there was no other exit. She grabbed her pack and Paula's and staggered outside under the weight of all of their belongings.

The chaos around her made her reel. Three rounded vans painted in outrageously bright primary colors sat on the road. Near them, at least five strangers and one small, white dog watched the ecobots secure the attackers with what looked like big nets that tightened around their arms and torsos, leaving their legs free. Coryn blinked at the number of attackers. Erich, Marina, the two men who had been holding her, three more men she was seeing for the first time. There was also a stocky woman who looked older than them all. Erich was the only one she recognized from the school.

Why send so many people after her and Paula? Where was Paula?

"Hey!"

Paula's voice. Coryn whirled, shivering with the release of fear. She let the packs fall and raced into Paula's arms.

"Are you okay?" Paula whispered.

"Now." She stepped away and looked at Paula. Other than a few hairs out of place, she looked exactly like usual. "They didn't hurt you, did they?"

"No."

Coryn's voice still shook. "They told me they reprogrammed you."

"They planned to."

The ecobots herded their captives up a ramp into a truck that Coryn hadn't even noticed. "What happened?"

"They stunned me briefly with something—maybe a beam weapon?—and dragged me outside."

"I didn't notice?"

The door slammed shut on the truck. The bed had a top, which the robots latched down. No one would be getting away.

"They were very quiet," Paula said. She smiled. "And you do sleep deeply."

"Not that deeply."

"Want to bet?"

One of the men who had been standing near the vans headed toward them. The expression on his face looked triumphant, which made Coryn smile. His wore his long black hair in a loose ponytail, a few silvery strands making him look a little older than his fit physique suggested. He wore jeans and hiking boots and a simple green shirt with rolled-up long sleeves. Most people she'd seen out here would look shabby in the city, but not this man. Paula leaned down and whispered, "Be careful," in Coryn's ear before she went back to prim and proper robot mode.

Coryn held out her hand. "Hello. I'm Coryn Williams. Did you help us?"

"Lucien." His deep voice rumbled from his chest. "Lucien Lapatsa." He took her hand and shook it. "We've been watching that group. We had enough evidence to have them arrested, and we were tracking Erich. So when we saw them intersect with you in the barn, we called for help."

Coryn glanced at Paula. "Thank you. Thank you very much."

"You're welcome." The string of ecobots and the truck pulled away, and she and the man—Lucien—stood watching until they disappeared from sight.

She had a stray thought. "How did you know we were in the barn?"

He blinked. "Satellite."

So it was more like home out here than she had thought. "Does someone always know where we are?"

"No. Not like in the city. Don't expect to be saved. One of our friends saw you in the school and suggested we watch out for you. Since we were here anyway, waiting to take down Erich, we did. What are you doing out here alone anyway? It's not safe."

"I'm heading for the Palouse to find someone."

"You just left the city? On your own?"

She might as well paint it in on her forehead. "Yesterday morning."

He sighed. "Okay. Well. Don't stay out by yourself. We're heading up the 90. Not as far as you're going, just to Cle Elum. But we can give you a lift."

Coryn felt lighter. A smile crept across her face, and she felt a little bubble of happiness rise. "That would be fabulous." If she understood the map right, that would make up all of the time they had lost so far.

He glanced over at the gaudy vans. "So. Lesson number one. This is a barter economy. Sometimes. You can't barter your way out of everything. Some people take credit against a future favor, but almost everyone takes trades." He watched her closely, as if assessing whether or not she understood. When she nodded slightly, he asked, "What will you trade for your ride?"

"I'm almost out of extra socks."

He blinked at her. "What?"

She laughed. "Sorry. You'd have had to be with us. If there's any hard jobs to be done, Paula and I can help. We can clean up your cars, for example. Do dishes. Paula's strong. We can lift things."

He smiled. "All good options. Lucky for you, I don't need even that much. I'll trade you the ride and some advice for news about the city. I grew up Inside, and there are days I still miss it."

She considered him, reminding herself that no one Outside had proven trustworthy yet. He was handsome in a far-older-man kind of way, a little rugged, and not particularly threatening. In fact, he seemed kind; both his voice and his gaze projected concern.

He had also just saved her and Paula.

She hadn't done so well on her own so far. Making it to Cle Elum would be progress. She held her hand out again. "I'd be happy to tell stories."

He shook it again and seemed to relax a little, pleased with her answer. She glanced back at the garish vans. "Can I sit by your dog?"

"Of course you can. His name is Aspen."

"Aspen? That's pretty."

"It's a kind of tree."

"I know that."

"The name doesn't fit him."

She found herself laughing a little. "Paula stays with me."

Lucien smiled. "Good. Let's get you bundled into one of the vans, and I'll see that Aspen and I are both near you." He gestured toward the vans. "Which one do you like the most?"

The front van was white with yellow and blue, the back yellow with bright red doors, and that middle one had a bright blue door and bright blue fenders on a faded red body. She pointed at it. "Is that okay?"

He smiled. "Sure."

Lucien led her toward the van she'd chosen. The vans were slightly rounded in the front and the back, like oval balls, and the wheels were almost as tall as Coryn.

"Why do they have such big wheels?"

"We're not always on roads. Even when we are, most roads in the rewilding areas are being let go, and some are being ripped out. We drive through some pretty rough country."

He opened the door, and she ducked into the van. Inside, it looked bigger than it had from the outside. A long table with bench seats full of drawers filled the nose, and the back half was given over to neat bedding, a small kitchen, and two chairs that stared at a blank video wall. Below the front window and just above the table, an interactive whiteboard had pictures and notes scrawled on it. Lucien pointed toward the front. "Have a seat."

The red plastic cushion softened when she sat on it, reacting to her weight and bending enough to be perfectly comfortable. The front was almost all window, thick enough that the images outside appeared slightly distorted.

Lucien appeared in the doorway, snapping his fingers. "Up!"

Aspen bounded in and sat, regarding her cautiously, his tail thumping the floor like a drum. He had pale bluish-gray spots and streaks over a short white undercoat, pure white legs, and a white head. One eye matched the blue in his coat and the other was a pale brown. She patted her lap hopefully, and he cocked his head to the side, reminding her of the wild dog she'd fed earlier.

"Go on," Lucien said.

Aspen hopped up and landed on her. He lifted his face and licked her cheek before turning around to sit on her.

"Good boy," Lucien said. "I'll be right back," he told Coryn, and then glanced at Aspen. "Stay."

The van pleased her. Everything had a place. The roof and upper walls and benches all had drawers or cabinets in them. Color splashed everywhere, primarily blues and reds that were lighter, less jarring versions of the outside paint.

Nothing about the vans was meant to blend into the background. Why did they try to draw attention to themselves?

Lucien came back with two other people, a woman just a few years older than Coryn and an older man with Hispanic features and warm brown eyes that matched his skin. They piled into the seats opposite, which left Coryn with no one next to her except Paula.

The man held his hand out. "I'm Pablo." He had a gravelly voice and scars all over the back of his hand.

She smiled at him and took his hand, almost letting go as she felt his rough skin. "Coryn. And this is Paula."

Paula said, "Pleased to meet you," in her warmest voice.

Pablo put his hands together in what looked almost like prayer and gave a small bow, just a few inches. "You must be a good person. Aspen is very picky."

That delighted her, and she clutched Aspen a little closer. He reached his little nose up and licked the underside of her chin.

The girl said, "I'm Lucien's cousin, Liselle. People often think he's my dad, but I'm older than I look." Sure enough, her thin face matched Lucien's in shape, and her eyes had the same grays in them, like morning skies just before the clouds opened to let in sunlight.

The vans pulled out and headed northeast. The blank wall sprang to life, filling with satellite images of the area, the vans highlighted in brighter colors. "Wow!" she said.

Pablo smile, an easy, soft smile. "We don't want to be surprised."

"I guess not." She forced herself to stop staring at the video. "Thank you all. I'm pretty sure I'd be dead."

Liselle shook her head, the black curtain of her hair waving across her shoulders. "More likely left behind or about to be sold for a slave. We've figured we'd catch Erich eventually—it's stupid to set yourself up as a lord that close to the city."

"Thinks he's a warlord," Lucien added. "He'd have sold you and your robot for money and bought whiskey with his profit."

Aspen seemed to sense her sudden dread; he leaned into her and rested his face on her chest. She looked down into his one blue and one brown eye, and drew her fingers though his unexpectedly soft fur. He was more fur than dog and actually surprisingly slender. "Thanks again for saving us."

Lucien leaned toward her. "You were lucky. If you'd run afoul of just any common thug we wouldn't have stopped them. So be grateful you drew the attention of a true bad guy. We've been out to catch Erich for a long time. Kidnapping you gave us direct evidence of a crime."

That caught her attention. "Do you work for the city?"

He shrugged as if to say *doesn't everyone?* But she recognized it as a non-answer and pursed her lips.

Well, Lou was out here. So was she. But she had thought the Outside was full of people who had never been in a city. Another thing she'd been wrong about. "Are you police?"

"Not exactly. You don't need to worry about that. But we haven't been Inside for a long time. Tell me some news?"

The trade. She suddenly felt tongue-tied. "How long do we have?"

He chuckled. "You can stay with us overnight up at Cle Elum, so you'll have as much time as you want. We'll keep our promises, too, help you out." He paused, as if thinking through nuggets of wisdom. "For example, you should dress Paula in clothes that a person would wear, not a robot."

It seemed so obvious in hindsight. *Duh.* "You're right."

"Do you have any?"

"No."

"We'll solve that." Liselle said. "Tell us about the city." She sounded almost as hungry as Lucien for news.

CHAPTER FOURTEEN

Coryn sat back, the dog warm on her lap, and realized she felt safe—really safe—for the first time since she'd walked out from under the dome of the city. Knots of stress she hadn't noticed released from her neck, her back, her gut. Telling a story about the city was small trade for such unexpected relief. "I don't know where to start. I mean, you're from the city, right? You know things, right?"

Silence fell, so all she heard was the gentle rolling of the wheels and everyone breathing. The dog's breath was surprisingly sweet. She started hesitatingly. "Well, we finally made it to ninety-five percent city-grown food, which means we could live inside the dome completely."

They showed no sign of surprise.

"You knew that. What else? Half of us are transitories. No home address but always a place to sleep, even if it's a little one. I was about to be kicked out of where I was living, since I'm an adult now. I would probably have become a transitory, trading chores for basic-basic or picking up a simple job so I could save for better schooling."

"Was that why you left?"

She found the question mildly offensive. "Of course not. I would have done okay with that life. I spent two weeks of my last summer vacation living transitory. It wasn't bad. Went north into Seattle proper. Paula helped me find small places we could afford, and I got to stay in a tent-camp at Volunteer Park for two nights. They had movies every night and free food."

Liselle smiled. "I love the botanical gardens there. And some of the trees with the loopy branches." She leaned forward. "How happy do people seem?"

"Most are happier than me." Aspen jerked in her lap and resettled. "I mean I left, right?" She paused, groping for words. She'd never tried to organize her own thoughts, her unrest, her sense of not belonging, into something substantial enough for words before. Now, they seemed to take on a life of their own, spilling out of her with increasing ease. "Everything's just too perfect in the city, too unreal. It's like stacked virtual worlds, one on top of the other, like you can be a physics geek or a dancer or get lost in reading and talking about books. But none of it felt real." She looked around again. Liselle smiled at her, and Coryn felt like it was a little encouragement to keep going. "Almost everyone is nice, in a cold-distracted way, but I didn't have anyone I was really close to unless you count Paula. She's my friend, but she's still a robot."

She hadn't really meant to say that much. She'd gotten confident and then gone too far, and now the sympathetic looks Lucien and Liselle directed at her crawled up her spine. "I don't need anyone to feel sorry for me; I mean, I'm just saying that's how it seems to me."

"Okay." Pablo smiled that easy smile again. "I think it was brave of you to come out here. After all, we did."

She cleared her throat. "Good." Out of the window, tall trees closed in around them, blocking the sun. "Look, do you have specific questions?"

"You said you're going to find your sister," Lucien asked. "When did you see her last?"

She swallowed. "Four years ago. We write to each other." She didn't like how the conversation kept curling back to her personal life. "What can I tell you about the city?"

Liselle sat back and looked thoughtful. Pablo asked her, "How happy are people other than you? Do you see protests? Can you tell if people are happy with how things are run?"

That was a harder question. What did she know about how other people felt? It wasn't like she'd ever tried talking to anyone about this kind of thing. "I think so. I mean, not everyone. There's never everyone happy, right? But, like I said, most people seem happier than me." She twisted her fingers through Aspen's fur. She'd like to give them whatever they wanted, if only she knew what that was. "I hear about protests on the newsfeed sometimes, but they don't seem to be very big."

Lucien looked up from a tablet he was poking at and asked, "What are the protests about?"

"What's it always about? Some people have too much."

"Do you think that's true?" Pablo asked. He leaned in a little, his curiosity genuine as far as she could tell. It still felt a little like a test.

"I . . . I haven't thought about it much." She took a deep breath. "No one's poor. Not with basic. Even if I never earned enough to go up in the job market, I'd have had food and doctors. Doesn't everyone in the city have more than most people out here?"

Pablo steepled his hands and leaned toward her. "Some people out here have a lot of power."

"Like Erich? That's why they want to steal Paula, right? She'd give him more power here."

Pablo reached a hand across the table and scratched Aspen behind the ears. "Robots confer status here more than power, and they seldom last long. The real power is in the NGOs."

She glanced at Paula. *Robots didn't last long.*

But Paula didn't appear to hear that. She looked curiously at Pablo. "What about the NGOs?"

Liselle answered, her voice tinged with bitterness. "They have all of the resources. Or 90 percent of them, anyway. They're like the angels and the devils, and we're all the ones in between trying to broker life and peace."

The van slowed for a moment and then sped up again. Lucien looked out the window before turning back to them. "The NGOs *are* the best and the worst things out here. But people like Erich kill more people."

Pablo grinned. "Only directly."

It felt like an old argument. Coryn filed it away to ask more questions about when she got a chance.

Paula spoke, startling Coryn a little. "They wanted to reprogram me. I have been pondering what that might mean. What did they want to program me to become?" She glanced at Coryn. "After all, if they kill you, then I'm pretty much available to be reassigned. But no one tried to kill you. Therefore, they wanted to make me something I'm not."

Coryn swallowed hard. *That* danger had never crossed her mind. "What if they didn't want any traces that you used to be mine left? So if they got caught later, they could make up any story they wanted?"

Pablo went to the sink and poured water for everyone. Coryn drank gratefully, using the time to think a little. "How come there aren't more robots out here anyway?"

"There's more than you see," Liselle explained. "Farms have some, usually. Some people have helper-bots for the sick or the old. They're expensive and hard to maintain, and having one can make you a target. So a lot of the tech that's out here is hidden."

"But you drive around in vans that look like kids' toys?"

"We want to be seen," Lucien said. "That's our mission. To help people that need help, and they have to be able to find us with stories. The bright colors tell them who we are—we're Listeners."

Coryn blinked. "Listeners? I never heard of Listeners."

"Well, there aren't any Listeners in the city. So why would you?"

"I did a lot of research," she snapped at no one in particular.

Liselle laughed and held her hands up. "Real life is different from stories. That's something we know. That's why we're out here, on the ground."

That made sense, kind of. "Do people try to steal the vans?"

Lucien laughed. "Not often. They're bio-chipped to us—no one else can drive them. Besides, we have weapons. They don't kill anyone, but people leave us alone after a try or two."

"So what kind of help do you give people?"

He grinned. "Rides."

"Why?"

"We need information. People trade us that for help."

Like she was doing. She still wanted to know if they worked for the city, but she was pretty sure they weren't going to tell her. "What do you do with information?" she asked.

"We watch for patterns."

She stared out the front window, waiting for them to ask her another question. The caravan of vans had turned twice, and now they were slowing down. They passed slowly up and over a makeshift bridge of stones that crossed a place where the road had been washed out. The van tilted one way, then the other. Aspen stood up on her lap and looked out, and everyone held onto their water glasses.

After the ride smoothed again, Pablo asked her, "So people inside are complaining about having less than the center people, right?"

"Yes." He meant the really rich people. Like Julianna. The ones who lived in the tops of the biggest buildings and looked down on the rest of the city.

"How do you think people out here feel?"

Pablo looked so earnest that she laughed. "Like they want my robot. But can't at least some of them get into the city?"

"Not many. There's so much tech they can't function."

They passed a tractor, one of the few things allowed to use gasoline any more. The plume of smoke coming from its pipes made her cough and choke. When she could talk again, she said, "I guess. I see that."

Liselle laughed, her laugh high and friendly and sweet. "It's a speed thing. In the city, everything moves fast. How long does it take you to go from Seattle to Tacoma?"

"Half an hour? Depending on where I start."

"That's right. On a train." Liselle flipped her hair away from her face with her hand. "How long would it take you to bike?"

"Maybe three hours. I'm pretty good on a bike."

Pablo said, "The distance between Duvall and Cle Elum is about twice as far as the distance between Seattle and Tacoma. How long have you been traveling already?"

No need to respond at all. A whole day and a half and she would bet they weren't halfway there yet. Well, maybe halfway. Pablo was a funny man. He kept making her think but he did it without making her feel like he was talking down to her. She liked him a lot.

"Time to get between places is one thing," Lucien said. "How many people would you pass between Seattle and Tacoma?"

She had to think about that. "A hundred thousand?"

Lucien smiled. "Add a zero and double it. That would be closer. And that's if you left out Seattle and Tacoma's population. Seattle is a million and a half all by itself. All of Seacouver is how many people?"

This time she was going to guess high. "Seven million."

"Almost ten and a half. Do you know why you care?"

She answered quickly. "Cause that's how many people have everything they need?"

This time, Pablo answered. "That's part of it. But it's not the most important part."

"What is?"

"Why don't you think about the differences?"

It felt like being back in school, and she'd been happy to graduate. Oh, she knew she'd take more school someday, but she hadn't expected her next school to be in a dusty red van with blue fenders and the smell of wild forests coming from beside the road.

"Stopping," crackled through loudspeakers she hadn't even known were built into the ceiling. And the van did, almost immediately. The others grabbed their water glasses, but hers spilled across the table and dripped onto Pablo's pants.

"I'm sorry," she exclaimed. Pablo put his fingers to his lips.

Aspen leapt across the table and planted himself firmly in Pablo's lap. The window and door locks snapped shut.

Outside, a long line of people walked down the road. Literally a line, one after the other as if they were single file waiting for the bathroom or something. Creepy. She spotted young people, her age and maybe even a little younger, and older people, and a man with a limp. Not an army. More like a huge family. Then, all at once, they stopped and stared at the vans. This wasn't casual. The people were about a person's distance apart, all standing one way. All watching. They had coats and bags and other things, but no one held weapons.

Paula put a hand on her shoulder. "Get down," she whispered.

"No need," Liselle whispered back.

Coryn swallowed and looked at Lucien. "Didn't you say people don't try to attack you?"

Lucien said nothing, but he glanced from her to the line of people outside, and she wasn't sure how to interpret the look on his face. Whatever it meant, it did make her feel unwelcome in the van for the first time.

CHAPTER FIFTEEN

For a few long, serious moments, most of the people outside of the vans simply stared at them.

Aspen whined, and Pablo shushed him with a hand run softly across his muzzle.

Liselle held a finger to her ear, her head cocked, listening. Her face creased into a tight frown, but then it opened up a little and she relaxed. "It's okay," she said.

"Who are those people?" Coryn asked. "They're so strange."

"They're part of a gathering army," Lucien whispered, speaking with great emphasis, as if he were trying to tell her something while playing it down. "They won't hurt us. But will you stay here while we talk to them?"

"All of you?"

"You'll have Paula."

"And Aspen?"

Lucien appeared to be amused by her attachment to Aspen. "Of course. No one will hurt you. Keep the doors locked."

She glanced at the line of people again. "I can't go with you?"

He didn't even hesitate. "No. We don't want to expose Paula, and you shouldn't leave her."

"Sorry to make you wait," Liselle said. "We should be back in half an hour or less."

"Maybe more," Pablo countered. He leaned down and picked Aspen up, holding him close for a moment. He kissed the dog between the eyes and was rewarded with a tongue in his ear. He handed him back to Coryn, and for a moment he looked genuinely regretful. "Stay safe."

She wondered why he was telling her to stay safe when Lucien had just told her she would be safe. Before she had time to frame a question, they had all left and closed the door behind them.

Aspen whined once and then settled on the wide bench, cuddling up next to Coryn. "Sweet boy," she said. "Sweet." He made this whole strange situation feel almost okay. Of course, she didn't like being left. *That* made her feel vulnerable and left out.

Beside her, Paula stared out the window, her eyes slightly narrowed and her mouth still. Coryn could almost see the electrons burning through her brain. "What?" she asked.

Paula waved a hand outside. "I think this is part of something bigger."

"What do you mean?"

"I think you may have chosen a particularly dangerous moment to come Outside."

"I'm not going back."

Paula merely looked briefly annoyed at that.

Lines of people still stood nearby, although they'd also apparently gotten the message to relax. They had gone from a single disciplined line to small groups of two and three that talked quietly together, still watching the vans. She counted at least twenty people, maybe twenty-five, and the line went up and down from there.

"Can they see us?" Coryn asked.

"The windows are tinted. So, no, not unless they come right up and peer in."

Paula sounded . . . careful, so Coryn asked, "What do you think is happening?"

"I can't tell. Not yet. But I think this might have been one huge mistake."

"Catching a ride?"

"Leaving the city."

Coryn knew better than to get angry with Paula. It did no good. She picked up the water glasses and went to the sink to wash them, letting the hot water take her frustration. "We'll get to Lou." She could see a little more of the crowd from here. Most of them looked shabby, but strong. Two families had small children, and there were at least four teens in the mix as well. What kind of army brought its children with them? To be fair, this wouldn't be a crowd at home; in fact, it would be a sparse grouping of people.

She still thought of the city as home. She shouldn't do that. "It looks like I'll have to protect you as much as you'll have to protect me out here," she told Paula.

"But I don't care if I die, except that it would mean failure to protect you."

Paula said things like that from time to time. True—she had volition only inside of a set of parameters. The robot couldn't just choose to stop being Coryn's companion, for example. If Coryn told Paula to do something else, she could do that. But if her job changed—say if Coryn sold her—she'd be reassigned, or maybe even reprogrammed, or, if no one wanted such an old model, taken down to her constituent parts and recycled. Still, Paula seemed so alive that direct reminders to the contrary irritated her. She looked Paula directly in the eyes. "Don't get suicidal."

"Of course not."

They sat quietly, watching the people move in a slow stream, or stop and talk, or drink water. It felt like watching a slightly boring scene in a movie.

"I don't understand these people," Paula said, almost abruptly, "not even the ones that saved us. I don't think they mean us any harm, but they want something."

"Do you know what?"

Paula returned to watching out the window. "No."

Coryn didn't know what else to say. She kept cleaning until there was nothing left she felt comfortable doing and sat back down. Pablo's question still bothered her. Why couldn't people who lived Outside go back Inside freely? They weren't—as far as she knew—expressly forbidden from doing so, although there were health checks, and they had to pass tests.

Lucien seemed like he belonged out here, as did Liselle. Pablo might even be a guest, like her. She couldn't quite tell. But he had gone out with the others, and no one had questioned him.

She tapped Paula on the knee. "What do you think Lucien and the others are talking to those people about? Is your hearing good enough to tell?"

"Probably."

"Can you tell me what they're saying?"

"I'm not supposed to do that."

"You can do it with an overriding command. So I'm giving you one. Tell me what you hear."

"I have to agree," Paula reminded her. "So tell me why you want to listen."

Damned privacy double checks. "I want to know if these people are safe for us, and for you."

Paula fell quiet for a moment, and Aspen snuggled in close to her. Coryn realized she could open the windows, and hurriedly did so. The van breathed; heat rushed out through the windows, and forest and birdsong and low murmured conversation rushed in.

Coryn whispered, "What do you think Lucien meant by the term *gathering army?*" After a moment, she added, "I'm curious about what they are gathering to do."

"If I learn the answers to those questions, I'll share them with you." Paula stilled, her gaze loosely focused on the people outside of the van, her body unmoving. Coryn kept expecting her to talk, but she remained silent. Aspen went to the window and peered out, wagging his tail.

Paula finally spoke. "I can't tell a thing from the crowd outside. They're not talking about anything important, probably on purpose. Lucien must be blocking the main conversation."

"Why?" It could be done, although it was hard, at least in the city. She wondered if it would be harder or easier out here in the land of far less technology. Maybe easier.

"I don't know," Paula said, somewhat unnecessarily.

"Maybe they'll tell us." Coryn paced around the inside of the van. She swept the surfaces clean, wiped up the few open cubbies, and eyed the drawers.

"What are you looking for?" Paula asked.

"Anything. How do I know these people aren't just taking me along to get you to go quietly? Maybe when we get to this Cle Elum they'll do exactly what Erich wanted to. Maybe they'll kill me for my robot."

Paula answered quickly. "Their body language isn't threatening. It's curious."

"Good." Paula was programmed to recognize microexpressions and slight modulations in voices; she could see and hear much that Coryn didn't. Coryn opened the door closest to the kitchen sink. After all, she could say she was looking for a knife. She found small speakers, a few board games, and an old roll-out video screen.

She slid a drawer out from under the bench she'd been sitting on. Fat notebooks filled it. Paper notebooks. They looked so out of place in the high-tech van interior that she leaned down and opened one. Schematics? She snapped a picture with her wristlet, turned the page and snapped another and then another. She sent them to Paula as she went, glancing back over her shoulder once. "What do you think these are?"

"Plans for something. Wiring diagrams, and maybe coding. Look in a few of the other books."

Paula was encouraging her? She'd expected to be chastised. "Watch out the window."

Coryn opened three or four more of the books, all she could get to without actually taking them out of the drawers. She snapped pictures of the first and last pages, and a few random ones for good measure. Even with Paula keeping watch, her skin itched with the fear of being caught. Her heart lurched at a slight thump outside the door. "That sounded like a footstep."

"It's okay," Paula replied.

Coryn took a deep breath and abandoned the idea of digging any deeper in the drawer. She carefully lifted the top notebook out and captured its complete contents in pictures, page by page. It took forever. Every noise outside sounded like the others coming back. Paula could do this faster, but it bordered on illegal and Coryn expected she'd refuse. Robots were more bound by laws than humans.

She finished the book and thought about starting another one, but too much time had passed. Surely they wouldn't leave her alone forever. She closed the drawer and climbed back onto the bench. Why was she convinced the contents of the notebooks were important? Because they were on paper instead of electronic?

She called Aspen to her. It calmed her to pet him, and she giggled when he licked her face. He hopped off her lap, went to the door, and whined, his tail thumping.

Now what? "Should I take him out?"

The door opened and Lucien stepped in, his face unreadable. Liselle followed and shut the door behind her. So Pablo was elsewhere.

The vans started up, and she glanced between the two. Their expressions were closed and hard.

They drove slowly past the string of people. She thought she saw Pablo in among them, wearing a funny wide-brimmed hat and slouching a little. She glanced up. "Where's Pablo?"

Liselle said, "He had to run an errand."

"He joined them," she said. "I just saw him."

Lucien glanced at her. "It was probably someone who looks like him."

"No," Coryn replied, suddenly not caring if they believed her. "It was him."

The silence in the van felt thick and uncomfortable. Lucien and Liselle had changed from the people who had freed her to people who kept secrets. They were both; she knew that. Whatever they were, she wasn't one of them. Besides, she had her own goals. Hadn't she already learned how dangerous people out here could be?

Liselle started the bargain up again. "So what about all the people living in the city? Pablo started you thinking, right?"

"Yes," Coryn said. "The more people you have, the more information they share, and the faster knowledge grows. Network effects." She paused, reaching to follow a thick thread of an idea. "Network effects brought us down in the first place, people falling into lies and believing them. That was the last gasp of the oil idiocy."

Lucien smiled, and added, "That's what brought down the old order. But from death comes life. . . . Without that last bout with stupidity, the cities wouldn't have risen, and the rewilding would never have started. If we hadn't had that hard patch, we'd have never made enough changes. We'd all be dead."

Lou believed that. She continued, "Later, network effects helped us resurrect ourselves with better science and more control of the message. Network effects drive the city forward every day. The city changes public spaces by consensus. It's like a constant vote." She stopped, the clarity of her idea waning as she tried to express it.

Lucien encouraged her. "Go on."

"Well, if you're part of the same network of ideas and people, then you know what to do. If you're not, you don't fit."

The cousins both stared at her. Did they want more?

It suddenly dawned on her. "I'm right. That's part of why Outside and Inside are so different."

"Yes," Lucien said. "You're right."

Liselle spoke softly. "You understand the main point. Network effects among groups can be good or bad."

Coryn frowned. "I probably left because I didn't absorb all the common city memes."

Paula chimed in. "You're a rebel." She sounded satisfied about that.

"Bad robot." Hadn't Paula been discouraging her from leaving? But then Paula was better at human psychology than humans. That had been true of companion-bots for a long time. This wasn't the moment, but if she remembered later she was going to ask Paula if she had secretly been hoping Coryn would come out here. But even so, could she believe her?

Could Paula lie to her?

The van rumbled and rocked, and Aspen sat warm in her lap, and she fell into a fretting doze. If the Inside and the Outside were really so different, and if the webs of what they believed were so different, did that explain why Lou seemed to have grown away from her? If so, what could she do about it?

CHAPTER SIXTEEN

The van drove up a smooth patch of road, with healthy-looking trees and no ecobots or long lines of strangers in sight. The blue sky looked as if the wind had blown it clean, even though the road itself was still stained with small branches from the recent windstorm. Clearly someone or something had cleared the serious fall—cracked and downed trees with recent saw cuts lined the low bank on the upward side of the road. In spite of the relative calm, Lucien seemed twitchy, pacing inside the small space.

Liselle looked at him. "Are you okay?"

"I think . . . I just want to go ride in front."

"You hate not getting all the news." Liselle made a shooing motion. "Go on. We'll be okay."

He looked grateful, opening the door the next time they slowed and hopping out.

Coryn wondered if she had failed as a storyteller.

She and Liselle rode in a slightly awkward silence until Coryn said, "I'm looking forward to seeing Cle Elum."

"It's nothing like Seacouver," Liselle warned.

They passed a deer standing frozen by the side of the road in a small clearing, its big ears twitching back and forth and its coat a luxurious, warm brown with pale spots. Coryn stood up close to the window, entranced, until it shook itself briefly and bounded between two tall trees.

"How are you doing?" Liselle asked her. "You just got Out. Is it too much?"

Coryn laughed, her first since the barn and the ecobots. "Too much information? Too much sky? Too many bad guys?"

"Too much of anything."

"I studied Outside before I left the city. I read about burned forests, storms, and bad soil. I talked to one of my friends about land with almost no people on it, and I saw pictures of roads with cracks and pits and holes in them." She hugged Aspen so close that he gave a small yelp and she let go. "I read about untended forest. I stared at pictures, but it's another thing entirely to smell it, to see it, to realize the vast emptiness. I hadn't been able to imagine that. I'm not entirely sure I can imagine it now, even though

I'm looking right at it. Since we're inside the van it's like vid, even though I know it's real. Like that deer."

"That's okay," Liselle said. "Give it time. It's hard to switch between. I was born out here, and I had to go to a city four times before it stopped making me sick. The first time I could barely walk."

"Sometimes the city felt overwhelming to me, and I was born there. But you get used to all those things that support you. I miss the traffic systems and the news and the AR—Oh, the AR—and . . . ." She let her thoughts trail off. She'd left that behind her, at least for now.

They passed through a reforesting zone, a vast open area with shattered stumps and rocks that had been scarred black by fire. She spotted a herd of huge animals browsing in the juvenile trees. "Are those deer?"

"Elk. You can tell by the white butts."

Sure enough. "Are they as big as they look?"

Liselle laughed, a high tinkly laugh full of friendly taunting. "Don't ever make elk mad. They'll chase you. A male is seven hundred pounds of muscle."

"People used to hunt them, didn't they?" They looked so beautiful. So majestic. "I heard we ate them."

Liselle frowned. "People still do. They're all microchipped, but some go missing every year. And then the NGOs hunt some on purpose, just to keep the right amount. You have to have the right amount of everything you know, and that's all up to people now."

"I thought we were introducing wolves."

"Returners kill them faster than they kill the elk."

Coryn had heard that term. People who resented the great taking and wished life was like it used to be. They passed a sign that said, SEVEN YEAR PLANTING. "Are those all cedars?" she asked.

"Over half are firs. See the darker ones with the slightly droopy leaves? Those are cedars. They were sacred to native people here. They made boats and baskets and art out of them. In fact . . ." She stood up and rummaged in a bowl, and brought out two carved wooden earrings. They were shaped like suns or flowers and had been sanded and rubbed so they glowed. "You can have these. Maybe you need something made from trees."

Coryn held her hand out, and the earrings landed in her palm. "They're beautiful." They were lighter than they looked, almost like feathers. She never wore her mother's earrings. She kept those in the box she often carried in her pocket. She did have on small nanofabbed earrings, something very trendy in the city, with clever geometric shapes. She pulled them out and washed them. "Trade?"

"You didn't have to." But Liselle looked pleased, so it was the right thing to have done. Coryn slid the wooden earrings into her ears and shook her head, pleased at the light touch on her neck.

Even though Pablo was warm and Lucien handsome, Liselle was the easiest to be around.

They passed a REFORESTING IN PROGRESS sign. Robots with buzzing, crackling saws at the ends of long appendages thinned small trees that grew close to each other, easily lifting fifteen-foot trees and tossing them into chippers or simply onto the ground to rot. Smaller round robots slashed at blackberry bushes. A mechanical army, every piece working together. In front of them, the forest looked ratty and wild. Behind them, it still looked wild but also like it had room to breathe and places for animals to thread through trees. "Are those also ecobots?" she asked Paula.

Liselle looked out the window. "Of a sort. They're workers—they can make decisions, but not hard choices. The ones that rescued you? They can decide if humans live or die. They have rights and power, within strict lines. These don't have nearly that much leeway." Liselle stared up at the forested hill and the robots above them, looking lost in thought. "What about your robot? What rights does she have?"

"Paula?" Coryn handed the question on.

Paula twisted in her seat and chose a relaxed position. "I have the right not be abused. I have the right to make decisions that are aligned with my basic framework of instruction, but not to violate that. For example, I am Coryn's protector. If you attack her, I can kill you. But I cannot kill her."

It sounded harsh, almost shocking, spoken out here that way.

Liselle must have thought so, too, since she changed the subject and started naming off tree species.

Fifteen minutes later, detour signs directed all three vans to rumble and rock up a steep ridge on a gravel road. As they wound upward, the reason for the detour spread out below them: a river of jagged rock had buried the road. A dark slash of mountain had given way, the edges crisp and surprisingly even.

Huge robots worked the rock fall, bots bigger than buildings, far bigger than the ecobots. Of necessity, bigger than most of the rocks in the fall.

The road ended abruptly, buried in rocks and dirt and crushed trees, and crawling with robots.

A shadow blocked the light of the front window. Aspen yipped; Coryn looked up. A robot towered over them. It seemed like she had to look all the way up to the gray, cloud-darkened sky. The robot looked vaguely humanoid, with four legs and four arms, all of them multiply jointed. In some ways it seemed more like a giant spider than a robot. Its metal body had been dinged and scraped, and here and there patches showed where it had been repaired.

If Paula hurt herself, self-healing nanomaterials would re-create whatever part of skin she needed, but this creature clearly didn't have such skills. It was expressionless, powerful, and yet it also looked worn down and slightly sad.

To her surprise, it reached out a huge hand and curled long, gripped fingers around the van, one of them draping itself along the window where she stood. Two large scratches marred the multicolored metal joint in front of her, and the side of one finger had been gouged by something sharp.

"Sit down!" Liselle snapped.

Startled, Coryn sat. Aspen leapt into her lap, his claws digging into her thighs. Her stomach fell out from under her as the robot picked them up.

It carried them with authority, as if they were merely another rock, but the van barely tipped. Nonetheless, she shoved her clenched fist in her mouth as the harsh rasp of her own breath filled her ears.

It set them down, and the van kept driving as if nothing at all had happened.

Coryn clutched Aspen close, unable to stop shaking or slow her breathing.

CHAPTER SEVENTEEN

High clouds faded from bright to burnt orange as they turned off of the interstate into Cle Elum. Coryn glanced over at Lucien, who had rejoined them. "The roads are good here," she said, surprised.

"The main one through town, anyway. Cle Elum is one of very few places with independent taxing authority between here and Spokane Metro. The others are Wenatchee, Yakima, Walla Walla, and Metro itself. There used to be seven Washington cities, but Leavenworth burned ten years ago. Flames the size of skyscrapers. Seared so hot there are rumors that tree roots are still burning underground today. They never rebuilt." He said it with a little nod of casual triumph, as if it was obvious that losing a smaller city was good.

They swerved to miss a big truck, and she clutched Aspen tighter. As they rumbled into town, they passed a decent sized shopping mall, a few trucks, and a ranger station surrounded by ecobots. Slightly run-down shared-living housing lined one side of the road, the bottom peppered with small coffee shops and common-things stores, and the tops full of apartments with ragged plants and bicycles and chairs on the balconies. Free bike stands lined the streets like they did in the city. They passed five riders with night lights just starting to glow on their tires.

It was getting too dark to see by the time they turned right again at the top of a little hill and turned again to slide the vans into three adjacent spots in an old cracked parking lot. Other vehicles had been there awhile; awnings stretched out over clusters of chairs full of people talking around small campfires.

Liselle said, "These are all family. You're safe enough here, with us, and everyone in this circle is safe to talk to. But don't leave. We'll give you a ride out of town when it's time. Cle Elum can be dangerous, and your robot is valuable."

"Paula."

Liselle grinned. "*Paula* is valuable."

"She is!"

"Good thing you're learning," Paula replied. "You haven't called me stupid robot for at least a day."

"Stupid robot."

"Come on," Liselle said. "We need to find something that makes Paula look more human."

Liselle led Coryn and Paula through the parking lot and up a small hill to a falling-down red barn with a faded picture of a horse-drawn carriage on it. Clothes filled one room, ragged and colorful cottons and bamboo. Old. None of them looked like they had been printed in the first place. "Find some for yourself, too," Liselle said.

Coryn frowned. "I like my outfit. I designed it just for this trip."

"You might as well wear a sign that says, 'Escapee from the city.' You can keep it if you can carry it." She led Coryn toward a floor-to-ceiling stack of shelves.

Paula had started picking through the clothes on the far side of the room. Her uniform was made exactly for her and designed to move where her joints moved. She probably wasn't going to be much happier than Coryn with the idea of wearing mass-market junk clothes. Coryn eyed a pile of shirts suspiciously. "How old is this stuff anyway?"

"Older than anything you've ever worn," Liselle said. "It's made better than anything from a 3D printer."

Coryn bit back a snarky reply.

Liselle started handing them things. Coryn held them up and shook her head: too blue, too ragged, too rough.

"Pick something," Liselle said. "I'm hungry."

Coryn sighed and selected a long, sage green shirt she could wear over her own tight-fitting one, and a pair of blue jeans with white stitched seams. The legs were too long for her, but Liselle rolled the cuffs up. If she had a mirror she could laugh at herself, but it probably *was* time to go native. She already felt a little less different than everyone else out here.

Paula ended up with brown pants, a navy blue sweater that her dark hair almost blended with, and a dull red overcoat that would make her easy to spot, but which also looked decidedly nonrobotic. It had enough pockets she could carry a number of her tools and things. After modeling her new outfit in the mirror, Paula held up a wide knitted black scarf that could cover some of her face. Liselle tugged it up around her neck and up over her chin, leaving only her nose and eyes uncovered. "There," she said. "Doesn't that make her look a little more real?"

Coryn didn't like the term. "She looks less like a robot."

Liselle narrowed her eyes at that but recovered quickly. "And you look less like a city girl. Let's go find food."

Paula stood her ground, staring at Coryn, until Coryn remembered her manners. "Thank you."

Liselle nodded at Paula while speaking to Coryn. "No problem."

The camp must have had a hundred people in it. Liselle took her around and introduced her to at least half of them. Twice they sat down and ate, once a salad and once an oatmeal cookie redolent with cinnamon. Coryn watched for Pablo but didn't see him. It made her even more certain he had stayed with the wandering army, or the gathering army, or whatever it wanted to be called.

Everyone around the campfire outside the colorful vans stopped talking as they approached. Liselle introduced her to the people who had been in the first and last vans in the little caravan. One of the women who had been riding in the front van, Kimberly, dished her out a thin vegetable soup and another man, Chizen, filled a huge bowl with salad. Most everyone seemed to be eating at once.

At first she didn't see Lucien, but then he stepped in from behind her. "I might have found some people you can travel with. They'll be here tomorrow."

She bristled. "I'm not sure I want to travel with anyone."

"It's safer," he countered.

She wanted to be up and moving as soon as it was light. They were back on track now—Cle Elum was just over three marathons from where they'd left the city. Less than ten marathons left to go. She chose not to argue until she could talk with Paula. As if he'd heard her unspoken thought, Lucien said, "You might as well sleep in the van tonight. We'll be right outside in tents. We can find a pillow and an extra blanket."

"Thank you." She looked forward to being alone. If only she weren't sure they were hiding something from her.

To her utter disappointment, they didn't shoo Aspen back in after them. As soon as Liselle finished helping her set up and closed the door, she asked Paula, "Well, what do you think?"

"I think they're outside talking about you."

"Why do you think that?"

"I still have very good hearing."

"You're an awful brat for a robot."

"Makes me a good match for you."

Coryn rolled so she was staring up at the roof of the van. "No, really. Something big *is* going on, isn't it? We left the city to look for the peaceful Outside, the one Lou keeps writing to me about, but that doesn't exist. And then there's that army Pablo went with."

"I never did figure out what they want. But they were going toward the city."

"Maybe it's a good thing we left."

"Maybe it's a tough time to be out here," Paula countered. "The city has more defenses than we do."

"I need to see Lou. I don't understand what, but I feel like something bad is about to happen. I want to be with Lou if that's true."

"We should have let her know you were coming," Paula said, for about the tenth time since they'd left the city.

"I want to surprise her."

"I want to find her at all."

"Stop being such a worried robot."

Paula didn't bother to reply.

Coryn worried. What if they didn't find Lou? What then?

CHAPTER EIGHTEEN

Coryn woke to the smell of coffee and eggs. Lucien stood in the open door, politely looking away as she pushed herself up off the bench and ran her fingers through her hair. His hair was tied tightly away from his face, making him look a bit severe. He radiated physical power and energy. He drew her the way a vid star or a singer attracted, with presence and something unnamable. "Good morning," she mumbled, trying not to express how awkward it felt that he'd seen her sleeping.

He spoke in a serious voice. "Do you have a few minutes to talk?"

Paula glanced at her and raised an eyebrow.

"Can I wake up for a minute?"

He smiled. "Use the camp bathroom. It's in the middle."

She gestured for Paula to follow her and climbed down the steps. Aspen wrapped himself around her calves and almost tripped her as she stepped onto the ground. "It's cold!" she proclaimed, pulling her arms around her. She gratefully took a light coat Paula handed her, although it only helped a little. Ice outlined every blade of thin grass along the path. "Is that frost?"

"Yes," Paula said. "It's cold enough to snow."

"I'd like to see that!"

"It's too dry. Maybe someday."

After she performed her basic morning rituals, she scrubbed at her face with her bare hands, trying to feel presentable.

Her long, reddish hair hung limply around her shoulders and bunched awkwardly where she'd slept on it. Even in the low light, her face looked splotchy and pale. "I need help this morning."

Behind her, Paula said, "You look fabulous."

"I pay you to say that."

"You do not."

"Any idea what they want?" Coryn took a last look, fluffed her hair in the vain hope of it doing anything besides lying down flat and stringy, and stepped out the door. Maybe coffee would help.

"None," Paula said. "They seem to have plenty of silencing tech. In fact, they seem to have a lot more tech than I expected. But they keep it hidden."

"It's not as if I thought everyone in the Outside would be living in caves." In the city, everyone and everything was festooned with subtle flashing and talking and beeping. Here, quiet. The tech seemed like bare bones scaffolding, and when something familiar and city-like showed up, it looked as incongruous as an evening party outfit on a commuter bicycle.

Dawn light washed the campfire pale. Liselle balanced a plate and cup and gestured for Coryn to sit in a folding chair. Coryn sat, and Paula stood behind her, arms folded.

This morning, Liselle was dressed in sky blue all the way down to her shoes, which looked like they had come from the same feed-lot as her shorts. Maybe they had, except surely none of it was printed. The same dye lots? It was out of fashion in the city to wear the same material or color on more than one part of your body, but they weren't in the city anymore, and Liselle did look good in blue. She handed Coryn a plate with fresh eggs and cooked potatoes on it. Coryn took it, slightly confused at being treated with what looked like deference.

They wanted something from her.

Well, they would eventually tell her what. In the meantime, the eggs smelled of pepper and hot sauce, and she ate them greedily before downing two cups of delightful, bitter coffee. The warm food tasted good; the warm cup felt like heaven.

After Lucien took her plate from her, he and Liselle both sat watching her.

Coryn fidgeted, unsure how to pass the test in his gaze.

"Look," he said. "I'd like to tell you more about us and offer you an opportunity. But only if you'll promise to keep what you learn secret."

"Secret from who?"

"Anyone you meet on the road."

"What about my sister?"

"She's all the way in the Palouse?"

Coryn hesitated. Everything else Lou had told her had been wrong. "As far as I know. That's where I'm going, anyway."

"You can ask us later, when you're close to there."

"How would I do that?"

"We'll show you." Lucien leaned closer to her. "First, do you agree?"

She swallowed, looked around, and then back at Lucien. "I agree to listen and to keep your secrets. But I can't promise any more than that. I need to find my sister."

Lucien began by repeating a question he had asked yesterday. "You left on purpose, and you don't want to go back. That's right?"

"Yes."

"Why?"

Coryn took a deep breath and thought her answer through before she spoke. "I can't find myself inside of all the people."

Liselle's voice was soft. "Was that all?"

Coryn's blinked away tears and forced herself to keep looking calmly at Liselle. "My parents died there."

Lucien knelt in front of her. "How?"

This defined her, but everyone wanted to know it. Julianna. Now these two. She took a deep breath and looked directly at Lucien. "They killed themselves. My mom never fit. I hadn't known my dad agreed with her, but he wasn't very emotional." Lucien looked quiet and thoughtful as he watched her. Listening. Maybe waiting, so she said a little more. "I don't want to become them. When I was little, I loved the city, but after they died, I didn't fit. I never really fit again. I tried. I still love the city, but it seems more important to find Lou."

Paula squeezed her shoulder softly, almost a caress, and Coryn fought back more tears she didn't want. This was no time to get emotional about things she couldn't change.

Liselle looked almost shaken. "I'm sorry."

"Is there anything else we should know?" Lucien asked. "When did your sister leave you?"

Coryn took another deep breath, getting some control, but still relieved when Paula spoke into the silence. "Lou left as soon as she could," Paula said. "She hated the city as much as their parents did. She wanted to do environmental things. She's been out here a few years. Her notes home are short and very positive, so much so that Coryn grew suspicious. And last summer they got shorter. Coryn no longer believes everything is okay, so she chose to come find Lou."

Lucien didn't respond directly to Paula but kept looking at Coryn. "Suicide is serious. Was there anything specific that made your parents ill? Were they depressed?"

What a stupid question. "Of course they were!" Coryn spoke a little too loudly.

Paula took over again. "Marianne, Coryn's mother, used to tell me that only the smart ones knew enough to notice how bad the city is."

Lucien laughed. "Maybe we're all brilliant." He swept his hand in the general direction of the camp. "Almost everyone out here wants to be here, at least on most days."

Paula asked the question Coryn hadn't quite stirred up the courage to ask. "What do you want from Coryn?"

Lucien looked at Coryn rather than Paula, and waited yet another minute or so for her to finish collecting herself and sit up straight. When he spoke, it sounded a little like a prepared speech. "As listeners, we can't take sides. But many people want the cities to change, the borders to open, and for things to be more equally distributed. There may have been a time when locking almost everyone inside of bubbles and keeping the rest of us out made sense, but there is a lot of anger and a lot of pain out here. There should be free movement, or at least more resources for the people who live out here. There's no reason some kid born in Cle Elum shouldn't get to go to a university in the city."

"Aren't some of the people out here from Inside, and just out to help? To do jobs?" Earlier, he had suggested a lot of people from Inside went Outside.

"Like your sister? Sure. Many idealistic people come out to work for the NGOs—who by the way, hire almost exclusively from Inside. But many children are born out here, and they have almost nothing. People from Outside never get jobs to run anything. Just to be strong backs, and mostly there're robots for that. For most, this place is dark and unconnected."

"What do you mean?" Coryn asked. "Specifically?"

"People who spend their lives out here get to see a doctor, on average, about once a year. They're lucky if they can find one in an emergency." He took a sip of coffee. "How often do you go to the doctor?"

"Whenever the city says to."

"So even someone on the lowest social rung in the city, an orphaned student with no significant financial resources, gets medical monitoring all the time."

It was hard not to bristle at his tone of voice. It wasn't her fault the city provided medical care. "Yes."

"You're not getting it now."

"I know that." Coryn got up and poured more coffee, buying herself a moment to think about what to say next. "Didn't you tell me you're from the city?"

"Just like you. The city is threatened by its wealth, and by the fact that it doesn't care what happens out here."

"Of course we do!" Coryn protested. "We know we depend on the wild."

"No." Lucien sounded bitter. "If the city knew that, it would help more. That's what we're trying to do. To help by gathering information."

Liselle watched her closely. "How does that make you feel? The idea of helping?"

A test. She thought about the army again, and the idea of Listeners being out here as a sort of security measure. "So do you work for Seacouver?"

"We work for peace. We work for everyone." Lucien pulled his ponytail out, thumbed a comb loose from his back pocket, and started untangling his long hair. "We collect and analyze data so we can get some idea of what is going on, both Inside and Outside."

"But you won't hurt the city?" she asked.

He winced as he tugged the comb through a knot at the back of his head. "We never hurt anyone if we can help it."

Not a very good answer. If the city ever wanted her, she might want it back. "I used to love the city. Even now, I miss a lot about it."

Liselle pressed her. "But what about the system? What about the way it works? Do you love that?"

"That could change," she allowed. "But there are a lot of systems. The city isn't one thing."

"Any concentration of power is dangerous," Lucien countered. "That's what we finally learned before we stopped the war on wildness."

The vehemence in his voice surprised her into silence. But she thought about the old robot that reported her to the orphanage's managers, and the forces that buried her parents. She thought about the center of the city, and the jobs in government that she would never have. "It feels that way. Like power can be tough."

"Okay." Liselle seemed impatient with the long conversation. She glanced at Lucien, who nodded. "Good enough. Here's what we want help with. We'll give you a way to communicate with us. You can use your wristlet—we'll just upload some new capabilities. We want you to tell us who you talk to and what they say. Take pictures. Tell us what you see, what people you talk to say. We're particularly interested in the ecobots, but we're also interested in movements of people."

"Is that why you were stopped by that string of people yesterday?"

"We could have driven by them." After she said that. Liselle looked away, biting her lip.

Coryn was convinced they wouldn't have driven by, and Paula had been certain the meeting with the silent army was planned.

Before she could decide what to say next, a couple bundled up in heavy winter coats wandered into camp and sat down, pouring coffee for themselves. The conversation turned to the continuing effort to clean up after the windstorm and a rumor that the power had gone out in part of Spokane Metro, although how that could happen wasn't clear. "Maybe part of it was on the old grid still," the woman suggested.

The man shook his head. "I don't think so."

Coryn was about to ask a question when she noticed a small shake of Paula's head. A warning.

As soon as the couple left, Lucien said, "We just want to know what you see and what you hear. We're recognizable. We know that. We chose to be bright and memorable so that people who want to tell us things can find us. But we also need an army of people who are just watching out there. We're Listeners. Loud, easy to find Listeners. Formal Listeners. But we also need secret Listeners."

She frowned. "And if I hear something I don't want to tell you?"

He smiled grimly. "We can't make you tell us anything."

These people had saved her life once already. She owed them. She didn't like it, but she should do this. In a barter economy, she might need help again.

Paula gripped her shoulder a little too tightly, like a warning. Coryn shook her off. They could talk about it later. In the meantime, she didn't see what it would hurt. "I'll try. But I'm not going off course. I came out here to find Lou."

"We would never ask you to give up on your family." Liselle held her hand out.

Coryn stripped her wristlet off, opened its security, and handed it over. Liselle stood, "It will just take me a few moments, and then we'll get you a ride out of town."

After she'd surrendered her wristlet, she wondered if they would see the pictures she had taken of the books in the van while the silent army surrounded them. But Liselle didn't even leave. She merely pushed a series of buttons and whispered commands at Coryn's machine. As she handed it back, she said, "I added an app. It's two taps below home. Try it."

Coryn held the machine out and tapped it twice. She saw her own face.

"You point it at whatever you're taking a picture of."

She pointed it at Liselle.

"Not us!"

She snapped a shot of Aspen, which whooshed off of her small screen as soon as she took it. "Is it still here?" She pointed at her wrist.

"Yes. In case we don't get it. But these pictures won't get in your way."

Coryn felt a little dubious, but at least they hadn't seen the other pictures she'd taken.

"You can get texts from us in the app and also send us short ones. So you can give us context for pictures."

"Okay."

Ten minutes later, Coryn and Paula stood in their used clothes with their packs. Liselle and Lucien shook her hand and Paula's. Coryn leaned down and gave Aspen a hug, whispering in his ear, "I hope I see you again." She probably wouldn't though. To her surprise, leaving Liselle stung, too. It had almost felt like they were becoming friends, and even though there hadn't been time to really tell, it had felt good.

Their ride turned out to be a truck taking apples out of a warehouse in Cle Elm and bringing them back to the city. So it wasn't going their way at all, except that it led them out of Cle Elum and back onto the highway. The driver treated Paula like a person, so much so that Coryn wasn't entirely sure he knew she was a companion-bot. Could such a simple thing as clothes make that much difference?

It was already late morning when the truck dropped them off, but Liselle had given them extra food for lunch and dinner and also handed Coryn a spare first aid kit. It had warmed some from the bitter early morning, and the air smelled of rain. As long as there wasn't any wind, Coryn was willing to deal with it. As soon as the truck was out of sight, she turned to Paula. "So you didn't think that was a good idea?"

"You could get into trouble."

"With who?"

"City police for one. Spying is illegal."

Coryn frowned. "At first I thought they were helping the city. I mean, they got the robots to save us."

"They got the robots to arrest Erich. Saving us might have been an unintended consequence."

"We know he was a bad guy. We know he was going to steal you and reprogram you."

"But we don't know why."

"Is everything about taking a side out here?"

"I'm not even sure I can define the available sides yet." Paula stared down the road, which was forested on one side with high trees and reforested with light green saplings on the other. "There seem to be far more than two options."

"True enough. But I don't think helping them will hurt anything."

"You're being stubborn."

Coryn smiled. "Maybe."

"You don't even know what they put on your wristlet. They could be tracking you."

"Do you want to look at it?"

Paula held a hand out, and Coryn dropped the wristlet in her palm. "It's okay if they track me," she said. "If they'd wanted to steal you, they could have done that right there. They saved us, and I'm willing to help them. If they can track me, they can save me again. End of story."

Paula peered at the wristlet, almost certainly sifting through data she'd downloaded from it in seconds. "I think it's just communication software. I can't tell for sure without risking breaking it."

Coryn took it back, feeling better when it snapped around her forearm. They had arrived at the interstate again, the road a crisp black ribbon under their feet. They walked along the side, heading downhill. From time to time, cars or trucks or skateboards passed them. Coryn kept hoping for a horse.

With luck, they'd be near Lou in two weeks. Less than ten marathons left. Maybe they could even make better time if the roads were good. There were hills between them, but they had just crossed the highest mountains and gotten a ride up the worst part. Maybe they weren't doing that bad after all.

CHAPTER NINETEEN

The first day out from Cle Elum had been memorable for a steady rain, but the next two had been full of blue skies and pleasant spring weather. Before they'd gone to bed in a copse of trees the previous night, though, the sky had darkened. Now, at almost midday, a heavy layer of black clouds pressed down on them, so close Coryn fancied she could reach up and touch them. Weather reports suggested rain and wind. At least there weren't any high wind warnings like the first day.

They were making good time, and they hadn't had any mishaps since Erich captured them in the barn.

Three middle-aged women passed them on the road, heading west. A few minutes later, they came up on a couple and two teenagers pulling an old-style metal grocery cart with clothes and goods in it. A small black dog in a ragged red raincoat balanced on top of the cart, trying to look in all directions at once. Coryn dutifully took pictures, even though neither group of travelers seemed remarkable.

The reliable little pings of thanks that scrolled on her wristlet screen every time she sent them a picture or a generic text made her feel like she was part of something, and reminded her that someone knew she and Paula were still out here, still moving.

An hour later they ducked behind a rock and hid from two ecobots heading east like they were, and ten minutes after that a whole pod of ecobots passed her head-on, rattling and rumbling as they dropped four legs each to get over a break in the road where a stream had washed the pavement away. A long string of bicyclists followed the ecobots, stopping at the break and tossing bicycles back and forth before struggling uphill too slowly to overtake the ecobots.

It took half an hour before they saw anything else. A coyote crossed in front of them, but she didn't take a picture of it. Whatever the Listeners were working on, it wasn't the environment.

Rain pelted her in big, slow drops and then grew faster and harder. Paula found a farm and beckoned her into the barn. "Aren't barns a bad idea?" Coryn grumbled.

"See anything better?"

"No. But no sleeping this time. I'm not willing to wake up with you gone."

They chose a reasonably dry stall, swept it out a little with a branch, and sat against a wooden partition.

Paula handed Coryn a handful of nuts and dried fruits. Coryn ate, washing the dry food down with water from her canteen. Rain leaked in through the roof and made small wet streaks on the stained concrete floor. Birds twittered in the rafters, and something small and four footed scampered around above them from time to time. The air stank of damp and something sour that Paula identified as mold.

Altogether, it made for a pretty miserable afternoon. She texted *Liselle: Are you all right?*

Of course. You?

Sure.

Silence followed. Who would have thought you could feel the absence of people? Before coming Outside, she had never been around an absence of people. She had thought she was alone in the orphanage, but she hadn't been. Not even close. She poked at her wristlet to turn on music, but the streams didn't run out here. She tried to sing a few of the songs that she knew, but her voice trembled, surely because of the cold.

Paula put an arm over her shoulder. "I'm sure the sun will come out soon."

"Stupid robot," she said.

"Stupid person," Paula replied.

"I am," Coryn said. "I got us way out here."

"Hey, that was partly for the horses right?" Paula arched an eyebrow. "You did want to ride a horse."

"More than almost anything."

"And not a city horse."

Coryn perked up. "Are there horses in the city?"

"South of Tacoma."

"I thought the city stopped at Tacoma."

Paula stood and looked out, as if worried by something. "It stops on the far side of a few horse farms."

"Why didn't you tell me that?"

"Because you said you were leaving to see Lou."

"I am!"

"So, perfect then? Right? We're exactly where we're supposed to be."

"I hate you."

"I know."

"Stupid robot."

Paula's eyes widened and she stood straight, looking toward the barn door. It slammed open and they heard footsteps. Paula ducked, gesturing Coryn down.

The owners walked casually, apparently unaware that Coryn and Paula were there. Coryn rose and peered carefully over the half wall of the barn stall. Two young men. They wore clean clothes almost nice enough to wear in the city. Water dripped down from the brims of their rain hats and onto their coats. One was tall with black skin, and the other was nut-brown, stocky, and short. The tall dark-skinned one said, "I counted ten in the last pod."

"Could you tell what they want?"

"How? They're just a bunch of silent dumb robots."

Were they collecting information like she was?

Paula cleared her throat and said, "Hello."

The smaller one jumped, and the tall man turned and squinted at them. "What are you doing here?"

"We came in to get out of the rain," Coryn replied. "The door wasn't locked."

There was a moment of silence before the taller one said, "Well, that's not a bad idea. After all, we had it." He grinned, his smile wide and big, and his voice big as well.

But if they came close they might see Paula was a bot. Coryn stood up and crossed the open room, holding her hand out. "I'm Coryn. That's Paula. And there were twelve."

"How do you know?"

"I counted."

He laughed. "What were you counting?"

"Ecobots."

He and the taller man exchanged looks. "We were counting cows."

"Cows don't come in pods," Coryn replied. "They come in herds."

"Don't be a know-it-all." There was another smile as the tall one held out his hand. "I'm Blessing."

"That's quite a name." She shook; he could have hidden two of her hands in his. Touching him warmed her, as if he burned a little brighter than she did.

Blessing gestured toward the smaller man. "It's even easier to remember his name. This is Day."

A huge crack of thunder rattled the barn from the top all the way down. "I guess it's good we're in here," Coryn murmured.

"So, you and your friend are traveling?" Blessing asked.

"We are. To the Palouse. What about you?"

"We're going the other way." She wasn't sure if it was her imagination or not, but Blessing sounded a little disappointed at that. Now that they were quiet and close, she thought they might be younger than they'd looked at first. Maybe just a few years older than her, like Lou.

They eyed Paula, who now stood in the open stall door and hadn't spoken since her initial greeting. Coryn swallowed hard. "This is Paula," she said carefully. "We've been friends a long time."

The two men dropped their packs by the door, walked over to her, and exchanged handshakes. As soon as Blessing was done, he turned, caught Coryn's eye, and said, "She's a robot."

Well. So much for crappy clothes. "Yes. She is. She's my robot."

Day's eyes had narrowed, although he looked more puzzled than anything else. "So how is she your friend? Is she a sex-bot?"

Coryn felt the blood rush to her face. "Of course not! She's been my companion since I was seven. My parents bought her for me."

Day laughed. "So she's like your mom?"

"No."

Paula clarified. "I'm a protector."

Day looked curious. "So you're so important you have a robot protector?"

Blessing laughed. "No. She's just from the city."

"Fucking city." Day drawled it out, a familiar slur.

"Come on," Coryn said. "You can sit in here. I'd rather listen to you than the rain." Maybe she'd learn something interesting for Liselle.

Neither Blessing nor Day sat until after Paula sat, and then they took the opposite barn wall. Day sat easily; Blessing looked a little more like he was folding himself down into place, all long thin legs and long arms. "So what are you looking for in the Palouse?" he asked her.

She hesitated, then said, "My sister's there, on RiversEnd Ranch."

Blessing whistled. "Really? That's dangerous. I did two years there."

Coryn tensed. Dangerous? "Lou never said that. She talks about riding horses and counting animals and watching the perimeter of the reserve they're on. It's huge—takes over parts of three states."

Blessing took in a deep breath, his thin chest rising and falling, and his face deadly serious. "Your sister's name is Lou?"

"Yes."

"What's she look like?"

"Red-haired, like me, only her face is thinner and she's taller. Her eyes are blue. She's intense, takes everything seriously."

"No kidding? If you're Lou's sister, you're my friend. She's a firebrand—you can't help but listen to her when she talks."

Coryn grinned, eager for more information. "Yeah. That's my sister. But what's dangerous?"

Blessing stretched his arms up and put them down, leaning toward her. "Did she tell you about the wolves and the bears?"

"No. But that's part of why she came Outside in the first place. She used to hang pictures of wolves up on her walls."

He smiled wide. "She still does. Did she tell you poachers almost killed her two years ago?"

Coryn leaned toward Blessing. "No. What happened?"

"She was riding a wildlife circuit when a tagged wolf pack took off, running like hell. She raced toward where they had just been, sending two drones ahead of her." A huge gust of wind silenced them all for a minute, and after it passed Blessing continued. "She had stationary cameras as well, but I don't think she took time to use them."

Coryn could imagine that. "She's always been passionate."

He laughed. "Some idiots were trying to kill the wolves. They'd missed all of them, but horses are a bigger target, and not half as bright as wolves, either. They hit Lou's gelding in the neck and stopped him, and she fell off. They shot her in the foot and would have done more, except one of the drones got a good shot in and dropped the leader. While the poachers were staring up at the sky, Lou pulled out her own weapons." He stopped, took a breath, maximized the suspenseful moment. "She didn't miss."

Wow. The word kept running in her head. Wow. Wow. "She killed someone?"

"Three of them. She's had to kill more than that."

Lou knew how to shoot guns? Coryn couldn't imagine Lou killing people. She stared at the barn door and listened to raindrops drumming on the roof. She'd known Lou was lying to her with her sweet little letters about nothing, but this was . . . more than a lie. "Nothing like that came in her letters."

The smile came again. It wasn't condescending, it was merely warm, and his voice sounded like he was sharing secrets with her. "You can't write down most of what happens out here."

"I suppose not. Are there police? I mean besides the ecobots?"

Day spoke up. "Ecobots will kill you faster than you know."

"Some saved me."

Blessing shrugged. "They do that too. Can't ever tell."

"Is Lou okay now? Is she safe?"

Another epic gust of wind rattled through cracks in the old, dry wood, and a chilly finger of it reached into the stall, making her shiver. Blessing spoke quietly. "She was okay when I last saw her. That was almost a year ago. Did she tell you about the Returners?"

"I read about them. I thought maybe they were a story someone made up to scare us into staying in the city."

Day looked at her like she was the best amusement he'd had in weeks. Unlike Blessing, the smaller man always seemed to be watching.

Blessing leaned back against the wall and stretched his long legs out on front of him. He looked around at all of them, pausing to be sure he had everyone's attention, even Paula's. The look in his bright eyes suggested he was setting them up for a story. "There are many people who hated the great land-taking that went with the beginning of the restoration and the rewilding. There were winners and losers. The people who owned land in the cities got to keep it, big cities and little cities alike.

"Landlords in Seacouver stayed landlords, shopkeepers in Cle Elum kept their stores. But the farmers? Out. All of them replaced by fake food and food grown in towers in the cities or put out of growing feed by the ban on eating big animals. Even though the great taking happened twenty years ago, people remember. The Returners took the money they were paid and used it to fight the government instead of moving into a city. Sure, some of the Returners live quietly on government land, and mostly they get ignored if they aren't doing harm. But others created little armies that roam the west trying to foil the ecobots and the NGO enforcers and everyone else working on the grand design."

He paused for breath, giving Coryn a moment to think. "So how many Returners are there? Didn't most people already live in cities before this happened?"

"Most still leaves out hundreds of thousands of people. This is a big state. Nobody knows how many live Outside. They travel and live in small groups." He put great emphasis on his words, making the story seem like something in an AR passion play instead of a real tale. Blessing dropped his voice to a loud whisper. "Perhaps, sometimes, they even live here."

Coryn giggled, a reaction to his theatrics, and maybe a show of nerves at the wind outside. The giggle felt out of place and she stopped herself.

Blessing didn't even seem to notice. He continued, "A lot of ranchers lost land when the Palouse became a reserve. It takes days to ride across the hills there, and often times we'd find small groups of Returners camped in the draws by water, or reoccupying barns that hadn't been burned down yet. Some days they'd just attack us. Volunteers and Wilders, regular people all the way, and the damned Returners would just attack us as if *we* took their land." He stopped and stretched again, folding and unfolding. He drank a little from a silver flask he pulled out of his pocket, wiped his long-fingered hand across his thin mouth. "Two of our work parties disappeared entirely. We think they were killed and buried, and some—"

A fierce gust threw the roof from the barn. Wood smashed onto the driveway outside, splintering and cracking as it fell. Wind flew inside, circling. It tugged at her, as if it could pull her up and away. She screamed.

Paula grabbed her, one hand pulling on a piece of barn wall and the other holding onto Coryn.

Blessing and Day scrambled away, staying low, wind yanking at them so hard she expected them to go through the hole in the wall like autumn leaves.

Coryn barely had time to think *tornado!* before it ripped through a wall and threw a ceramic pot at another wall. The pot shattered, and flying shards hit her, one slicing through her new jeans and into her flesh. Hot blood spurted onto the shreds of cloth and trickled down her leg. Instantly, Paula's hand pressed on the cut, stopping the blood.

The wind stopped as abruptly as it had appeared, as if that final fury had spent all of its energy.

Blessing stared at the broken pieces of barn. Day went to his pack.

Coryn's voice came out in stammers. "Was that a tornado?"

Day came back with a blue towel that he ripped in half, looking up at Paula. "It's clean."

Paula took it.

"It must have been," Blessing said. "I've never felt wind that could pick me up."

"Last week's storm was almost as bad," Coryn countered.

"Half," he said.

She didn't argue.

Paula wrapped the towel around Coryn's leg, being careful that only Coryn's jeans touched her skin.

Well, now she'd look even less like a recent refuge from Seacouver.

The clouds had opened into blue sky above them, and beyond there were fewer and higher clouds, although some still looked like rain. A sudden gift of late afternoon light washed over everything and turned it sparkling and clean. Blessing looked even darker in the natural light, and taller and thinner, and she and Paula looked soaked. Day grinned. "We're safe. Not dry, but not as wet as we might have been."

"You always see the good," Blessing said.

"And you tell a great story."

"Someone's got to talk. Stories out here need to be told."

Day merely grunted.

The moment felt awkward. If they were done sheltering in the barn, and they were really traveling in two different directions, they should split up here. "So you were saying that two work parties disappeared . . ."

Blessing led them to some large rocks that had been dragged into a line by the edge of the gravel drive that led to the barn. They had to work their way around parts of the shattered roof. He perched on the tallest rock, making him much taller than Coryn, especially once she sat down on a smaller rock near him. It was damp, but so was she, and the sun was the best chance they had of drying off. Day also sat. Paula stood, her back to the barn, watching across the street as if trying to be sure no rabid groups of Returners came on them unawares.

Blessing started in again. "So two work parties disappeared from the farm, and one more was ambushed and everybody but one was killed."

Paula interrupted him. "How many people work on the farm?"

He closed his eyes and tilted his head back. "Maybe three hundred and seventy or so all the time. Fifty or sixty more in the summer." He glanced at Coryn. "That's what you're going for right? Summer work?"

"Sure. What else happens out there? How dangerous is it?"

"Do you have a contract?"

She stood up, which still left her below him. "Blessing, how dangerous is it?"

"Hold onto your curiosity and sit back down. You can't have the whole story in the one answer to a question. That's no way to understand."

Coryn glanced at Paula, but there was nothing in Paula's face that gave away her thoughts or provided any advice. Ever since Coryn turned into an adult, that was the face Paula chose to present the most. She'd wanted it to be that way, but there were times she hated it as well. She sat back down and chewed on a fingernail.

"So Lou is a boss," Blessing began again. "She's got to handle Returners. They're pathetic, wanting to go back to the way of living that almost killed us all. But there's children with them and families—you can't just kill all of them, or even lock them up. Sometimes the Foundation sends cops, but more often she's got to rely on the ecobots, which means she has to convince them to uphold the law."

"Isn't that what they do?"

"They can act when it's about protecting the land. They're forbidden from getting between humans and humans unless they get orders from on high."

So why had they helped her? "How hard is that? Getting someone to give the ecobots orders?"

Day laughed, one of the few spontaneous things she'd seen him do.

Blessing said, "The ecobots mostly tell us what to do. Out here, there's the Wilders—that's us and people like Lou who work for the NGOs, and a bunch of other people—and there's the robots that work with for the Wilders, or the Wilders work for them—hard to tell on any given day but I would call the ecobots Wilders, and there's the Returners."

"Is that all?"

"There's wanderers, like you."

She sighed. Maybe she shouldn't have asked such an open-ended question.

"Scientists," Day said. "They travel in packs with protector-bots." He added to the list. "A few people out for the adventure of it all."

Blessing thumped his thumb on his thigh like a drum. "Crazies."

Day grinned. "Loners. Gotta remember the loners."

"Everybody that doesn't fit anywhere else is out here somewhere," Blessing said. "Psychopaths, too. And saints. We're all Outside."

"There's psychopaths in the city, too. Trust me."

"But we were talking about Lou," Blessing said. "She's sane as anything. Lou protects the land she's responsible for from the Returners. That's her job. It can take days to ride it all. She's got wildlife cameras and sometimes ecobots to help her out. At least once a month, she rides the whole place. She's put more Returners into jail or sent them into cities than anybody else."

"She sent them into cities? Does that work?"

"The little cities. Like Cle Elum. Sometimes they like having hot showers so much they never come back out. Other times they turn into escapers, like you."

She stiffened. "Just a minute ago, you said I was a wanderer."

He laughed. "How would I know what you are? All I know is you're my friend's sister."

"You guys have a label for everyone? I came to find Lou. Not to escape."

"So you were happy in the city?"

"Ecstatic."

"Thought so." He stood up and stretched, a tall thin tree trunk of a man with a wide smile, and at the moment laughing at her. "Go on." He glanced up the same road that they had walked down. "We'll see you again. The Outside is not as big as it looks. Nowhere near as big as a city."

Her throat tightened. "I'd love to hear about your life someday."

He leaned over and gave her a hug, his cheek warm against her forehead. "I'll keep an eye out for you. Outside is big, but it's also small."

Day shook her hand, and then Paula's, and started off first, his gait smooth and easy. He reminded her a little of the coyotes she'd seen. Lithe.

He looked eager to be wherever they were heading to. Cle Elum? Maybe they'd see Lucien and Liselle. Blessing wasn't too far away yet. She took a few quick steps after them. "If you see some particular Listeners, Lucien and Liselle, tell them I'm okay so far. And pet their dog for me."

He stopped in his tracks and stared down at her. "Who would have guessed?" He bent down and planted a completely unexpected kiss on her forehead, and then turned and jogged after Day.

She stared after him for a long time, her forehead burning. Paula came up beside her. "There's only an hour or so before dark. We should go unless you want to stay here for the night."

Coryn glanced at the debris pile from the barn and then back up after Blessing and Day, but they had rounded a corner and vanished. She took the pack Paula held out to her. "Just a minute." She hadn't sent Liselle any pictures of Blessing or Day, or anything else since the storm had gotten worse late that morning. She sent a short message to say she was okay and took a picture of the broken barn and sent it along with a short description of the tornado. She felt a little guilty for not mentioning Blessing or Day. Before she stopped staring at her wristlet, she added a question. *Are you okay?*

When there was no immediate answer, she started walking. If it was an autobot, why hadn't it answered?

CHAPTER TWENTY

The cedar above Coryn swayed ever so slightly in the early morning breeze. Birds that had woken her an hour ago grew louder, as if the puff of wind was a signal for extra volume. Back in the city she had used bird sounds on her alarm clock, but they had always obeyed her wishes explicitly.

These birds refused to be muted.

Paula's arms curled around Coryn's torso, the robot's stomach warming her back. Paula put off a tiny bit more heat than a human, and being close to her helped keep the worst edge of cold away. Coryn was pretty sure she'd slept no more than three or four hours all night in spite of the fact that it had stayed clear and quiet.

She stretched the leg that had been cut the day before. It felt stiff, and moving it brought a twinge of pain. Still, it wasn't as bad as she had feared.

She pushed Paula's arms away and they sat up at the same time, Paula looking considerably more refreshed than Coryn felt. Coryn grumbled, "You could do me the favor of sleeping badly some night." Not that Paula slept at all.

They crawled out from under the tree to find the morning sun painting stars of light on the stream that ran down a short bank in front of their sheltering tree. They sat side by side on a rock, and Coryn drank water from the river she'd purified and rubbed her arms together, trying to get warm.

At least there was no wind or rain.

"Any messages during the night?" Paula asked her.

Coryn peered at her wristlet, then stiffened. *Help us! We're under attack.* "Oh! Oh my. Oh. We have to go." She stood up, still staring at her wrist. There were coordinates.

"Why?"

Coryn was already heading for the packs. "Liselle sent me a text. They're being attacked."

"Where?"

Coryn stopped, reread the note, whispered a few short commands. "About ten miles I think. They're ahead of us, same road. We have to hurry."

"Really, why?" Paula threw her pack on and kept Coryn's in her hand. "You'll be faster this way. Go."

Coryn made a grab for her pack. "I want you to go now. Get there as fast as you can."

Paula got her no-nonsense look on. "That's a bad idea."

She wanted to argue, could argue, but the look on Paula's face suggested it would take a while. In truth, she was probably right.

Coryn took a deep breath. "Then let's go."

She started a little slower than she usually would, controlling her breath to keep her panic down, lengthening her stride. After the first mile, she found a comfortable, quick pace. She avoided her fastest run, though, staying slow enough to react to holes in the road and to last that distance. Almost half a marathon. Paula jogged easily beside her, carrying all of their gear. "I swear," Coryn said, panting a little, "some days I'd rather be a robot."

"No," Paula replied, "you wouldn't. Every day I want to be human."

"That's a cliché."

"Doesn't make it a lie."

"Stupid robot. You should go ahead. We're not going to get there in time to help them." She thought about making it an order, forcing Paula, but she didn't want to lose sight of the robot, not out here.

"Look how much you care. Humans. You break on each other."

"You care."

"How do you know?"

Coryn refused to take that particular bait. Yes, Paula was programmed to care. But what was genetics if not programming? Still, she'd lost the argument before, and right now she needed her breath.

They kept running. Coryn's breath soon became too hard for conversation anyway.

She kept glancing at her wristlet, losing a little speed every time. No new messages came in.

She started slowing down, finally dropping all the way to a desperate, fast walk. Paula made her eat a handful of nuts and a gel energy pill. "It might be okay," Paula said. "Didn't they tell us they had defenses?"

"They never said what they were."

"They're better defenses if no one knows about them. Get your breath. Drink water."

Coryn gulped a few mouthfuls, then they were running again, the road fairly straight and long. It hadn't gotten warm, but Coryn ran with her coat tied around her waist.

At almost eleven o'clock they came up on the caravan. If they hadn't been looking they would have missed it. But they *were* looking, and the garish colors gave the vans away.

All three vans had been shoved nose-in to a copse of trees in full leaf. A small stream ran under the front wheels of the yellow van. Lucien lay on the ground by the stream, under a dogwood full of cascades of fine white flowers going brown at the edges. One hand trailed in the water.

She had seen death in games and videos, and once a suicide had jumped close to her, although Paula had hustled her away before she could get close to the broken body. Lou had seen their parents dead, and she hadn't. Still, she knew immediately that Lucien was gone.

Paula grabbed Coryn's arm and pulled her to the side, behind the edge of the trees. "Wait. It might not be safe."

The robot flared her nostrils to draw in a deep sample of air. "Stay here," she said. She loped around the periphery and then cut through between the vans, moving like running water. She made no sound, as if her feet weren't even hitting the ground.

Birds twittered and sang, high up in the trees, clearly more in touch with the sky than the ground. Would they be singing if the attackers were still here?

She hated not being able to help. Her frustration turned to slow anger and then worse. She couldn't stand still forever. She edged forward, taking small steps.

Most of the van windows gaped open and smashed. Tiny bits of glass littered the ground, dull and wicked looking as the first few raindrops pinged against them.

Even from the periphery, Coryn spotted three other bodies. Kimberly, who had made them soup, face up, staring at the rain. Two others she recognized, but whose names she'd never learned. They had fallen right next to each other, the dead man's arm over the dead woman's face.

Paula stood staring into one of the vans. She didn't react as fast as Coryn expected, and when she did turn around there was a warning all over her face and in the way she held herself. "Back up."

"Is anyone okay?" She noticed her own wording. Anyone instead of everyone.

"No."

"Liselle?"

"Dead." Paula was using her most metallic voice. "Don't touch. This will be a crime scene."

Coryn's thoughts raced. She and Paula had to be the first people here except for whoever had done this. "I don't see that they defended themselves."

"I don't see any dead strangers either, although there are a lot of footprints."

"Can you tell why this happened? Were things stolen?"

"I'll look." Surely a robot shouldn't be affected as strongly as Paula looked, but maybe that shocked, blank face was really for Coryn. "I won't leave any DNA behind, but you should back up so you don't. We should call this in."

On her way out, Coryn knelt down to look at Lucien's broken body. He didn't look peaceful in death, or pretty. He just looked gone, all the animation and structure lost with his life. She had to walk around to see his face. It had been smashed, his cheekbone exposed in one spot. Coryn raced for the bushes and heaved and heaved, tasting bile and fear and anger all at once. When she stood, she felt dizzy.

A whimper came from the bushes.

"Aspen?" Coryn called softly. "Aspen, is that you?"

He didn't come.

She listened but she didn't hear anything else.

Paula came up behind her. "That's an impressive pile of DNA."

"I couldn't help it." She knelt in front of the bushes. "Did you see Aspen? Was he . . . over there?"

"I didn't notice. He's small. He could have been under something."

A thicket of blackberry vines in front of her were wicked with last year's thorns and just beginning to throw out bright green leaves, so she picked at them gingerly. "Here, boy," she called.

"I do hear an animal," Paula whispered.

"Aspen?" Coryn plucked at another cane, drawing blood all down the inner part of her forearm and snagging the cuff of her jacket. "Aspen?"

A nose poked out.

It was him. She had to catch him.

He ran past her, stopping on the road and looking back at her.

"He's scared," Coryn whispered. "Poor thing." She glanced up at Paula. "Did you see any dog food? Any treats? I need something to attract him."

"I wasn't looking."

"Please?"

Paula frowned at her, but after a heartbeat she snapped, "Be careful," and left.

Coryn sat on the ground. Aspen sat as well, although he left a solid ten meters between them. His pink tongue hung out of his mouth. He panted, looking around as if for danger, his eyes darting this way and that, his little body shaking.

Coryn shushed at him and clicked softly and talked to him, her words jumbled. "It's okay. It's not okay. I'm sorry. My voice is shaking. I'm sorry. It's not okay, not okay. I know. I'll take care of you." Hot tears ran down her cheek, and she held her hand out to him. Her fingers trembled.

Damn.

Liselle.

Aspen didn't move.

Liselle would be glad he was alive.

She had liked Liselle, thought maybe they had been—in some small way—already friends. "Please let me take care of you. I like dogs. I liked how you sat on my lap. I could use a friend, and you need one now. I know you do."

What had she done? She'd almost lost Paula, she'd almost been blown away by wind, and now she was desperate to save a dead family's dog.

Everyone around her died.

Her stomach rumbled again, turning so sickeningly twisty she had to work to stay seated.

Aspen took a step closer to her.

She looked at him and whispered, "Please."

As if he finally understood, he bounded to her and fit himself into her arms.

She clutched him tightly, chest heaving, tears falling on his white coat.

CHAPTER TWENTY-ONE

Aspen trembled and yipped as Paula came up behind them. Paula held a bag of kibble, a water dish, and a few unopened bags of dog treats. She also had a cloth bag stuffed full of things. "I found the dog food." She dropped a bag of treats on the ground. "And I brought a few other things we can use. One is a raincoat. For you. I called this in. I had to."

"Thanks."

"I had to. The mass murder of multiple people is near the top of the list of things authorities expect travelers to mention."

Coryn wasn't sure if that was an attempt at humor on Paula's part or not. At any rate, she didn't laugh. Her hands shook as she reached for the treat bag with her right hand, keeping the fingers of her left hand wrapped through Aspen's collar. "I want to know who did this."

Paula's clothes were covered in droplets of rainwater. "It looks like it was a surprise to them. No one seemed to be in a defensive posture, and they didn't have weapons." Paula's voice sounded robotic and calm, like it had the day Coryn's parents killed themselves. "There are so many footprints I couldn't tell the story from the aftermath. Someone ripped all of the drawers out of every van and spilled everything out of every drawer."

"So they were looking for something?" She held her hand out, with two treats in her palm, and Aspen gulped them, the edges of his teeth raking her hand lightly. "He must be scared. At least he's eating."

"They must have been. I wish I knew what was in the drawers."

Aspen struggled in her grip, and she dropped a few treats on the ground and let him take them one by one. "What about the one I found, with the notebooks in it?"

"All gone."

"Maybe that's a clue. Maybe someone killed them for information." She glanced at her wristlet, which had at least one notebook of data stored on it. She wished she had been bold enough to take more pictures. "Did you see a leash?"

"I'll go look. Put on your coat."

"Bossy robot." She fed Aspen two more treats and then closed the bag.

He seemed a little calmer, so maybe having something familiar like the treats helped. She turned to look at what Paula had stuffed into the bag. A coat, a fresh pair of pants, and an inner plastic bag that held snacks, water, and a little more dog food. She shrugged into the coat, which was bright red. Just like the Listener's vans. At least it was too big, so it probably hadn't been Liselle's.

Paula wouldn't have taken anything in the city. The logic that drove Paula's choices seemed to be shifting.

Fair enough. Coryn wasn't exactly the same person who had walked up out of the city three days ago either. She stroked Aspen's chest and the soft fur by his nose. "Do you understand death?"

For answer he licked her fingers, then curled into a small comma-shaped ball, with his nose resting on the base of his tail. "How could you not?" she asked him, and then she fell silent. Lucien and Liselle and the others had been alive right here—maybe they had sat in this same place, talking and looking at the dark clouds last night, wondering if it would rain. They had made camp in this place and slept here and gotten up, and then they'd been surprised. It couldn't have taken long—she'd only gotten the one text. "Where were you, boy?" she asked the dog. "What happened?"

Paula walked with heavy steps now, moving more like a human than a graceful robot. Coryn took a leather leash from her and clipped it to Aspen's collar. Paula stuffed the food and extra clothes into their packs until they bulged and carried the packs back up to the road while Coryn carried Aspen after her.

"They'll be here soon," Paula said. "You'll have to tell them you rode in the vans." She set the packs down. "You probably left hairs or skin cells behind on our trip to Cle Elum. But don't say too much, or get involved. We don't want to get stuck here."

"Or blamed," Coryn said. "I want to get to Lou."

"Contact her."

Maybe she should. Her original plan looked childish and stupid about now. So far she hadn't been able to get through a whole day without some kind of trouble.

Paula put a hand on her shoulder, as if to encourage her. "It will be immediately clear we couldn't have done this."

"Even you?" Coryn whispered.

"Even me. Not alone. It took a lot of people. Or robots. But I think it was people."

"Why?"

"It wasn't always efficient."

Coryn shivered at those words, and the cold, and her losses. They sat on damp rocks under some trees and waited for the police. Hawks or some other kind of big bird circled high overhead. A deer wandered through, upwind, and then saw something that startled it and bounded away.

A half hour passed before two ecobots and a truck full of policemen rumbled up the road and pulled to a stop. Two policemen—both men—surrounded them and started asking questions, while four or five more walked slowly in toward the scene, careful, guns up and pointing at air.

One of the policeman took Paula away, while the other questioned Coryn. She stumbled over her words at first but eventually calmed as she described finding the vans and Paula going in to see if she could help while Coryn stayed outside. She kept a tight hand on Aspen's collar the whole time, unable to stop fidgeting.

She had answered every question at least three times before one of the men led Paula back and sat with them while the other went to help poke through the mess of the vans. The cop who stayed with them was dark haired with a long dark beard, a black cap, and a hard face full of angles and scars.

Paula got up and stepped a little bit away, making a show of watching the bots and the people.

The cop didn't seem very interested in Coryn or even in the proceedings surrounding the vans. He looked sad, and maybe also a little nervous. He kept looking behind them as if he expected someone else to show up. After a while, he cleared his throat and said, "You shouldn't associate with Listeners."

"Why not? If you're police, aren't you on their side anyway? Aren't Listeners and police the same? Both of you want to follow the grand plan and support both the cities and the rewilding, right?"

"We've found other Listeners dead in the last few days. Maybe this is all of them. If you were riding with them like you told us, you could have been killed, too."

She hadn't even thought about that. She would have, eventually. Surely she would have. "So why is it safer to be police than a Listener?"

He looked like the question unsettled him, but after a moment he said, "We have more protections, for one. Someone's always tracking us, and people know that."

He was making sure she knew it. "What else?"

He laughed, a huff of breath without humor. "Listeners hide what they're doing. They don't work directly for the city. I do. That's who pays me. Listeners are paid for by the NGOs and the rich, mostly, and the money trail isn't clear. You can't trust them the way you can us."

What came to mind was that the Listeners had saved her life and the police had been nowhere near her, but she managed to stop the words before they came out of her mouth.

"You look nice enough," he said. "I think you're honest. You'll be safer in the city. A lot safer. You should just go back."

She didn't bother responding directly to that. "Do you know who did this?"

"I don't," he said. "Something's happening out here, and I wonder if you know what it is."

She shook her head. "I just left the city a few days ago. I'm trying to find my sister. I don't know anyone out here except her and the people I met on the road like Liselle and Lucien." She glanced toward the overturned vans. "I guess I don't really know them anymore, either."

Aspen sat panting in her lap, and she wondered if he was thirsty. She dug in her pack for a small cup and filled it from her canteen. "Do you believe me and Paula?"

"Maybe. But you should believe me. It's dangerous Outside, and it's getting more dangerous. You're a target out here, don't mistake that . . . two women." He looked at her slyly, like he expected her to say something. When she didn't, he plucked at the grass with his fingers. "Get yourself killed."

She couldn't tell if he'd spotted Paula as a robot. Probably. Aspen sniffed at the water. "Look," she said. "I'm meeting my sister. She's expecting me. Can we go?"

He gave her a long look. "I'm not supposed to let you go until someone tells me I can."

"You're not going to need us for anything. If you do, you can always reach me at RiversEnd Ranch in the Palouse. That's where we're going."

He offered her a patronizing smile that made her wince, but once more she held her tongue. She didn't want to find out how powerful a policeman was out here. She needed Lou. Without Lou, she couldn't make sense of the Outside. At least not so far. "Please let us go on. I don't like being around all this death."

His features softened a little. "I'll go ask, if you promise not to run while I'm checking."

"Thank you."

"If you run, I'll chase you."

"I won't run."

She watched him head down the little rise to the vans and the swarm of people. A gust of cold wind plucked at her purloined coat, and she shivered some more.

She walked over to Paula, lightheaded and cold. Aspen stuck close to her feet. "I want to leave," she mumbled.

"I know. We will."

"I need Lou."

"You need to eat and rest."

She glanced up at the sky. "We can still go at least five more miles. We should start out."

Paula's voice softened. "I know, sweetheart. I want to go, too. But we can't go until the nice men let us go."

"Stubborn robot."

"Smart robot, if you ask me," Paula replied.

The three officers kept talking to each other, and from time to time they looked at her.

"I'm scared," Coryn said. She hadn't realized until she said it, but she'd been growing more scared every day since she left the city. Now the fear was a solid thing deep inside of her. Maybe if she got food and time alone with Paula and Aspen, she could be strong again. Getting to Lou could make her strong again. Maybe the fear itself could even make her strong, but in that moment she felt weak and small, and a little dizzy.

Lou could explain.

The sad policeman walked back up and over to them. He held his hand out. "Coryn, if you need anything, please reach out to me." There was a small card with his contact data in his hand. "My name is Sam Dinsmore."

She looked directly into his pale blue eyes. "Thank you." She would remember his name. She could think of him as Sad Sam whom she met on the worst day of the trip, and on the second-worst day of her life.

She and Paula picked up their packs. She clutched Aspen's leash in her right hand. After they'd walked for about ten minutes and couldn't see anything except the police cars out in the middle of the road, Paula asked, "Are you okay?"

"I'm dizzy."

"Should we stop?"

"Not yet." She made it for another hour, one foot in front of the other. That was all she could focus on, that and Aspen, whom she picked up and put down and picked up again. When she held him, she ran her fingers through his fine white fur and whispered lies to him. "It will be okay," she said. "We'll be okay."

‡ ‡ ‡

The next morning, she woke to sunshine that warmed her eyelids and to Aspen's warm, raspy tongue on her cheek. One arm was thrust out of her sleeping bag, and she'd pushed her pillow away so she lay with her head right on the ground. Her fingers felt cold, and she tucked them back in for a moment, warming them against her stomach. She looked up at Paula, who had spent the night standing guard and holding onto the end of Aspen's leash. "Paula?"

"Yes."

"We still have a few days left, don't we?"

"Probably. We might get to the edge of Palouse Country, but that's not the same as finding Lou. Of course, it might help if you tell her you're coming."

"But what if something happens and I don't get there? Lou wasn't telling the truth—not if Blessing was right about what her life is really like."

Paula handed Coryn's canteen to her. "I think we should tell her."

"I'll tell her tonight." She could only think about one thing, going forward and finding Lou. "Do we have anything other than his food bowl to give Aspen water in?"

Paula handed her a plastic cup Coryn had never seen before. It must have come from the vans. Coryn filled it half full of water and Aspen sniffed it and looked away.

Surely he was thirsty.

"Put some water on your fingers," Paula suggested.

Coryn did. Aspen licked them dry and then drained the cup.

Coryn sat up and looked around as she drank her own water. She'd slept in a shallow ravine between two hills, only a little out of sight. But between having a dog and a robot to watch over her, even a little cover was a lot.

Open country surrounded them: green hilly pastures, a small gray-blue river crowded with two lines of trees, and, here and there, the remnants of broken fences or abandoned houses. "Let's wait until we're closer."

"Your sister lied to you."

Coryn felt tears sting the edges of her eyes. "Not very much."

"Don't kid yourself. She lied about almost everything."

"You always did like me better than Lou."

"It was my job to protect you, not Lou. When your father bought me, Lou said she didn't want me, but you did."

"I remember." She ran her fingers through her hair. "I got lucky." She smiled at Paula, as if she were human enough to care.

Paula smiled back, warm. Just right. She, too, was looking out over the landscape, scanning it. "Call her soon. We don't want to wander around out here for weeks and miss her."

Coryn looked up at Paula, and made sure Paula was looking back at her. "What if . . . I'm afraid she won't want to see us." She pushed the last of the blanket off, folded it into her open pack, stood all the way up, and stretched.

"Really?" Paula frowned. "I suppose that could be true."

"It might. Now that we've gotten this far I'm going to find her. Nothing will stop me. Nothing. Not tornadoes, not regular windstorms, not wannabe warlords, not ecobots, not snow if it comes. Nothing. Let's go."

"Breakfast?"

The thought of food made her stomach roil, particularly since she'd just talked through the litany of dangers. "I'll stop soon."

"Suit yourself," Paula said. "But if you fall down from exhaustion before you decide it's soon, don't blame me."

Coryn took another long swig of water and started off. She was tired after so many days of walking. Her feet had swollen so much her shoes barely closed. The scab on her leg itched. She'd lost track of how many marathons were left, but every step took her closer to Lou.

She could hardly wait to hug her sister. If Lou would let her. She banished the thought.

For half an hour, she counted steps. At just over three thousand, they came near another river and three deer bounded across the road and away, and she lost count, laughed, and stopped bothering. The deer pleased her. Surely if there were wild deer here, the restoration was going at least all right.

After another hour, Paula said, "I think there's a little lake over there." She pointed toward a copse of aspen a few hundred feet off the road.

A spring bubbled up inside of a circle of trees and rocks. Coryn admired the convenient placement of the rocks. "This is so pretty it must have been designed by someone."

"I agree. But there aren't any houses nearby. There were a few resorts and guest ranches out here that got taken down, though. This might have belonged to one of them."

The day wasn't quite warm yet, but Coryn stripped off her clothes anyway and stepped into the water, using her bare hands to scrub at her skin. The bottom of the pool felt mossy between her toes and cold from her knees down, and somewhere near the middle, it fell away to nothing—she had to flail her arms and kick to stay afloat since there was nowhere to put her feet.

She splashed the top of the water, trying to convince Aspen to come in. He could use a bath.

A fish bumped her, and she yelped.

"Coryn," Paula hissed in her warning voice.

"Yes?"

"There are people coming."

Coryn swam over to the edge of the pool and pushed herself up from the rocks, dripping, her skin breaking out in goose bumps and her blood running fast and hot. "I don't see them."

Paula pointed.

Coryn squinted, one hand reaching down for her underwear and jeans.

Calm, calm, she told herself. Maybe it's someone more like Blessing and Day.

"There, see, on the edge of the meadow."

Whoever it was headed straight for them, and also toward the road. They were coming down from the hills on a path. They were too far away for her to tell much about them. But Paula could see far better than she could.

She scrambled into her clothes, and when she looked again the movement had clarified into a group of maybe twenty-five people coming toward them. Tall men, mostly, scruffy looking. There were a few women. "Should we run?" she asked.

Paula shook her head. "They have robots with them. They'd see us—they've surely already seen us. If we run, they would think we are worth catching, and even if I can outrun the robots, you cannot."

They'd trapped themselves for a simple bath. She shivered, and her knees felt soft. Liselle and Lucien had died near water. But she wasn't a Listener. Thankfully, she wasn't shaking too much to ask, "So you think they see us?"

"Probably. They're going to hear us if you don't keep your voice down."

She whispered, "Are the bots as fast as you?"

"How can I know that?"

A light wind rustled the aspens and chilled Coryn's damp skin. She should never have brought Paula. "Then I want you to run."

Paula's head whipped around so she looked directly at Coryn from only a few inches away. "And leave you? I cannot."

"If they're friends, I'll be safe enough anyway. If they're not, you're the one they'll want the most. So if you run, you keep me safer."

"I don't think so. I can take that many."

"Even robots?"

Paula had gone completely still, looking for all the world like a human woman taking some time to puzzle things out.

"Run," Coryn told her. "And take Aspen. Please."

For a moment, she thought the look the robot gave her might tear her in two. She remembered the day Lou left, and how they'd dragged it out so it hurt more than it had to. "Go now. Then you'll be free to rescue me if I need it."

Paula stared at her. "For the record, I disagree with you. I'm not supposed to protect your dog. I'm supposed to protect you."

"Leaving me will protect me."

"Stupid human."

Coryn almost laughed, but she looked back at the oncoming group of people. They frightened her. Not just because they were strangers, although out here that might be enough. But they looked severe and serious. She had the distinct impression they had a goal. "Go."

Paula went. Without Aspen, without her pack. She hunched down and fled the trees and raced *toward* the incoming people.

Damn it. She was trying to draw their attention! "Fucking robots," she whispered under her breath. She should have made it an explicit, completely clear command instead of saying please.

She left her pack as well, clutched the little dog, and sauntered out of the trees as if she didn't see any of them, the people or Paula, and then pretended to suddenly notice that she had company. She stopped right out in the open and watched to see what would happen.

Paula glanced at her, and even though she was so far away that Coryn couldn't see the look on her face, she was pretty certain Paula looked pissed. She wouldn't really be, she was a robot, but she had been taught to feign certain emotions, and right now she would look angry.

Fine. Coryn *was* angry.

She got an accurate count. Twenty-two. There were five she suspected might be robots. Paula had given herself away from a distance with her gait.

Why hadn't Paula tried to fool them?

She only spotted five women. They walked behind the others, heads down. A robot walked behind the women, watching them. The men were so big and so . . . unkempt that Coryn suddenly wished she had run. Or hidden.

She wanted to run.

Paula stood her ground in front of the oncoming people, but stopped approaching.

Coryn's blood raced, and she licked her lips. Paula had trapped her, but Paula was brilliant. Might as well play it out. She walked right toward the people, coming up beside Paula. When she stopped, she smiled and waved.

"Hello!"

CHAPTER TWENTY-TWO

The man in front was tall and pale-skinned, with long black hair and a long black beard and black eyes. His clothes didn't look right out here— he wore form-printed jeans with a designer logo on the front pocket and a mint-green wired coat. Printed. City stuff. AR glasses dangled from a string around his neck.

What would he do with those out here?

He walked so confidently and so clearly in the front that Coryn felt sure he was the leader. He smiled, but he didn't wave back.

He did keep coming without breaking stride.

Carefully, fingers shaking, she snapped two pictures and sent them off. Maybe someone was still listening.

Paula's ears were good enough she would hear anything Coryn whispered in spite of the distance between them. So she whispered, "Run. Now."

The group came closer. The man who walked beside the leader looked similar, except browner—browner skin, lighter hair, and a shorter, better trimmed beard. He also wore modern clothes.

Coryn whispered again. "Please." Her voice shook with fear. Fear for Paula, fear for herself, fear of what might happen if Paula didn't understand why she had to stay free. "Now. Take Aspen. Go."

The men were close.

Paula glanced at her.

There was no time for the robot to fight her own inner programming inconsistencies. "It's an order."

Paula's face went neutral, but she crossed the short distance to Coryn, grabbed Aspen, and raced away.

One of the men took out a stunner and fired at Paula's back. Either he missed, or it simply didn't bother Paula. Her robotic body had been created as a bodyguard, long before this personality had been uploaded and set to protect Coryn.

The leader of the group's face twisted up in anger, and he barked, "Catch her."

Two men and two robots took off after Paula, the robots quickly outracing the men. Paula shot back through the trees, using them for cover, and emerged on the grassy meadow on the far side of them. Coryn stood on tiptoe, watching Paula run. She had a head start, but would it be enough?

A hand grabbed her around her right arm, just below her elbow. The man's words were clipped and cold. "Are you alone?"

She almost laughed. A weird reaction to her fear. "Now I am."

"Where is the robot going?"

Coryn shrugged. "I really don't know. I sent her away until I'm sure you're not planning to do us or her any harm."

He stared at her. "Call her back."

Coryn just stared at him.

"We'll find her."

"Who are you?" she asked, trying for a tone that suggested everything might work out all right and they really should just let her go on her way. She didn't sound confident even to herself.

"None of your business. But now you're coming with us."

"People are expecting me." There. Better. He couldn't know she lied.

He shoved her at the brown-bearded man, who stripped her wristlet and stuffed it in his pocket, unclipped a set of plastic restraints from his belt, pulled her arms behind her, and locked her wrists together.

She struggled, and the man cuffed her on the shoulders. "It will do you no good."

The gravity of her choice to leave the city struck her then.

She could die. Aspen could die, too. Paula could be destroyed. She had taken responsibility for the dog, and now she might have killed him because she'd been too stubborn to listen to Paula. She'd walked right into trouble. Even after Liselle died, she hadn't thought that *she* could die.

Now she did, and it made her feel liquid.

The men started moving, the brown one, who was probably second-in-command, pulling her beside him. "Walk quietly," he said. "Do not draw attention."

Attention from what? It didn't matter; at that moment she couldn't have spoken out loud if she'd had to.

It required concentration to walk without stumbling, and her fear gave way to that focus. She stopped shaking and walked, surprised by how much the loss of her arms' freedom of movement affected her gait.

At least they were walking east, which was generally the way that Coryn needed to go anyway. It was away from Paula, though. Or at least away from the direction she had chosen to disappear into. Paula could run a long time—she recharged her energy storage systems with her motion and the sun, and she was very, very energy efficient.

After a while, Coryn tried to slow down to end up back by the women so that she could talk to them, but her assigned watcher kept her right in front of him.

It was hard to walk slightly bent over. A rock caught her foot, and she went down onto her knees. The brown man slapped her on the cheek, and she understood why the two women behind her looked down. She started glancing down from time to time, but she kept her head up. She was going to get to Lou and instinct told her being submissive wasn't the right answer.

She grew thirsty. The slosh of the water in the canteen on her captor's back sounded like an unscratchable itch. The midday sun beat down on them. Sweat trickled between her bunched shoulder blades and stung her eyes.

They followed a clear trail that wound through the cracks and valleys of hills, never getting near the crests, and sometimes blessedly in the shadows.

It took a very long time before one of the men and one of the robots returned. The man said, "She got away. She took down Bryce and Mer."

The leader's eyes widened. "Dead?"

"Mer is. Bryce stopped responding to any commands, but he can probably be reloaded. I had to leave his body, though."

So Mer had been a human, Bryce a robot.

The brown man bunched his fists, but the leader put a hand on his arm, restraining him. "Wait. She is not her robot. We have more important things to worry about."

The line of people thinned out and returned to walking in silence. From time to time a boot scraped on rock. Birds flew overhead, calling, and once a great V of geese flying north crossed low above them; she managed look up without tripping. Another thing she had seen pictures of but hadn't ever seen in person. They flew even more precisely and even closer than she had expected. Beautiful.

What other beautiful things might she miss if she died out here?

Her feet were numb by the time they stopped. She flopped to the ground, desperate for water.

The man who had been walking her drank from his own canteen and then poured a small cup for her and brought it over. She couldn't make herself refuse, and the water tasted wonderful. Thankfully, he poured a second cup.

The others had made a big semicircle, and she was basically part of the circle. She could see them all well now. Most were dressed in drab clothes that belonged out here, but all of the men had at least one or two things that belonged in the city. Bright colors, earrings, AR glasses. The women all wore modest clothes that covered their chests and arms, and two wore veils that hid their faces. The men splayed comfortably across rocks or the open dirt, but the women all sat reasonably straight, and together, across from her. When they glanced at her, they didn't look very kind, but at least one looked as curious as the others looked cold.

Returners? She hadn't heard that they were patriarchal, though. A few articles had suggested religious groups. Maybe they were that. They used English, and it seemed to be native to them, but the dialect was a little off from the city, the words cadenced oddly.

She wanted food. Funny how she almost always refused food from Paula, but now that Paula was gone, she felt starved. The leader came over and sat on a rock a few feet in front of her. "Where are you going and who are you meeting?"

She struggled for something from her research that wouldn't endanger Lou. "I'm going east. I'm meeting some friends from school. We're going to help with the burning this summer."

"Idaho."

"Yes."

He didn't look like he believed her, but he also didn't look like he cared. "Will your robot come back for you?"

Which answer was safer? "Maybe."

"Will she?"

"Why does it matter?"

He looked bemused. "You owe me a robot now."

"Because you chased mine?"

He slapped her across the cheek, hard enough to sting. "You are like a city kid. She's metal and a program. Just tell me if she'll come back. If she will, maybe you'll be bait. If not, maybe you'll be dead."

"She might." That was really all she could say.

"Then you might live tonight." He stood up and walked away, stopping to talk to two of his men in low tones.

She swallowed and blinked back tears. Damned if she was going to let these people see how much they frightened her.

Had *they* murdered Lucien and the caravan? Was she walking with Liselle's murderers?

She shifted so she sat higher and looked around. If they'd taken anything, it would be in a pack. She couldn't tell if the men's high-tech gear had belonged to the Listeners, but that might explain why they had AR glasses out here where there shouldn't be anything to see with them.

Without her wristlet, she couldn't take pictures, but she did her best to memorize faces and features.

She also looked for anything she recognized from the vans. It reminded her of a memory game Paula used to play with her when she was little. She used to bring her a box with real things in it and have her look at it for a few minutes and then write down what she remembered. Only this time, when she'd been looking at the box she hadn't known she was playing the game.

She couldn't do it. There wasn't anything she recognized from the van. And, after all, there was no reason to assume these people were the murderers. Maybe there were multiple bands of dangerous people who didn't think much of human life wandering around out here.

Lou had lied and lied and lied.

Even though she didn't see or hear any signal, the entire line of people started putting their things away at once and standing up, getting ready to go.

Without her wristlet, Coryn couldn't tell time. It felt like hours before they stopped again. They came upon a small circle of lean-tos and tents nestled near some large rocks and under a band of trees near a thin, cold stream. Two women and three men were already there, the men sitting on an old low wall that had probably once been paired with a big house or resort, talking. A group of women chattered and fussed over a large pot of soup that smelled like pepper.

They took her cuffs off and shoved a bowl of the soup toward her. Her hands felt so weak she almost dropped the soup on the dirt before she managed to rest it on her knees. She shook her tingly right hand to get enough control to lift her spoon. She tasted potatoes and celery and milk, and way too much pepper.

After she ate, two hard-eyed women came and stood a few feet away, and one offered to take her to the latrine. Two men watched them walk through the center of camp, trailing them at a distance. "My name is Coryn," she said. "I just want to leave safely. I don't wish you any harm."

They kept their faces down and ignored her.

"Will you tell me your names?"

The taller of the two women barked, "Silence!" in clear English. The other woman held a weapon of some kind, maybe a stunner or maybe even an old-fashioned gun with bullets. Whatever it was, the woman carried it with authority.

The latrine turned out to be a square room with three tiny, stinking stalls and a single metal sink, but it was stocked with paper. A small mirror showed Coryn how unkempt she looked, and after she finished using the facilities she ran water on her hands and brushed sweat from her cheeks and ran more water and started in on her hair.

The taller woman said, "Stop!" and Coryn took another swipe through her hair. As she walked back, she kept her head up even though the shorter woman held the weapon to the small of her back. The hard metal barrel poked at her if she slowed even a little. Fear of it made Coryn almost lose her footing twice. Blood thrummed through her ears and jaw, and she swallowed over and over and watched the path closely.

A flash of light blue caught her attention. One of the women they passed wore the soft blue shoes she'd loved on Liselle. They were more scuffed than they had been in the van, but they were the same shoes. They had to be. The color was too unique.

Her breath fluttered and she almost choked. At least she knew something; she knew who had killed her friends.

Hopefully Paula would show up soon. But she'd almost certainly wait until after people had started going to sleep.

The sun still slanted through camp, giving everything a dusky golden look and making it appear almost pleasant in spite of how hard and poor it actually was.

The silent women took her pack and put her in a tent near the front and center of the encampment. The man who'd chased Paula sat in front of her tent, cross-legged on the ground, angled so he could see if she tried to get out or if anyone tried to get in from the front.

She sat in the tent doorway behind a zipped mesh panel and looked out at whatever passed in front of her. Most things happened behind the tent, which was probably exactly how her captors had designed it. A few people walked by on the way to the latrine and back. A brown dog with a crooked tail hopped past the tent on three good legs, favoring the other one. The air smelled faintly smoky from the cook fires.

She had almost nothing. No Paula. No food of her own. Nothing from her pack. Only the small box with her mother's earrings in it. She resisted touching it.

By the time the sky faded to true dark, the camp was also dark, all of the fires doused. Here and there, soft, diffuse beams shone down from cupped palms as people walked in front of her. From time to time, someone exchanged murmured greetings with her taciturn guard.

As it grew quiet, she started to shake. She imagined Paula and Aspen coming for her, and Paula getting caught in nets, or Paula getting shot, or Paula being captured in some other way and reprogrammed. The more tired she grew, the more jumbled things became, until she saw Paula lying on the ground the way Lucien had, one arm in water and part of her face gone, blood all around.

Paula was a robot. She didn't have red blood to leak. But Coryn still saw it coming from her, and struggled not to cry, holding her hands tight to keep them from shaking.

When people came by it felt a little better, even though they were enemies.

She fell asleep sitting up and cold, but so bone tired that even fear and curiosity weren't enough to keep her from falling deeply asleep and dreaming of the city. She woke with tears gathered in the corners of her eyes and looked out through the mesh. The camp was quiet now, except that her guard lay right in front of the tent, snoring.

Stars filled the sky. This had become her favorite thing about Outside, the Milky Way looking like a soft blanket covering the sky and the bright lights of stars, planets, and space stations barely indistinguishable one from another. Tonight, it was as beautiful as she had ever seen it, but it didn't make her happy in the way it usually did. She felt numb.

Surely Paula would come soon.

She watched the stars, fighting tears and swallowing sobs, struggling to keep herself strong. Once, she spotted a flaming meteor streaking right to left near the horizon. Planes flew overhead, red and white blinking lights accompanied by a dull roar.

She must have dozed off again because she woke to a less-than-black sky that hid the Milky Way from her but still allowed for the brightest stations and planets to shine.

Her hands had stopped shaking.

The slight hum of electric engines seemed to come from at least two directions.

She couldn't see them.

Her guard had woken and moved to his old spot, and he stood, staring.

The sound seemed familiar, low and throaty and efficient.

Then she saw them. Three ecobots, their outlines an unmistakable silhouette against the barely lightening sky.

CHAPTER TWENTY-THREE

One by one, ecobots drove right past her tent and parked. She counted five of them before it dawned on her that they hadn't come to save her. They didn't know she was here at all, and if they did, why would they care?

There was another clue. Even though she couldn't see most of the small, ragged village from inside of her tent prison, the camp sounded quite pleased to see the ecobots. People chattered excitedly, and two of the younger men near her actually clapped.

She didn't understand. She sat mute while more ecobots drove by in front of her and parked.

She couldn't stand up in the tent, but she scooted as close to the front as she could get, pressing her nose against the mesh. People cheered and stamped.

The leader's voice shushed them. She'd come to recognize it, gruff and deep, full of authority. In spite of that, there was a tiny bit more cheering before the camp went quiet. She could only hear some of his words, but she got the impression that ecobots coming to camp represented a victory of some kind. It also apparently represented work, as people started walking by her with more purpose than she had seen before.

Her guard glared at her, and she moved an inch back. He returned his attention to the caravan of ecobots and trucks. They seemed to be gathering behind her in what would be the center of the overgrown campsite. A few rattling trucks that looked like they had come from farms trailed the line of ecobots. They seemed to be occupied by humans, although she wasn't really close enough to tell whether they were human or the most humanoid of the ecobots. Although if they were bots, she reasoned, there would be no need for them to use the trucks.

What was happening? What could these outlaws possibly have to do with ecobots?

She tapped on the mesh in front of her and said, "I'd like to use the restroom."

The guard shouted "Female guards!" at someone she couldn't see.

It took longer than it had before, but two came and stood beside the opening of the tent as she crawled out. At first, her legs felt so stiff from sitting all night that it was hard to stand. She had to shake the leg that had been cut a few times before it held her weight comfortably.

It was colder outside than it had been in the tent. A few very high clouds were just beginning to lose the sunrise tints and fade to pale white in the otherwise-clear sky.

"Hurry," the same woman who had told her to be quiet the previous night commanded. "Look down. Keep your eyes down."

As before, the women flanked her, and this time her guard walked behind her.

So she wasn't supposed to see? At first she hadn't really needed the restroom; she had come out to see who and what had arrived. Now she had to go so bad she wanted to stop and cross her legs. A deep breath banished tears that wanted to overwhelm her.

How could she find out what was going on?

"I'm thirsty," she said. She would have to lift her head to drink, and they had always given her water when she asked.

"When we get back," the woman said.

The younger woman who walked on her far side was new, and not much bigger than Coryn. Maybe there was some advantage there. She scuffed her foot and tripped over a rock, rolling so that she managed to glance at the newcomers as she fell into the other small woman, hoping to knock her down.

No luck. The woman pirouetted away, turned and kicked her.

She managed not to pee her pants.

Her other guard growled.

Coryn got up onto all fours, sharp stones digging into her palms and knees. She looked up, quickly, assessing.

There were more people, now. Ten or twelve new ones as far as she could tell, although the new people had started mixing with the old. The ecobots had parked themselves beside the road in a long line, and some of the people from the camp were swarming up and down the big metallic bodies.

Her mind couldn't quite wrap around that.

The woman who had kicked her lifted her up, and the man who had been walking behind them snarled at her, "Keep your head down."

"Why are there ecobots here?" she asked.

"Shhhh. Like us, they are serving a purpose. You do not."

"What purpose?"

No answer.

She walked slowly and demurely the rest of the way to the bathroom, keeping her head down and listening as well as she could. Multiple low conversations went on all around her, all in English, but none quite understandable. She heard the word "city" more than a few times, and also "plans" and "freedom" and other connector words that made no sense out of context. She also heard the word "Wilders" more than once, and wasn't that what Lou was? A Wilder? Certainly these people weren't wilding anything.

They seemed excited though. Laughter welled out of groups of people here and there, and voices exuded a sense of pride. About the appearance of the big robots, for sure, but why?

She made it to the bathroom in time. Each of the two women took advantage of the opportunity as well, one by one, everyone moving so slowly they must be stalling. They did not talk to each other or to her. Coryn had the distinct feeling that they were following orders.

They weren't doing anything nice to her or for her, but they probably couldn't risk that even if they wanted to.

The only comfort she took from their presence at all was that the older one's look grazed hers, their eyes meeting for maybe a second or two, and there was no hate in them at all. More like compassion and resolve.

The reason the women had stalled became clear when a third woman handed a square of cloth into the bathroom. They tied it tight across her eyes, an impenetrable shield of cloth that hung down over her nose and smelled of soap.

They marched her forward, and for a heart-stopping moment she felt like there was a target on her back. She held her breath, bracing, although nothing happened.

She couldn't look down, so she kept her head up and shuffled her feet. Someone took each arm. Probably the women, since their hands were small and strong. They pulled her along, and she lost her sense of direction. Only after what seemed like far too long, she realized they were back at her tent. They pushed her so she fell into the tent, rolling toward the back.

As they zipped the opening shut, the guard instructed her to leave the blindfold on.

"Water, please," she replied, surprised at how strong her voice sounded.

"In a moment."

It took more than a moment. Eventually the tent door zipped open, and a cold cup bumped against her shoulder. Water. Odd that she could smell it.

She drank, then handed back the cup, asking, "More?"

No more came, and no food, and so she sat blindfolded, hungry, and still thirsty.

The ecobots had come to the barn at Lucien's request. They had saved her and Paula and taken away their attackers. So what were the ecobots doing here with the people who had killed Lucien and Liselle?

‡ ‡ ‡

No more water came, and no breakfast. She dozed fitfully and listened as much as she could. Her guard changed. Another man.

Sometime in the early afternoon, it appeared that someone had bothered to remember she might have needs. The front of the tent unzipped, and small hands tugged the blindfold off. Light assaulted her, and she had to blink and blink in order to actually see. The same women who had helped escort her to the bathroom handed her a plate with bread, a small, dried apple, and a handful of nuts on it. She took it. "Thank you," she managed. "Water?"

A full-sized flask of water came in as well. The two women sat right in front of the tent, looking away from her. She thought about whether or not the flask could be a weapon, except that it made no sense to attack these two, who were clearly following orders. Not in the daylight anyway, since she couldn't outrun the group's robots. She ate and drank and, mostly satisfied, passed the plate and flask out to the women, who disappeared.

They hadn't made her put her blindfold back on. A small win. She tucked it into her pocket reflexively. When you have nothing, take what you can get.

She really, really missed Paula, and the city, and the multiple AR worlds and the bridges and her bicycle.

If she wasn't careful she was going to break down, and that wouldn't help her or anyone.

Maybe she missed the bicycle the most, except for Paula and Aspen of course. If she had the bicycle she could escape. Where was Paula anyway?

If only she could ride away from this damned tent and take a long downhill and feel the wind in her face.

At least she hadn't called Lou.

Damnit.

‡ ‡ ‡

As it grew close to evening, the leader of the group peered at her through the mesh. He looked more tired than he had but also more confident. "Your robot isn't coming, is she?"

"Of course she is," Coryn replied. "But she's not going to break into a camp that's this big. She's out there watching for me."

"If she watches for you too long, you may not be here to find. We will be leaving early in the morning."

Coryn licked her lips. "I'm worth more than robot bait."

"We're not taking new recruits right now, and we don't rape. We value the women we keep." He actually looked slightly regretful, although perhaps in an exaggerated way. She wouldn't call it a caring look.

"Then let me go. I have things to do."

"Yes, you do. You can call your robot in, and you can pray."

She wanted to ask what god he prayed to just so she could be sure and pray to another one. When she had said nothing for a long time he stood up and walked away.

Half an hour later, more food and water came, and she got another blindfolded trip to the restroom.

They left the blindfold on again. She reached up to take it off and her guard tied it tighter.

What were they afraid she would see?

She stretched out and started testing all of the tent's seams. Metal poles held it up from outside, so there was nothing that would possibly make a good weapon inside. The near end had the zippered mesh and the guard. The far end had nothing but nicely done, tight, double seams. She ran her hand along the bottom of the tent, hoping for a weak spot or maybe a sharp rock under it.

Nothing.

She had her shoes and her coat. They had her wristlet, which they probably couldn't get into since she was careful about security. She needed it to reach Lou. Without it she might have come all the way out here and risked all this only to wonder lost around the Palouse for years.

So many mistakes. Clearly city smarts and books counted for almost nothing Outside.

What would any of the vid heroes she knew do?

For starters they'd have more resources. Maybe she could make friends with a guard. She scooted up toward the front, feeling for the mesh with outstretched fingers. There. She knew better than to reach for the zipper, but she called out, "Hello."

"Be quiet," the man said.

"I don't understand why you're holding me."

"Be quiet." His voice was soft and very, very firm.

"You could have just let us go when we saw you. We were going different directions. It would have been much easier."

He returned only silence.

Someone came up and talked to him in hushed tones. After the person left, he said, "This is not your lucky day."

She sat with those words. "Is anyone going to bring me dinner?"

He laughed a little. "I don't think so."

Okay. But she needed strength. "Do you have any water?"

He hesitated, but then said, "I'll call for some."

She had been hoping he would carelessly hand her a glass, and she could bite him or pull him down. He did call, "Female guards, please. Bring water."

Before the guards got there, she heard something. Horses' hooves. She tried to figure out how many horses. But she'd never heard them for real, and video representations of horses hadn't taught her enough.

More than one, anyway.

She reached up and ripped her blindfold off. The guard wasn't looking directly at her, but was squinting in the direction of the road. She reached up for the zipper, her heart pounding.

Her movement must have caught his attention since he turned back to her.

Damn. This was just a tent. She was being held prisoner in a tent by one man!

She wanted to see the horses.

No one was going to hold her hostage in a tent. She stood up and rushed at the door, only to be kicked in the face. Blood ran down her lip, tasting of metal and fear.

She sat, swiping the blood off her face, rocking. Listening.

More horses' hooves. Something else they didn't want her to see? She called out to the guard. "Can they bring rags with that water? You busted my lip."

He didn't answer her. Probably fascinated with whatever he was lucky enough to see out there.

At least the blindfold was still off. She peered out, but it had started getting dark, and pretty soon it would be too dark to see.

There were new voices. A female. She strained.

It could be Lou. It had been years now, but she knew Lou's voice.

It made no sense. The voice came again.

It could be Lou.

And then, for no obvious reason, she was certain. She took in a deep, slow breath and bellowed "Lou!" with all of her might.

CHAPTER TWENTY-FOUR

Coryn's scream seemed to rip the very air in two. All of her anger, all of her fear from the last two days, all of her despair, and even the small, sharp pain of her split lip, all of it came out in that single aching screech. "Lou!"

The mesh door of the tent ripped open. Her guard reached in, trying to grab her.

She scooted away, her hands sliding through the blood from her lip, boots scraping at the tent fabric, barely getting any purchase at all. She kicked at him.

He stepped back, ripped the rest of the mesh free, and came in after her.

She managed to scream again, a wordless animal shriek.

He reacted to the sound with fury in his eyes.

Good, he hated screaming. She screamed again.

He scrabbled around on the floor, searching for something. The blindfold, but she'd put it in her pocket. He backed up, and she kicked his face, catching his chin with a glancing blow.

He grunted in pain. *Good.* She tried for a better kick. Missed. He backed all the way out of the door. *More good.* She twisted and dove, aiming for the door, hoping to follow him.

He grabbed her arms and pulled her out like a landed fish, the toes of her boots scraping on the ground. He smelled of sweat and anger and dirt, his scent strong enough she nearly choked.

She twisted one arm free and punched him in the stomach. He gripped her arm again, nails digging into her flesh.

Pounding feet raced toward them. He held her face against his chest so she couldn't see, and she braced, certain someone or something was about to hit her. The leader barked a command. "Stop!"

The footsteps stopped and then came forward again.

"Let her go," the man growled, sharp and hard.

Her captor released his grip a little, still tight enough to keep her from running.

"Let her go," the other man repeated. He did, dropping his hands so she staggered.

She turned. Lou. Walking slowly up the street to her, moving casually and smoothly. A bigger Lou, muscled and tanned. Even though she'd always been confident, there was something more than confidence in her walk and her carriage. Maybe *command*? Other people besides Lou watched her. Her red hair curled around her face and across her broad shoulders; her lips were tight and thin, her walk full of purpose. She wore odd-looking tan pants, loose across the butt and thighs, tight at the ankles, and a flowing long-sleeved shirt the color of firewood bark.

She met Coryn's confused smile with a command to *be still* on her face.

Lou had been telling her that all her life in one way or another; she obeyed.

Lou kept coming, a casual smile playing across her face. The setting sun shone from behind her, masking the fine details of her features, haloing the back of her head. An angel come to Earth to save her sister.

She was saved. Lou had saved her. Not Paula, but Lou.

She wanted nothing more than to run to her sister and bury herself in her arms, but the look on Lou's face held her back. Lou reached a hand out and touched her cheek. "It is you."

"Yes." Coryn tried to read her sister's emotions, but she got nothing. No relief, not even surprise.

"Come with me." Lou spoke directly to the leader. "Thank you, Bartholomew," she said evenly, as if she were thanking a minion. "We'll meet after dinner."

She turned and walked back the way she had come, clearly expecting Coryn to follow. Coryn did, relieved and still frightened, her clothes in disarray and smeared with blood. She tried to straighten them. At least her lip had stopped bleeding.

As they approached the small town, Coryn struggled to take in details. Ecobots lined the edge of the road, parked docilely on a hard surface that had been created out of wood and stone and gravel. She hadn't even noticed it on the way in. A single cook fire gleamed dully in the dusky light, with three women bending over it. One sprinkled in spices, another stirred, and a third held a tasting spoon. Such a strange, old-fashioned way to cook.

Lou slowed down enough for Coryn to catch up. She whispered, "We will eat with these people. You will say nothing unless I ask you a question."

Coryn swallowed. "Okay."

They stood outside the cook tent, watching for a few long moments as a line gathered. Lou handed Coryn into line behind the last of the men and the first of the women, the tall one that had given her orders when they gave her restroom breaks and had tied the first blindfold over her eyes. Coryn nodded at her, and she nodded back, her face still and blank but her eyes dark with emotions Coryn couldn't quite read. Maybe curiosity, or even resentment.

Bartholomew stood in front of the line, but waited. He gestured, and Lou walked in front of him, taking the first bowl.

Wow. She replayed the tiny scene in her head a few times. It seemed impossible. Equally strange, none of the women around her said a thing to her. They were not nice. Not polite. But neither were they mean or condescending.

Coryn got her food after the older woman who had guarded her. So whatever was going on, Lou was in first place, and she was second among the women. That had to be because of Lou; she'd been a prisoner and maybe about to die.

Now she stood in some place she didn't understand at all, free of the tent and free of her death sentence and more confused than she'd been an hour before.

Had every one of Lou's letters been a lie? Everything? Had Lou started down whatever path she was on before she even left the city?

People grouped around low tables to eat. Coryn approached Lou, who sat with the leaders, all men except for the one woman Coryn had been put right behind. Lou gave her the *not now* look, and she sat by herself, on a rock, eating the soup. It had more vegetables in it than yesterday, and some pasta, and it tasted a little more of herbs than pepper, and it was fabulous. As an experiment, she took her bowl and cup back and went to the restroom by herself.

No one followed.

She used the blindfold and the thin stream of cold sink water to wash the blood from her face. She was getting a substantial fat lip. But she would live.

She would live.

She let that thought sink in, and only as the idea of life sank in did she realize how sure she had been that she would die.

What had happened anyway? How did Lou know these people, and why did they defer to her? They were murderers.

What was Lou doing with the people who had murdered Liselle?

CHAPTER TWENTY-FIVE

Even in the dim light, the scratched mirror in the latrine suggested she looked better than she had as a prisoner, other than the burgeoning fat lip and the beginnings of two respectable black eyes. She walked back to camp, still a little shocked that no one stopped her. She paced up and down the road, trying to stay warm and awake and to understand her situation.

Lou and the leaders sat apart from everyone else, talking and making notes on a slate. A group of three people wandered from ecobot to ecobot, using clipboards and climbing up and down on the machines, looking tiny on top of the biggest of the bots. During this, the ecobots did nothing.

She walked toward the big robots, but one of the drably dressed women, who had clearly been watching her, blocked her way. "Do not go there."

Coryn stood her ground for a moment, but then remembered the tent and the guns. It wasn't worth disobeying. She looked the woman directly in the eyes, which were a shocking blue, the color of Lou's eyes, and wide with intent. "What would I see if I did?"

"Nothing you would understand. Go."

She went. Maybe Lou would tell her what was happening.

She paced awhile longer. People watched her, but from a distance. The cook fires were out again, the camp dark, the stars spread like fancy sea salt on the sky.

The ecobots began to emit a low, electric hum. They rolled away, one after the other, a long line of a dozen big machines. She heard them long after the darkness had swallowed them.

Once they were gone, she stood up and walked around. No one bothered her, so she started making bigger circles, looking for anything more interesting than watching Lou talk with the man who had killed her best friend.

Near the edge of camp, she spotted five horses in a small pen. A low light had been rigged so that she could see them even in the almost dark. They were smaller than she'd expected, and noisier, stamping their feet and tossing their heads. They whickered as she approached the makeshift corral. She put a hand out, and a voice said, "Flat. They'll nip off your fingers."

A relieved heat bloomed in her center as she turned to step into Paula's embrace. "You're okay." Her whole body shook with relief. "I hate being separated from you. Let's just skip that next time, okay?"

"You're the one who made me go," Paula pointed out.

"I thought they were going to kill me. They . . . they said my luck had just about run out. The . . . they weren't going to feed me dinner. The only reason they didn't kill me is they wanted you to come back so they could capture you." She withdrew a little from Paula's arms, looked up into her face. It was so good to see her. So good. "Do they know you're here? They were using me as bait for you, and they wanted to hurt you or keep you, or maybe reprogram you, like Erich." She grew cold at the thought. "Don't let them see you."

"These people are doing work for Lou."

"I guessed that. But really? Killers work for Lou?"

"I don't yet understand the situation."

"That makes two of us. But are you safe here? Should you leave?"

Paula shook her head ever so briefly. "I'm safe enough as one of Lou's minions. No one's even noticed me." She flicked a low light on and flipped it up to illuminate her face. "They helped me look less like a robot."

A jagged scar that simply couldn't be real ran across her nose, and she appeared to have dark circles under her eyes. Her hair had two streaks of gray in it. "What possessed you to make me leave you in such danger?"

"I didn't want them to hurt you."

"I'm not human," Paula reminded her. "I will not feel the pain of death."

Coryn touched her cheek. "I would feel your death."

Paula shook herself. "We'll talk of this later. Let me introduce you to the horses."

"Wait—where's Aspen?"

Paula smiled. "He's okay. You'll probably see him later tonight."

"Where is he?"

"I can't say. Not here. Trust me."

"Of course, but tell me what's happening? Who is Lou? What is she doing here? Why do these people listen to her?"

"Lou should tell you that. Besides, I share your questions." Paula turned toward the animals. "Come, meet the horses."

Coryn stepped close to them, surprised at their solidity. They felt bigger than they looked.

Paula must have seen her hesitation. "Horses are prey," she said. "That means, in the heart, they are fretful beings. They are afraid that wind is a wolf, that a snapping coat is an eagle, that a rustle in the bushes is a bear. You must calm them, and that starts with being calm."

Coryn took a deep breath and reached her hand slowly out toward the nearest horse.

"That's good," Paula said. "If you are calm and can learn to tell a horse what you want, almost any well-trained horse will give you everything they have. They'll burst their heart for you."

Coryn smiled as she ran her fingers through the dark mane of a dark brown horse with a white nose. "She's beautiful."

"He," Paula corrected her. "Most of these are geldings. They're usually easier to manage." She pointed at a huge light tan horse with dark stockings on its feet and dark ears. "That's Mouse. She's Lou's horse, and the only mare in this group."

"Where did you learn so much about horses?" Coryn asked.

Paula smiled. "I've had all day with them, and I asked questions."

And of course she had databases full of experiences as well, most of them not her own. Paula had always been able to learn almost anything. "I thought Lou had a pinto, like an Indian horse."

"She did. It died."

"An awful lot of things die out here," Coryn muttered. "How did you end up with Lou?"

"As soon as I was free, I started looking for people. The first people I saw knew Lou, and the second knew where she was. Lucky for us, she wasn't very far away."

Coryn remembered. "Did you really kill a man?"

"And a robot."

She was very matter-of-fact about it. A killer robot in the city was destroyed quickly unless hard evidence proved they had killed in defense of their charge. A slight chill touched Coryn's center. Paula had only had to act like a bodyguard in small ways before. She had shouldered people out of the way, put herself between Coryn and a car that had lost its brains, and reminded Coryn to be aware when anyone Paula deemed as dangerous came too close.

Funny how something you knew like the back of your hand changed on you suddenly. "Did you mind killing?" Coryn asked, switching horses to touch noses with a gray.

"It makes me less safe, and thus less able to keep you safe. I mind that."

"Thank you." She turned around to look for Lou. It had gotten to be full dark, and as usual the camp was dark. She listened, hoping to hear something that way.

No sign of her.

"We're not staying here tonight are we?"

"No. We would have stripped the tack off the horses if we were."

"The saddles?"

"Yes. We did take the bridles off, and those halters are for when they're penned or hobbled so they can eat."

Coryn fingered the leather bridle on the gray. "Lou is so different now."

Paula moved a few steps closer to Coryn, worked on the mane of the lightest brown horse. He had a white stripe down his forehead, which flared out over his nose, and one leg was white to the knee. "This is River. I rode in on him, so you're likely to ride out on him."

"I like the gray one."

Paula laughed. "He's not yours to ask for. Now, as for why Lou is different, how different are you from when you left Seacouver?"

Coryn didn't have to think very hard. "Oh."

"Here she comes."

Two flashlights showed Lou walking over to them, deep in conversation with Bartholomew. Behind her there were three other people, one woman and two men. She couldn't see them in the dark. Lights shone down from their hands, but all she could see was their feet.

Coryn was suddenly afraid to talk to her sister. This whole trip had been about this moment; while she had imagined a meeting over horses and beside Paula, or maybe a slow walk along a path, side by side, talking, she never suspected that they would be surrounded by a camp of killers. Of course, she hadn't expected to have almost lost her life to storms and been saved by robots, that her own robot might have changed into a killer, or that the whole world would feel tilted.

How had she been so naive?

Lou and Bartholomew shook hands very formally. He turned away without even glancing toward Coryn, fading back into the black of night. Lou came up to Coryn, her face tense. "I don't know how you managed to get in so much trouble so fast. Can you ride?"

"How do I know?"

"Okay. Stand aside while we get the horses ready."

She obeyed, watching Lou and Paula and two other people slide bridles on in the dark. They left the halters, but took the long ropes and coiled them, tying them to the saddles. They tightened big belly bands on the horses, touching them, whispering to them.

Lou gestured for her to come over. "Paula will help you mount."

That was all? No *hello, how are you, little sister?* No *glad to see you?*

One of the people she hadn't been able to see came up close to her, flashing his light on his face for just a moment, illuminating his bright smile.

Blessing.

"I'm so happy to see you." It came out of her mouth, but as soon as she said it she realized she didn't know what to think. Hadn't he been going toward Cle Elum?

He sounded exactly the same, like a happy showman, confident and funny and a little light for the situation. "I didn't think I'd find Lou before you did."

"How did you?" she whispered. "You were going the other way."

"We decided to be gentlemen and follow you—we were worried about whether or not you'd be okay. After all, you were new out here, and walking around with companion robot Outside is like wearing a coat with a target painted on it."

"I think I understand that now." Here she was, almost laughing a minute after seeing him again.

"We tried to find you but couldn't do it. But it seemed like a good idea to tell Lou you were out here."

"Well, yes."

He reached for the gray horse, which made her grimace, although it only took her a moment to forgive him for having the prettiest horse. Of course he did.

She felt a little shy. "You probably saved my life."

She couldn't see his face, but she heard his laughter. "You still have a few things to learn."

"Day's here?"

He pointed. "Over there."

She had drifted to River, and Paula came up beside her, holding her hands together, clasped and low. "Step here."

She did.

"Other foot."

"Oh."

"Put your hand on the saddle horn."

She reached up and grasped the worn leather. It fit her hand perfectly. Paula boosted her and she swung her leg over inelegantly, her foot catching on the horse's rump before she tugged it over where it belonged. The horse was wider than he had looked from the ground; her legs splayed awkwardly.

Paula touched her leg to draw her attention, make sure she was listening. "Stay calm. This isn't a bicycle. River knows what you're feeling, and you need to learn what he's feeling."

She took another deep breath. "Okay. I'm ready."

Paula handed her the reins, also leather. "Don't pull on those unless you want him to stop." She fiddled with both of Coryn's stirrups, positioning her feet so the heels pointed down just enough to be uncomfortable.

Coryn looked around. Everyone else seemed to be waiting for her. Just then, Day's horse almost bumped River, and the horse kicked, rocking her in the saddle. She gripped the horn tighter, and River tossed his head. Day looked quite calm about the incident. "Just follow us," he said. "Don't let River too close to Monkey, here. Blessing will ride beside you, and Paula will walk close by. It'll be okay."

"You named your horse Monkey?"

"No. Someone else did that. It fits him, though."

Lou took the front. Coryn and River were next to last, with Paula right by River's bridle as if she expected to have to grab him.

The horses walked, rolling gently back and forth with each stride. "We're not going to go any faster?" Coryn asked Paula.

"It's not safe. Lou doesn't like to ride in the dark at all. But this is an extraordinary circumstance."

For the first hour or so, her senses seemed extra attuned to everything, the feel of the cooling air, the calls of night birds, the small animals rustling in the low scrub or grasses that they rode through, the clunks and pings of the horses' hooves when they stepped on stones. Eventually, her eyes grew so heavy she closed them. Paula poked her, and she jerked straight. "Stay awake," Paula admonished. "Never underestimate the challenges a horse can present you with. They're easily scared."

"Mmmmmm . . . ." Coryn said, and struggled to stay alert. She had so much trouble that eventually they devolved into a rhythm where Paula would poke her every few moments.

Stars spilled across the sky above them, and the moon rose almost full, making it easier to see the faces of the other riders. Everyone stayed as quiet as the entire camp had been at night.

It made her wonder what they were all hiding from.

The horses stopped all at once, startling Coryn out of a daze. Lou unlocked a wide gate in a tall metal fence and gestured them forward. After it closed behind them, Lou locked it and climbed back on Mouse. As they continued riding, low and excited chatter started up among the riders. Coryn thought about approaching her sister, but Lou was surrounded by the others, and she'd have to muscle River in. She wasn't sure she had that much control over the horse.

"Do you know where we are?" she asked Paula.

"Home," Paula said. "RiversEnd Ranch."

Dawn began to break as they turned up a slight hill. Pale light spilled onto a barn that sat a respectable distance above a riverbed lined with trees and cluttered with rhododendrons dotted with a few of the last spring blooms in pinks and whites and a brilliant purple. The entire line of horses had already been speeding up, but when the barn came into view River tossed his head and tried to rush past the front horses. She had to hold herself on by clutching the horn with both hands to keep from falling.

Paula grabbed River's bridle. He twisted sideways once, before settling and allowing himself to be led.

The barn towered over them, far larger than it had looked at first. Paula led River in last, and they all bunched loosely in a tall, covered area with wide open doors. Tack festooned the far wall: saddles and bridles and blankets and buckets and ropes and things she didn't recognize at all. One door opened onto rows of horse stalls.

Ever since she'd left the city, her life had been full of barns.

Paula reached up to help her off of River. She almost fell, but Paula took most of her weight and let her stamp her feet to get the blood back into them. They felt like fire, and she was surprisingly unsteady. They walked together around the barn until Coryn could walk with no help, and then once more for good measure. Everything about her legs and butt hurt except the bottoms of her feet.

The barn's roof ran high and supported bales of hay, and the long rows of stalls held at least twenty other horses. Each animal occupied a private box with hay strewn on the ground and a bucket of fresh water. Coryn started up the rows, peering over stall doors. A few were empty, but many held horses she hadn't seen. "Where's Aspen?"

"In the house." Paula put a hand on her shoulder. "First, you have a horse to put away."

She shook free of the foggy feeling of finally being on the ground, and noticed Blessing lifting a saddle free from his gray horse and Day carrying a brush in one hand and a halter in the other. She sighed, wishing for a quiet place to lie down. But all of these horses had come to save her, and River had carried her here. She headed back to River, and Paula gave her precise directions without offering any other help. This was typical when she thought Coryn needed to learn something, which probably meant she would be riding again. Hopefully not for a few days; the inside of her thighs felt raw.

She put the saddle and bridle away and brushed the saddle marks from River's coat, cleaned his feet, and gave him a few handfuls of grain and a flake of fresh hay. After he stood eating contentedly, she followed Paula into the house.

They were the last ones out of the barn. She turned to Paula. "Horses are a lot more work than bicycles."

"They're not more work to ride."

"I disagree. My inner thighs feel like someone set them on fire."

"There's that."

"Stupid robot."

Paula smiled. "Stupid Coryn. What would I have done if you got yourself killed?"

"Found another human to keep."

"But I might not like them so much."

"Stupid robot."

The others had gathered in a great room in front of a roaring fire. A few of them clutched hot cups of coffee, looking as if they might just skip sleeping. Blessing smiled at her, and the strangers in the room looked at her with intense curiosity but didn't approach her.

Coryn went right for the fire and held her hands up, grateful for the warmth. Paula came up beside her and dropped Aspen into her arms. The little dog yipped and leapt free, running around the room twice and making her laugh. Finally, he jumped back into her arms and stayed there.

Aspen and the fire warmed her. She was alive. For the moment, it was enough.

Lou drew her from the fire and performed introductions. She knew Blessing and Day and Paula, of course, but there a woman named Matchiko and a man named Daryl, as well. Both were older by a few years and fit Coryn's expectation of cowboy types, with rugged good looks and wrinkled faces and even flannel shirts.

"Thank you," Coryn said.

Matchiko blushed a little, and said, "You're welcome." Daryl simply nodded.

Lou also introduced her to a thin and slightly bent old man named Justin, who handed out tea and coffee and set out plates of bread.

Coryn helped herself to both tea and bread. The still-warm bread smelled of cinnamon, raisins, and nuts. The food and the hot tea combined to fill and soothe her, and fatigue began to slow her movements. She hadn't felt this safe since she left the city, not even in Cle Elum.

She had made it. Lou had found her instead of her finding Lou, but now they were together. Nothing had been like she'd thought, except that the trip had somehow taken about as many days as she expected.

But Lou was not at all what she had expected. Coryn silently watched her sister move through the small crowd, realizing that she had complete and utter charge of these people. She seemed to be a casual and capable leader, encouraging and laughing and stopping to ask questions.

Now if she could only get Lou to talk with her.

CHAPTER TWENTY-SIX

Lou pulled her and Aspen away from the fire and into a corner of the room as far from everyone as possible. She looked into Coryn's eyes. "I'm glad you're safe. I have to meet with my crew. I'm going to take you to your room. This is . . . a difficult time."

Coryn blinked for a moment, realizing that Lou meant she might be an inconvenience. After all that had happened to her, she was being handed a dismissal from the adults' table. "I can stay up for a while," she stammered.

Lou's expression softened a little. "Come on. We can talk for a few minutes."

Coryn followed her, partly out of habit and partly because she was truly exhausted. Aspen padded behind her. Paula remained in the room by the fire, almost certainly at Lou's request. Maybe she'd learn something useful there.

The room Lou led her to was far away from the fire, and almost as cold as the outside. But it had a sumptuous-looking bed piled high with blankets, a small attached bathroom, and fresh clean clothes that had been laid out for her. She hadn't realized how much she needed each and every one of those things. She fingered the heavy coverlet. Stains marred one corner, and the middle had been patched more than once, but it smelled clean and felt soft.

She hadn't been warm at night for a long time. Maybe she could stand to miss whatever conversation Lou intended to keep from her after all.

Aspen leapt up and curled into the middle of the covers like a king on a throne.

Lou stood in the door, watching. The differences in her were even clearer in this light. She looked like she'd aged ten years instead of four. She had filled out, all of it muscle. Even her face looked fuller and stronger, more alive. Something had knocked her nose a little crooked, and there was a small scar right on the bridge of it. "Did you bring the dog all the way from the city?"

"It's a long story and you don't have any time."

Lou stiffened and shook her head. "I have a job to do. I can't help that, and we just lost an afternoon and a night."

Stung, Coryn stood completely still and tried to keep her cool.

Lou noticed. "I'm sorry. It's not my fault so much is happening right now, but it's not your fault, either."

Coryn walked over and touched Lou's cheek. "Okay. Thanks. That was the hard way to find you, though. Not everyone gets captured by raving murderers in order to find their sister."

"They're hackers, not murderers."

"They killed my friends. And they were planning to kill me."

Lou's lips thinned. "Maybe. Life is harder out here. You should have stayed in the city. It's safer there."

Coryn took a deep breath. Whether or not Bartholomew was a murderer could wait. "You're the only family I have. I had to find you."

Lou closed her eyes and chewed on her lower lip. "I think about you every day. But I knew you were safe with Paula. I knew you were okay. Damn you, now I don't know that anymore."

"Yes, you do. I'm right here." Anger curled up her spine. She tried to control it, knowing that she was too tired to make any sense of things. Hackers. They'd been hacking the ecobots. That's why they were so excited when the robots rolled up to them like pets. "Aren't you about to attack the city?"

Lou's eyes widened, as if shocked that Coryn had deduced the obvious. "Portland," she said. "Only Portland. I'd have warned you before we got to Seacouver."

"Damnit, Lou." Her anger dug in deeper. "I didn't come out here to fight; I *miss* home. I can't tell you how much I miss it now that I've left it. I don't know what you're part of, and I didn't think things would be so bad out here, but your notes didn't exactly warn me. I want to help make it better."

Lou stayed still, just inches from Coryn, a slightly shocked look on her face.

"I'm willing to help rewild. Isn't that what you came for? To rewild?"

Lou just laughed. "You don't know anything." She crossed the bed without touching Coryn and sat down on the edge. "Living out here, we forget."

"Forget what?"

"How little anybody in the cities know. They're keeping you distracted."

Coryn bristled. "I read the papers. I know Portland just changed mayors and Rio just became the biggest city in Latin America with no one below the poverty level. No one!"

Lou sighed. "Maybe you are my sister after all. I didn't used to see this much fight in you."

"I'm not your *little* sister any more. I'm a full adult."

Lou braided and unbraided her own hair, brighter red and longer than Coryn had ever seen it, almost down to her waist. The old habit made her seem a little more like Coryn remembered her.

"You have no idea how much you have to learn," Lou said, her voice so soft that the words didn't sting very much.

"So stay and tell me a few things. I'll shower and you can talk to me and then you can tuck me in and go talk to your friends without me."

"If it weren't for Blessing, you'd be dead."

"Okay, our friends." Coryn starting stripping off her filthy, bloody clothes. She looked for a hamper, but didn't see one.

"Drop them on the floor. They're trash anyway."

Maybe it was a good thing she'd gotten old junk clothes in Cle Elum.

Aspen crept across the bed to Lou's side and nosed her until she started petting him. "I'll wait. You can't take long showers here."

"So tell me something I should know." She stepped into the small bathroom and turned on the standup shower, holding her hand under the water to test temperature. Her fingers nearly froze, but the cold woke her up, got her thinking more clearly. "What's wrong with the cities? I would have thought you'd defend them. Concentrated population so the wild can be wild and all that. The efficiencies of the many. You know the stories."

"There's some truth." Lou spoke louder now, to get over the sound of the shower. "But that doesn't make me love the cities. No one should, not really."

"Really?" Coryn asked, grabbing a towel and positioning it near the shower. "Billions of people should hate their homes?"

"The city killed our parents."

"You never did like home as much as me." The water changed to tepid. "But then I left, so I guess I don't know what I want. Not really."

"So why *did* you leave?" Lou asked.

Coryn took a deep breath and ducked under the shower head. She held her bruised face up, let the water wash the blood and grime of the last few days away. She found soap and started slathering it everywhere, stinging her lip with it. "The city's a lonely place." She set the slippery soap back down. "And I missed you."

"That's one problem." Lou spoke slowly, as if afraid Coryn would miss a word and misunderstand her. "The city drains you of your soul. I felt it. You felt it about the same time. Our parents killed themselves because mom couldn't bear the city anymore."

"I know our sordid family history. Is there shampoo?"

"The pink bottle."

Coryn found it. "But a lot of the people in the city *are* happy. When I go back, if I go back, I think I could find a way to be happy. I miss my AR games and being able to run for hours safely. I bet you didn't know that I won marathons last year."

"I didn't."

"At home, I don't have to worry about getting killed every five minutes."

"But do you agree that the city isn't an easy place to be happy?"

She focused on washing the grit from her hair. The water finally felt warmer. "I always think everyone else is happier than me."

"Maybe everyone thinks that. All this time, I thought you were happier than me."

Coryn couldn't think of any way to refute that statement. She rinsed her hair.

When Coryn didn't answer, Lou asked, "What about out here? Is Outside like you expected?"

Coryn stood on firmer ground here. "You pretended you were out here riding horses through the hills and planting native plants."

"I do that."

Soap stung the inside of her thighs. "You're leading a revolution."

Lou's answering laugh sounded a little bitter. "I wouldn't go that far."

"You were just bossing around the people who killed my friends." She should have saved that comment for when she could see Lou's face. "That dog, Aspen, he's all I have left from the first people who were nice to me out here. Those people—Bartholomew and his creep women—killed my friends."

"Be careful who you make friends with."

"You too."

"Let it go. You're safe now. Shit happens out here, and you live or you die. I'll try to teach you to live, but out here we appreciate every day."

Coryn put the top back on the shampoo bottle and turned the water off. "Why is it so bad out here? Why all the violence?"

"There aren't any big corporations killing things out here anymore, but there are a lot of people trying to kill each other and trying to stop us. I've lost two wolf packs this year. Two. The Returners hate the cities more every year. If the cities don't stop staring at their navels and start paying attention to the great wilding, it's going to fail, and we're all going to die. It's like we've become two different planets instead of part of the same whole."

Coryn opened the shower door and stared at her sister. "It does feel like that." She should have a million questions, but the simplicity of the statement struck her like a truth and set her mind racing. Everyone was on sides here, although there were far more than two. She toweled off, the rough nap bracing against her skin. The inside of her thighs were bright red, too tender to rub. It probably wouldn't do any good to complain. She glanced at Lou. "That doesn't mean we should hurt the cities. Or the people in them."

"I hope it doesn't come to that."

"So tell me. What are you going to do?"

"I will."

"When?" Coryn winced as she patted her thighs.

"Soon. You're safe enough for now. We're home. I'm able to keep some order here. But don't ever think we're ahead. We've lost a lot of the rewilded land to squatters, and there are stealth towns and small armies like the one that caught you."

"Weren't they your friends?"

"I don't make friends with religious fanatic hackers. But I need them."

"For what? To catch me?"

"No. You're only here because of raw, stupid luck. And Blessing."

Coryn hung up the towel and started getting dressed. "What about the Listeners? A group of them called the ecobots that saved me and Paula from a self-styled warlord when we were just a day or two Outside. They seem like a force of order."

A brittle laugh escaped Lou's lips. "So you almost died on day one?"

"That was day two."

"You can't trust Listeners. They work for so many masters they don't have any."

Coryn frowned. "What do you mean by that?"

Lou sighed. "I can't teach you everything. Not all at once."

Coryn ran a brush through her wet hair, warm from the shower and sleepy. "You sound like you don't trust anything about the cities." None of it made sense right then, but she was exhausted. All the sleep she'd had was in the damned tent, and under the trees, where she'd woken up a few times at night when things scurried close to them, and before that in the barn before the ecobots saved her and before that . . .

Lou took the brush. "Let me."

It was something she used to do for Coryn, something Paula had taken over whenever Coryn didn't want to do it herself. It felt good. In spite of how confused and sore she was, Lou brushing her hair felt like she had thought this whole trip might feel, and she had to struggle not to cry. "That feels good," she whispered. "Thank you. And thank you for saving me. Blessing isn't really the one who did that."

"We're a team out here," Lou murmured. "We have to be." She stayed longer than Coryn expected her to, brushing and brushing and saying absolutely nothing. Once, Coryn noticed that her hands were shaking as she held the brush. When she stopped, she whispered, "I'll bring you something. Stay put."

Coryn managed to sit still and wait, although her hands shook a little and she felt light and exhausted but awake.

It took Lou ten minutes to come back with a cup of water and a single pill in a bottle. She handed it to Coryn.

"What's this?"

"Something for PTSD. You know what that is, right?"

"Yes." She didn't feel that bad right now, but she didn't want to go to sleep very much. Almost every time she slept something bad happened, like getting caught by Erich or having Liselle killed. "I don't know that I have *that*."

"It's a danger for all of us out here. Things happen. The more things happen, the more it builds up. This is new, but it works, especially if you take it right away."

"Like the windstorm that almost killed us on day one?"

Her sister whispered, "You didn't tell me about that."

Coryn took the pill and drank the water. "I haven't had time to tell you half of everything."

"Tomorrow." Lou kissed her on her forehead and tucked the heavy cotton covers around her. She left quietly, and Coryn lay still and wondered what it would feel like for the medicine to work. Aspen stood, stretched, and then lay beside her, warm and alive and comforting.

Moments later, Paula opened the door and slid quietly in. "Are you okay?" she asked.

"Mmmmmm. Did you learn anything?"

Paula set an extra glass of water down on the small bedside table. "Only that some people thought Lou was crazy for rescuing you and some people think she was a hero."

"Which side was bigger? Crazy or hero?"

"Hero," Paula said, walking around the bed and climbing onto the far side.

Coryn turned toward her, burrowing her head into Paula's side. The robot's slender fingers stroked her damp hair, and Coryn gave up on not crying and wondered if the medicine and crying went together and then stopped wondering much of anything. It was good to be in Paula's arms, with Aspen at her back and in a big, safe place with a window they could escape through if need be.

Even better, they weren't in a barn.

CHAPTER TWENTY-SEVEN

The urge to cry had left her entirely by time she woke up. God, she must have needed sleep, and maybe also that pill Lou gave her. Her legs felt so stiff from riding that she had to hold them up and grab them to stretch them out before she could move fluidly enough to get out of bed. The air chilled her, and her bare feet slapped against the hard, cold floor. The gentle light of early morning spilled through pale curtains that did nothing to muffle the birds singing outside.

The room was empty; Paula must be off on an errand, and Aspen must have gone with her.

She went to the window, threw it open, and gulped fresh air, damp and filled with the scent of hay, horses, and damp grass. Rolling hills looked like they had been dusted with a fine sage-green sugar as the sun lit up the morning dew. Here and there, low yellow flowers ran in loose lines, like erratic stripes of paint. The hills went on and on, graceful and full of gentle curves. Even though she knew there had to be mountains somewhere, there was nothing sharp in her vision except the edges of the roof, a corner of the barn, and the pointed ends of a flock of small dark birds that wheeled over the land like punctuation marks.

Other than looking out toward Puget Sound from the highest bridges and buildings, or looking back toward the city right before she left, this was the widest vista she had ever seen.

The door slid open and Lou poked her head in. "Good morning."

Coryn turned to her. "No wonder you want to save this."

Lou stood beside her, and they looked out of the window together. A soft smile played on Lou's face. "It goes like this forever. You can ride for days and see nothing but this, nothing but land and sky and river, hill and sky, river and sky, mountains and sky, always sky."

"You sound poetic."

Lou's cheeks pinked. "Open land does that to me."

"I never imagined a place could be this empty."

"It will change you. It changes everyone."

"Like it changed you?" Coryn asked.

"Maybe differently than me," Lou mused. "The wild has its own way with everyone. All you can do is be open to it."

"Like I had to be calm for the horses?"

"Like that. You've got be aware. Aware of beauty." She pointed out the window. "And aware of dangerous things as well. You get an opportunity to die at least once a day out here."

"I know."

Lou turned to face her. "Don't. In fact, for the next few weeks, don't leave my side without telling me. It's perilous here. It's always been, but it's far worse now. I can't keep you safe unless I know where you are. This is my own fault for not telling you how it really is out here, not telling you to stay home." She crossed to the side table and picked up the brush again, her voice losing some of its intensity. "Here, you've gotten all tangled."

Lou hadn't usually been this tender to her. Maybe she was glad to see her after all? Or in spite of whatever else was happening.

"Do you promise?" Lou slid behind her and started running the brush through Coryn's sleep-mussed hair.

"To tell you if I go anywhere?"

"To do what I tell you."

The tone in Lou's voice crawled up her spine. "I'm not a kid anymore. I don't just do what I'm told."

The brush caught in a tangle of hair, and Lou resorted to her fingers to free it. "If Blessing hadn't told me where you were, and if Paula hadn't found us shortly after, so I actually believed him, you would have died last night. They were going to kill you."

Coryn swallowed. "I think I knew that. But why?"

"There's no time for distraction now. That's all. Another time, they might have ignored you or encouraged you to join them or even simply helped you. You were a distraction, and a liability. You saw the ecobots in the camp. If you talk about that, you might ruin all of our plans." Lou found another tangle. "I know you won't talk about it."

Coryn felt cold. What would Lou think if she found out she had spied for the Listeners? But she was learning not to say the first thing that came to mind anymore. "I won't talk about it. Except maybe to you. I want to understand, though. What were they doing there anyway?"

Lou ignored, her, lost in her own train of thoughts. "I may not be able to save you next time. You'll learn, eventually. Like I learned. Like everyone who survives learns. But right now, you know nothing."

Stung, Coryn took a deep breath before she spoke. "Teach me. I'll stay near you, and I'll even promise not to leave without telling you. But I can't promise *not to do anything you don't tell me to do.*"

"You've gotten more stubborn than you used to be," Lou muttered.

"The orphanage wasn't always a great place."

Lou stopped in mid-stroke, clearing her throat. "I'm sorry. I've always regretted leaving you. But if I'd stayed in the city, I would have killed something or someone."

"I didn't blame you most days. I was lonely, but I didn't think it was your fault. It was just how my life turned out." She took the brush from Lou's fingers, looked into her eyes. "Your eyes are the color of the sky out here. You belong here. You always have. I don't know where I belong, not yet. Maybe with you, maybe in the city. At any rate, when I chose to leave there, I came to find you, to understand you."

"Okay," Lou said. "I'm amazed you survived, and that I found you at all. I'm amazed I've survived so long. But let's just back down some. I know a lot that you don't know, and I'm going to watch out for you."

Her sister sounded like someone trying to calm a child. Coryn tried not to let it upset her.

Lou drew a breath and spoke slowly, weighing her words carefully. "We deal with what's real out here. For now, it's a work day. Come out and have breakfast. I'll find you some boots that fit."

"Boots? What for?"

"We leave in an hour. We'll call you a prospective volunteer. That way you get the right to take a horse. You can ride River again today."

"My legs are still sore from yesterday!"

Lou grinned. "Not yesterday. You slept a day and a night. We have to go soon, and you have to come with us. I have my own pursuits at night, but if I want food and horses and a roof over my head, I have to work during the day. You didn't think I owned all this, did you? It's the Foundation's, every bit of it."

Of course it was. "All right. I'm coming." Had she really slept that long? "Is there food?"

"Lots of it."

Coryn's legs complained when Paula boosted her up. Eight people rode out, with Lou and Blessing in the lead. Day rode beside Coryn, a calm, comfortable companion. He felt good to be near, steady. She decided she had underestimated him when they first met, letting Blessing's outgoing personality mask Day's calm competence. Aspen trotted behind them.

Paula rode a nearly black horse almost as big as Lou's Mouse. When she came up beside her, Coryn asked, "Why'd they put you on a horse today?"

"So people won't know I'm a robot." She smiled. "No human can run like I can. I can sit a horse a lot like a person, though. I probably look more natural than you. Straighten your back and hold your hands a little lower."

"Bossy robot." But Coryn obeyed, bemused. She did feel more comfortable this way. River's slightly rocking gait felt more natural when she wasn't slumping. "Do you know where we're going?"

She swore Day smiled a little as he said, "No."

Coryn enjoyed watching the sun-laden hills and the huge blue sky. The path they followed sometimes allowed for two horses to ride side by side, but mostly they rode in a long, lazy line that wound up and down hills. At least once every hour, Lou stopped them. She took photos and picked up dirt and grass samples, putting them in bags and labeling them before tucking the bags into pouches on the back of her saddle. After a while, Paula started dismounting and helping. Blessing and Day stayed on their horses, looking in different directions, acting like guards. Without any further instructions, she stayed on River as well. Besides, it might not be possible to get back up.

Matchiko appeared tightly partnered with Lou. She got on and off her horse every time Lou did, and gathered samples right beside her. They talked in tones too low for Coryn to hear, Lou's red hair and Matchiko's black blending in the wind as they stood side by side.

Once, a huge bird circled well above them. Lou stopped dead in her tracks and lifted the binoculars she carried around her neck, conferring with Matchiko. They took pictures and chattered excitedly.

Lou dropped back, her face excited. "That's a vulture. We don't see many of those."

"I've seen a few big birds," Coryn said.

"Those were eagles. We saw two lone goldens, and a mated pair of bald eagles flew over earlier. They live near the Snake River."

"How far is that?"

Lou smiled. "You'll see."

"Is everything a secret?"

"Think of it as a surprise."

"So are you counting wildlife?"

"Yes. And collecting grass and scat to measure nutrients and look for illness. And watching for signs of people who shouldn't be here. This is a preserve, and everyone on it should work for the Foundation, or have the Foundation's permission, or be one of the few natives allowed here, and we know who those are."

"And when you find someone who shouldn't be here?"

Lou smiled. "Then it depends on what my deal with them is."

Coryn swallowed. "You have a deal with the people who kidnapped me?"

"It's more accurate to say that many of us are benefitting from a deal between others. I'm the enforcer of that deal, in this place, at this moment. But if we see anyone . . . even Bartholomew and his family, you do what I say."

There Lou went, treating her like a two-year-old again. "They're a family?"

Lou offered her a complicated smile, an expression that seemed to say *it's way too complex to explain to you now.* Aloud, she said, "More than a blood family." Lou's smile relaxed some, and she began to sound like her old self. "Besides, yesterday was a good day. I managed to get some business done and rescue my hapless little sister all at once."

Coryn smiled at the teasing tone in her voice. Maybe Lou was finally relaxing a little bit. "When are you going to tell me more about what you do at night? About why Bartholomew and his family let you tell them what to do?"

Lou's face tightened.

"When, Lou? You said you'd teach me more to keep me safe."

Lou looked irritated, but then relented and softened some. "I'll ride by you for a while after lunch. We'll start then." She clicked Mouse to a trot, looking back over her right shoulder directly at Coryn. "Relax. Enjoy the ride. I'm going to show you a real treat."

‡‡‡

Coryn's stomach rumbled with hunger by the time Lou led them up over the biggest hill they'd climbed yet. Her back hurt, her legs had stopped screaming at her only because they'd gone numb, and she was pretty sure that she'd do well to fall gracefully off of River. Whatever had she expected riding a horse to be like, anyway? Paula was right, River was no bicycle. If he was, she'd have come this far and still be fresh and happy. Frankly, since they'd been walking all morning, she'd be ahead of them on a bicycle, too.

Well, except this hill would be tough. It had a false crest, so it seemed like they went up and up and then up again.

Horses did climb well.

Near the top, the grasses were low and thin, the ground rocky, and the flowers small and lacy.

Eventually they reached the real summit. Lou pulled Mouse to a stop and the others stopped as well. Coryn could see farther than she ever had, even farther than from the Bridge of Stars. She forgot she was hot and tired and hungry and could barely stand to be on horseback another minute. She almost forgot her name.

On the far eastern horizon, mountains created a jagged skyline accentuated with gray and black scarps angled into the sky like blades. Dark green forests laced with the lighter colors of spring leaves fell down below the high faces like a cloak. Just to her right, row on row of white windmills turned slowly in the light breeze. Directly in front of her, a thick navy blue ribbon wound through the bottom of the river valley. Even though they were far, far away she could tell that the river was wide and slow and worthy of respect. It had to be the Snake. She leaned forward and whispered between River's ears. "That's what you're named for. That's a river."

One ear swiveled back toward her.

Close by, Blessing sat easily on the beautiful gray, a dark man on a lighter horse, both tall and long of leg, both beautiful enough to take her breath way. He glanced at her with an amused look on his face, and she blushed.

Blessing laughed. "Go on, keep looking. You still haven't spotted your sister's surprise."

"It's not the river?"

"Keep looking."

The low hills between the rise they stood on and the river below were browner than the hills on the other side, almost chocolate. It looked. . . . She breathed, confused.

The shifting mass of brown was the shaggy backs of thousands of animals.

Alive. Hooved. Horned.

Lowing softly, the sound barely carried on the breeze.

Animals.

Buffalo.

A wild herd of buffalo so big that it covered her field of vision. With some difficulty, she maneuvered River to Mouse's side and looked up at her sister. "That's the most beautiful thing I've ever seen."

Lou was already smiling, her face alight with joy, bathed in light and warmth. "That's what we're here for. I needed you to see them, to understand them, to know that this is why I'm doing some of the hard things I'm doing."

Coryn could barely stammer out, "Thank . . . thank you."

They sat and watched together. Paula, Lou, Blessing and Day, Matchiko, Daryl, and a broad woman named Shuska who hadn't been with them the night before last. Seven humans, a robot, a small dog, and thousands of animals, the horses shifting their feet, the buffalo moving across the plains, the long river far away and past the beautiful brown beasts. Golden eagles flew above and thin, pale grass grew like a carpet of spring under their feet. It all came together to be magic, to be like the moments Coryn had only experienced on the highest places of the city when everything looked bigger than her, and she was part of all of it, when she understood what it meant to be human.

CHAPTER TWENTY-EIGHT

Exactly as she had expected, Coryn had to be lifted off of River. She leaned on Paula and stamped her feet while pins and needles raced up her nerves. Aspen curled around her, almost tripping her, making her laugh, worry in his mismatched eyes.

Lou led her away from the others, saying, "I promised my sis I'd have lunch with her."

The others dutifully took their own lunches and created a small party a few hundred feet away. Lou pulled out dried pears and peanut butter and jelly sandwiches, handing a fistful of pears and a whole sandwich to Coryn.

Coryn chewed on a pear, looking down at the buffalo and the river, and even looking down on circling raptors. She gave Aspen some bread and peanut butter and water, and a little of the dog food Paula had rescued from the caravan. She wanted it to last. As they ate, Coryn asked, "They're beautiful, but why buffalo?"

"They're hoofed. Herds of hoofed animals can restore prairie and wild places faster than anything humans can do. Their feet churn up the top of the soil and mix up the grass seeds, and their dung moves seeds around and provides food for animals and insects. The whole Palouse—all of it—was meant for hooves. A lot of it was cattle for some time, and that did all right, but buffalo are even better. They're naturally healthier and haven't been overbred for color or virus resistance or anything. They're only lightly modified at all, much less than the horses."

Coryn grew thoughtful. "What about horses? Were there wild horses here?"

"There still are. We're tracking two horse herds. But horses were never native to the Palouse, and buffalo were, before our ancestors shot them all for fun."

Coryn flinched, staring down at the herd. "I can't imagine wanting to shoot them."

"Good. Even though climate and land use change habitats, one of the tenets of wilding is to stay close to history when possible. In this case, we could. So we did."

"We? Surely this herd started years ago."

"We Wilders. The Foundation."

She heard a stiff pride in Lou's voice, a sense of belonging that tied her to all of the humans that had watched over this herd before her, that had watched for birds like the vulture they had seen earlier, and that had counted the eagles. Lou cared for this.

Coryn swallowed a lump in her throat, recognizing it for a useless snip of jealousy. Did it matter if Lou loved this work more than she loved Coryn? At least she wasn't despondent like their parents had been. She was happy. "I'm proud of you," she said. "It looks exactly like the vids show us. That's a healthy herd on healthy land."

Lou smiled. "The Palouse is one of the biggest wilding successes. But the land between here and Seacouver is stained with nests of survivalists and Returners. They come through here from time to time as well—Blessing said he told you about the worst encounter."

"Did you really kill someone?"

Lou's face hardened. "I had to."

"So *you* have to be careful. You, too. Not just me."

"Everyone out here has to be careful."

Coryn touched the lip her guard had kicked back in the camp. It still felt tender and a little swollen, and it cracked a little as she smiled. "I have a reminder."

"We were lucky," Lou whispered.

Not something Coryn wanted to dwell on. "So what do you want from the cities?"

"Resources. They have everything, and they don't give us enough of anything. We have the right laws, but no tools to enforce the laws. We can't help the people out here who need help. We can't help ourselves some days." She sounded bitter. "The Foundation has enough money to run the Palouse ecosystem. But nothing more. There was supposed to be an NGO for every part of the world that was aggregated, every piece of land we took, every necessary wildlife corridor. But there isn't. Some rogue cities have just restarted. The old roads and buildings that were supposed to be ripped up and recycled are being reused again. There's a hundred little groups of religious nuts with odd skills like the hackers that captured you, only less useful. A few are even more dangerous, and treat women like sex slaves."

"And no one stops them?"

"I'm the law out here, me and the ecobots. I *have* stopped some of the crazies; I had to. The ecobots can't do anything to humans that aren't hurting the environment."

"So how come the Listeners could get the ecobots to save us?"

"The Listeners have resources. You were lucky they were your friends, even though I don't want you to see any more of them."

"They were my friends after they saved me. Not before. I think they saved me to—" She thought about telling Lou she had been sending the Listeners pictures. But she held back. She wasn't part of their secret army any more. They were dead. "Because they help the people on the bottom. I was so stupid when I first came out. Why does everyone here want to steal Paula?"

"To sell her."

"They wouldn't have used her? Reprogrammed her?"

Lou laughed. "Could she be a sex-bot? I thought she didn't have the parts for that."

"She doesn't. But someone could give her a vagina." Lou kept changing the subject by focusing on the wrong parts of the story. "The hackers didn't seem preoccupied with sex, and they looked up to you. They let me go because you told them to."

Lou picked up a rock and tossed it to Coryn. "This one has a nice white vein of quartz in it."

"Lou."

She looked almost guilty. "Trust me. Please. I can't tell you more than I'm telling you."

"*Because you don't trust me?* Or because you're doing the wrong thing?"

Lou turned away for a moment, and when she turned back she looked collected. "I'm happy to see you. I'm telling you as much of the truth as I can. But your timing might have been better."

Coryn stood up. "I almost died to find you. And you saved me. Both of those things should be worth something."

"They are." Lou looked absolutely miserable, her mouth a thin line below red cheeks. She almost spit out the words, "There's too much at stake." She pointed down at the buffalo. "All of them. Every single one. All of the people in the cities. There's you. I *am* fighting for you. There's the whole goddamned world."

"You can't save the whole world!" She thought about Julianna and all of her resources and all the power she used to have. Julianna wasn't trying to do as much as her crazy sister. "Maybe you need to slow down," Coryn said. "Maybe you need to save one thing at a time, or a few things."

"No time." Lou glared at her before she bagged up the remains of her lunch and shoved it in Mouse's saddlebags. "There's a lot more story to tell you. I just don't have time yet. None of us has any time."

Coryn picked up Aspen and held him while she shook her feet out, getting ready to remount. She had helped Lou before, right before she left. She had been the strong one on that awful night when they learned how their parents died. She could help her again. She stood beside Lou and held her for a moment. "Thank you for showing me the buffalo. They're beautiful."

A trace of a smile touched Lou's face. "You're welcome."

Coryn limped back toward River. She grabbed the saddle horn and canted her foot up, hopping awkwardly. River turned his head and stared at her.

"Trust me," she said.

The horse gave a look that she swore was skeptical, but she tried again, succeeding in shifting her center of gravity enough to force her foot forward into the stirrup and pull on the horn at the right time. She stood in the one stirrup, facing sideways, and swung her right leg over the back of the saddle.

River startled, but she managed to keep her seat as he lunged forward, and even to pull him back so that she was in her proper place in line. "There, boy," she said. "We did it."

He flicked his ears at her.

It hurt to sit, but there wasn't anything else to do. She looked around. Aspen stared up at her.

"I don't think I can give you a ride," she said.

Paula hadn't mounted yet. She came over. "I can carry him if he'll let me."

"Would you? His little legs must be tired."

"Sure."

Paula scooped him up and managed to make mounting look easy, even while carrying a dog.

Lou started off. Coryn urged River forward and dropped in right behind her sister. She was going to stick to Lou until she figured out what was going on. Lou was just going to have to deal with it.

CHAPTER TWENTY-NINE

They rocked and swayed down toward the buffalo herd, following a thin, switchbacked trail, the horses careful of their footing. Coryn leaned back in her saddle at the steepest spots after Day whispered at her that it was easier on the horse. In some places, the edge of the trail crumbled under River's hooves. The sun soaked sweat from them all, the only occasional release a slight wind that blew the tangy scent of buffalo dung and trampled dust up as it dried their brows.

They rode single file. She could watch Lou's back and Mouse's swinging black tail and powerful golden hindquarters, but she couldn't actually talk to Lou. Seeing her sister had devolved into dynamics a lot like the ones she and Lou had stuck to when she was five and Lou was eight.

Maybe family was always that way.

Right after they found out how their parents died, she had been the strong one, at least for one day. Lou had needed her. No matter what Lou said right now, or how childish they both acted on the surface, it felt exactly like that time. She couldn't put her finger on exactly why, but she knew Lou needed her.

Riding hurt. Riding down the steep side of a hill made her afraid of falling. Based on how everyone else was acting, riding *shouldn't* hurt. Blessing and Day talked back and forth easily. Blessing turned around casually in his saddle from time to time. Matchiko sang softly under her breath, as if singing to her horse.

When they finally reached the bottom of the hill they rode in shadow, since the sun had fallen over the top of the hill without much notice. It still lit up the scarps and crags of the far mountains with magical golden yellows. Heat turned quickly to chill, and if it went through a comfortable phase she didn't notice it.

They rode close to the herd but not inside of the river of backs and snorting great noses. The ground was so torn up by hooves she wasn't sure how Blessing, who was in the lead at the moment, could see the trail, or even *if* he could see it.

She directed River up beside Mouse, looking up at Lou. "What are our plans for the evening?" she inquired through chattering teeth.

Lou glanced down at her. "We have two more hours on the clock. I'll be taking pictures of this—" She swept her hand down toward the ground, indicating the torn-up dirt. "—then we'll ride to one of our smaller outposts and spend the night. It's about an hour away. We'll have dinner there."

Coryn smelled secrets. "And what happens at the smaller outpost?"

Lou didn't look happy. "It's Bartholomew."

"The one who was going to kill me and steal my robot?"

Lou's reply came sharp and fast. "The one who is doing some work for me."

"Aren't you snippy." Coryn frowned. Why was she losing it like this? Maybe just because her legs hurt and she was tired. "Sorry," she told Lou. "I'm cold and hungry."

"That happens a lot out here. You'll have to get used to it."

"I'm trying."

Lou glared at her, and Coryn decide to change tactics. "Are you happier out here? I can't tell."

Lou seemed surprised by the question. "I . . . of course. It's more real out here."

"But clearly you could die."

"Some of my friends have." She pulled Mouse to a stop and called out, "Fifteen minute break! Blessing and Day on guard."

Everyone else dismounted. Coryn swung off by herself and fell on her butt. She managed to get up, red-faced, before Paula or anyone else could get to her. "But you're still happy? Would you be happy if I had died?"

"Not if I'd known about it."

But she probably wouldn't have. That was something to chew on later. "Will you ever go back to the city?"

Lou smiled. "Ever is a long time."

"How come you never answer any direct questions?"

Lou reached up and pulled her camera from Mouse's saddlebags and gestured for Coryn to come with her. They had left the buffalo behind now, although they walked beside the churned earth of the herd's passing.

When they were a few hundred feet away from other others, Lou spoke in a harsh whisper. "Look. I have a reputation here. More, I'm saving the fucking world. I know you don't understand, and I promise—I promise with *everything* I now am—that I will tell you why and what it's about. But . . . it's complicated. I can't give you three sentences and have you understand. It's not possible. So I need you to just relax." She snapped a few pictures, some quite close to the ground. "Follow directions. Don't challenge me in public. Let Paula look after you."

Coryn refused to answer that at all. She stopped right where she was and watched Lou walk away from her, taking pictures. She moved with purpose, a lone figure with more energy and anger than size. The light had almost left the tops of the mountains, and it was becoming hard to see fine details and easier to hear the river, the birds, and the stamping of the horse's feet.

The bad energy between her and Lou could ruin everything.

She found Paula, took Aspen from her, set him down and let him run. At least he was smart enough to stay away from the horses' feet.

When Lou had to pass her to get back to Mouse, Coryn used the same harsh whisper Lou had used on her. "I love you, but don't expect me to take your orders and shut up. I *know* it's complicated. So was our parents' death. So's the city. *Everything* is complicated as far as I can tell. But secrets and lies are more complicated than anything else." Her voice rose, her words coming out faster and tighter. "If you're the only family I've got, then I'm the only family you've got. You might want to consider that."

Lou stared at her, open mouthed. "You haven't heard a word I said. Your life may depend on listening to me and to Paula." She gave Coryn the big-sister look. "Drink some water," she said. "Horseback riding is more work than it feels like."

"Fuck you," Coryn muttered, too low for anyone but Lou to hear. She handed Aspen back up, wriggling, to Paula. He yipped and squirmed so much that Paula handed him back. "I think he wants to run."

"Okay."

Coryn climbed up a little more gracefully this time, and waited for Lou to lead them off. Lou made a clucking sound with her teeth as she and Mouse surged ahead of Blessing, taking the lead. Mouse tossed her head and held her tail up so it streamed in the wind.

Blessing drifted back to ride beside Coryn. "Not many people can piss her off so easily," he said.

"It's a talent I have."

He laughed, the laugh clear and light and brightening.

She smiled. "Did your mother name you Blessing, or did that become your name because you make everyone smile?"

"I don't remember my mother," he said. "And I don't remember how I got the name, but I like it."

"How'd you meet Day?"

"I can't remember a time I didn't know Day." He turned toward her, his expression uncharacteristically serious. "Please don't unbalance Lou. There's a lot of very hard things going on, and a wrong step could cost us years of planning."

So he was in Lou's keep-it-all-secret camp, too? "What do you mean? What could I do that would hurt?"

"If you distract her, she could make a mistake."

"So will you explain some of this to me?"

His lips thinned, although not enough that he lost any of his ethereal beauty. "I'll answer questions."

"Okay. Tell me why I didn't know anything about this from Inside? All the stories are good stories, or no stories. Or once in a while whispered real horror stories, stuff like *everyone who leaves the city dies*, or *the ecobots will kill you if you litter*. Nothing I learned Inside was *anything like* the truth. And I did research!"

"That's a good question." He didn't answer it right away. He rode quietly, looking around. After a few minutes, he asked her, "Where did you do your research?"

"On the Internet. In libraries."

"Did you ask any librarians for help?"

"No. Should I have?"

"Depends on the librarian. I know some wicked good ones."

"So you're from the city? I had the impression you were from here."

"One of my friends on the farm used to be a librarian in the city, and she told me they knew how to find all the real news. I thought that was pretty cool."

"Were you born out here?" Maybe she could at least understand this one person, and if she understood enough people out here she could understand the place as a bigger entity.

"Outside, but in California. I worked my way up here slowly. I worked for the farm before Lou did, though, taught her to ride."

"All right. But I searched every newsfeed and website I could find."

"Do you know who owns most of those?"

"No." But why would Blessing know that? River stretched his neck out, trying to eat some tall dry brush.

"Don't let him do that," Blessing cautioned.

She pulled back on the reins, and River stopped.

"Now tell him to go."

She made the same clucking sound that she'd heard Lou make, and River broke into a trot. She gasped, bouncing in the saddle.

Blessing's voice sounded warm and patient. "Lightly pull on the reins. Lightly."

She did. When River slowed, she smiled in relief. "Thanks." She took a deep breath. "I guess the feds own some of the websites, and the city some, and the big corporations, too."

"That's close to right. Add in a few individuals, some of whom are more interested in how many people believe their stories than in the truth."

That made her think of Julianna Lake again. If only she'd been able to spend more time with her. His tone of voice puzzled her. "You sound bitter."

"Sorry."

She was still puzzled. "Don't we have free speech? Like we can ask the librarians and they can tell us. We have free news—news-bots are more protected than anything else in Seacouver."

"Someone has to care enough to talk for free speech to matter." His face looked almost as bitter as his voice sounded, and the whole conversation made her uncomfortable.

She frowned in frustration. "That still doesn't explain why no one told me how bad it is out here. People care."

"How did you search?"

A bird flushed from just under River's nose, and he crow-hopped a little under her. She nearly fell off and had to take a moment to calm him. "I must have run hundreds of searches. Not one site gave me the idea I could be killed any old day out here." She fell silent for a while, listening to the horses' hooves and the wind in the small trees they were riding through. "If they told us, we'd be afraid, and they don't want us to be afraid."

He smiled. "That's good. And what do they get by not telling you?"

They rounded the line of trees and came up to a low bank that ran down to the Snake. Up close and in the near dark like this, the water looked almost black. It raced along inside its banks, one whole edge white-capped where a quick current met wet rocks. "If they keep us in the dark, they get people who aren't afraid. But it's worse than that. They get people who don't know they should be afraid."

"Are you afraid?" he asked her.

"Now? Yes." She was, too. "The world isn't at all what I thought it was."

Lou and Mouse had stopped in front of her, and she and Blessing came up beside them, and then the others, Paula on the end, looking as close to human as Coryn had ever seen her.

"It's beautiful," Coryn said, kind of speaking at once to Lou and to Blessing.

Blessing sidled up next to her. "And what would happen if everyone in the city knew that it was still so dangerous out here?"

"We'd panic."

"Maybe. What else?"

"We'd question."

"What do you do now?"

She thought about all the reasons she had been happy once but hadn't been happy recently, the reasons her mother had hated the city. All of the small things that didn't matter individually but added up. Endless ads, constant opportunities to play games, being watched and watching others, which was in truth both a comfort and a pastime and bit creepy. Maybe that summed the city up—lots of energy and growth and entertainment, like a constant high point, like a dance, only if you were just a regular person you were dancing for all of the others.

She didn't want to talk about her parents or her vague unease with the city, so she answered simply. "Now? Now I look at the Snake River and I wonder where it goes. Not to Seacouver. Not, I think, to Portland. Then? At home? I watched a lot of entertainment, went to school, played games, rode my bike for fun, hung out with people. I spent my allowances on whatever I wanted."

"And isn't that exactly what they want you to do? Buy stuff? Be docile?"

She scowled. "That's pretty dark."

"They'll tell you that you don't have to know it's dangerous out here, you just need to know not to go out. But what if the Outside comes in? Will the city be prepared?"

Prepared for what? "The city has defenses."

Blessing changed the subject. "The Snake goes where all water goes, to the ocean. It does go through Portland, only by then it's gotten married to the Columbia. You can't tell what drops of water came from which place by the time it's all mixed up in the ocean. The water has no choice about where it goes. But you do."

Instead of answering him, she stared at the dark, gurgling water.

CHAPTER THIRTY

The sky darkened into a velvet blanket pricked with a million lights, maybe more. Coryn felt like she could reach up and touch the small hard diamonds of the stars. Looking up gave her a crick in her neck, but she didn't care. The cold and the stars and the clop of the horse's hooves in the vast emptiness made her feel alive.

Cold had crept into her arms and legs until her whole body shivered, surprising her every few breaths. They rode toward a large house with an attached barn that perched on a hill overlooking the moving black ribbon of the river.

Barn and house were so dark as they approached that they had to use hand-lights to find the barn door. Coryn ran water, and Shuska and Blessing pulled feed down from the rafters, which Day and Daryl delivered.

After the horses were cared for, they all trooped together into the house, where Matchiko fed fresh logs onto a crackling fire. The warmth felt searing and welcome. She almost collapsed with exhaustion before she made it to a spot on the end of the dirt-brown couch. The couch had an overstuffed arm, and she rested her head on it, pillowed on her coat, breathing in deep lungfuls of warm air and horse sweat from her sleeve. She stank. No help for it.

The next thing she knew, Paula shook her arm.

"Mmmmmnnnnn," she heard herself say, as if from very far away.

"We have visitors coming," Paula whispered.

Bartholomew! Coryn sat up quickly, startling Aspen out of twitching dog-dreams.

The door opened. Aspen lifted his small, white head and barked. Three people walked in: Bartholomew, his number two, and a small woman no bigger than Coryn herself but darker, with nut-brown skin, dark curly hair with a bright streak of yellow sheeting down the left side, wide lips, and a tattoo around her neck of a chain with a broken link.

Coryn hugged Aspen close to her, paying close attention to names as she was introduced. Bartholomew's second—the man who had marched her into camp—was Milan, the woman Jersey. Jersey sat beside Coryn and immediately began petting and cooing at Aspen.

He licked her fingers and greeted her with a wagging tail. Traitor.

Jersey smiled at the dog. "I'm glad someone took him in."

"So where did you see him?" The answer almost had to be at the massacre.

Jersey made a vague shrug. Lou give Coryn the *be quiet* look.

The conversation began with stilted small talk, greetings, and a plate of dried apples, cheese, and crackers shared out on the kitchen counter. Something hot and savory bubbled in a pot on the stove.

Day threaded through the crowded room and brought her a tall glass of water and a bowl of thick soup. She smiled at him. "Thank you."

He sat on the arm of the couch while she ate, making a friendly barrier between her and her previous tormentors.

The soup was a sickly green, with the occasional carrot it in, but it smelled of ginger and beans and tasted fabulous. She let Aspen lick the bowl and then got up to see what else she might feed him. Moving was hard, but apparently the soup had something magical in it, because her legs obeyed her.

When she took her bowl into the kitchen, Day traded her a clean bowl of bread scraps and carrot ends. "That's for Aspen." He looked hopeful. "We didn't plan for a dog."

"Thanks." Aspen took the food from her hand bite by bite, constantly trying to lick her fingers. As she finished hand-feeding him, the people in the room settled into a rough circle.

"All right," Bartholomew said. "Let's report out."

Lou glanced at Coryn. Coryn smiled back as sweetly as she could. It wasn't as if Lou could exclude her easily, not in front of everyone. Lou sighed, looking torn, but she didn't order Coryn into the back bedroom or give her some stupid chore in the barn.

Bartholomew spoke first. "We're ready. The hack worked, and it should be spreading at about five percent an hour. There's no sign of detection yet. We have two more rolling versions ready to start on your command."

He had to mean the ecobots. It made sense. They hadn't been hacked (or at least hadn't been hacked by these people) when they saved her at Lucien's command. But they must have been hacked before they started pouring into Bartholomew's little makeshift town the night before last.

At some deep level, this frightened her. She'd always been taught that the ecobots were the saviors of all mankind, and that humans relied on them to enforce the various climate frameworks. Without them, everything would burn and flood and die.

But then, the city had clearly lied to her about many things. Just like Lou had.

The conversation moved on as Lou asked Bartholomew, "What about other city systems? Which ones are finished?"

He smiled and said, "Enough of them."

She said, "No. Tell me."

"It's not your business."

Lou let out a long sigh. "Part of this deal is that we share information."

"And blame," Bartholomew said. "What you don't know is good for you and for us. It is enough."

Lou leaned forward as if she planned to press her point, but then she stood and got water. When she came back, she asked, "Perimeter security systems? Do we at least have those?"

"We do."

Bartholomew and Lou stared at each other for a long moment, the faintest nods showing mutual agreement to back down.

Lou shifted her attention to Jersey. "Are you ready?"

"Sure." That was it. No one else in the room seemed to need more information. Coryn glanced at Blessing, trying to extract an unspoken promise that he'd fill her in later, but he looked away.

Great.

Lou asked, "Are you staying the night?"

To Coryn's relief Milan and Bartholomew said no, although Jersey stated that she'd be glad of the warm fire. Nevertheless, no one left for a while. Bartholomew and Milan both had flutes with them, and Lou produced a guitar from a closet in the house. She glanced at Coryn, who shook her head; she had lost her flute when she lost her pack. Matchiko brought in spoons, and Paula sat opposite Lou and started drumming on a wood table, which sounded satisfyingly hollow.

Paula used a steady, fast drumbeat to start them off, and everyone else joined in, the whole musical thing a jazz-like improvisation. Then Lou called for a conservation song Coryn had never heard before. Bartholomew offered a hacking song from the old days of Anonymous. Lou called on Jersey, who sang a high-noted and incredible version of a song about parking lots that she claimed was an early protest song. Without her wristlet, Coryn couldn't look up the name of the original singer. It didn't really matter. Jersey's voice was incredibly high and sweet. Blessing and Day sang two duets so polished they must have sung them in front of audiences before.

The singing didn't die down until past midnight, when Lou clapped her hands and said, "Stop now. We've got to sleep some."

Bartholomew and Milan packed up somewhat noisily. Just as they started for the door, Coryn stood up and intercepted them. She did her very best to stay calm and look Bartholomew in the eye. "I'd like my wristlet back. You put it in your pocket."

He smiled, his breath smelling like old beer. He whispered, "I gave it to your sister."

Coryn blinked after him, not sure what to say. He smiled again, the smile slightly creepy, and pulled the door shut behind him and Milan.

Lou let out a long sigh of relief. "You can have the couch," she told Coryn. "Paula will stay with you, and the rest of us will sleep in the barn with the horses. There's not enough beds here anyway."

Coryn choked back a snippy comment about her wristlet, even more disturbed because now they could have a meeting without her or Paula, and there really wasn't any way for her to prevent it. So she smiled as widely as she could, and simply said, "Thank you."

When everyone except Paula had left for the barn, she realized she needed to move to stay awake. There was so much to think about. Well, there was still a mess in the kitchen. She got up and started in on it, which prompted Paula to join her.

As she stacked dirty plates, Coryn asked, "What do you think is going on?"

Paula raised an eyebrow. "Regarding?"

"Well, first of all, right now."

"They're all talking as they get ready for bed." Paula started running the water, dipping the tips of her fingers into it to test the temperature, which she could read precisely. "I doubt they are talking about you, but I suspect they are saying things they don't want you to hear."

"I'm shocked." She went to the table and finished gathering the glasses and cups. "But why? Is it that secret?"

"They don't trust you."

"I was afraid you'd say that." It hurt as much as she had expected it to, making her chest feel full. She set the dishes into the sink more loudly than she'd planned, her cheeks hot. She never had understood why she could feel embarrassed in front of a robot. "Do you know why? Because I'm from the city? Because they don't trust anyone?"

"Your timing appears to be uncannily convenient to something big going on. Blessing is on your side, Lou is silent, and the others are split."

"Even Day?" She started washing, building a pile of clean plates and little tipi of forks.

"Day is closer to Blessing than anyone else, and he'll do whatever Blessing asks of him, of course. But he thinks the timing is suspicious as well." Paula rummaged through doors until she found a towel. "Just as they get ready to act on long-term plans, Lou's little sister shows up with a robot and a fancy wrist machine. It is kind of hard to see it as coincidence."

Coryn rinsed in silence, handing Paula plate after plate, fork after fork. She didn't need to ask Paula how she knew—the robot was fabulous at reading body language and microexpressions and often acted bemused that Coryn didn't do it nearly as well as she did.

The door banged open, and Lou came in. "Hey—" She noticed the dishwashing. "You didn't have to do that."

"Someone had to," Coryn replied.

"Paula could have done it."

"Paula's not my personal slave," Coryn replied.

Lou stood there with her mouth gaping.

"And while I'm at it," Coryn said, "I'd like my wristlet. It might be handy if I get lost. I'd have a way to reach you."

Lou's face paled. She stammered, "Not now."

"Do you have it with you?"

"Look." Lou headed for the refrigerator. "I just came in to grab a few beers." She hesitated, cocked her head. "You can have one if you want."

Coryn sighed. "I don't drink. And I'd like my wristlet."

Lou separated her feet a little and leaned toward Coryn. "And who would you call?"

"You. If I get in trouble."

"Who do you call in the city?"

"No one. I never made friends at the orphanage. Call them homework buddies on a good night."

Lou's chin twitched as she clenched her teeth.

"Really," Coryn said.

"You don't need to call me tonight. I'm right outside."

A cold certainty grew in Coryn's chest. She let it grow silently, watching Lou stand still and stare at her as if staring alone might make her suddenly compliant. But if she was going to do anything about it, she couldn't tell Lou what she worried about. "Promise you'll give it to me tomorrow?"

"I promise." Lou's face softened a little at the win. "Go to sleep. Paula can finish the dishes. We'll be riding all the way back tomorrow."

"Ouch." She smiled at Lou though, using her best trust-me look. "I am tired."

Lou lifted the four beer bottles she had in a salute and walked back outside. The night had grown foggy, and wisps of it crept in through the door during the brief moment when it was open, so cold that Coryn rubbed her hands together to warm them.

She went back to the kitchen and took up washing dishes again.

"I can do this," Paula said.

"I know."

"It doesn't matter to me," Paula said. "It's not as if I sleep."

"It matters to me."

They finished the kitchen quietly, and when they were done Coryn ignored the urge to sweep the floor and made up a small bed on the couch.

She didn't, however, climb into bed or get undressed.

CHAPTER THIRTY-ONE

Coryn hunched outside under big open tack room's large square window. The night wind drew goose bumps onto her arms. Light spilled out from the barn, so she stayed low and listened. She couldn't make out most individual words, so she crept carefully around the building, looking for a better window. On the far side, a door led to the two rows of horse stalls.

She tugged lightly. It swung out three inches. Unlocked.

She tried to think. None of the stalls were empty. River had been stabled near the front. He knew her. Would he let her share his stall?

Could she even get into the barn quietly?

Maybe if she just walked in like she belonged, so if she got caught she could make up something she'd come to tell Lou about? After all, they hadn't forbidden her from coming over here. Not directly.

What?

She could tell her about all the bicyclists. There had been a lot. Too many to just be all out from the city, or at least she could pretend she thought that.

If she didn't get caught, she could slide into River's stall and see if she could hear better from there. It would also be warmer.

To her relief, the door didn't creak as it opened. She swallowed and stepped in, closing it behind her. It creaked then, but no one leaped up or even stopped talking. There was a bend between the stalls and the tack room. Unless someone was coming down to check on the horses, there was no reason for anyone to catch her.

Her steps sounded loud in her ears.

She passed Mouse and Blessing's big gray, Shadow, and opened the door of River's stall. On the far side, he raised his head and whickered softly.

She should have brought a carrot.

He nuzzled at her as she shut the door. The voices were easier to make out here than they had been from beneath the window, although they were still muffled. She sat as still as she could, listening.

Snippets of sentences . . . Seacouver and Portland and ecobots, Bartholomew and news. Eventually the voices separated into a clearer conversation.

Blessing: "—gotten to her, and why?"

Lou: "No one did. She's clean. I know my sister."

She hadn't really expected Lou to defend her. It warmed her.

A higher voice, probably Matchiko: "I'm running diagnostics. We'll know what she knows soon."

On her wristlet?

Lou again: "Is there news?"

Shuska. The big native-looking woman with the long brown hair and the small brown eyes like dark half-moons: "Portland's Listeners have almost all been captured or disappeared, and the city noticed."

Someone—maybe Day, maybe Daryl: "Should we be worried? I never heard about hurting Listeners as part of the plan."

Coryn felt overwhelmed with relief.

Blessing: "Who would hurt Listeners? I have Listener friends—they're mostly harmless."

Shuska. "I'm trying to find out. It's hard."

What could they find on her wristlet? Pretty much nothing. Years and years of recorded time with Paula, schoolwork she hadn't gotten around to erasing yet, and the messages between her and Liselle.

Nothing about Julianna.

Pictures of Bartholomew, but she hadn't sent those anywhere.

The stall door jerked open. She looked up, into Shuska's eyes gazing directly at her, dark and big like the woman herself. Eyes the size of coins. She looked meaner that Coryn remembered. "Come on."

There was only the one door to the stall, and Shuska occupied the whole thing. Coryn smiled and stood up, brushing hay and dust off of her jeans. "Sure. Just visiting River."

The horse ignored her.

Shuska pulled her out of the stall and into the main room, in the middle of six pairs of eyes. "Look what I found listening to us."

Bedrolls had been laid out on the floor in rows on the other side of the barn, and for now people sat on hay bales holding half-empty beers. A few LED lanterns shed pale light upward, washing everyone's faces to an ill color and making large shadows dance on the walls behind them.

Lou looked perturbed, her mouth thin in her thin face, her skin whitish in the odd light. Blessing's eyes were round, Day's flat. Matchiko looked pleased, or maybe vindicated would be a better word. Daryl showed no emotion at all.

Shuska carried a scratched up wooden stool to the middle of the room. "Sit here."

Coryn sat, her pulse racing with a combination of anger and shame at being caught.

Lou's look turned to frustrated fury as she watched, and Blessing's to confusion.

Matchiko stared at Coryn from her perch on a bale of hay. "Good timing. I just got my diagnostic back on your wristlet data."

Coryn took a deep breath. "I didn't give you permission."

"This isn't the city. Spies have no rights."

Who did they think she was spying for? No point in asking. Probably the city. Lou stepped over to Coryn's side, clapped her on the back, faced the others. "She's not a spy. I keep telling you that."

Matchiko looked like she felt sorry for Lou. She drew a square in the air and touched a button on her shirt; a screenful of information appeared in the air in front of her.

No one seemed surprised by the blatant display of technology.

"And?" Anger and fear were fighting for points inside of her body; she rooted for anger.

Matchiko's fingers swiped the air, batting the photos around. "Well, you keep a lot of crap."

"Who doesn't?"

"You sent messages back and forth to some pretty well-known Listeners."

"She told me about them," Lou said.

"Did she tell you she was a spy for them?"

Lou fell quiet and looked at Coryn.

"They were nice. They asked me to count ecobots for them. Since the ecobots worked for them, it didn't seem like there was any harm in it."

"You just did whatever they wanted?" Daryl asked. He looked genuinely puzzled at that, as if only an idiot would ever do what a Listener asked her.

"Yes. But I didn't do it for long, and I didn't know better. They gave me a ride in trade for that, and it seemed like a fair deal. Look. You'll see I only sent a few days' worth of messages."

She remembered how Blessing had kissed her when she asked him to say hello to Lucien and Liselle. She'd thought it was because Blessing knew them. She looked at him, thoughtful, but he was looking at the pictures, clearly focusing on the images she'd chosen to send.

She didn't say anything. She didn't know if she was right, and she didn't know if the Listeners were good or bad anymore, just that they weren't on the same side as Lou.

Blessing extended his hands in a *relax* gesture. "It doesn't look like she sent anything that mattered."

She knew what the last two pictures would be though. Bartholomew and the other hackers walking toward her.

Was Blessing taking her side because he was on it—he liked the Listeners? Or because he liked her? Or both?

Maybe she wasn't on her sister's side at all. She swallowed that thought. Of course she and Lou were on the same side. They had to be.

Shuska glanced at Matchiko. "Maybe that's why the Listeners are in trouble." She frowned at Coryn. "Are there more people spying for them? I mean, it wasn't just you spying, was it?"

"How would I know?" Coryn countered. "Look, I just came out here to find Lou. That's all. I met people. Some helped me; I helped them back. If they hadn't helped me, I probably wouldn't have gotten this far. They saved me from a thief who wanted to steal my robot. You saved me from the last people who tried to steal her."

"And what are these?" Matchiko asked, drawing attention to her screen. "What?"

The pictures of the schematics she'd taken in the caravan flashed up.

"I found a book in the Listener's caravan. I thought it might be interesting, so I took pictures of the pages."

"Stop scrolling!" Shuska leaned in and peered closely at the image. "Another."

Matchiko advanced the page.

Shuska took a step closer. "Another."

"Another."

She stepped back. "Do you have the whole book?"

"I think so. I was in a hurry. I might have missed a page. Do you know what it is?"

"Don't you?" Shuska asked.

Coryn shook her head. "I have no idea."

"It's schematics for the most current version of the ecobots. Bartholomew would kill for this."

Coryn swallowed hard and stood up, stiff. "I think maybe he already did. Paula looked through the Listeners' caravan after they were killed, and the books were gone. There were more."

A quiet fell over the barn as if this news had gotten people thinking pretty hard. Finally Lou asked, "So you think Bartholomew killed the Listeners you made friends with?"

"One of his women had Liselle's shoes on. I know that much. They were blue." Lou gave her a skeptical look. She frowned back. "A very particular shade of blue. Trust me, I know."

Silence fell again, Shuska and Matchiko watched her closely. She felt like any movement or anything she said might be misinterpreted.

Lou moved next to Coryn and broke the silence. "Is there more news?"

"Hang on," Matchiko said. "Let me finish looking through this."

Lou frowned at her. "Only if it means you'll leave my sister alone. She doesn't mean us any harm."

Matchiko sighed. "You're too trusting."

Lou didn't bother to answer.

Matchiko kept staring at the data feed as if it was going to spit out a great big scarlet letter. Lou held her breath, certain she'd find the pictures of Bartholomew and his group.

Something drew Matchiko's attention away from the display and to her own wrist. A wide grin spread across her face; Lou checked her wrist and Shuska did the same, all three women grinning and then standing. Lou called out loudly, "It came. We got the call!"

CHAPTER THIRTY-TWO

Lou stood up on the stool Coryn had been sitting on and stared out at her crew. "All right. You all know what this means. Pack up and get some sleep. We'll ride out as soon as it's light." Shuska was already picking up empty beer bottles. Daryl helped her. Day watched everyone. Matchiko watched Lou, her face tight with worry. She pointed a thumb at Coryn. "Is she going with us?"

"Yes."

"And the dog?"

"And the robot. I can't leave them."

Matchiko looked she'd eaten a lemon. "Your choice."

Not for the first time, Coryn wondered at the relationship between Matchiko and Lou. It seemed half best friend and half bitter lover, with a dash of rivalry thrown in.

Lou addressed them all. "Please be ready. I'm going to sleep in the house. I need to prepare Coryn."

About time, Coryn thought.

Shuska spoke up. "We're ready."

A smile spread across Lou's face, jubilance and joy filling her. "Thank you. Thank you all for helping us get here. We have a chance to change the world." She hopped down off of the stool and went to Matchiko's side, holding out her hand.

Matchiko looked at Lou's open palm. She let out a sigh deep enough to fill the barn. "We don't know that she can't do us any harm. Especially now. Wait another day."

Lou glanced at Coryn. "No."

Coryn's wristlet fell into Lou's hand. She immediately handed it to Coryn, who strapped it on.

Good.

No one spoke as they walked out, although they all watched her, and Coryn was sure the barn would erupt in conversation as soon as they left. Barns were never a good thing.

They found Paula in front of the fire, playing tug with Aspen.

"Good thing Paula doesn't sleep," Lou said.

"Why? Not that I don't agree."

"She can take care of Aspen when he wants to play. He probably sleeps less than you do, right?"

"He ought to be exhausted. He walked almost as far as the horses today."

Paula looked up. "He is. He'll settle now that you're here." She nodded toward Lou, her voice shading toward disappointment. "Nice of you to come back."

Lou ignored the comment. "We're leaving at dawn. So we're going to go to bed soon. Can you make up a second bed?"

Paula gave a slight curtsy, which Coryn interpreted as robot irony, and headed toward the closet. Lou and Coryn sat together on the same brown couch Coryn had fallen asleep on when they first came in for the night. Coryn turned slightly in place to face Lou. "So what does getting the call mean?"

"I'll have to start earlier," Lou said. "I told you this is a bad time for you to join us. Things are serious out here. We're failing. The wilding is failing. There's too much to do. We don't have enough resources. We don't know enough to do this. We can't keep the predators alive. Wolf packs and mountain lions get shot. Or they die. We can't get a grizzly population started, even though this used to be part of their native habitat."

Lou's staccato statements felt like slaps. "You're planning some kind of war with the city because the wolves keep getting shot by Returners?"

Lou leaned back into the couch, putting her hands over her face for a moment and then dropping them. "We could do this. We could restore a functioning wild. Maybe not the one we had, but one that didn't need us. But to do that, we need an army. Bots and people. We don't have enough people and the robots keep getting hacked."

Coryn decided this wasn't the moment to point out that Lou herself was hacking robots. Maybe that was just what people Outside did for entertainment when they ran out of wolves to save or shoot. "You're going to declare war on Portland?"

Lou laughed so hard she held her stomach, a high nervous laugh that didn't seem much like her at all. "Think of it as a major protest action with teeth. Obviously we can't beat the cities."

At least Lou hadn't gone completely crazy. "How do you plan to get people's attention?"

"That's why we have teeth. And what Bartholomew is for. Victor says it will keep the Foundation's fingerprints off of the serious stuff." Los hesitated, glancing at Coryn, something unreadable that wasn't happiness in her eyes. "Victor is my boss."

"Serious stuff like security systems?"

Lou looked sharply at her. "You should forget you heard that."

"How did you get involved in all this?"

"I got recruited to help almost as soon as I got out here."

"So why'd you write all those flowery things about how peaceful and happy it is Outside? You made me think it was all pinto ponies and knocking down old barns."

"No one's allowed to write the truth, especially not and send it to the city. It's a shared fiction we use to survive. People who talk about how bad it is out here get shot."

Coryn almost protested, but then she remembered Lucien lying under the flowering tree with all the life drained from his body.

Lou stood up and started pacing in front of the slowly dying fire. "A lot of work is coming to fruition right now. Not just us." She waved her hand in the general direction of the barn. "Not just us. But the Foundation, which is really big and has a lot of resources. That's part of why it's so tricky. The foundations need us, and they need the cities, and they need to make all of this work. I think some of the other NGOs are in on it, too, although no one will tell me. And other groups out here who don't like the cities any more than we do."

She remembered the silent army, bent on something, and how Pablo had gone with them and survived. "What about the Listeners? Whose side are they on?"

"Listeners? They're like cops covered in sugar. They pretend to help, but they're really spies."

Coryn stiffened. "Are you planning to hurt anyone?"

Paula came back in, her voice and face both set on some variation of cheerful. "Lou can sleep in the back bedroom, you can take the couch, Aspen can sleep in front of the fire. I'll watch the door."

"We're not ready to sleep yet," Lou said.

Paula held her hands up. "The bed will be ready when you are."

"I didn't see a bed back there," Coryn said. "Are you going to hurt anyone?"

"It pulls out of the wall." Lou leaned forward, looking into Coryn's eyes. "It's not likely that we can take a whole city hostage without someone getting hurt."

Coryn leaned back against the couch. "A whole city? Portland?"

"Yes."

"Why?"

"I told you. The cities swore to give us enough money and people to finish the wilding. It's not stable, nowhere near stable. We've got a few species doing okay—mostly ones that were okay without us. Eagles. Mice. Two species of bats. Two. A few frogs." She looked and sounded bitter. "Rabbits. The rabbits are doing great. And the coyotes and the coydogs."

"Okay, but it's only been what—twenty years? Since the great taking?"

"That's time for a lot of failure. The cities don't care. If they could make themselves into starships and just fly away, they would."

Coryn leaned back, trying to picture that in her head. It made her giggle, but it might be true.

"But they can't," Lou continued. "They need the wild, and the wild needs them, and if we fail out here, we will all die. Everyone. We'll all die together."

Coryn heard the passion in her sister's voice, but she thought the Outside was beautiful. "That buffalo herd looks great."

"They *are* doing great. And they depend on us to live. We kill off the weak and some of the young, and most importantly the ill. We pump water to some of the places they go, fill artificial lakes for them. We track most of the adults. They're not wild. They need us, and we don't have what it takes."

"What do you mean?"

"I'll explain on the way to Portland."

"You mean Vancouver. The Washington one."

"Yeah. There's no point in crossing the Columbia. I have some authority throughout the state. Most of us do. That's why we're working the Washington side. There was . . . something that happened. Portland needs us to go defend it, and so that's what it means that we were called up."

Coryn stared at the fire, which had shrunk to bright coals.

Lou stood up. "Want some water?"

God, did she ever. "Yes."

Lou came back with two full glasses. "You still don't drink anything stronger?"

"This doesn't seem like the time to start."

That made Lou smile.

Aspen stopped following Paula around and jumped up into Coryn's lap. She made sure Lou was looking at her. "So what you're saying is Portland is calling you to help it, and you are going to use that to get in close enough to attack the city?"

"We can't change anything by telling the truth."

Maybe Lou couldn't hear herself. She didn't want to ruin the moment or send Lou running back to the barn, and she wanted some more time to think. So she sat and drank her water and stared at the fire. It felt good to be sitting by her sister even though she wasn't sure how to feel about this new Lou.

Maybe this moment was the one most like all of the moments she had imagined back in the city.

Lou seemed to have pretty much come to the same conclusion, since she sat quietly as well for a long time.

"Is there anything else I need to know?" Coryn asked.

"Probably a lot. For one thing, you need to work for me in order to go along. I presume that's okay."

"Sure. Who doesn't want to work for her big sister?"

Lou gave her a funny look.

She grinned. "I'm teasing you. I'll do it. I had to give up my basic when I crossed the border."

"I forgot about that. Consider it done. I have ten open positions. You're now a—" She stopped and rolled her eyes up into her head, her way of saying she was thinking. "Let's make you a wrangler."

"Do I have a choice?"

"You can be a wrangler, a cook, a bookkeeper, a botanist, or a biologist. If I make you a bookkeeper, I'll have to send you back to the farm."

"What if I *want* to be a biologist?"

"You don't have the credentials."

"Fine."

"Well, wrangler Coryn, let's go to sleep. I'll set you up to get data on our networks starting tomorrow. Your wristlet will be your best friend."

"Can you do that now? What else do I need to know?"

"Sleep. We leave in four hours."

"I guess I did need to know that."

Lou shared a genuine smile with her before padding into the back bedroom.

And now what? She'd been ready to leave her city and never look back if that was what it took to get to Lou, but she'd never in her wildest dreams imagined she might attack a city.

Aspen snuggled up to her. She felt his warm, soft breath against her cheek. What was she doing?

CHAPTER THIRTY-THREE

The sun beat down on Coryn, making her slightly nauseous. She turned in her saddle, checking on Aspen. He balanced in front of Paula, looking like he was telling the robot what to do. Coryn slowed down so they rode side by side. Paula's horse was a good four inches taller than River, so Coryn had to reach up to touch Aspen's nose.

"You're getting a lot better," Paula said. "You almost look easy on a horse now."

She'd had a lot of practice recently. They had been riding and camping for two days. "It only hurts a little."

"Pretty soon it will feel harder to walk than to ride."

"Not for you."

"Silly human."

Coryn smiled. If they weren't riding toward a fight the day would be perfect. Instead, all of the things that she still didn't understand circled in her head. So many unanswered questions.

She glanced down at her wrist. She'd been able to check that it worked, but that was about all. There had been very little connection out here the few times she'd tried, and she really couldn't stare at the thing while riding. River sensed distraction and tried to eat grass he shouldn't or get too close to Mouse or Shadow, or, worse, to Monkey. Monkey liked to kick at him.

Up ahead, Lou called for a halt. She had told Coryn that they were nearing Yakima, which, like Cle Elum, had survived the culling of the cities.

A stream ran next to the road, thin in a wide and rocky riverbed. They walked the horses carefully down the steep hill from the road to a clear, wide beach surrounded by scrub oaks and alders. There were only seven of them; Daryl had gone back—reluctantly—to keep things running at the main house. Lou and Matchiko and the ever-looming Shuska, Blessing and Day, Coryn and Paula. At least two people at a time stayed mounted to act as guards while the others watered their horses.

Coryn wasn't asked to guard, or Paula, even though Paula would have been better than any of them. That bothered Coryn a little, but she let it go. She settled for watching the others. They were all good hands with the horses, confident. Shuska seemed the best. When they camped, her dark bay horse, Max, followed her with no lead line and seemed to do whatever the big woman wanted with no need for direction. Max stood as tall as Mouse, and broader.

They ate handfuls of nuts, dried apples, and stale bread for lunch. Instead of getting back on the road, they seemed to be waiting.

A group of five other riders met them, led by a stocky man on a nearly-black horse. He had short hair above a square face, and a decided air of authority. As that group began the same routine her group had been through, Lou brought the man over to where Coryn waited, scratching behind River's ears. "Coryn, this is Victor. He's one of my bosses, and while you work for me you also work for him."

Up close, she could see that he was a week away from clean shaven, and a scar started at the right side of his mouth and travelled almost to his ear. His left pinky finger was missing. All of his breadth looked like muscle. He had an easy but surface smile, and his eyes were warm as he held out his hand. "Pleased to meet you."

"Likewise," she answered.

He knelt down and held a hand toward Aspen, who had been watching him from a few feet away, staying clear of River's hooves. Aspen regarded him for a moment, then presented himself to be examined and then petted.

While he was scratching Aspen under his chin, Victor looked up at Coryn. "You know we won't be able to stop for him. You have to keep him safe, or not."

She swallowed. "I might stop for him."

"You can't separate from us. If we had a safe place to leave you, we would. I need to make sure you understand that. Do you?"

She stiffened but managed to get out a single nod.

"See, I don't care about you, at least not yet. But I do care about your sister, and I don't want her distracted. So you have three jobs. Stay nearby. Watch your dog. Do what we tell you and only what we tell you."

He sounded like Lou. She said nothing.

He stood up and glanced toward Paula. "Will you let us give you orders for your robot?"

Paula stood by the river, at least a few hundred feet away. She had clearly been listening. She turned her head toward them, her expression so blank Coryn couldn't read any clues about what she should do there. She looked back at Victor. "Can you give me an example?"

He shook his head.

He was trying to control Paula! Everything in her resisted, and she finally looked him directly in the eye. "I won't order her into any danger."

"We're all going into danger."

"She's going to protect me."

Victor stared at her. "What if Lou needed protecting?"

Coryn swallowed. "I could ask her to do that."

"What about Blessing?"

"That, too."

"What about me?"

She took a long time to decide how to answer. "If Lou and I are safe, and it wouldn't put Paula in too much danger."

He narrowed his eyes. "You do know she's a robot?"

"She's mine. She's been mine since I was a child."

His face tightened so hard and fast that she expected him to argue. He started to turn away, but then, as if it were an afterthought, glanced back. "What if you had to choose between saving your robot and your dog?"

The question stopped her cold. "I hope I never have to."

"You should decide before we get closer to Portland."

After he had walked away from them, she clutched Aspen to her and whispered in his ear. "I don't like that man. I really don't."

‡ ‡ ‡

About five minutes after Victor finished his conversation with Coryn, a string of bicycles came down the road toward them. The riders wore matching black spandex and bright yellow tops and braked to a neat stop just opposite them. They waved hello and carried their bikes over their heads down to the trees, where they propped them carefully against branches and trunks. One even hung his bike from a branch, as if the dirt might contaminate his wheels.

This was the man Victor walked over to and greeted with an enthusiastic hug.

Coryn found Lou, and asked her, "Bicycles?"

"We use tours from the city to get people out here."

"Out here to do what?"

Lou shook her head ever so slightly. "What do you think?"

"Well, so you have more people who see what needs to be done out here."

"And so we can stay up to date on what's happening in the city. But we're past using it for a recruiting tool. These are all regulars."

"They've got nice bikes," Coryn observed. She led River over toward the water, which put her in closer earshot to Victor and the head biker. She noticed the word "Lead" running up his arm, and looked reflexively for the other two positions. One woman proclaimed herself as "Sweep" and a taller, thinner one as "Float."

Victor noticed her and led the man he was talking to farther away.

Coryn watched River slurp up water, then took him back up to Paula. She patted her leg and Aspen followed her over to the sweep. The woman was stouter than a typical bicyclist, although she had the muscled thighs and calves. She looked like she was older, maybe even in her forties, with thin lines of wrinkles surrounding green eyes. Her hair had been cropped short, and curled close to her head. Coryn held her hand out. "I used to ride with the SeaVan bike club. I always liked to be sweep."

The woman smiled. "It's my favorite position."

"So you're good at changing tires."

That turned the smile into a laugh. "Yeah, I'm good at clean up. But I leave the really slow ones."

"Even out here?"

"No slow riders get to come with us."

Coryn grinned. She had seldom wanted to leave riders behind when she was with the club, but the more experienced ride leaders had made her. It would be fun to be on a ride where everyone was professional. "Where did you start from?"

"Seacouver."

"Seattle proper?"

"No. Old Vancouver, the Canadian one. Actually by Surrey. It took us three days to get down here."

"That's fast." Coryn figured it would take her five. But then her gear had never been as wickedly strong as this looked, all dull black metals and big wheels. She'd have killed for the money for a bike like this. She ran her fingers along the smooth metal frame. "Are these wireless shifters?"

"Yes. No wires anywhere."

"Even on the brakes?"

The rider pointed at her bike. "Do you see wires?"

"How are the roads out here?"

The woman unclipped a gel tube from her belt and snapped off the top. "Good if you know where to go. That's why the tours. We use roads the cities keep up." She lifted the gel to her mouth and sucked at it.

"I wish I'd brought my bike."

"Can I pet your dog?"

"Sure. His name's Aspen. I'm Coryn."

"LeeAnne."

"So, do you know my sister, Lou?" She pointed toward her.

LeeAnne scooped Aspen up. He started licking her arms, making her smile. "He must need salt. I never met Lou. But I know of her."

"Victor?"

"Of course." LeeAnne's face didn't light up at his name. "Did he tell you how long it would be before we ran into trouble?"

Now she was getting somewhere. "He didn't. I heard we're skipping the mountains with the horses and going by the river."

LeeAnne glanced west, even though distant clouds obscured the Cascades. "The gorge is beautiful, but it may be harder."

"Why?"

"It's easier to defend than to get through."

"Will we have to get through defenders?"

"It depends on how well the hack jobs hold. The damned ecobots have been hacked so many ways from hell in the last decade I have no idea if what we did will hold."

"I thought Bartholomew did the hacking?"

LeeAnne handed Aspen to Coryn. "Were you listening? Everything's been hacked so many ways it's hard to tell who's running what machine on any given day."

"So you're going to join us in Portland?"

"We'll go ahead. Take the gorge. Ride in. This was just a chance meeting and you never met us."

"I'll forget your name tomorrow."

LeeAnne grinned. "You can forget it in an hour."

✝ ✝ ✝

Coryn watched the bicyclists pack up their lunch trash and prepare to depart. She supposed they would go soon, too, but she didn't see any of Lou's crew near the horses. Maybe she had time to stretch her legs before climbing back on River.

She called Aspen close to her and left quietly, walking along the weedy stream bank until she found a place to pick Aspen up and cross the water with a long jump. They walked along the far bank looking for tracks. She spotted some that were probably coyote, then the double oval of deer tracks. She wasn't certain, but it looked like a doe and a fawn.

As she knelt to run her fingers around a muddy track that might be a cat or a coyote, a breeze carried heated voices from somewhere behind her. She turned, listening carefully. One was Lou. The other? A man. At first she thought of Bartholomew, but then she decided it must be Victor. She scooped Aspen up, holding him tightly to her chest. She walked quietly toward the conversation, listening.

The words were muffled with distance, but full of anger and sharp tones. The voices were so visceral they drove a cold shiver up inside her even though it was perfectly warm now standing in the midday sun.

"—your sister and the dog. Take the robot. She's from your family. She'll go with you."

"No. Who would keep Coryn safe?"

"Then leave them all. She's not going to make good press. Can you imagine? Child runaway with dog and companion robot part of Portland takeover team?"

"I can't leave her out here. I'm not missing this. I've been planning it too long."

"*We* have." The male voice rose. "This is many of us, hundreds of us, not just you. This is directed at all the cities everywhere, not just here. You have a part, and you have to play it."

Lou spoke so softly that Coryn had to strain to hear her. "I'm in charge of my team, and Coryn is on it."

Coryn grinned at that. Lou defended her more to other people than to her face, but at least she defended her. Coryn stopped, afraid that if she got any closer they would hear her, or maybe see her. A thicket of blackberries and alders blocked her view of them, and she assumed it blocked their view of her. She kept Aspen close, hoping he wouldn't bark.

"I told you to drop Shuska, too."

"She's my backup, my protector."

"She's a wildcard."

A pause.

Victor didn't seem comfortable with silence. "Besides, you don't need protection. Not from me, you don't. Stand your ground and listen to me. You work for me. I can change that any time."

Lou's answer to him came out steady. "You can't change that today. Today is action, and you need me." Some rustling of bushes suggested movement Coryn couldn't see. "We all need each other. You do your part," Lou continued. "I'll do mine."

Coryn wished she could see their faces, see what they were doing. Were they close to each other? Far apart? Was Lou's face as tight as her voice sounded? Was she in any kind of danger? Although surely not. Coryn was already convinced Lou was a far better leader than Victor. People liked following Lou.

When the silence held, she started to back up, still holding Aspen.

Lou burst out of the trees that had blocked Coryn's view of her and Victor. She stopped right in front of Coryn, tears streaming down her face. She held her hands up to forestall conversation and swiped frantically at her cheeks as it removing the tears would wipe Coryn's memory of them.

Before either of them said anything, Victor came out. He stopped, about ten feet away, his face red with anger and his jaw tight. One fist was clenched and one arm raised.

Lou stepped toward him.

He stared at both of them, still, his raised fist slowly, very slowly, unclenching. "Be careful," he spat at Lou. "Nothing is guaranteed in this world. If you do your job maybe you can keep it. Leave soon—it wouldn't do for you to be late." He left, going back the way he had come.

Lou stared after him. After she could no longer hear his footsteps, Coryn set Aspen down and leaned over and opened her arms to offer Lou a hug.

For a moment, Lou hesitated. But then she stepped into the hug, returning it with strength even though she stepped back out of it quickly. "Don't tell the others," she said.

"Why not?"

"He's been gone a year now. It's better that way. I don't want them to be afraid that he might come back. He's just mean because that's all he knows. He's on the same side we are."

Coryn disagreed, but this didn't seem like the time to say so.

Lou started back toward camp, glancing over her shoulder and saying, "You heard the boss. It's time to go."

CHAPTER THIRTY-FOUR

Halfway through the next day, they stopped at the top of a hill festooned with fast-spinning white windmills and peered through a face full of wind to more hills on the far side of the Columbia River Gorge. The river sparkled in the noon sun, choppy with whitecaps.

They rode alone again. The bicycles had left an hour after they came, and Victor and his riders had chosen to go up and over the mountains on Highway 12, leaving Lou to lead her group through the gorge. Coryn had been pleased to see the last of Victor.

She took a deep breath and savored the fish and salt smell of the river, keeping her horse pointed directly into the wind even though it made him prance. Lou, beside her, squinted downward, one hand over her eyes for shade. "Do you have any news?" Coryn asked her.

"Nothing useful. There was a fight between two groups of ecobots outside of Seacouver. Then one whole side just stopped, like their programming stuck."

"How did you learn that?"

Lou glanced at her own wristlet. "I get news from the Foundation."

The mysterious Foundation, yet again. So many things she half-understood. "Are the bicycle people really hackers?"

"Everyone's a hacker these days. But yes, some of them. I saw you talking to LeeAnne. She's supposed to be one of the best. The government trained her, back around the time of the great taking. She had to learn a lot of operating systems."

"You sound like you wish you had studied computers." Coryn stood in her stirrups to get a little more of the wind.

"I'd have been terrible at it. Mostly it just irks me to be dependent on people when I don't understand what they do."

"You know none of us can stand up to an ecobot, right? If we get into a fight with them, we die if they want to kill us."

"I know." Lou headed Mouse down the paved road. Coryn let them get a little ahead. Blessing brought Shadow up beside her, holding him back so his pace would match River's. Coryn slowed River even more, letting additional distance open up between them and Lou's big buckskin. She smiled up at Blessing. "How's your morning?"

He started whistling a tune. "Like that. Happy as any last morning."

"Last morning?"

"I had a teacher once who taught me to treat every minute like my last. Works pretty good."

"Almost every morning out here could have been my last. So is today any different?"

"That's the point. Do it. It helps."

If she'd been smart enough to treasure every day in Seacouver she might not have had so much trouble with the last few years. "If I can."

"Do you want me to remind you when you fuck up?"

"Ouch. Sure."

He cocked his head and smiled. "Just wanted to know, ma'am."

She laughed. "Did you know Lucien? You sounded like you might, that day we were all in the same barn with the tornado."

He didn't answer for a long time. "I know a lot of people who have died out here."

"You're ducking my question."

"So tell me about yourself."

"Not until you answer me."

He must have seen that she meant it. "I met him. A few times. That's all."

"Did you like him? I liked him."

"I like everybody. Tell me about you so I can like you."

"Funny how people need to know each other's secrets to like them."

"I'm just making conversation."

She doubted Blessing *just did* anything. But she wasn't interested in being the one withholding secrets. "You already know my sister is a raging lunatic who plans to attack a megacity. You know I just left a city, not long ago. When I'm not running around on a borrowed horse, I ride bicycles and I run marathons and I never made a lot of friends in the city. But I kind of miss it. I'm starting to be afraid they won't let me back in."

He laughed again.

"What's so funny?"

"Stupid city is afraid you'll get infected if you stay out too long."

"Well, I am trying to attack it."

His laugh inspired her, right along with the situation. Here she was, riding down a steep hill, leaning back to keep her weight off a horse's kidneys and laughing like a crazy person.

As soon as they made it down to flatter ground, he asked her, "Do you want to go back?"

She didn't have a yes or no answer. It wasn't all that clear inside her anymore, more like a jumble of mixed memories and feelings. "I miss being part of something. I mean, in the city you're part of this great big system of systems. It protects you and it holds you and it feeds you and it traps you all at once, you know?"

"You're part of something out here."

She leaned forward and patted River on the neck, realizing after she sat back firmly in the saddle that it had been an easy thing to do, and that she and the horse were comfortable with each other. "If nobody will tell me what's going on, then am I really part of it? I think I was even more clueless about the city when I lived Inside. But can you tell me why we're attacking a city? I get the whole *they don't give us what we need to save nature* thing, but doesn't this seem a little extreme?"

"That's an easy answer. It's to be noticed."

"Noticed? I suspect we're risking more than being noticed. Isn't it illegal to hack ecobots and send them in to attack the city?"

His lips thinned, and he looked uncharacteristically serious for a long moment. "Remember, we got called in to help."

"We work for the city. The same city that we're lying to about coming to help, because we really just want to breach the borders so that we can— what? I really don't get it."

"We're going to get attention. Think of it as a demonstration. We're not planning to hurt anyone. Maybe you're thinking too hard," he told her.

If she owned River she just might go off by herself. Not that being on her own had worked out so well. She took three deep breaths. "Maybe you need to think harder."

He frowned at her and went silent, apparently a little miffed at her suggestion that their plan appeared crazy. She liked him; she liked him best of all the people she'd met out here. Right now she might like him even more than Lou. But she felt uneasy around him as well. He was out to help her—

he'd proven that by saving her life. But she wasn't at all sure what he really believed about the crazy politics of Outside, or how loyal he was to Lou.

After a while, she turned to him. "Promise we're not going to hurt anyone."

"How could I promise that?"

"Promise we don't mean to? That we're peaceful?"

He looked solemn. "I promise."

She extended her hand.

He encouraged Shadow to get close to River. They managed to touch fingers, which she figured was as good as shaking hands.

The road neared the base of a wide bridge that spanned the Columbia. Lacework struts lined the bridge deck. It looked quite stable and very pretty.

Roads ran along both sides of the river. Lou pulled Mouse to a stop in front of the bridge and waited for them. When they caught up, she pointed across the water. "That's Oregon. The bridge is new—the old one washed out after a wicked fire got followed by a storm that dumped half a mountain on it. If you look, you can see parts of the old bridge under the water."

Coryn looked, even though the sky had started to cloud up. Nothing.

Lou continued. "The Columbia used to be heavily dammed. It still is, but all three of the big downstream dams are gone. The John Day, the Dalles, and the Bonneville Dam are gone now, and that's restored a lot of salmon. There's footage of all the dam destruction. It's pretty beautiful to see an old engineered thing blown up and watch how fast the water forgets it was ever there."

"You speak pretty." She smiled at her sister. "Are we ever going to get a break with real tech where I *could* watch it?"

"You have your wristlet back."

"But there's nothing to see."

Lou glared at her.

Coryn didn't feel like going into a long conversation on AR. She had always loved it, and Lou had always hated it, swearing that it made her sick. "Can we still see where the dams were? In real life?"

"You can still see the scars of the old lake-beds, and there's lodges perched in strange places. But the river is better. The first summer I was out here we did a two-month study on it. The salmon runs are doing great, and of course we don't need hydropower anymore."

"Why did we?"

"No one understood the sun or how to store it. Neither of us has ever had to charge a battery, but Mom told me she had to plug her tablet into a wall when she was a little girl."

"Are we crossing the bridge?"

"Maybe on the way back. We're supposed to be rushing to the city's aid. I doubt they want us to stop and sightsee."

"Fair enough."

Everyone had gathered close, even Shuska on her draft horse. Lou called out directions. "We're going to keep going for about a mile." She pointed down the road on the near side of the river. "There's a big rock there on the left and some picnic tables. We'll stop there and bed down. It's a little early, but I know there's water for the horses and I want them fresh for tomorrow. Besides, the light leaves early here."

Coryn looked up at the steep hillsides they'd come down. That was easy enough to believe.

It would be good to rest. Coryn rode next to Blessing as they grouped up to get in the last mile. She reined River close enough to speak to him without having to shout. "I think you want the city to do okay. I think you were helping the Listeners. But you want Lou to do okay, too. I want to figure you out."

He narrowed his eyes, looking perturbed. "Let me know what you find, okay?" He pulled Shadow up so in a moment he rode by Day. She was on her own, left to try and puzzle out the unspoken words that seemed to be riding right alongside them in a cloud of dust and airy words.

CHAPTER THIRTY-FIVE

After sleeping near it, and riding alongside it for a whole morning, Coryn found herself more accustomed to the Columbia. Still, every once in a while, some magical element of the river would catch in her peripheral vision, as if calling her. An island. A young buck on a beach. A lone man in a yellow kayak.

They stopped and ate together on a bluff, then rode west along the river again, the road a flat ribbon carved into the middle of a cliff. Coryn pulled River up beside Mouse, encouraging him to speed up a little to make up for his shorter legs and slower natural gait. "Will you tell me where we're going?" Coryn asked.

"The Foundation is ordering us to Vancouver to defend it from a possible ecobot attack."

"Which you engineered."

Lou laughed, sounding more excited than nervous. "We're going in through the Camas Gate if we can, and then to the Portland-Vancouver Bridge." Lou glanced at Coryn. "And you love bridges, don't you? That's the PV Bridge for short. It's beautiful. If we can't get in through Camas, we're to report why, and we may get orders to engage wherever we the city stops us. Could even be *at* the gate."

"Your life is so convoluted my brain hurts."

Lou raised an eyebrow over a wry smile.

"What about weapons? How do we stand up to city security, much less ecobots?"

Lou's said, "The Foundation will get us anything we need. We're going in to protest, not to bomb the city."

"That's good. I was getting a little worried there. Seacouver has protests all the time. Peaceful ones. It's a hobby, mostly for old women. Why do we need hacked ecobots to protest? Just because we're outside the dome and need to get in?"

Mouse had gotten far enough ahead that Lou had to turn in her saddle to look at Coryn. She said nothing, so Coryn kept asking questions. "But this is real, right?" Excitement, fear, and even dread rioted through her now that they were close. "We could get hurt."

Lou gave her a long and quite calm look. "We could. But I hope there isn't much physical fighting. I expect it will be more hackers and systems, one against another. We have whatever Bartholomew has done, whatever other helpers have done, and we'll be fighting the city's systems people. Our best weapons will be our brains." She pulled Mouse back so she rode right beside Coryn again, "And our hearts. Our hearts matter the most."

That sounded like the sister she missed. "I don't know much about hacking." She'd never even been a terribly good programmer. She swallowed. They were getting close, and that made her nervous. Did she really want to do this? "What should I do?"

"Stay out of the way."

That stung. Ever since she left the city, she'd been over her head. Maybe she'd always been over her head. After all, now that she'd left it, she knew the city was far more complex than she'd thought. Coryn tugged on River's reins to slow him down, pulling them away from Lou and Mouse. She didn't breathe until she was at the back of the line, riding beside Blessing and Day, with only Shuska behind them.

Shuska acted like a sweep in a line of bicycles. She rode silently, always behind, never pulling up by them. In some ways that made Coryn feel protected, but she also felt boxed in.

They rode beside a long, low wetland and beyond that, to their left, the Columbia. High rocky cliffs shouldered them always toward the river, the color palette all the myriad browns of dried grasses, periodically punctuated with yellow or white daisies. Hawks circled overhead, and twice Blessing pointed out bald eagles.

Later in the afternoon, the sun speared them in the face and the horses slowed to a plod. They stopped for another short rest. The river had narrowed to a quarter of its usual width, maybe less. Water roared through the narrows, plunging in a symphony of sound and strength, singing down into a huge pool before leaping and jumping down another cliff. The power of the river showed here, as if all of the rest of the ride they'd been going by a vein of water, and now they'd stopped to watch the river's pulsing heart.

Paula came up beside her, and said, "Celilo Falls."

She let out a long breath, momentarily stunned. "I remember that story. I understand, now. I don't think I ever did. What a crime to have taken this away." It was in her history books, the de-damming of the river, and the great celebration among the native peoples. A banner action for the great rewilding, for the human race undoing some of the damage it had done. "Isn't there a big reservation around here then?"

"A few. They're actually a little inland. We'll ride through a small part of the biggest reservation, since there's access to the water, but they're not allowed to do anything with their access except walk on it. The wildlife corridors around here are more important than the Indians."

"Really? I thought they had rights to the fish?"

"They traded those to have the falls back." Paula had stopped a moment, leaning over and watching the falls. "If they want to fish, they do it like everyone else, with a permit. That was their part of saving the world."

Coryn couldn't stop watching the falls. "I'd like to meet a Native American."

"You have. Shuska is native. Mostly."

"Oh. I don't think she likes me."

"She would love to see something happen to me," Paula said.

"I had never thought about that." She'd thought they were safe, and here they were, in danger from their sister's protector. "She's intimidating."

Paula looked back the way they'd come, as if making sure no one came upon them and disturbed their conversation. "The tribes are powerful. They stay out of overt politics. They're still sovereign, which means they don't really have a say in our world. But the reservations *are* wilded, and more successfully than anything the NGOs have done."

"I'd like to see that." She stared at the brilliantly falling white water, trying to imagine the river slow and placid here, to picture how strong a dam it would take to cover up such powerful falls.

Aspen was beside her, leashed because of the sheer cliffs, and clearly wishing he wasn't. He pulled at the leash. His nose twitched in the wind, looking for all the world like he wanted to ride a drone or wear a flying cape and sail down to the river.

Coryn spotted a stone bench that looked like it might offer an even better view of the falls. She took Aspen there, sitting with him on one side, keeping a hand on his collar. Paula sat down on her other side, her legs folded up against her chest and her arms wrapped around them. She must have felt pretty safe, since she usually stood. Or else she was really hoping for a conversation with Coryn. That was fine—Coryn could indulge her. "Paula?"

"Yes."

"If there's fighting, will you save Aspen?"

"You will be my first priority."

She couldn't identify why that irritated her so, but it did. "I'm giving you different directions. Save me too if you can, but save Aspen first." As if he knew she was talking about him, Aspen leaned up and licked her cheek.

Paula's face had gone deadpan, a sign she hated Coryn's orders. "What do you want me to do with him if you die?"

"Keep him."

"I can't."

Rules. "I bet you can out here. Make sure he's safe. I feel like that's up to me, and thus up to you."

Paula stared at the water, still in ways that robots could choose stillness. "It's not safe for the dog to take him into battle."

That stung. "What else can I do with him?"

For all that Paula's posture was relaxed, the tone she chose was not. She sounded wary. "We could all do something else."

Coryn laughed. "Don't tempt me."

"You found Lou. That's what you came here for. But Lou's up to no good. Being here isn't safe."

Coryn had thought the same thing a few times over the last few days. Still, she clamped down before she could accidentally agree. They weren't leaving Lou. It was the robot talking—always when Paula became impossible to understand it was the robot in her. And only at times like this did Coryn remember she didn't really have a human side. Her job was to keep Coryn safe, and Coryn needed her to switch loyalties. She let out a long sigh. "You have a directive about safety. Keeping me safe." A family walked by the falls on the other side, tiny from this distance. No threat, but their presence made the river feel more domestic. "And we know the city's not safe."

"Safer than here," Paula interrupted.

"And Outside isn't safe. And being here isn't safe. Maybe nothing is safe until the unrest gets figured out, until we stop fighting because we fix our problems and don't have to fight anymore. Maybe I'll be safe when the city gives up more to help the wilding."

She was on a roll now, seeing it in her mind. How it might be if everyone had the resources they needed. Chubby children played outside and rode on ecobots. "Maybe Lou is right, and we can succeed. The cities can go on and evolve and people can come and go, and no one needs to be hungry for anything. We can craft peace. That will be better than running around to find the safest place out of a lot of places that aren't safe."

Paula just stared at her.

"It could work." The brief spark of hope she'd felt flickered, draining out.

Paula still looked at her. "Didn't you study history?"

Coryn frowned, suddenly empty instead of hopeful. "Just keep Aspen safe if anything happens to me. If you have to choose between me and Aspen, pick *him*. He's innocent."

Paula hesitated, her "I'm calculating" hesitation, her expression briefly flat. She chose her serious voice. "This isn't a way of committing suicide, is it?"

That stunned Coryn. "I'm not my mother!"

"Have you lost some of your sanity out here?"

"Uppity robot." She said it lightly, but it gave her pause. "Mom was too depressed to care about me and Lou. I don't think she cared about herself either. And dad followed her. I'm not depressed, and I care greatly about Lou and Aspen. And you." She put a hand on Paula's shoulder and leaned in. "Promise? It's not about me dying, it's about me protecting someone I love. I'll take care of myself, and I need to you take care of Aspen. That's an order." Even if she wasn't doing it "right," a direct order was supposed to work with the robot. She was an adult now, and Paula could only refuse orders that put Paula in danger or violated laws.

Paula nodded. A jerky nod, but a nod nonetheless.

Coryn shivered. She looked down at the soft top of Aspen's white head and his small brown nose, and a surge of protectiveness filled her chest, pushing away the unease about changing how she treated Paula.

CHAPTER THIRTY-SIX

Lou led them down a long gravel driveway past a series of No Trespassing signs. Three young women, maybe even still teenagers, came forward and took their horses. Two older women and an older man led them to some picnic benches in a grove of trees. There, they quietly handed each of them weapons, and plied them with water, dried apples, and cranberry-flavored energy bars. The whole exchange was almost silent and only took about twenty minutes. The man drove them back down the driveway in the back of a big truck. In thirty minutes, they were back on the road, on foot.

Coryn felt the weight and heft of the stunner in her right pocket and the thin lethality of the knife in her back pocket acutely. These were new things, and far more foreign than a new pair of AR glasses. They made her a new person, forced her to look around more, to stay aware of her surroundings, to walk carefully.

Aspen trotted at her feet, looking pleased to be rid of the horses.

The river ran wide and slow here, and the cliffs had moderated their steep attitudes, although the land still sloped up to their right, covered in small trees. Obviously, this area had been deeply scarred by the post-taking fires.

Matchiko had made the promised update to her wristlet and now that she wasn't on horseback and carrying a dog, she could play with it. She had access to a few of the basic news channels she was used to, although she didn't want to distract herself just yet. She had contact information numbers for everyone in her party, including Paula. She tried that, and after a few moments Paula said, "Yes?"

"Just seeing how this worked."

"It works fine. Watch the road."

"Spoilsport."

"I know." They started up a long, moderately steep hill. They had to be getting close, but she couldn't see anything over the top of the hill.

"So will you tell me what's in the news?"

"Of course." Yet Paula hesitated for so long that Coryn was about to say something snarky. She looked serious. "All the gates into and out of Portland are under attack from ecobots. They haven't taken down the roads or hyperloop between Seacouver and Portland, nor has either city closed them."

"So they're not that worried?"

Paula shrugged. "The city is starting to fight back, and a few ecobots have been destroyed, but not many."

"How do they destroy ecobots?"

"With other robots."

Oh. "Like a robot fight?"

Paula hesitated. "Yes. But that's not happening at Camas, which is a small gate."

"Are people being hurt?"

"I don't think so. If so, it's not really making the news. My bet is the ecobots' hack isn't allowing them to hurt people. So far people aren't panicking, and the news isn't the lead story, although it's creeping up. People Inside are getting curious and shares and retellings are increasing."

"Is Seacouver being attacked?"

"Not so far."

That was careful language. Still, she felt relief. "Do you expect it to be?"

"I don't know."

A command from Lou flashed across her wrist. *Be quiet. We're almost there.*

Coryn glanced at Paula and mouthed, "Anything else I need to know?"

Paula still looked like a study in solemnity. "Nothing is what it seems."

She hesitated before whispering, "I know." Coryn sped up so that she rounded the next corner just a little behind her sister. The walls of ridge on their right flattened out considerably, and the river ran placid and golden in the setting sun.

The low angle of the sun forced Coryn to shield her eyes as they came near the gate. Unlike the simple gate she had left Seacouver through, an actual wall went from the edge of the river some ways inland. The gate itself had a big artsy sign proclaiming it the CAMAS GATE and two large metal doors with thick vertical bars and fancy scrollwork tops. Open, the gate dwarfed the two ecobots that stood on each side like sentries. They didn't appear to be letting anyone in or out, and no one seemed to be trying to attack them.

She recognized the dome as a slight shimmer in the air, a faint bend of the sun's rays.

Nothing looked like a fight about to happen.

Lou smiled, stepped close to Coryn, and pantomimed turning off any electronics. She sounded theatrical, like she was confiding a secret. "So the city thinks we're here to attack the ecobots. The Foundation thinks we're here to attack the city."

"Everyone in the Foundation?"

Lou raised an eyebrow. "You have been thinking, haven't you?"

"You didn't answer my question."

"Let's go surprise a few people."

Coryn considered Paula's advice, but it was too late to turn back. Clearly she was just going to have to trust Lou and Lou's friends and hope that it all came out all right. Not that there was any reason for her to think it might be all right, except maybe that the ecobots waited there, docile and quiet, and the gates stood open.

‡ ‡ ‡

As they neared the Camas Gate, Coryn felt small. She probably would have felt small even if they were still on horseback. The gates were that tall and thick.

Lou walked in front, Matchiko behind her, Blessing and Day side by side behind Matchiko, the difference in height again obvious as they walked instead of rode. Coryn followed them, with Paula right beside her carrying Aspen. Although no automated sensor system in the word would fail to identify Paula correctly, her scarf covered her face and with the squirming dog in her arms she looked as human as Coryn had ever seen her. Shuska kept the rear, as always.

Aspen shouldn't be here, but there was nowhere else for him to be. The same could be said of her. Two of kind. Rescued interlopers. Lou was walking into the city on a mission, but Coryn was merely following Lou. So far. Maybe with time she'd come to hate the city, but as it was, she'd been swept into a river of dangers she hadn't chosen.

It didn't matter.

She was here. She had Lou, and somehow she would turn Lou back into family. Whatever she was now, commander or revolutionary, it wasn't Lou's whole life.

Coryn just had very bad timing.

For now, she inhabited a surreal and strange moment she'd never imagined, when she and her dog followed her long-lost sister, when she carried a stunner and a knife and wore combat boots.

She felt as if she'd walked into a movie and couldn't tell if it was an adventure movie or a horror movie or a family drama.

A small army of drones perched on top of each ecobot, ready to fly toward any enemy. She caught brilliantly illuminated flashes of light on the bridges of Portland as the sun prepared to fall into the river. Closer in, the thin edges of the ecobots' drones looked like golden knives.

She half expected the drones to rise up and block their way. They didn't. The ecobots—and the drones—might as well have been statues. They stood still and silent as the small party approached. If it weren't for cameras on one of the bots' heads turning a slight bit to watch them, she would have thought the ecobots were dead. But the one did watch.

Paula put Aspen down and he trotted over to Coryn, staying close to her right foot.

Coryn couldn't see the dome, but she imagined she felt it. The temperature warmed ever so slightly and the air smelled staler. The road under their feet shifted from the rough gravelly Outside surface to a hard ribbon of reflective road filled with solar sensors and pale lighting. No birds sang. The wind stayed still. Coryn heard her own footsteps and the footsteps of the others with her and Aspen's small footsteps.

They walked between the huge ecobots, which felt heavy with menace. She reached out and touched one, expected a reaction. She got nothing. She touched another one. Only metal, and a little grease on her fingertips.

Her wristlet buzzed as they crossed over the midpoint of the gate, and a message scrolled along the bottom of it. "Welcome to the Portland Metroplex. You have been granted free entry in order to perform a service. You have a three-day visa."

Well, here she was, back in a city. Not home. But already it felt familiar and frightening all once, full of stimulation. News-bots flocked down from above them, coming in for close ups.

Lou glanced at her, a wry twist in her mouth signaling concern and maybe even regret.

Coryn smiled back at her, doing her best to look sunny. Lou shook her head, bemused, but quickly turned her attention forward.

Coryn turned to Paula. "I always wanted to see Portland."

"Really? You never told me that."

"I'm sure I asked you to look up marathons down here at least once."

Paula grimaced. "We're about to be greeted."

Sure enough, a group of people stood in the road. They were far enough away that they looked small. "They don't want to get too close to the ecobots."

"Do you blame them?"

"I still don't like to get close to them." The people, who were clearly waiting for them, stood their ground, and as they got closer it became easier to see that at least half a dozen were uniformed city police, and many more looked like city police doing their best not to look like city police. A few of them wore AR glasses or expensive AR buds pulled down over their eyes. Coryn imagined an arrow with her name on it identifying her to each of them. The rest had AR gear riding up on their heads, ready to pull down, hanging around their necks, or tucked in pockets. Coryn almost drooled. It had been so long! There must have been twenty new games released since she left, things she would have already mastered by now.

She shook herself out of it.

A squat man with long, well-kept blond hair stepped forward. Next to him, a black woman stood at least a head taller than he did. Her hair was plaited into two long, thick braids and her high cheekbones and large eyes were colored with rainbow dust. She was familiar enough Coryn must have seen pictures of her, although she didn't have a name to put with her.

Small drones hovered above and behind the couple. Probably a protection detail.

Three men trailed behind them. One of the men looked like a bodyguard, one like a politician, with makeup and well-groomed hair and silver data earrings. And in the middle, a simpler man dressed in jeans and a shirt. Stocky. She realized who it must be just as Paula whispered, "Victor."

As they passed the gate, she spotted a line of full-sized ecobots on this side of the gate, sitting and waiting quietly. There must be at least twenty. A few drones rose up from each of them, a flock of dark machines in a dusky sky.

Streetlights turned on, a few self-propelled and bobbing around obnoxiously and shining faint golden light on whatever was below them.

Paula scooped Aspen up.

Lou reached the blond man and the exotic woman and extended a hand. Matchiko stayed near her, a protective half-step back but close enough she could touch Lou if she needed to. Coryn shivered with a brief and unexpected stab of jealousy and clamped her mouth tight. She would know more soon, and then she could be more helpful. Matchiko made far more sense as Lou's second right now.

Everyone waited until the two groups made a sort of circle around the four—Lou and Matchiko standing inside, as did the blond man and the black woman.

He didn't reach his hand out, but his voice carried quiet, warm power. "I'm Jeremiah Allen."

These weren't politicians. They were NGO legends. Lou's bosses. Her bosses, too.

The man turned to the woman with him. "This is Mary Large."

Oh. The only reason Coryn hadn't recognized her was that she was totally out of context here among beaten-up ecobots, tired Wilders, and multiple flavors of law enforcement. Mary Large belonged on stage, in concerts that filled up huge venues, or dancing and singing in exotic locations and sharing her deep, throaty voice in AR videos. Coryn seemed to remember that she had married wealth. Maybe this was how she had done it.

Coryn reached for Aspen. If they needed to run or fight, Paula should have her hands free. Aspen was happy to leap into Coryn's arms, and gave a little yip as he did.

Mary Large glanced at them, a curious look on her face. She whispered something to Jeremiah, who then asked Lou outright, "Can Mary see the dog?"

Lou gave Coryn a warning glare, but gestured her forward.

Mary Large tilted her head and asked, "Can I pet him?"

"If he'll let you."

Coryn was a little afraid that Mary's elaborate armbands would frighten the dog, but Aspen stayed still at first, and then leaned a little into her long-fingered hands. Coryn smiled up at the performer, slightly awestruck to be so close to her.

Jeremiah addressed Lou directly. "Thank you for coming." He gestured toward some of the law-enforcement types that still stood behind them, watching. "Some of these fine people work for Portland Metro and some for the Foundation. They've been analyzing the ecobots' behavior. They have some information to share with you."

Jeremiah was talking for the cameras. And everyone watched him, letting him. He gave Coryn the creeps, at least a little. He felt fake.

He continued, "We're going to step aside for a moment and catch you up to date on what's happening at the other gates and see how you might be able to help us restore the ecobots to their original programming."

Lou swallowed, and her nod was stiff. Her eyes darted toward Victor, who stood behind Jeremiah and Mary Large, but she didn't acknowledge him or talk to him directly.

It felt like things were off plan.

Aspen wriggled a little. Mary opened her arms and the dog slid into them.

Coryn glanced to either side. Shuska looked more worried than Lou. Blessing and Day seemed small, silent, and uncertain. Some of the men had headed around behind them; the entire small party was now circled by people Coryn felt certain meant trouble. The lights that had been bobbing around them moved together and grew brighter, making it hard to see anyone outside of the small circle of their party.

Coryn reached for Aspen back, but Mary Large had stepped out of the light with him. Panic hit Coryn, and she searched the crowd. To her right, Aspen yipped, clearly unhappy. Coryn lunged that way, spotted Mary and Aspen. Lou barked at her to stop, but she snatched the dog back into her arms before she turned around.

Two men had stepped between her and the action. She had been cut off from everyone in her party.

CHAPTER THIRTY-SEVEN

People surrounded Coryn. There was almost no space between them. As soon as she realized she had no place to go, Coryn glared at Mary Large.

Mary looked back, placid. No apology at all, and also no fear.

Coryn kept Aspen close. Men crowded in close to her. She turned back to look for Lou, who could be heard speaking a little too loudly with Jeremiah. She tried to duck through the men blocking her way, but they might as well have been a wall; they closed together and suddenly she lost sight of her sister. She bit back a scream. She couldn't lose Lou now.

She put her head down and dodged right, Aspen clutched close to her chest.

One of the men knocked her down with an expert tap. It didn't even hurt—it just dropped her right to the ground, banging up a knee.

Shouldn't Paula be coming for her?

A slight sound drew her attention upward. A drone spun three feet or so above each of the men who had been blocking her.

Some of the lights that had been shining down shifted to shine up on the bottom of the drones. They glowed, their whirring engines and rotors catching the light and throwing it around, so the sky seemed full of glitter.

Lou called to her. "Sister. Come here."

Coryn pushed herself up awkwardly, still holding the dog tight. She took a last look at Mary Large, who smiled softly at her, something almost like compassion in her eyes, but maybe it was worry.

This time, people parted for her, glancing up as if to confirm the drones had made their choices for them.

Lou leaned in toward Jeremiah, her words clipped. Coryn recognized anger. "If you'll just have your men step aside, we'll go right on past you. We're merely doing what your own Foundation needs. We won't harm anyone."

Jeremiah's face had gone red, and he held his ground.

Victor came up beside him, his face completely unreadable.

Lou's voice sharpened until each word cut like a knife. "If you don't step aside on your own, we can make sure you do." Her eyes flicked up toward the drones. Two of them started whirling faster, making a slight screeching noise.

"You're fired." Victor spit out the words, as if trying to get them out before Jeremiah could. His boss—for Jeremiah had to be that—looked at him in surprise but still held his ground.

Coryn had to give the older man points for bravery. He glanced directly at the news-bots. "The Foundation doesn't stand for harm to the cities in any way. We disavow use of any of our technology for any purpose other than self-defense."

Lou nodded. "I know. We will keep that promise of yours."

Victor glared at her.

Jeremiah said, "You signed a contract."

"The cities signed contracts with us, and more importantly the cities signed contracts with *nature*. That's all we came for, to gently remind the cities of those contracts. Surely that is in your interest as well."

Many of the news cameras zoomed up and back, looking for a wider shot. One ran directly into a drone and both fell, the drone bouncing off Matchiko's shoulder. With her usual silent calm, Matchiko simply watched it crumple to the ground and returned her gaze to Jeremiah. They were both beautiful, Lou and Matchiko. Two strong women taking on the world.

The drones began to make sounds. Small, alarming sounds. Warnings?

Jeremiah stepped out of Lou's way and gestured for his men to do the same. Mary Large came to his side, acting for all the world like a silent witness.

Lou and Matchiko started up the road. The others all filed behind them in the same order they had come through the gate. Blessing smiled at her. "Glad you didn't get lost."

He looked like he had expected that. For a moment, she wondered if she was watching a show concocted for the news-bots. Then she was certain, and then she wasn't. Well, she wasn't going to ask, not now. It left her unsettled.

Most of the ecobots that had been waiting inside the gate moved with them. As they stepped into the suburb of Camas itself, the bots formed a sort of wall, traveling on each side of them and behind them.

Maybe twenty ecobots and slightly fewer people, all proceeding quite slowly up the open and empty road.

Coryn glanced back and caught a glimpse of Shuska's face. She didn't look at all happy to be hemmed in.

This side of the gate continued the same highway they had come in on, with the same basic view: river to their left, and now Camas to their right. The road was good and flat, and empty except for them, the ecobots, various news-bots, and lights that lit as they approached and dimmed behind them.

The lights and bridges of Portland glittered in the distance, still far off.

"Are we going to stop?" Coryn asked Lou.

"Not until we get to the PV Bridge."

"How far away is that?"

"Fifteen miles."

Over half a marathon. That was a long way, even on a city-quality street. Especially in the dark. But a few moments later, Lou stopped and grinned at her. "Brilliant, little sister."

Coryn didn't know what she meant until Lou called a brief break. She and Shuska conferred for a few moments, just far enough away to be out of earshot. Shuska thumbed her wristlet and spoke into it, and then everyone waited, the pause full of the activity of news drones and ecobot drones. As still as they were on the ground, the sky thrummed and buzzed and sparkled.

Clouds thickened above them and a bright wind carried cold knives between the robots, forcing Coryn to stand with an ecobot between her and the river for shielding. Blessing came over and stood close to her. He stared at the robots, the sky, the lights, the drones that spun and whirred softly above them, the occasional news-bot. "How come the drones don't shoot the news-bots down?" he mused.

She smiled. A reminder that he wasn't from the city. "It's illegal."

"Aren't the drones illegal?"

"Sure. Ecobots are also illegal, at least in the city." She thought about that. "Well maybe. They're usually not in the city, anyway. But no one violates the news. Honest."

He laughed. "I guess not."

"I didn't think I'd be back so fast."

He stepped closer to her. "You know, if we hadn't stopped in that barn, I wouldn't be here."

"I might not be here either."

He laughed. "No, you might not."

His closeness felt electric. But surely the middle of a cold road with robots all around you was no place to feel this. She glanced all around. No menace in sight. She took half a step back and looked up at him. "Thank you for stopping. And then for saving me by turning around."

He gave a little bow, smiled broadly, and said, "Here's to us all being here tomorrow." He scratched Aspen behind the ears, and the little dog nuzzled him back.

She smiled and whispered to Aspen, "Do you love everyone?"

"Hey!" Blessing reached over and gave her a hug, the first overt affection he'd shown her since the strange kiss right after the barn, when they separated. He smelled like river and fresh air and little bit like horse, and she breathed in deeply and realized she liked it. She returned the hug.

Lou whistled, loud and piercing.

Two of the ecobots had rolled into middle of the road.

Each extended arms and laid them on the road, so the hands were flat and the arms at a reasonable angle for walking up. Lou and Matchiko scampered up one of the front arms, and Shuska went up a back one, using a hand-over-hand method based more on strength than speed.

That left Coryn, Blessing, Day, and Paula to scramble up onto the back of the rear ecobot. Blessing gestured for her to go first, and she ran as fast as she could with the dog in her arms, not losing her balance even once. On top, she looked around while Day and Blessing climbed up behind her. There were no chairs, but they could sit cross-legged on the available flat surfaces. Blessing and Day took the outsides, so she sat in the middle, between and a little in front of them. Paula settled herself on the back, sitting down and looking behind them.

The ecobot's broad back had plenty of room; it could have taken at least five or six more people. There wasn't much to hold onto, and Coryn worried a little about sliding off until the bot curled one of its many extensible arms around her and made a sort of uncomfortable but secure chair.

She wondered how many appendages the ecobots had. A lot.

The ecobots started off, the ride smooth and easy. Wind bit at her face, and the air started to feel damp with impending rain.

She glanced at Blessing. "We would never allow so much wind."

"They're not allowing it."

That puzzled her. "Did we break the dome? Or the weather system?"

"No. Someone sent this for us."

She'd have never thought of it. The city had always acted to keep her safe. But right now, she was its enemy. She shivered with more than the cold. "I hope they can't send any really nasty weather at us. Surely they can't do much."

"Why not?"

"Well, the buildings. The gardens. They won't want to ruin things."

"Are you kidding?"

She sighed. He was right; she had to change her thinking. It helped a little that this wasn't *her* city. She called over to Paula. "What do you know? Can the city send weather against us?"

"Probably," the robot replied. "The city spends much on weather control. It is blocking every attempt I make to connect to the companions' newsfeed, so all I have is public news formatted for unaugmented humans like you."

A reminder that she would need AR and identity to see anything important here. Although maybe the pass she'd gotten would make glasses work if she got them?

Even with the clouds and wind, the ride was spectacular. Boats plied the Columbia, hulls, masts, and wakes outlined in white lights that shone on the dark water.

Portland grew closer. She tried to make out details. They were coming up on a bridge that spanned the wide, wide river. Dim lights outlined the structure, and it, too, looked dark and empty. Her wristlet informed her it was the 205 bridge.

She oriented herself using the tiny map on her wrist, identified the airport, and pointed out a large plane coming in for a landing.

The road stayed empty.

On a normal day the bridge must be thick with traffic of all kinds. Even the bikeways were empty.

They crawled up a freeway interchange and rumbled over a wide set of exits with brightly lit signs that identified a bullet train station, a hyper-loop station, and a light rail station. The interchange was attached to the high, wide bridge.

The road stayed empty on the far side of the 205. More houses and businesses crowded up to it, and in a few places it swept inland of the river and tall buildings rose on both sides of them for a while. She spotted lights on in many of the homes. Sometimes families stood glued to their windows, watching the strange long line of robots pass.

The clouds thickened.

The temperature dropped.

Every moment, Coryn expected them to be stopped, or at least that something would try to stop them.

With no warning, rain sluiced down on them, harder and faster than she had ever felt, even Outside. She couldn't see the ecobot in front of them anymore.

The surface grew slick with water and the bot's arm tightened gently around her. She held on. She stuck her tongue into the rain and tasted it. She had to yell to be heard. "It's just water."

Blessing yelled back, "It won't hurt us."

"We're good," Day added.

Her hair was soaked, her eyes, her clothes. Everything.

At one point, she felt a familiar hand on her shoulder and looked up to see Paula's face close to hers. "Keep your head down."

"Why?"

"Just do it." Paula stayed crouched by her.

Coryn listened through the rain, trying to use her feeble human senses to detect whatever had just alerted Paula.

CHAPTER THIRTY-EIGHT

Rain pelted Coryn. Paula clutched her hand and Aspen huddled in as close as he could, whimpering, his cold nose on her neck. The rain fell at odd angles, driven by unnatural winds. Coryn bent her head to the side to look up, only to have Paula press on her. Paula yelled loud enough for Blessing and Day to hear. "Keep down. Drones. Cover your necks."

Coryn shivered, staying as still as she could under Paula's heavy hand, listening. The same dull engine sound of the ecobot drone cover army still existed, but it had been joined by higher-pitched sounds.

It hurt to keep her head down, and she couldn't stand being unable to see. She carefully tilted her head enough to see to the side. Rain soaked her cheek, and she had to blink it away. Even with lights illuminating the clouds, the rain blinded her. She struggled to make sense of what little she could see. The lights must be from news-bots. Autonomous drones wouldn't need light, and surely wouldn't want it right now. The news-bots, on the other hand, were illegal targets. They could wear neon if they wanted.

Coryn fingered the butt of her new weapon, her fingers shaking. How could she pick out what to shoot at? The drones moved as fast as birds. One plummeted in an uncontrolled spin and bounced off the slick, wet top of the ecobot just to her right. It shone for only a moment before it was gone, leaving no mark whatsoever on the robot's thick metal skin. Had it been an ecodrone, a city police drone, or something else?

The rain stuttered and then stopped.

Moving lights came in closer and brightened. Small spotlights from drones hurt her eyes and threw concert-lighting spears across the sky, a variety of colors that illuminated the machines moving through the dark night. The myriad logos of popular newsfeeds and newsies decorated the sides of some of the drones.

The rain sputtered to a halt. The clouds stayed, far paler in color, bereft of ammunition. The lighter sky made it easier to see the drones darting through her peripheral vision like small flocks of birds: Five to nine drones at a time flew so close it looked like you could barely slip a piece of paper between their wings.

Next to her, Blessing sat up straight. "Wow," he whispered.

Coryn sat up, too, surprised that Paula no longer tried to restrain her. Just above them, lights bounced off white clouds. The lights of news-bots shone directly on them, ruining her peripheral vision.

It felt like they existed in a movie set, just the smoothly lumbering ecobot with the robot and the three people and the dog on its back, and a few hundred drones of many shapes and sizes shining and flashing in highly variable lights above them.

The ecobots' drones were mostly shaped like arrows, while the city's police drones were cylinders, copters, and small planes. Nimbler machines, in general. The ecodrones were bigger, heavier, and more menacing and didn't flinch as the smaller machines dove at them.

Something pressed into her palm. She looked down. Safety glasses from Paula's infinite store of useful things.

She sighed and put them on, the colors dulling a little. Too bad Paula didn't have any AR gear.

Aspen tugged at his leash, jumping and barking at the drones. It was unusual for him, and it took her a moment to scoop him up. After she got him tucked safely in her arms, she glanced back up as a swarm of ecodrones herded about five other drones too close to each other. One rotor snapped and a small bot tumbled down. Two more slammed into each other and shattered. Something dropped from above the level of the fight, knocking an ecobot drone off course so it smashed into another one. Both fell, wings clattering and bumping into each other. Something a drone had dropped on purpose?

Phalanxes of ecodrones flocked steadily around and above them. They didn't seem to be firing at the other drones, just knocking them down or herding them off and away.

Day screeched, and she looked behind to see his right hand cupping his cheek, blood welling between the fingers. Had one of the drones accidentally hit him with a shot meant for another drone?

Blessing lunged for Day, but the ecobot held onto him, pulling him back. Coryn tried to move, but the ecobot arm supporting her tightened ever so slightly, pinning her. None of the three of them could move. Protection?

Fears stuttered through her. What if the shot had hit his eye? What if a drone laser hit her? What about Lou?

She leaned over and whispered into Paula's ear. "Will you go check on Lou?"

"I shouldn't leave you."

The robot had better eyesight than she did. "Can you see the other bots?"

Paula shook her head.

Coryn changed it to an order. "Go to the edge and see if you can see them from there."

Yet again, Paula looked like she might disobey, as if she were trying to dissuade Coryn from enforcing her order. Coryn barked at her. "Go!"

Paula went.

Coryn turned toward Day. "How bad is it?"

He shook his head and offered a thumbs-up.

Blessing struggled against the robot arm that held him in place, cursing.

"It's okay," Day yelled. "It's just bloody. I'll be okay!"

Blessing shouted and pointed behind Day. A uniformed woman scrambled to the top of the ecobot. City colors. Blue and white. She ran toward them.

Another. A man.

Aspen lunged, snapping and barking, twisting so fast Coryn almost lost her grip on him.

The ecobot's head rose and swiveled toward the officers.

The woman stared at Aspen, fear and surprise flashing briefly in her eyes. Her face made a hard flat plane in the strange light. She braced her feet and pointed a gun toward Coryn. "No one move!"

Aspen slipped free and slid across the slick surface. As if it knew to help her, the ecobot's arm opened just a tiny bit, and Coryn sprang after him. She grabbed Aspen's collar with one hand, cupped her other under his belly to pull him back, and looked up to find Paula standing just behind her.

Paula leaped at the woman. The officer's eyes flared in shock; a blast from her gun hit Paula but didn't even slow her down.

Paula plucked her weapon out of the woman's hands and threw it, knocking a drone out of the sky. Paula kicked a similar weapon from the man's hand.

As one, both officers reached for additional weapons, but Paula grabbed them by the elbows, pinning them to her. "Drop your weapons."

The man did, but the woman waved hers as if it were stuck to her palm. Paula tightened her grip until the woman screamed and fell to her knees. The gun clattered down with a dull, plastic thud.

"Tell me what you want," Paula demanded.

The woman looked incapable of rendering a sentence through the pain. The man spat out, "We have orders to capture all of the Wilders."

Day winced. Blessing still struggled against the robot arm. Coryn had the absurd thought that the city police didn't need to trap them since the robots already had.

The man's eyes flicked over them, across the width of the ecobot's back. Paula questioned him sharply. "Are there more of you?"

He shook his head, but the woman's eyes widened.

"I think so," Coryn warned.

"Off!" Paula demanded, yanking her captives to the edge of the ecobot.

"It's too high!" the man yelped.

Paula shoved him from the edge of the bot and he disappeared, landing with a thud.

"Is he okay?" Coryn asked.

He answered by screaming for his wounded partner. "Jump!"

Paula let go of her arm, and for just a moment it looked like the woman was going to leap toward Coryn and Aspen, but she cursed, turned, and jumped.

Paula stood staring off the end of the still-moving ecobot. "They're okay."

"Did you find out anything about Lou?" Coryn asked her.

She shook her head. The scarf had come off and trailed from one shoulder, snapping in the breeze. She looked more like a robot again. "Thanks," Coryn said. "I've never seen you fight before."

"I know. I'm going to go look for Lou." She walked off, looking quite sure of herself.

Blessing stared after her, wide-eyed. "She was awesome!"

"She fights well." Day turned toward Coryn. "Are you okay?"

"Yes. I'm fine." He had turned the bottom of his shirt up and started scrubbing the drying blood from his cheek. "Maybe I'll have a good scar."

Lights drew Coryn's attention back upward.

A huge drone—or maybe something else—some flying thing—

blocked the clouds. It was almost as big as the ecobot they rode was long, if far slenderer. Another joined it, and another.

If these weren't on their side, then they were in trouble.

The ecobot drones seemed to come to exactly that conclusion. They made a last flourishing, flocking movement, and then three shot off and up as if on a reconnaissance mission, while the rest started settling back down around Coryn, Day, and Blessing, carefully nestling into the places people weren't.

Paula stepped around the ecobot's metallic head, still tucked against its body. "The others have been taken."

Coryn stiffened. "Lou? Taken?"

"There are soldiers on the top of the ecobot, and it has started going the other way."

Cold filled her. "Soldiers or police?"

"I think they're soldiers. They have on green uniforms."

She had no idea who wore green uniforms. Who knew where they'd take Lou? How could this have happened? "Are there any soldiers near us?"

"I don't see any," Paula said.

"And we haven't changed direction?" She was sure they hadn't, but the drone fight and the storm together had been disorienting. The drones close to them shuddered from time to time, as if adjusting themselves or preparing for something.

She glanced down at her wristlet's small screen. "Can you get any news?" she asked Paula. She had contact info for Lou. She tried to send a note. *Are you Ok? Where are you?*

No answer.

"Primary news sources suggest the city is being attacked and identifies hackers and Returners as the bad guys. They don't list the farm or Lou. They claim the situation is almost under control." Paula glanced up, reminding Coryn of the large and almost eerily silent drones that tracked them now. The drones had done nothing, although Coryn kept expecting them to fire. She felt vulnerable on the empty road with the huge drones above her.

Day asked, "By primary news sources do you mean what the city tells you?"

"Not the way it should. I'm searching video and AR logs."

"What about the social webs?" Blessing asked.

A moment passed before Paula answered. "Rumors. Some say the city's systems have broken down, and the city won't tell them that. There's some truth to that one—Camas and Vancouver seem to be out of power."

"That's why it's so dark."

Paula nodded. "There's also some people who think the city is being attacked by Seacouver."

That was an old fear, that the megacities would fight each other. They never had. Still, it came up every few years. "If the power is down, is the dome up?" she asked.

Blessing answered. "Yes."

She remained unsure where his loyalties lay. "What do you think is happening?"

He pointed up. "I think those are defending us."

"Oh." She had thought they might attack. "They're on our side?"

"I hope so," Blessing said.

She prodded Paula. "Is there news about Lou?"

"No."

"Damn. Damn." She felt like she should be doing something to save Lou, but from what? Without the ecobot's help, she couldn't climb down, and in fact she couldn't move out of her makeshift chair at all right now. Her wristlet showed that they were almost at the PV bridge.

Where had Lou been taken, and who had taken her?

CHAPTER THIRTY-NINE

They rode their strange steed toward the PV bridge. Thick clouds obscured the bridge itself, but Coryn spotted other ecobots from time to time. Three long cylindrical drones flew close together right above them. Others hovered nearby. The clouds broke for a moment, and it seemed like there were far more, that perhaps a hundred drones went with them, a sky-army of flying machines.

They had no markings. She tried finding a name for them by taking a picture with her wristlet and running a search, but nothing showed up.

Banned knowledge?

Aspen huddled in her arms, and she wished for Lou, or at least for word of Lou. She still hadn't received any answer to her query.

Blessing and Day looked around with shocked faces and wide eyes. From time to time, Blessing smiled.

Why was he smiling? Was it his strange desire to beat death back daily with acceptance, or did he recognize the drones? Is so, he wasn't telling her what he knew. It bothered her. If only she could talk with Paula about him. Did the robot see red flags in the details of his expressions and nuances of his voice?

Whatever Paula might be sensing, she seemed to think they needed a release. She spoke in a light voice. "Here's the latest from the social webs. The city is being attacked by refugees from the Koreas. The city is not really being attacked at all. The city is being attacked by aliens."

Coryn laughed at that last, grateful for the humor.

A few minutes later, Paula said, "Here's a good one: It's mutiny— Vancouver is trying to separate from Portland. The ecobots have been directed to come into the city and eject the PV police by force."

She shivered. "Let's hope not."

"You know that's not true," Day objected.

"I know nothing." Well, she knew some things. The clouds were a weapon. She half-expected rain to fall when they reached the bridge, but it started long before. A deluge pounded their heads and the bots, struck the drones above them, and dripped from metal wings and tails. Every possible crevice on the wide top of the ecobot filled with puddles.

As soon as the sky finished hurling water down at them, the clouds blew away. The pale yellow-gold of the PV bridge superstructure glistened in the fresh air. "So they are finally letting us see something," Coryn muttered.

"More likely they want to see us," Paula said.

Coryn swallowed, trying to look brave. Surely their pictures were being displayed everywhere. She sent another message to Lou. *Are you OK? Where are you?* She tried to find a news story with their pictures.

"It's beautiful," Blessing whispered.

She looked up from her wristlet screen. He was right. The bridge crossed the river in three graceful arches, one for cars, one for people, one for the hyperloop between cities. Lights showcased the four great pylons that plunged deep into the river and the four on each side of the land. A ribbon of bright wire designed for zip-lining ran on each side, making a large X shape above the bridges.

All of it looked empty. The night smelled of water and wind, and the peculiar clean smells of the city. Vancouver smelled far more like Seacouver than either smelled like the Outside.

She reeled Aspen close. "Stay with me," she whispered in his ear. He circled three times and settled into a small ball, his chin on his paws. She asked Blessing and Day, "What do you think is going happen? The city obviously knows we're going to the bridge—I'm sure it's no different from our bridges in Seacouver. There should be traffic. We haven't talked to anyone except that weird greeting party, and cities are not this quiet."

Blessing shook his head. "I suspect we are too complex for automated systems to make all the decisions. The wealthy are trying to decide what to tell the city to do. And people are being hurt."

She froze. "Lou?"

"How would I know?" He shifted his gaze past her toward the bridge. "But I doubt it. Someone may use her as a scapegoat. If this goes bad, they need someone to blame."

"Could Victor have blamed her?"

The silence that followed her question suggested she might be right. She tried another question. "What about me? Everyone wanted to blame me, back in the barn."

Blessing laughed. "You're too naive."

His comment stung, but she didn't have the energy to argue. She'd lose anyway. "What's going to happen?"

"Remember what I told you back on the trail, just as we headed down to the river?"

She swallowed. "It's a good day to die."

"Not quite. But live every day like it could be your last. Then you'll be ready for anything."

What could it hurt? She took a deep breath. Chanted inside her head. *I could die tonight.* The ecobot rolled so smoothly over the slick road it created the optical illusion that the bridge approached them. Some of the ecobots that had been following them stayed behind as they climbed up the empty ramp to the bridge, still dogged by the bigger drones and followed by four other ecobots. *I could die tonight.*

The silent parade of climbing bots and the drone escort frightened and awed her at once. She was worried sick about Lou, and frustrated that she was being taken for a ride. It wasn't as if the ecobot had stopped and extended its arms so she could get down. There were no choices being offered to her. None.

Blessing must feel the same, but she couldn't see it in his body. He rode relaxed and kept flashing his wide smile. He spoke softly, "Let's figure this out. What do you think you know? Tell me."

She stared up at the bots and the flashing lights, and then out across the dark river. What did she know? "We, and a bunch of other Wilders, recruited from the NGO teams . . . " Was that right? Probably. "People are breaking into the city in order to get attention. While we're at it, we're assuming the city won't kill us and that it will in fact listen to us."

He nodded. "Close enough. Add in that there are a lot of players. Just like Outside has the Returners and Listeners, there are factions in the city."

She sighed. "Before I left the city, I wouldn't have recognized a faction if I met one."

"At least you have a sense of humor," Day observed with humorless calm.

Their ecobot led the others up the bridge. They quickly climbed far enough to see both cities. Vancouver sprawled behind them; Portland gathered and rose ahead, clearly well over twice the size of Vancouver, with far taller buildings. Portland Metro spanned Washington and Oregon like Seacouver spanned Washington and Canada. Her wristlet screen showed the red line of the state border not far ahead, over the center of the Columbia River. She glanced behind her again. The other ecobots still followed them. "There's another way to look at it. We're being restrained by robot claws as we ride machines that could be controlled by anybody to some destination we don't understand, and the people we thought were our leaders—including my sister—have been abducted and taken who knows where."

"Also true," Day said. "Or we're just on a pretty night ride over a spectacular bridge."

Paula smiled at her. "You like bridges."

"Crazy robot." But she smiled back and tried to think like Blessing and Day. If only she knew Lou was safe. Lou had led her here, but she had stupidly followed. She could have stayed back, refused to go. Maybe if she'd refused to come here, Lou would have thought twice.

As they approached the state border, a small sign turned on. "Welcome to Oregon."

If she had an AR set, there would be a lot more data. She was enveloped by silence and also blind.

Two large metal gates had been pulled shut across the bridge. She could see where they usually rested open, and how the tall arched and filigreed metals would create a work of art when it stood in the open position. Now it made an effective barrier. The top of the arch of the bridge had a flat space just between two gates. Two small covered buildings filled the space on each side of the road.

The ecobot stopped in front of the gate. To her surprise, the arm that had been holding her released a bit, and then a bit more. Aspen barked at it, as if surprised it could move. Drones scuttled away from the metal appendage, and it moved further, so that she had all of the freedom she needed. Her stiffened legs refused her command to stand; she had to push herself forward onto her knees and use her hands to push from there to her feet. Blessing and Day stood, too. They did not look nearly as mystified as she felt. She looked up at Day, her voice shaking. "What do you know?"

"Look at your wrist."

She touched it to turn on the light. A message. Lou? How had Day known she had a message?

Go with my Blessing and do as he says. Julianna.

Her heartbeat sped up. She had dreamed of seeing Julianna again, of running with her and asking her questions. But this felt—bad. "How? Where is she?"

Blessing whispered, "I don't know."

"But you know her."

"Yes."

"Even though you're not from the city?"

"I wasn't born here."

"You're a Listener?"

"Not quite. But how do *you* know her?"

She wasn't about to tell him anything. Besides, Julianna was her secret.

If Blessing had just betrayed Lou, Lou might very well think Coryn had been in on it the whole time.

Dammit. What should she do? She had to go, didn't she?

Aspen tugged on his leash, drawing her attention. He tugged harder, and she sat to counterbalance him, falling on her butt with her legs wide, giggling at the fall and then at the fact that she was giggling when nothing was funny.

Blessing laughed with her. He reached a hand down for her and she took it. He pulled her up and briefly in close to him, saying, "It will be all right."

She couldn't agree, not now, so she pulled away from him and climbed down the ecobot's arm, already lying at an angle she could walk down carefully with Aspen in her arms. The end of the ecobot's flat appendage rested right at the edge of the gate. She stepped onto the hard surface of the bridge and waited for the others.

The gate slid far enough open for them to enter. Blessing led her through, followed by Paula, then her and Aspen, and lastly Day.

Once inside, Blessing stopped and stood, looking as lost as she felt. She had no idea whether or not to believe his body language, or anything else about him for that matter.

To think she'd wanted to kiss him.

The gate gave a soft clink as it shut behind them.

Aspen lunged to the right, and Julianna stepped through the door of the little hut on that side of the bridge. She looked older and more resolute than when Coryn had last seen her. Sadder. Dark circles stained the skin under her eyes, and her hair had grown longer and grayer. Coryn would be willing to place bets neither of them was in the running shape they had been the last time they saw each other.

Blessing walked right over to Julianna and gave her a hug, which was returned unreservedly by this woman who had always kept some distance from Coryn. She took a step back.

Day smiled at Julianna, and got a return smile.

It took her a moment, but Coryn said, "I didn't expect to see you here."

Julianna pulled free of Blessing. "I've been protecting you."

"I don't think so!" she said. "I almost died three times."

Julianna glanced at Blessing. "Later. We'll talk later. For now, we need to get you away. All the gates are under attack. That's the only reason I was able to guide you all up here."

"With the drones?" Coryn asked.

"Yes. They're mine." She glanced up at the sky, where the long drones flew low circles over the ecobots just on the far side of the fence.

"Why'd you take us to the top of a bridge?"

"I need you on the Oregon side. As soon as you step though that gate, you'll be there. I only closed it so you'd have to stop."

"Are we supposed to get back on the ecobots?"

"No. We need to disappear. First, we have enough time to get some food and water into you all. You'll need it."

Coryn gestured at the busy sky. "How are we going to disappear with all those news-bots?"

Julianna smiled at her. "That's my problem."

Day licked his fingers and scrubbed at his cheek again, even though it was mostly clean. Then he ran his fingers through his unruly black hair. As usual, Blessing spoke for both of them. "Are you coming with us?"

"Lou." Coryn spread her feet and crossed her arms. "What happened to Lou?" Did Julianna even know who Lou was? "My sister. They took my sister. Soldiers."

The older woman put a hand up as if to forestall questions, crossed to the building she had come from, and brought out a bright blue plastic bag. She pulled four water bottles from it, keeping one for herself and handing the others out. Next, food bars. The first bite seemed impossible, but the second tasted good and the rest of the bar disappeared quickly. Coryn washed the bar down with water and felt hungrier than before she'd started it. Julianna handed her another one, and she ate that, too. "What next?"

Julianna glanced at Paula. "She can't come with us."

Coryn went cold. Julianna couldn't mean that. "She stays with me."

Julianna stepped toward Coryn and put a hand on her shoulder. "She can't come with us," she repeated. "Send her to the other side of the gate."

"I can't. That's not fair."

"Your robot just attacked two policemen. When she gets caught, they'll decommission her. You need distance from that."

Coryn struggled to find words, to think quickly. "But . . . but won't she be hurt over there? Can't we take her with us?"

Julianna didn't reply, nor did she soften. She just watched Coryn.

Coryn felt pinned. She had nowhere to go. She had never seen this side of Julianna, the woman who led cities to merge and took on a federal government. But Coryn couldn't give up. "She just saved us. Without her, we wouldn't have gotten here."

"I'll get you another one."

It took two breaths for Coryn to even parse that. It hit her in the middle of her stomach. "Another one wouldn't be Paula."

"I can send you both out there." Julianna nodded toward the ecobot and the circling drones on the Vancouver side of the gate.

Coryn's mouth hung open. She clamped it shut and held onto Aspen. She'd been warned of this choice, but this wasn't how she had imagined it. Robot for dog. She rejected the choice. "Will you take Aspen? Keep him safe and find him a home?"

Julianna blinked at her, as if trying to understand what she meant.

"I'm responsible for him. If I keep him with me and Paula, he might die. I'll lose him, anyway." She glanced at Paula, who watched her closely. Paula winked at her, a small gesture, probably seen by the others, but familiar and soothing.

Paula took a few steps closer to Julianna. She was taller by a head, but the expression the robot had chosen to wear was gentle. "If Coryn doesn't go with you, if she goes back through that gate by herself, what happens to her?"

"She'll be locked up. Or they'll kill her." Julianna stared out at the city, her face bathed in the sickening and uneven lights of her drone army. "Probably they will only lock her up. That's if she walks out by herself. The more people she has with her, the worse her chances become."

"And if she walks out with me?"

"The police or—other powers—may kill you both. They have reason now. You hurt one of them."

Paula nodded. "You knew all of that when you directed our steed to trap all three of them and bring them up onto a bridge, a place with no options but up or down."

Julianna glanced to both sides, and Coryn almost expected her to say, "Down or down, from here." She didn't. She merely waited. Had Paula gotten her motives right? Julianna was here, on the top of this bridge. It was completely improbable. And was one side of the bridge really that different from the other?

Paula continued. "And if I walk out by myself, that will make me a target. But I might be able to keep their attention."

Julianna nodded. She took a step back and gestured toward the other building with a come-hither gesture.

Coryn's head snapped around. Four people came out of the building, each with two bicycles. LeeAnne, two of the others that Coryn recognized from their encounter on the road, and someone she hadn't seen before, a tall man with a long, graying ponytail.

Paula stepped close to Coryn. She leaned down. "You must go."

"I can't leave you!"

"You must."

Coryn shook her head, wanting to bury it in Paula's breasts, to hold her and be held by her.

"You made me promise to protect Aspen. You didn't mean I should leave him with strangers while you die with me."

Coryn blinked at her, shocked.

Paula reached a hand out and touched her shoulder, and then leaped up and over the closed gate. She climbed on top of the ecobot that had brought them here, and sat, cross-legged, almost exactly where Coryn had been sitting on the ride up.

The ecobot didn't move or acknowledge its returned rider in any way.

Drones did not rain bullets down on her.

Nothing happened. Paula sat with her back to Coryn, looking out at the city, unwilling to allow Coryn any hope at all.

A sob broke in Coryn's throat. She let it out and then clamped down, turning to Julianna in rage.

Julianna's hands were already up. "Don't hate me. Paula is of the city. All of its robots are of it, and they are all unsafe. This is necessary."

Coryn swallowed.

"You are no longer a child."

They stood there, she and the old woman and the others. Wind whipped their hair. The lights of two cities shone at the feet of the bridge.

Blessing and Day said nothing.

Aspen licked her face.

LeeAnne brought her one of the extra bikes. It looked like LeeAnne's, thin and strong and fast. There was a good-sized pannier on the side, and LeeAnne held it open while Coryn slipped Aspen into it and clipped his collar to a chain. LeeAnne showed her how to zip it so his little head stuck out but his body was reasonably well contained. "There," she said. "He'll probably be safe enough." She held a helmet out to Coryn.

So Julianna had known about Aspen and planned for him, but she had planned to murder Paula?

Numb, Coryn took the bike, glancing back at Paula. The moment seemed completely unreal, like she should be able to move and talk normally, but everything insisted on being slower than usual. Her breath. Her tears. Everyone else's movements. The slightly pitying look on Julianna's face and her own boiling anger. The movement of her hand and elbow as she pushed the helmet on her head and felt it clamp around her perfectly. She leaned down and tucked her pants into her boots, hating herself for it, but unable to stop moving forward.

She could only go forward.

Julianna nodded at her.

She glanced at the gate and at the ecobot and Paula, who still looked away from her. She looked back at Julianna. "Where's my sister?"

Julianna merely shook her head.

The other gate had already swung partway open.

Suddenly, she had to move. She could no longer be here. Time shifted from slow to fast. She threw her right leg over the bike, pushed off with her left, and raced down the bridge. Lights and wind whipped at her. Aspen yipped. The bridge angled more steeply as they came away from the top, and the bike picked up speed. Coryn screamed into the wind of her passage, her breath burning in her empty chest.

She didn't even look to see if the others followed her. She couldn't give a shit.

CHAPTER FORTY

The PV bridge was so long and so smooth that the bicycle reached thirty-five miles an hour before Coryn noticed a faint—frightening—wobble. The bike transformed from a stable gyro to an unstable one, and she struggled not to tense and lose her balance.

She reached for the expected lever and found it missing. The bike sped faster as she tried two or three other places carefully and quickly. At forty, she could only move a little without de-stabilizing the bike. *LeeAnne told me the brakes were wireless.* She gripped the ends of the handlebars. The bike started slowing. Stability returned, but she kept the brakes on for a while more. No one caught up with her.

She realized she didn't want them to.

She let go at twenty-five, gaining speed again, whooping into the wind until she reached thirty-five once more, and repeated that three more times down the long hill.

Near the bottom, the PV Bridge crossed over another bridge, and another, and then plummeted down through a set of tall buildings, leveling a little as it crossed above a park. Near the bottom, the bridge split out for walkers and riders. She had no idea what to do, but it wasn't possible to hesitate at this speed, so she took the first bike off-ramp and spiraled down onto a busy street, finding herself inside of a crowd of people instead of alone.

Julianna came next, then Blessing, two of the other riders, Day, one more rider, and, true to her title of sweep, LeeAnne came in last, a wide grin pasted across her face. She pulled up next to Coryn. "You're crazy." But it sounded like jealousy, and maybe welcome.

"Nice bike," Coryn responded.

LeeAnne reached for her water bottle. "You almost lost it."

Coryn's cheeks grew hot, but she grinned. "You have no idea how good it felt to be on a bike instead of a horse."

"I might."

People had gathered on the street across from them, staring.

Julianna glanced around, her lips thin, her movements smooth. She nodded at the man with "Lead" scrawled on his shirt. His bike bulked a third again as big as Coryn's, and his legs seemed to come to Coryn's chest: a classic bicycle build that contrasted with her slighter form and LeeAnne's stocky one. He might even be bike-modded, with extra muscle in longer legs.

He touched his wrister, which was easily three times the screen size of Coryn's smaller wristlet, glanced forward, glanced back at Julianna and waited for her nod, and then took off. He went from a dead stop to fast, like water falling from a roof.

Coryn glanced down to check on Aspen, and in that one short moment Blessing passed her. She cursed under her breath and took off after him.

Ten minutes later, she stopped worrying about catching Blessing and simply tried to hold on and keep the lead in sight. In a normal ride, the lead would pick a pace and stick to it, the other bicyclists following him or her in a long, steady line. This man dodged between people and cars, barely smooth enough not to upset the transportation system. Coryn had to use every bike skill she knew to keep up with the varied pace and the dodgy, fast turns. A few times she lost sight of the lead entirely and followed Blessing as best as she could. Then she lost them all and slowed, searching.

She must have missed a turn. LeeAnne came up beside her and drove her left.

Her inner thighs and her arms chafed against her regular clothes.

Portland flew by. Her impression was of old houses mixed with new, busy gardens stuffed full of pink and purple azaleas and red rhododendrons, and the scent of lilacs. The street illumination was bright, and the bars and dance halls and coffee shops and lecture halls lit and filled with people. The streets themselves were less crowded than Seacouver's, and the people she saw were mostly of a type: casual, slightly unkempt, and almost all smiling. Many bicyclists. More people on bikes than in cars or on scooters, although walkers outnumbered them all. Twice, Aspen barked at dogs.

She kept expecting drones or news-bots, but if they were following the group they did it from too high up for her to see. Maybe the police were using street cameras. Someone had to be watching.

She stayed straight again when she should have turned. LeeAnne caught her again, breathing hard. "In your fork pack!" she yelled. "Glasses!"

Coryn fumbled the pack open and grabbed a pair of dark brown lenses with bright orange frames. As soon as she put them on, her helmet grabbed the ends, pulling them against her face. The world took on a brighter glow, everything slightly amber. Living things like trees showed brighter than dead things like streets. A green course-line glowed in front of her nose, close in, and a directional arrow for her next turn blinked just above it. *Right. 300 yards.*

Beside her, LeeAnne glowed brighter yet, almost blinding, a brilliant neon green. She glanced around, looking for the others.

"Watch out!" LeeAnne screeched.

Coryn braked automatically, glancing at the real world through the virtual overlay in front of her just in time to miss hitting a bollard. Aspen barked, complaining about the sudden near stop. She cursed and reoriented, found the lead three streets over and going a different direction.

LeeAnne yelled at her again, "Follow me!"

Coryn cringed. She was a true fuckup if the sweep was keeping her behind. But she leaned into the wind, the bike responding as she adjusted to the AR. She noted her speed—twenty-one on the flats. Nice.

The other riders glowed bright green, and her exercise stats showed up in black. The real world had become a series of yellows and pale browns, dizzying.

She'd only been gone a few weeks. How could she be so unbalanced by AR so fast? But within ten minutes she began keeping up better as her brain made its initial adjustment to the enhanced world.

She rode hard, the AR world around her making the physical effort of the ride easier. She almost emptied the water bottle in easy reach and couldn't tell if there was another one. Her calves and thighs burned. Each breath ripped into her lungs and blazed out. Each team member had a symbol; she puzzled out who was who. She looked like a dog.

Julianna, a wolf, kept up just fine, moving fast, two bicycles behind the lead, and making every turn on time. In spite of the pain, Coryn forced her body to move fast enough to catch up to LeeAnne and pass her. "I've got it," she yelled. "I can see the route."

"Make the next turn!"

The lead disappeared in front of her. The route line stayed, a bright green arrow blinking in front of her nose. She slid right with it and entered a tunnel, the entire world darkening around her except for a string of pale lights on the ground that she kept just to the right of her front tire. She swallowed, trusting, legs pumping, riding through near dark with Aspen tucked safely beside and just behind her, her bike wheel spinning sounds that bounced back at her from the top and sides of the darkness. Bright green lights ran in a straight line ahead of her. The glasses dimmed in the darkness to preserve her real sight but helpfully laid in the outlines of the tunnel. They jogged left, and a few minutes later right and up a hill, everyone slowing, and then a left again and downhill, using brakes to stay under twenty.

She lowered her head and dug further, focusing on keeping her heels down and her upper body still, on using her quads and glutes to power through the darkness.

The tunnel angled up so steeply she barely managed not to grind to a halt as she ran through gears, finding a low that let her stay above fifteen miles an hour. Her legs turned faster, almost a blur, and her lungs burned even harder. Just as she thought she couldn't keep up the pace a second longer, they turned again and rode left, flattening out, still enveloped in darkness. The other riders' breath sounded almost as loud as hers, and at least one rider had even more trouble than she did, his or her breath ragged and wheezing.

Light beckoned. The lead sped up. They all followed suit, emerging onto a clean concrete pathway. A raw dawn spilled yellow-gold light onto purple, pink, and white flowers that lined the path. Beyond them, carefully kept lawns were decorated with more paths, benches, and fountains.

The lead called out "stopping," and she braked with the others; they gathered in a circle, panting, and watching the sky. He nodded at them all, his gaze lingering on Coryn for an extra second or two. "Nice job, all."

LeeAnne grinned at Coryn, and Coryn nodded back. She was too tired to return the smile, though, and too heartsore. It had been well over twenty-four hours since she slept.

One by one, the others reached for water or cracked open snacks. She took the cap off of her almost-empty water bottle and poured a little into it for Aspen. He lapped it up, and to her amazement he seemed happy to stay tucked into the zipper of the pannier. His small pink nose stuck out, curiously sniffing the air. She leaned down and whispered to him. "We'll find Lou again. She'll be okay." It felt like lying through her teeth, like saying her parents would come back, which she had done a few times right after they killed themselves, even though she'd known it wasn't true when she said it.

Paula. She'd left Paula, who would never have left her. Except she did—she made Coryn leave.

Coryn reached down and touched Aspen's nose. Victor had had the right of it, after all. She had been forced to choose between her robot and her dog.

LeeAnne handed her a post-ride gel and she sucked it down, immediately feeling a slight easing in the taut muscles of her lower back and neck.

Julianna seemed at home. She led them all to a big shed and helped them park their bikes. Everyone waited patiently, almost no one talking, as Coryn let Aspen mess up the beautiful lawn. Julianna didn't even wince.

They walked up a gentle hill toward a sprawling white house. Halfway up, they turned left to follow a narrow gravel path. Coryn gasped as she saw a pool the size of her old orphanage. A low bungalow on the far side of it proved to be a set of bathrooms with showers and changing rooms. The others—including Blessing and Day—seemed to know where to go. Julianna led her to a shower stall, where towels and clean clothes had been laid out on a low shelf. "These are for you."

"Where am I?"

Julianna began pulling her hair out of its gray braids. "One of my houses."

"Do you know anything about Lou? My sister?"

"She's safe."

Coryn tensed at the stilted answer. "Do you *know* that?"

Julianna crossed her arms, watching Coryn carefully. "You could thank me for saving you."

Coryn crossed her own arms, mimicking Julianna. "You could have saved her."

"Your sister or your robot?"

She didn't hesitate. "Both."

"Hardly." Julianna looked almost like she was holding back a laugh. "Your sister made herself a powerful target. She rode in full of demands and stupidity and the brashness of the young. She also rode in with no support, and, worse, with enemies. You're still not much of anything, hardly on the radar. Neither are Blessing and Day. Even so, it was barely possible. I had to pull favors to route you to me."

"How did that work anyway? Weren't we all alone on a bridge and visible to everyone, and couldn't any drone have followed us?"

"That's what the tunnel is for."

"Surely people saw us go in."

"We've got shields up over the neighborhood. That's enough for you to know."

Right. Because if she knew anything at all for sure, the world might end.

She wanted out of her sweaty clothes, but she didn't want to stand around naked. "So why did you bother? Why save me at all?"

Julianna started stripping off her clothes, obviously not suffering from any of the shyness that enveloped Coryn. Her body was hard and muscular, although her skin sagged at the arms and around the knees. When she got down to bra and underwear, she stopped and smiled, maybe noticing Coryn's discomfort. "Not many people have run with me and asked for nothing."

Coryn bit back a reply. She heard a slight hesitation, almost vulnerability, in the old woman's voice. Something breakable. But that had to be wrong. Surely she was just so tired and hair-trigger that she couldn't read Julianna right. "Can I shower?"

Julianna gave her a little bow and backed out of the changing room, pulling the cheerful blue-and-pink-striped curtains closed behind her.

The water felt like heaven. The shampoo smelled of gardenias. The towel was as soft as summer sun. She had come unwashed and exhausted into the world of the powerful, utterly alone except for a scruffy, lovable dog. No Lou. No Paula.

She sobbed into the shower, trusting the running water to cover the sharp sounds in her breath. Why had she *wanted* to find Julianna? Maybe even missed her?

CHAPTER FORTY-ONE

Coryn woke stiff and sore and full of the starvation that followed marathons. "Aspen?"

He licked her face.

"Okay, okay."

The strangeness of the bed and the unfamiliar scent of flowers wafting in the open window tugged at her. Late morning light? She looked for Paula before she remembered her last sight of the robot on the far side of a metal gate. She fell back into the bed, staring at the ceiling, blinking back tears.

There was a hole in her life.

Her thighs throbbed from the bike ride. Someone had handed her a chicken sandwich and a tall glass of water after she showered, and she had finished both as if they were the last food and water in the world. After that, LeeAnne had led her to this room with its comfortable bed.

She felt as if she had forgotten who she was, as if she'd journeyed to some place far away and hadn't quite come back yet. But maybe grief had made her sleep.

Maybe she should sleep forever.

Her belly rumbled a strong disagreement at the idea of going back to sleep. Aspen was no more help than her stomach; he sat at the foot of her bed and whined.

She pushed herself out of bed. When he hopped into her arms, she hugged him close. A pair of comfortable beige drawstring pants and a loose white shirt had been laid out for her on the dresser, as well as sandals and underthings. The clothes were seamless—clearly printed on something high-end—and they hung comfortably on her sore body. The distressed purple shoes fit and looked fabulous.

The fancy clothes didn't make her feel any better.

She stalked down the corridor. Aspen followed at her heels, looking for a place to take him outside. The first door she tried led to a long, groomed lawn lined with dogwoods bathed in late morning sunshine.

She spotted Paula standing on the far side of the lawn, looking up at the flowers.

How could she have gotten here? It didn't matter. Her feet moved in spite of her doubt, carrying her toward the robot. "Paula! Paula! How did you get here?"

The robot turned toward her, wearing a smile that Paula often wore.

"Stupid robot," Coryn said, and then repeated it. "Stupid robot."

"Excuse me," the robot replied. "I am not stupid."

Coryn looked into her eyes, suddenly certain it wasn't really Paula, hoping she was wrong. "What's the name of the bridge we stood on when I graduated from junior high?"

"Excuse me?"

Coryn's fist balled. She'd never hit a companion robot, but in that moment she wanted to.

She dug deep and mustered enough self-control to turn around and walk away. She grabbed Aspen and buried her face in his side. Why care so much about a robot when she had a breathing, living, happy being who loved her?

Somewhere nearby, Julianna called out, "Coryn!"

She lifted her head. Julianna stood almost beside her, watching her. "I hate you."

"I told you I'd buy you a replacement."

Coryn stood, shaking. "You can't replace Paula with a robot."

"Paula was a robot."

She shivered and hugged Aspen tighter. "Was?"

"She fought a group of police and their drones who were trying to get through the gates and follow us."

Coryn set Aspen down and swallowed hard, a wave of disbelief and dizziness almost making her fall. "Of course she did."

"I can show you."

Coryn took a deep breath. Her bottom lip quivered and she bit it. "Send it to me. I can't watch it now. Not yet."

Julianna nodded slowly. "I understand. She died to help you."

"What do you mean, died? What is dead for a companion?" Coryn knew she was reaching for the impossible, but she kept doing it anyway. "There are backups. Surely there are backups."

"They shot her. It took five shots to stop her from giving commands. By then she'd killed two policemen and used one of the bodies to knock three drones from the sky."

She could remembered Paula on the ecobot, calmly knocking the policemen back. She'd gone out fighting. The gentle companion who'd told her stories and followed her around city streets as she ran, keeping her safe, had died fighting for her. A slight smile tried to escape onto Coryn's face but she denied it. "She was my protector. That was her job."

Julianna shook her head. "Robots who kill frighten the city. You wouldn't be alive now if the ecobots had killed anyone after they came through the dome. No one would have cared if you got hurt. Not compared to the danger of a killer robot. You have no idea how much effort the city expends to keep itself safe from automation."

Coryn knelt and petted Aspen, looking down so her hair covered her face.

Julianna words remained unrelenting. "Paula killed people. That means each and every copy anywhere will be erased forever, and it will be illegal to own one or to load one into any body."

Didn't this woman think she knew the laws around robots? Coryn looked down and kept petting Aspen, who nudged her hand with his cold nose and wagged his tail. The angry lump in her throat was too fierce for her to push words past.

Julianna's voice softened. "We made up a story about Erich, that he actually reprogrammed her when he had her. That he was the reason she went killer. So if you hear that, you'll know why. It's to protect you."

Coryn blinked for a moment. Julianna knew about Erich? How?

Julianna finally had the good grace to fall quiet.

Coryn couldn't keep the image of Paula sitting on top of the big rumbling ecobot out of her head. Heat broke across her chest and spilled out through her limbs, flushing her face and making her hands tremble. "You had no right." She stood, looking into the old woman's eyes. "I don't care who you are, you had no right."

"I'm not the one who brought her robot into a war. I'm not the one who got into a war she couldn't get out of." She paused, searching Coryn's face. She looked gentle in spite of her harsh words.

Coryn stared back. Surely Julianna felt Coryn's anger—so deep and hot it almost had to scorch her. If she did, she didn't react to it, or step back, or anything. Coryn took a step toward her. "I don't remember a time in my life when she wasn't there. She fed me and proofed my homework. You can't replace that." She pointed at the fake Paula. "I know they look alike—you had to have done some work to find that body, to make her hair the same. But Paula wasn't a wristlet, or a piece of jewelry." To her utter shame, hot tears gathered in the corners of her eyes. "I don't care if it's breaking the law. Surely there's a copy somewhere. You can get one. You can do anything. You're the great Julianna Lake." She knew she was going to regret her words, but they kept coming out. "You could have let her come with us. She wouldn't have hurt anyone."

Julianna reached a hand out toward Coryn's face.

Coryn slapped at it.

Julianna trapped the arm that had come toward her easily. She turned Coryn so that she looked away and then she trapped Coryn's other arm.

All the force of Coryn's body pointed away from Julianna, her balance tipped away so that only Julianna's strength kept her from falling.

Julianna's body conformed to hers, pressing out and pulling, in ways that kept Coryn from reaching her or from getting away.

Coryn struggled anyway. She tried to kick the older woman, the tears falling now, hot and embarrassing. Nothing she did freed her. Nothing she did hurt Julianna in the least.

Julianna simply stood there, holding Coryn immobile, letting her rage and cry.

Aspen danced around them both, yipping.

She wasn't going to win. She simply looked ridiculous, pinned in place by an old woman's cunning and strength. She took deep trembling breaths. "You can let go now."

"Can I?" Julianna sounded as if she were having a quiet conversation over breakfast. "Do you promise not to hit me again, ever?"

Coryn nodded.

"Say it."

"Yes."

"Yes, what?"

Was Julianna a bully? "Yes, I promise I won't hit you again or hurt you. I'm sorry I did at all. I just don't understand."

"Sit down, and I'll tell you what I can."

"Okay." She probably wasn't a bully. She was rich and powerful and trained. "I'm sorry."

"Don't touch me again, though, not right now."

"I promise."

Julianna let go of Coryn's arm, and Coryn sat on the grass, Aspen wriggling between her legs.

Julianna sat a good five feet away, waiting until Coryn looked at her and said, "All right. Explain."

"Companion-bots are not really your friend. Or at least that's not all they are. If you stay in the city and stay healthy, and you don't do anything suspicious, they *seem to be* your friend. The law says they belong to you, but it also says they must report back to the city's systems."

A rabbit hopped across the lawn, and Aspen pulled away, eager and excited. Coryn started to get up, but Julianna said, "It's okay. He can't catch it; it's faster than he is. There's a fence."

Coryn loosened her hold. With a yelp, the dog shot off her lap, racing after the fleeing rabbit. Coryn watched without really seeing either dog or rabbit. "So what? I always knew she'd report me if I broke certain laws. I mean, that's why kids don't steal candy, right? We reported it when the Listeners were killed. Doing the right thing doesn't make her evil."

"Companion- and assistant-bots are always connected to the city mesh. Distributed nodes take in data from all the city systems. They collect feeds from the water system, from the dome's billions of almost-invisible sensors, from the vertical farms, from the cars and the bikes and the streetlights. The only thing the city doesn't collect data directly from is you. Unless you let it, and then it does that, too."

"Like fitness monitors?"

"More often like *security* systems. Not all of them. But some are marketed by the city departments."

Dog and rabbit had vanished somewhere. "The city always knows where I am." Coryn stood, looking for Aspen. "That was the weird thing about being Outside. No one knew where I was, except Paula."

"Then the city probably *did* know where you were. At least, anytime she was connected back to it and had any priority on the net. The connectivity out there is allocated by priority and small lost girls probably don't have much."

Coryn swallowed at the description, but she said nothing. It was correct.

"And inside the dome, the city knows what you say. Laws protect your privacy from other citizens, but not from the city itself." Julianna looked around. "He'll come back. Don't worry."

It made Coryn nervous not to be able to see her dog. She craned her neck.

Julianna smiled at her and kept going, her confidence only reassuring Coryn a little. "All companion robots report everything. If what you say doesn't matter, the city doesn't care. It dumps the details a few days after the conversation. But it records things that happen to influencers or even that happen near influencers. So Seacouver already knows you've run with me more than once. It's already watching you. If Paula had come with us, the city would know where we are and what we say; neither of us would have any privacy."

Aspen trotted out from under a wide bush with varicolored red and green leaves and tiny white flowers, and Coryn sighed with relief. "Here, Aspen!" He looked at her and started over, so she turned back to Julianna. "Surely the city knows where we are all the time. It knew when I skipped school, even if I left Paula at home."

"It didn't know where either of us were after we entered the tunnels."

Anger about the fake Paula still burned through Coryn, but at least her voice had stopped shaking. "How? Surely you can't keep sensor dust out of the tunnels?"

"We do. We must have been wearing dust on our way in, since that had to have come with the rainclouds, if nothing else. But none of us had live dust by the time we arrived here."

Coryn fell silent, puzzled, waiting for Aspen to come back to her. He didn't, quite. He stopped a few feet short and flopped down on the grass, watching her. Maybe he didn't like to be close to her anger. Someone had told her that once, about dogs. "Did you build the tunnels?"

"Yes."

"Why?"

"So we could be safe from the city if we needed to be. We didn't know what we were creating back then. A self-healing city run by linked smart systems? Billions—billions of billions—of real-time feeds online? Millions of people interacting with a computer every day and not really knowing it, so they'd still be people? No one had ever tried anything like it. So we built physical back doors into the city upgrade plans. We had that power, early on. They're all over Seacouver and here, at least."

Julianna stopped, looking around as if seeing her gardens with fresh eyes. "Not that we need the tunnels in the way we thought we might. We were afraid the city systems might fail. Or attack us. But it works. The city works. Mostly. Everyone has enough to eat and enough power. Almost everyone has a job to do. We still have elites and creatives and entrepreneurs . . ."

Julianna looked proud as she glanced over at Coryn. "I suppose that only makes some sense to you. There are issues. You've seen those. The problems—the deep ones—they're with human psychology, not the infrastructure. We're trying to understand that now. But even though it works, it's smart to have a safe place. The tunnels and our other shielding makes it impossible for the city to watch our every move. It's not stupid, the city." Julianna glanced up, as if the city existed in the sky.

Given that they were in the open and under the dome, that wasn't too far-fetched. Not really. Coryn shivered. What the city really a single entity? Were the cities connected?

"It knows approximately where we are. But it can't hear this conversation. I couldn't bring a part of it—Paula—into this place." She gestured toward the fake Paula. "She's been scrubbed of the usual connections to the city. Every robot in my households has been scrubbed. Any I take outside as guards have not; they need the city connection."

"My Paula was more than a connection to the city."

"Of course she was. And you are more than your bones."

Coryn hesitated. "Maybe we would have been okay if I'd stayed with her."

"Maybe you would have been. But you have to grow up someday." Julianna pointed at Aspen, who watched them both, his eyes flicking back and forth even though his head rested on his crossed paws. "The dog is strange, and probably an impediment. But you love it, and it's worthy of love. A program isn't."

Coryn knew Julianna was right, at least about that last. But refused to let the water pressuring the dam of her resistance break through. She'd lose it if that happened. "What about my sister?"

"That's a good question. I'm trying to find out what happened to her."

"How?"

"I have people—and programs—looking."

"I thought programs were for children."

"Emotional attachment to programs is for children."

That stung. "So half the city is made up of children."

Julianna smiled. "Exactly."

CHAPTER FORTY-TWO

As the second day without Paula dawned, Coryn climbed immediately out of bed. She had to find Lou, which started with finding Julianna and seeing what she knew. Running clothes lay at the foot of her bed: lovely dark green compression pants with pale green highlights and periodic bright white blocks for design, a black bra, and a bright yellow shirt. Clearly printed. They fit her exactly. She stepped into expensive running shoes that conformed to her foot so tightly that she sat for a moment, wriggling her toes, relishing the sensation. No wonder the old woman could outrun her. The shoes and clothes felt so soft and supple they seemed like skin.

Julianna had ordered food for them outside yesterday, and then Coryn had passed out again. From the angle of the light, she had slept all night and through the early morning. She smelled baking bread and followed the scent down a long hallway lined with pictures of animals. She knew the black rhino was long extinct, and one of the types of elephants. Maybe everything on the wall. The pictures were all close-ups, focusing on the animals' structure and beauty, taken in a way that made each seem unique. She remembered the huge herd of buffalo Lou had shown her, and how Lou had said that, in spite of that success, failures beset them.

None of the others were in the kitchen, not even Blessing or Day. Not Julianna. A human woman she had never sat quietly at the end of a large wooden table, as if waiting for her. She had simple features and light brown skin, unremarkable except that there was an ethereal air to her in spite of the obvious muscle that defined her body. Her hair was caught up in a colorful scarf. She looked up and greeted her. "I'm Eloise."

No robots. Even in the orphanage, the servant would have been a robot. But she let Eloise bring her rehydrated food for Aspen and a plate full of toast and eggs and cut-up mango for herself. As she finished, Julianna came in, also dressed in running clothes. "I thought maybe we could run. Are you recovered enough?"

What was this? Boot camp? "Do you know how Lou is?"

Julianna poured two glasses of water. "Let's go outside. Bring some water."

Eloise handed Coryn water and a bag of dog treats, which she tucked into a pocket in her running shirt.

Coryn followed Julianna, suddenly apprehensive. Why were they about to go running instead of finding Lou?

Julianna led them to a small purple table under a dogwood in full bloom. White flowers cascaded around them, the grass underfoot softer than carpet. The air smelled of lilac, and hummingbirds darted through the trees on either side of them. Julianna watched one of the tiny birds for a while, her eyes flicking after it every time it reversed direction. When it flew away, she turned to Coryn. "I've asked about Lou. I was able to verify that the only orders the city has were to allow her to be detained and hidden."

The wording puzzled Coryn. "Orders the city has? Did the city arrest her?"

"The city maintains everyday detentions. I suspect that, in this case, the allowance was for one of the NGOs. I haven't found out yet."

"RiversEnd Ranch, I suspect. Her boss was angry with her. Victor. Do they have Matchiko, too, and Shuska? They're always together, them and Lou, like Blessing and Day."

"Everyone she was with, except you three. Blessing and Day were already mine, as I'm sure you've figured out. It wasn't too hard to ask them to keep you nearby."

Had they? She hadn't felt manipulated. Maybe they had arranged to keep her away from Lou. Maybe they'd even arranged it with Lou, since Lou seemed so distracted. Her sister might have liked that. The thought left a bitter taste in its wake. "I have to find her."

"I have good information systems. I'll let you know when and where she turns up."

"What about the others? Weren't all the gates attacked?"

"All of the attacks failed. It will be forgotten by tomorrow. The news-spinners are already working up other distractions."

Coryn frowned. "So what good did we do?"

"It's too early to tell. Probably not much."

"Do you have other news?"

Julianna pointed up. "See the pair of hummingbirds?"

"They're so fast." The birds were nearly impossible to see as they moved from place to place, so when they stopped to hover it seemed almost like they materialized out of thin air.

"The ecobots are still in town, theoretically being examined to see how they were hacked. I have a better question. How was the city so ready for you?"

She hadn't considered that. "Was it? How do you know?"

"No one got hurt except the two city police that Paula hurt, and one policewoman that fell off an ecobot near a different gate. Fell. No infrastructure was seriously damaged. They even got to test their weather systems." She smiled. "Maybe Paula told the city you were coming."

Paula wouldn't do that. But she had no proof, and never would. "I need Lou. I almost died to find her. More than once. I saw dead people. It was terrible. But if I have to do it all over again, I will."

"Is she worth that?" Julianna watched another hummingbird. "Blessing suggests Lou found your visit inconvenient."

She bit back a gasp. Not that the idea was new, but this confirmation hit deep. "We're sisters. I found it *inconvenient* when she left the city. She found it *inconvenient* when I left it and went to see her. She's still the only family I have."

"I don't have any. Not anymore. But I do have friends."

Coryn just stared at her. She couldn't think of a single person besides Paula and maybe Blessing and Day she'd list as friends. And Blessing and Day had turned out to have hidden agendas, like getting her here. She had thought Julianna might be a friend. She wasn't sure right now. Maybe she didn't have any friends at all.

Damn it. She couldn't think that way. It led down to the ledge her mom had fallen off. The ledge that felt closer without Paula, but that didn't mean she was going to jump off of it. Not her. She took in a deep breath and channeled Blessing as well as she could, pasting a smile on her face and looking polite.

"What matters the most," Julianna said, "is ideas. We haven't saved the earth yet. What was the goal of the great taking?"

"To rewild half the earth to protect biodiversity and mitigate climate change."

"Well." Julianna laughed out loud. "That's the textbook definition."

"Isn't that right?"

"In principle. As we were selling the idea, our nickname for it was 'last-chance lifeline.' The words you just used are sterile, meant to pull the fright and immediacy out of a messy and desperate situation. The fact that whole cities full of people think it's going far better than it is scares the shit out of me."

Coryn almost jumped at the word. Julianna didn't swear.

"We don't have the half-wild yet, we don't even have healthy cities yet. We haven't stopped the extinctions, or the migrations, or the deaths from new tropical diseases born of who-knows-what." She waved a hand around at the gardens. "This is all managed by me and my staff. Everything in the city is managed."

"I know. I used to weed."

"So you understand the concept of invasives?"

"I'm not an idiot," Coryn snapped.

"Sorry." We don't have a just society yet. Your parents died of social ills."

"They killed themselves."

"Because the cities are pretty, but diseased. They're a success—we pulled a lot of people out of places they were poisoning or that had been poisoned by other people. We made the rewilding possible. Some people thrive —we have fabulous art and dance, we have a good space program, we have great sciences. We're healthier than ever, physically. Better."

"Like you."

Julianna tilted her head back and laughed. "I suppose." She smiled at Coryn, an almost-intimate smile. "And you. But only about half the people in the city are thriving. The others?" She took a sip of water and stared at another hummingbird. "Our new diseases are nuanced diseases of the heart and mind; they're loneliness and boredom. Loneliness in a city of billions, boredom with more free education than ever, more things to see and do." She stopped a moment and then took a deep breath before she said, "I researched your parents. They didn't fit anywhere. They tried and tried and they failed. Our suicide rate has been rising since 2010, and you mom and dad were typical of one common cohort."

Coryn stood up, circling the table to dump energy. Aspen followed her, weaving in between her legs; she sidestepped to avoid tripping over him.

Julianna watched the two of them, her face a study in patience.

"Okay." Coryn didn't want to talk about her parents any more. "But not everyone in the city is sick. I know about the failed Auties and the disaffected. Who doesn't? I mean, we see the drones follow them everywhere. And none of us got to the orphanage by having a great life or being one of the rich. In spite of that, I met a lot of kids at school who will be fine, and our old neighbor worked in tech and he loved it. One of my friends from school has a brilliant Autie brother that three tech companies are courting." She sat down again. "A lot of the people I used to ride bikes with—and run with—seemed happy."

Julianna sighed. "Some people have low expectations."

Coryn's voice rose. "There's all the AR. I missed it a lot; it felt great to put it on. And you're fine."

Julianna let a bitter laugh escape before saying, "You're justifying."

Coryn took a deep breath, tried to slow down. "I may not have a lot of friends, but the city has infinite opportunity. I just can't reach it. But I can see it all around me, people succeeding. Look at what you have!"

Julianna made a sour face.

Coryn laughed. "I just don't know how to get to happiness yet. I needed to find Lou first, anyway. She's family."

"You chose to have a barrier between you and most people."

Coryn stopped, unsure what Julianna meant, and then decided it was the same thing the woman couldn't let go of. "Paula?"

Julianna didn't even bother to answer. So yes.

Julianna stood up. "Ready to run? We can talk on our breaks."

Coryn glanced down at her empty glass. Julianna obviously didn't understand what Paula meant to her. Being without her was like going through a day with half of herself missing.

"Leave your glass."

"I'm used to cleaning up after myself."

Julianna didn't bother to reply.

She didn't feel like running at this moment. Julianna had always disappeared on her. She had always come back, but what if she left today and didn't come back for weeks? Coryn had so many questions. She swallowed and tried to figure out where to start. "Can I leave here if I want to?"

"Yes."

"Don't you have robots?"

"As few as possible. I use them for guards when I run outside in the city. Only a fool would expect human guards to save her from an attack by robots."

"I bet you use robots to guard this place, too."

Julianna hesitated. "Point."

"Paula kept me safe for years."

"You needed her when you were three," Julianna snapped. She took off, starting slow.

Coryn hesitated.

If she didn't run with Julianna, she might not see her again.

It took Coryn a full five minutes to catch up. The path was just wide enough for the two of them, a soft pale-yellow surface that looked brand new. The conforming shoes felt light on her feet and took impact well. They *did* make her feel faster.

They ran silently for a while. They were naked—no AR, no electronics. Since no robots followed them, they must be on Julianna's—what had she called it? A compound. It wasn't an infinitely large space; after about a mile it became clear they were doing a circle as they passed in front of the table again. Their water glasses had been filled, but they didn't stop yet. As they started the third mile, Julianna said, "I'm sorry. I know you must be worried about your sister."

"Of course I am."

"Tell me about her."

They slowed to an easy talking pace. Lou was so much. How could she describe her? "She used to hang pictures on her bedroom walls, kind of like the ones you have on your hallway wall. Only scraps of paper, not framed. Extinct animals, threatened animals." A bird flew up in front of them, startling her, and she laughed at the timing. "She used to brush my hair and braid it." Lou had brushed her hair for hours that night in the farmhouse, that first night, even though she'd said she didn't have time. "She was always tough, but she's become something more now. She can tell powerful people what to do. I mean powerful for the Outside. Not like you." She was rambling; she had to bring it back in. "She's passionate about animals, and about things being fair. We had an argument over my last junior high school paper. She said the rewilding was failing, and I thought it wasn't."

"What do you think now?"

"She was right." The path turned, and she had to call Aspen off a lawn and back into place beside her. "But that's not what matters. What if Lou gets hurt or she loses her job? It would kill her to be stuck on basic in the city. That works for some but not for her. Not for me, either. I couldn't think of what to do even though I wanted to stay in the city." She stopped talking to catch her breath and take a drink. "It's not okay if she gets hurt. I have to protect her."

"Why?"

"If I don't do it, who will?"

"When you're older, you'll understand that not everything gets done."

"This is my sister!" Anger drove up her spine, shooting a rush of speed down her legs; she surged ahead of Julianna for the first time ever. She stayed ahead for a long time, forcing it, feeling the pain. The sound of Julianna's footsteps faded behind her. True, it might be the rasping of her own breath that hid the older woman's steps, but it surprised her; she slowed a little. When Julianna drew near her, she noticed tears on her cheeks.

She hadn't though the woman *could* cry. "What's the matter?"

"It's the little things that matter. I used to know that. That's what that picture gallery is for. To remind me of things we've lost, things we've stolen." Julianna paused as they neared a corner, jogging in place. "But when you stay involved in the big politics for years, when you care about *all* the species instead of one of the species, you forget the politics of family and the individual elephants."

"Is it all politics?"

"That's not what I meant to say. I meant to say it's all about the little things."

This time Coryn managed to bank her anger so it didn't translate into her calves, into running away. "Saving Lou is not a small thing."

Julianna stayed silent for a long time, and whenever Coryn glanced over at her she saw the tears continuing in a slow stream, controlled, but present nonetheless.

They reached the table again, now at the end of the seventh mile. This time, Julianna came to a stop.

Refilled water glasses and food had been set out for them: figs, potatoes, peeled eggs, and bananas. The older woman sank into her chair, her words rasping from her throat. "I'm sorry."

Coryn drank her water, waited.

"I love ideas. I've always loved ideas. That's how we started Seacouver, with ideas about seawalls and shared green infrastructure and shared commerce where no one could out-vote or out-tax our needs." Julianna's voice calmed, her face softened. "Those were all ideas. But implementing them cost us. Maybe I lost so many people I forgot what it's like to love a single person."

Coryn nodded and started peeling a banana. "What are you going to do about it?"

"Add resources."

"What resources?"

"Will you trust me?"

Coryn finished her banana in silence. "Not until you trust me. Withholding information doesn't show trust. I can't trust you if you don't trust me."

Julianna picked at a purple fig, exposing the deep mauve pulp and tiny dark seeds inside. "There are some things I can't tell anybody."

"You knew Lou and the ecobots were coming in. You had to, or you wouldn't have had a plan in place to get us out. Did you also know they would be stopped and captured?"

Julianna sucked at the fig and wiped her chin before she answered. "I didn't suggest that they come in. If I'd been there, I'd have told them they didn't know enough to go in anyway."

"Lou wouldn't have listened. I don't know anything—she doesn't trust me either—not anymore—but she was following a plan. I think it was cooked up by Victor, and by other people that worked in other parts of the wilding. Someone gave them an all clear but I don't know who." Coryn stood to stretch, trying to think through the possibilities. Someone above Lou was directing this. Was that Victor? Or someone above him? "Maybe the Foundation people sold her out. Victor, her boss. He seemed to hate her."

Julianna smiled softly. "Blessing is almost trained, and he didn't put it as well when he tried to explain what happened. But he did say Victor was jealous of Lou, that he has been for a long time. Blessing used to work with Lou."

"I know. Isn't the Foundation running the wilding? Why would they tell Lou to come in and then sell her out?"

"*They* didn't. The people who work in the field, like Lou, are fierce. They want to save the world. The people who live in the city and run the NGOs are a mixed bag. Heroes and villains."

"Lou said something like that."

"Some people with power are ruthless. The people who started the foundations were old when that happened, way back when we made Seacouver together. They were allies. They cared a lot—they were all heroes. Big ones. They spent huge personal fortunes to save all of us. They could have built private enclaves and let the poor die off, but they didn't." She picked up another fig, holding it up and admiring it. "Most of them are dead now. In some cases, the heirs don't understand what their parents did. So maybe someone in the field bragged about the protest, and it got upstream and they decided to stop it, or maybe Victor wanted Lou out of the way so she wasn't a threat to him. Something happened, but I don't know what. Not yet."

"Lou fought with Jeremiah Allen at the gates."

"Did you hear what they said?"

"No."

"Too bad."

There was so much to learn. Coryn let a long silence go by. "Is Day?"

"Is Day what?"

"Trained. You told me Blessing is almost trained. Is Day all the way trained? He seems so sure of himself."

She laughed. "Day has worked for me since he was ten. He's one of my best; I notice the quiet ones. He thinks the hackers might be the problem. That maybe they took the NGOs money and sold them down the river."

How many other Lous had been captured? Was there someone like her with every convoy of ecobots at every gate? And if she spun out the conflicts in her head, how many were loyal like Lou and how many were really part of the group that meant to attack the cities and bring them down? And that, of course, forced her to confront the idea head on. "Could someone really take a city down?"

"Enough people might." Julianna reached for a towel and dipped it in water to wash her face. "There's a lot of fail-safes, but then there's a lot of hackers out there, too. Every city depends on programmers. That's why they're our elite. Programmers are the architects of our infrastructure."

"I never wanted to hurt a city."

"I didn't either. Don't either. I built the damned things—at least Seacouver—and in some small ways, this one."

There was so much to think about. She lifted her hands over her head, feeling the stretch in her back and sides. "What about the silent army?

When I was with the Listeners, we stopped by this long line of people who were on their way to Seacouver. I think one of the Listeners went with them. I never figured out what they were trying to do. Do you know?"

"No."

Coryn stopped stretching. "Can we walk? I don't want to get cold yet." Aspen waited at her heels, looking up at her.

In answer, Julianna stood and started walking along the mile loop.

Coryn watched the rigid back in front of her for a few paces, then sped up to move alongside, where she could see the other woman's face. "No one ever told me. They called them a silent army. They were on their way to get into the city peacefully."

"Well, that can be done, you know. The dome isn't impermeable."

"But the dome registers every entrance and exit, right? No matter what?"

"Yes."

Coryn picked up her pace, still walking, but far faster. "Back to Lou. If you had to guess, where do you think she is?"

"She's might be in the main jail, but I can't verify. Not yet."

"If she is there, will you help me get her free?"

Julianna cast a raised eyebrow at her, eyes widening. "You want me to break her out of jail?"

"Well." Coryn glanced at Julianna. Her eyes lit with a strange delight Coryn hadn't seen there before. This must be what she loved—figuring out how to manipulate things. She hadn't been in office for a long time, but clearly she had a lot of power and contacts.

"Yes," Coryn said. "I do want you to help me break her out of jail."

CHAPTER FORTY-THREE

Coryn walked out of her post-run shower into a glorious early afternoon complete with sunshine and a light, city-sanctioned breeze. Blessing, Day, and Julianna were laughing together at the same table she and Julianna had used earlier. The water glasses had been replaced and a new pitcher set out by fresh bowls of nuts and fruit.

The snacks alone would have been a week's food allowance on her student budget.

Coryn really wanted some time alone to think about what else she needed to know, but when Julianna waved her over, she went. Aspen trotted at her heels and curled into a quiet ball by her feet, watching for treats or crumbs to drop from the sky. "Do you have any news about Lou?"

Julianna stopped laughing and looked serious. "No. I'll tell you if I learn anything. Willing to debrief?"

"Debrief?"

"I'd like to hear your story. I want to know all the details of what happened while you were Outside."

Didn't Julianna already know? Clearly she had talked with both Blessing and Day, and clearly she had been both getting reports and giving instructions to both of them. "Mostly, I just tried to get myself killed," she said, as airily as possible. She waved a hand toward Blessing and Day. "And these two saved me at least once. I kind of stumbled my way to Lou, and then I played bad detective trying to figure out what she was up to, and then I joined a revolution I didn't know much about, got rescued from that, and managed to get separated from my sister all over again."

Blessing grinned at her as she talked. She hadn't decided what to think about him, again or maybe even still, and it made her stumble over her words. She was trying to be funny, but in spite of his smile, the look on his face suggested she wasn't managing it. "And I lost my companion, who I should never have taken Outside in the first place. So I don't really see how there's much to talk about."

Blessing spoke before anyone else could. "Perhaps you bravely left the safety of the cloying and difficult city to find your only family member. From there, you survived natural dangers like windstorms and tornadoes, had the good luck to be rescued from a dangerous warlord who tried to capture your steady and faithful companion robot, made friends with the Listeners who rescued you, and acted as a secret spy for them. You made friends along the road—" He grinned and pointed at himself and Day. "—And then discovered your employers—the Listeners—had been brutally murdered." He stopped for a sip of water and then continued, exaggerating his dramatic delivery. "But wait—there's more! After you discovered the brutal murder, you took on extra responsibility and adopted the murdered Listeners' abandoned dog. In spite of the dangers you'd already encountered, you kept searching for your sister. You got captured by a dangerous retro-religious hacker gang that treats women like second-class citizens. But your faithful companions—" He waved at himself and Day again. "—and your long-lost sister saved you just in the nick of time. Even though you found your sister at the worst possible time for her, you convinced her to let you come along, and you joined her well-coordinated attack on the city."

She couldn't help but laugh at him.

He rose, throwing out his arms in a sweeping gesture. "But little did any of you know, the notorious hacker had other plans, and he betrayed your sister and many others for the sake of money, paid to him by evil people in power. You were rescued by your friends once again, in order to fight on."

Despite herself, she burst out laughing in earnest.

"See why I keep him around?" Julianna said. "But really, even though the truth has to be in between those two stories, I'd like to hear the details. Who did you meet? What happened? It might help us figure some things out. Are you willing?"

She wondered if that made her more like Blessing and Day than she wanted to be, but she nodded. "Sure."

Julianna took her through question after question, lingering on the dynamics in the schoolhouse, and on everything about the Listeners. "Pablo. Did you get his last name?"

"No."

"Did he seem to be in charge?"

"Lucien seemed to be in charge. At least he was the person who talked to me the most, except for Liselle, and Liselle was only a few years older than me." The memory hurt.

"Pablo wasn't killed?"

"He left the caravan long before that. He went with the silent army, in disguise."

"Are you sure?"

"Yes, although Lucien tried to convince me he didn't."

Julianna used a slate to show her a number of pictures. She identified Lucien, Liselle, and even Bartholomew before she found Pablo. She smiled when she saw him, remembering that he had seemed friendly. "That's him."

"You're sure."

"I'm sure."

"And he got away?"

"Yes. You don't have to ask me twice."

Julianna smiled. "Sorry. I'm just relieved."

Coryn leaned forward. "Tell me more about Bartholomew."

"When we get there. I want to go through your story in order, so we don't miss anything."

It took another hour to get to Bartholomew. When they finally got there, Coryn walked through everything, including talking about what it felt like to be in the tent guarded by an armed man and to think she was about to die. By the time she finished that story, her hands and voice shook. "Do you think they would have killed me?" she asked Julianna.

Day spoke up. "They killed a friend of mine a few years ago." He said it in his usual flat tone, but Coryn heard the slight stutter in it.

She touched his hand. "I'm sorry."

He smiled back at her. "I'm glad they didn't kill you."

"What would they have done with the body?" Blessing asked.

Julianna gave him a withering look, and no one answered.

Coryn cleared her throat. "Bartholomew. Tell me about Bartholomew."

To her surprise, Day was the one who answered. But maybe, because of his friend, he knew the most. "First, that's not his name. People think he's Mike Smith, only he didn't want to be anything so ordinary. So he took on a saint's name—Bartholomew was one of the disciples. Are you familiar with the Bible?"

"Only a little."

"Well, I don't think *Bartholomew* is either. But he likes the idea of a patriarchy, and you can't have that inside the cities any more. So he made one. I don't know why his followers put up with it, except maybe because he's such a brilliant hacker people have paid him a lot of money for a long time. Some of his male followers are techs, too. He has a reputation for being brilliant and for never talking to anyone about who hires him. He also has a less well-known reputation for taking money from more than one client who may have conflicting interests."

"So then why do people pay him?"

"Because he can do things they can't. Systems are pretty complex, and he can get into some that the best cracking programs can't. There aren't very many humans who can outdo programs anymore."

She reached for a handful of nuts. "And the people who would prefer a human are the bad guys, right?"

Day smiled at her. "No. But they're rebels. Anyone fighting the city. But, as we know, the city may need to be fought, or at least some people in the city may need to be fought. That's a talk over a beer. Yes, he would have killed you, but the Foundation probably needed him to get the ecobots into the city."

Julianna interrupted. "Assuming the protest was a good idea at all. But it wasn't."

"There's that." Day raised an eyebrow, looking a little comical about it.

"Well," Blessing asked Julianna, "what would you have done in Lou's shoes? She didn't know much, and she was being fed a mix of truth and lies and sent off to be a hero."

"I'm not blaming Lou." Julianna directed Coryn back to the hour-by-hour recital and seemed really interested in the eagles and the buffalo and everything Lou had said about how the cities weren't supporting the wilding enough for it to succeed.

After she got through the part where Bartholomew suggested he might have control of utilities, Julianna took a long look at Coryn. "Take a break. Have dinner. Sleep. We'll finish this after our run tomorrow."

Dinner? Coryn blinked up at the sky, amazed to see how low the sun was. "You really do run every day," she said.

Julianna grinned. "Almost. I have a feeling there will be a few days coming up when it's hard to run." She got up quickly, and was gone.

‡ ‡ ‡

They didn't see Julianna again that night. Eloise called them to dinner and fed them salads and huge slabs of vat-grown meat and even a glass of wine each. Afterward, Coryn took Aspen out, slightly dizzy from her first wine.

The garden smelled almost cloying, and Aspen raced in circles around her feet, periodically stopping and simply putting his head up and taking in deep breaths. "I can only imagine what this must smell like to you," she told him.

"Coryn? Can we talk?"

She turned to find Blessing walking across the lawn toward her. She still wasn't ready to talk to him alone. Not yet. She let him come without giving him an answer, but as soon as he was close enough to hear, she spoke. "You lied to me. You said you were from Outside, and all along you were working for Julianna, taking notes for her, pretending to be one thing and not being that at all."

He grinned. "I was born Outside. I already told you that. I never promised to have always been there. Think back carefully."

She glared at him. "Your smile isn't going to save you."

His smile merely widened.

"Maybe this is your day to die," she said. She wanted to hold onto her righteous anger, but the overstatement of it made her grin, and then laugh. "Why did you do it?"

"Why did you spy for the Listeners?"

"They asked me to." Aspen started chasing a rabbit, barking at the top of his lungs, and Coryn sped after him. Blessing passed her, scooping the little dog up.

"You and those damned long legs."

"You kept up pretty good on the bike."

"Don't complement me, you asshole."

He handed her the dog. "I didn't come out here to argue. I have something serious to ask you."

"Okay."

"Can we sit down?"

She didn't really want to sit next to him. Part of her wanted to hit him, and the other part to hold him and be held by him. She didn't want the weaker part to win. She followed him to a white-filigreed bench anyway. Why were men so difficult?

The tiny pink roses surrounding the bench released a soft, sweet scent into the warm air. Blessing sat sideways, gazing at her. At least that helped her keep a little distance. "I want to get a better look at the data on your wristlet," he said. "I suspect Matchiko still has a copy, but I want to look as well. I want to be sure we understood everything."

She held her wrist against her heart, sheltered behind her other hand. "Why?"

"Partly a hunch. But back in the barn, I wasn't as sure those were ecobot schematics as everyone else was. Or at least, I'm not sure that's all you took pictures of—I saw a few things that looked like ledgers and maybe even programs. It has to be important, since they were keeping it on paper."

She tucked her knees up inside her arms and stared up at the sky turning pink and purple above them. "Can I give it to you in the morning?"

"I don't know if we'll be here. I just want to make a copy. I'll give you back your wristlet right away. Five minutes."

She swallowed, still watching the sky. It was easier than watching his face. She unbuckled her wristlet, still without really looking at him.

He took it, and then he reached toward her face.

She flinched.

He stopped. "I didn't mean any harm. I had already turned around to see if I could get you to Lou safely before Julianna recognized you and gave me orders to get you back to her. You just seemed like a nice kid who needed help, even if you did have your robot. You were both naive."

She swallowed. Why did he have to say that?

"And I shouldn't have said it that way. I really like you. A lot. I'm glad we're both here. I never meant to lie to you."

She swallowed, a lump in her throat. "Please, just go copy the data."

"Can I take it off, too? Just for safety?"

She stiffened. "Are you going to copy all of my personal data?"

"No. Just the pictures. They might get you in trouble."

"Damn you. Okay."

He stood up. "It'll only take ten minutes."

"You said five."

"I'll be back soon."

The sky turned from pink to a bright magenta, then to a blinding gold that stunned the bottoms of the clouds. Just as the last color started fading, Blessing came back. He handed her the wristlet.

She took it. It didn't look any different. "It's okay," she said. "You taught me a lot. I forgive you. But I want you to promise something."

He whispered. "Okay."

"Never lie to me again."

"I never did lie to you."

"Promise."

"I promise."

CHAPTER FORTY-FOUR

Just to the right of a dogwood that hung over the patio table, two bright green hummingbirds fought over a crimson rhododendron flower. "Isn't there enough for them both?" she asked Julianna, leaning on the table while she caught her breath. They were back in the same place after another night with no word about Lou and another morning run. Julianna still hadn't promised to rescue Lou, although Coryn was sure she would. Not that she had any idea why she was sure.

"Nature—and humans—fight for resources even when they don't need to." Julianna reached for another fig. Her wristlet screen lit up with pulsing red light. It looked angry. She dropped the fig, frowned, and tilted her wrist so Coryn couldn't read the screen. As she stared at it, her face hardened.

"Is it about Lou?"

Julianna shook her head.

LeeAnne, Blessing, and Day emerged from behind a lilac tree, striding purposefully toward them. They wore regular clothes and looked clean and deadly serious. Even Blessing wasn't smiling. Julianna stood and paced out of earshot, whispering at her wristlet.

Coryn tapped her own wristlet for news, hoping to learn something before the other three arrived.

Alerts scrolled up the tiny screen in a multitude of reds and yellows. She popped one up and her mouth dropped open.

Portland Metro's gates had been breached again, only this time the ecobots *were* firing on people. Killing people. Regular people? Police? The news reports were confusing. The tiny pictures didn't tell her if they were the same ecobots they had ridden on.

She thumbed quickly through headline after headline, popping up a bigger virtual screen so she could read a few paragraphs here and there. Border guards had died, police had died, ecobots and city enforcer bots had been destroyed. Someone had shot Jeremiah Allen—she couldn't tell if he was dead or in the hospital or okay.

People in power were seriously angry. Rich people.

Poorer people were migrating inward from the edges of both Portland

and Vancouver, crowding streets, carrying belongings. A crowd had trampled a little girl in the Rose District in Portland, killing her in spite of a valiant attempt by her companion-bot to save her. Screens flipped by too fast to catch details.

Most of the news here came from Portland, but a few stories came through from Seacouver. The dome had stopped working on the eastern edge.

Julianna paced, still talking into her wristlet and periodically pawing it with her right index finger.

The other three reached the table, faces grim. Day—the usually silent and watchful Day—spoke first after Blessing took half a step to the side and yielded him the stage. "The same hackers who captured you—and others like them—have gathered Returners and hackers and wanderers and the silent army you reported and some of the people from the smaller towns like Cle Elum and Yakima where there's not enough economy to feed everyone. Probably half the nearby population of Outside." He paused, waiting for her to absorb it. After a few breaths, he blurted, "They've come in to do damage."

"There can't be that many of them, can there?" The city had billions of people and a lot of security.

"It depends on how many people they've recruited."

"Recruited?"

Day's voice sounded sad. "Recruited from within."

Oh. She sank down in one of the chairs. Would the city's own people attack it? Hard to imagine. Of course *she* had attacked *Portland*, kind of.

Would Julianna attack her own creation? There was no way to answer that.

LeeAnne said, "Jeremiah Allen is dead, I think."

"What about Mary Large? Is she dead, too?"

Day wrinkled his face a little, like the question surprised him and he had to adjust to it. "I think I'd have heard. She's more famous than Jeremiah."

Good. In spite of the small fracas at the gate, Coryn wanted her to be okay. She liked her singing. "Why attack so hard? They still can't win, can they?"

Day looked past her. He often did that, as if it was easier for him to think if he weren't looking directly at whoever he was talking to. "I bet they want to do exactly what they are doing. They want to make the cities panic."

Coryn realized she was rocking in her chair, and that she wanted Paula. She stood up to dispel both feelings. She couldn't afford nerves, and her companion was gone forever. "What do they want?"

"What have terrorists always wanted? They want to scare the city."

She sat down again. Terrorism was an old term. But she knew what it meant: an attempt to spread fear and mayhem. Terrorism had been a cause and casualty of the creation of the megacities. It happened, sometimes, in other places. Never here. "Is the news calling them terrorists?"

"They're starting to."

Blessing stepped closer to Coryn, almost touching her. She could feel his closeness like electricity on her skin. "Are you okay?" he asked.

"I need my sister."

"Then I think you should go get her." Julianna's voice came from behind her. Coryn turned; Julianna had finally put the phone down. "I just got the message. She's being detained, but not in the main jail."

Coryn felt a jolt, as if she needed to go right then. Lou was okay. Probably. "Is she okay?"

Julianna looked almost as pleased as Coryn felt. "I think so. I'll give you all the coordinates, and Day will bring weapons. He is a weapon as well; he'll surprise you."

"What?" Day? A weapon?

"I have to do other things. I promised I'd help you break your sister out. I will. I'll send you with three of my staff—" She nodded at Blessing, Day, and LeeAnne. "The four of you should be enough. If you need more resources, Day can reach me anywhere, and Blessing and LeeAnne both know how to leave messages for me."

Coryn closed her gaping mouth. "Thank you."

"Go," Julianna said. To Coryn's utter surprise, she gave each of them a hug.

She saved Coryn for last. Coryn clutched her back hard, inhaling the scent of clean sweat and figs. "Stay safe," Julianna whispered in her ear. "And come back. Remember that you're here on a temporary chit and you need to get back to me. Or get out through a gate."

"Okay."

"Leave Aspen. You'll be conspicuous with a little white dog."

It made sense. She knew it. She wanted to resist, but she forced a nod out. "Okay. Thank you."

"I'll take care of him."

"Can I have him back?"

Julianna glanced at Aspen. "I don't want the silly thing."

Coryn smiled.

Julianna looked *into* her, a long, hard look that stripped Coryn bare. "Thank you for reminding me that you matter." Before Coryn could answer, she turned around and ran up the path at full speed.

Blessing gave her a hard, fast, sideways hug. "We'll find your sister. Between us, we know a lot."

She looked up at him and smiled. "Let's hurry."

LeeAnne started off in the same direction Julianna had gone, walking fast. "Eloise is packing for us."

Aspen yipped. Coryn picked him up, snuffling his fur. "I'll come back," she whispered. "I'll see you again." She glanced at Day. "You know where Lou is?"

"It's already been sent to your wristlet," Blessing said. "She's in a safe house in the Pearl District, down by the river. It's just an hour away, and it should be a pretty easy place to get her out of. Compared to the main jail, anyway. *That* would have taken an assault force."

"Are we riding?"

LeeAnne grinned. "Whenever I can."

Coryn could already hear her thighs complaining. She glanced at Aspen and then smiled back at LeeAnne. "I'm ready."

"We need to leave in an hour. I want to finish this before dark."

"I told you. I'm ready."

CHAPTER FORTY-FIVE

After a full hour of furious riding through tight quarters they halted near a metal door. A few other bikes lay tangled against the wall beside it. LeeAnne dismounted first. "Leave the bikes."

Coryn took a long drag on her water bottle. They'd just finished a long climb in the near dark inside of the tunnel, and she could hear her breathing more loudly than any of the others. They stacked all four bikes just past the others that were already there, keeping them close to the wall.

A light above the door glowed red, then orange. LeeAnne leaned into the door. The light went back to red, then orange, then green. LeeAnne swung it open.

They came out beside a small square building in a park. Shade trees surrounded the building, their shadows long in the afternoon sun. Although the excited giggles and squeals of children playing came from nearby, the path near the door was empty.

Coryn leaned over to LeeAnne. "How many entrances are there?"

"That would be giving away secrets." LeeAnne fastened the door shut. It didn't look much like a door from this side, more like a decoration; there was no obvious handle, and a mural of two placid deer had been hammered into the metal. "We don't have any tunnels that cross the river. We add to the network with big street projects, but there's been no excuse to get under the river. There's no bridge big enough for a secret tunnel inside of it. Besides, the city needs to know who crosses its bridges."

Did that mean the city helped build other places that were shielded from it? Sometimes she thought of Seacouver as a single entity, but of course it couldn't be, nor this city or any other. More like an aggregation of constantly changing systems. "Are we in the Pearl District?"

Blessing laughed. "No." He started down the path, and when they emerged into light, he pointed downward. "The Pearl is by the water. At least it's all downhill."

Some of the land below them was already in shadow, although light still sparkled on the river and the far side of the bridges that crossed the river that cut Portland in two, the Willamette. The PV bridge, of course, crossed the wider Columbia. "Do we have a plan?"

"It starts with surveillance." He pulled her to a stop while they waited for Day and LeeAnne. "Tell me what you see," Blessing asked her, his voice low.

"Children." She'd heard them, but now she could see them on a wooden play structure with bright blue nets just to the right. Two companion-bots stood talking to each other while watching the children. "The companions mean its safe right here. Everything looks pretty calm, until I look farther away. I see smoke. Is it from the fire by the Camas Gate?"

"I think that's closer." He pointed. "Camas is pretty far that way."

"It's still on the far side of the bridge." The PV bridge was easily the most visible landmark, rising three times as high as the other four bridges she could see, and twisting through the sky on only a few supports. She closed her eyes for a moment. Paula had died there. "She was just a thing," Coryn muttered under her breath.

Blessing must have understood what she meant since he gave her a quick hug. "What else do you see?"

"I see drones." She spotted them as much by the bright flashes of sunlight winking in strange places in the air as anything else. "But I don't hear them. I hear sirens. And I don't know how busy it usually is . . ."

Day came up behind her. "People are scared. The fighting is on the far side of the river. So far. We've picked a route. When we leave the park, I want to look like two couples. So hold hands and talk to each other."

"I'm horrified." Blessing arched an eyebrow and pulled her closer to him. He kissed her forehead, leaned down and whispered, "You are even more beautiful than Lou. And that says a lot. We'll find her."

"I'm not nearly as strong as Lou."

"No one is. But you are strong."

She shook her head at his utterly inappropriate comments and pulled a little away, but reached for his hand. It felt warm. His fingers were so much longer than hers that they curled around her hand. She liked how they looked together.

As they started down the hill, a cool breeze hit them directly in the face, stinking of river and fish. Blessing said, "You'll know we're getting near the Pearl District when you see signs for artists' lofts and performance poetry and when we're surrounded by big old brick buildings."

The streets were quite empty. She reached for her wristlet, but Blessing stopped her. "If there's news we need to know, Day will get it. You and I should pay attention to what's going on around us."

"I never even see Day reaching for a device."

Blessing smiled a little smile that seemed to indicate that he had a secret about Day and devices.

"Don't keep secrets from me," she whispered.

"I tell you all I can."

She managed to squeeze his hand instead of kicking him in the shins. Since they were supposed to be a couple.

A dog ran across the road in front of them, tugging a small boy behind it on a red leash. They passed an older man hobbling downhill, and five bicycles passed them sweating uphill. Otherwise, the streets were pretty empty. They were also steep enough she had to pay attention to walking.

Hopefully Lou was okay. Hopefully Lou was wherever they were going. "Do you know who has Lou?" she asked. "Do we know if she's okay?"

"We're not sure of anything that I know of." Blessing squeezed her hand. "Julianna will tell us if she learns anything important."

A staccato series of explosions popped off in the distance, the sounds directionless, diffuse, and startling. Coryn stepped closer to Blessing.

"Guns," he said.

Only the police were allowed guns with bullets in the city. And they didn't use them much. "Where did they come from?"

"Gunshots are hard to read."

Day and LeeAnne came up on either side of them. "Julianna sent a message," said Day. "They're bringing some captives from this fight into the same safe house where Lou is being kept."

Blessing smiled. "Do I smell a possible moment of chaos?"

Day grinned back, the easy friendship between the two men visible again in this moment. "Yes, it could provide an opportunity. It's not a house, it's a loft. There's a sniper on the roof."

What were they going to do about a sniper? She shivered. "Doesn't the city know who and where we are? How do we sneak up on a safe house? Or get past a sniper?" She shivered, her excitement as the idea of rescuing Lou shifting to cold fear.

He smiled softly. His voice was low but full of a deep humor she hadn't heard from him before. "Of course it knows. We've got a team working to help it think we're no danger at all. So be careful what you talk about where the city can hear."

"Yes sir. I'll watch my mouth." How many people were always trying to manipulate the city, anyway? "You keep talking like the city is one being, like it's a big robot or something."

"It's not," LeeAnne said. "I know. I talk to it all the time. It's a million million connected systems and almost as many rules that tell those systems what to do. It's hackable because it's *not* one thing, but from the outside, to a normal person, it appears to have one face."

That was a long speech for LeeAnne. A set of police drones whizzed by above their heads, small sirens warning them to look away.

The ground leveled out below them. Day almost whispered, "The streets will probably be more crowded as we get closer. The building is coming up on our right. We're going to walk in front of it like we're on our way to somewhere else, and we won't look up unless a sound gives us a good excuse. Stay ready for anything."

She tried to walk quietly and notice everything. They passed a French restaurant, a bar full of people watching news videos and dancing, which seemed utterly improbable while the city was under attack. A silent car crossed in front of them and went on.

Another car came toward them, its lights already on in the dusky street.

She couldn't tell which building. Day and LeeAnne were behind her and Blessing, so she didn't get any cues from them. She was afraid to look up, but wanted to. What would she see anyway? The tiny barrel of a gun three stories up? Probably not.

She tried to sense her sister. It did no good.

The quiet dull hum of surveillance drones grew a little louder right above them.

Three men loitered near a streetlight, all of them wearing blue uniforms. Not police; more likely some kind of utility worker. As they walked past, Coryn raised her hand and gave a little wave, and the tallest of the three waved back.

"Ignore them," Day whispered, closer behind her than she'd thought. "You want to be background on cams."

Were these buildings lofts? They were square and two to four stories and had big windows. The lofts she knew about in Seacouver were on the tops of big buildings, and only the super-rich lived in them. People like Julianna.

The car stopped one building in front of them and two uniformed police officers climbed out. Blessing let go of her hand.

One of the officers opened the back door, and the other held a gun on the door. Two more officers appeared as if from nowhere and stood in front of her and Blessing, stopping them. "Hold on just moment, Miss Williams."

"Of course." He had used her name.

LeeAnne and Day had stopped right behind them.

Blessing pulled her a little bit to the side.

A man in a restraining shirt slid awkwardly out of the car. Bartholomew's second. Whatever his name was. Milan.

The coincidence stunned her.

The officer in front of them wasn't watching the car, just them. He stood casually, smiling.

Drones she had neither seen nor heard poured from a window in the building and more swooped out of the sky.

The officer looked up. Then he crumpled down to the hard sidewalk as if all if the structure had come out of him. Day leaned down and caught his head so he didn't crack it, an expert, fluid move.

Day hadn't touched him before he fell. He hadn't even really moved.

Every other officer looked up, but Day and Blessing focused on the street level, so Coryn tried to watch what they watched.

The uniformed man guarding Milan pulled him toward the building. One of the drones tagged the guard with a shot, and he fell to the ground. A door opened, and a man came out and helped Milan into the building.

Coryn winced, wanting to duck and cover her head, but Blessing tugged hard on her hand and they raced toward the building.

Day flattened against a wall and gestured for them to do the same. A door to the left opened, spilling out more uniformed people. Not the door Milan had gone in through.

Day's eyes flicked back and forth as if counting the people leaving. LeeAnne watched the sky.

Coryn was certain attentions would shift to them any minute. Instead, two more cars pulled up, tires screeching.

Blessing stayed flat against the wall, looking forward.

She copied him.

Some magic number had been reached; Day slid through the door. Blessing pushed her after him and then came right behind. LeeAnne came in last, pulling the door shut behind her.

CHAPTER FORTY-SIX

As they entered the building, Coryn searched frantically for threats to avoid. Maybe a guard, or a drone about to blow her down into a boneless fall just like the two men outside.

Nothing.

They stood in a dimly lit hallway with concrete stairs leading up and a single black metal rail with peeling paint. The brick walls were completely bare. The only light came from dim bulbs recessed in the ceiling.

Muffled noises spilled in from outside—shouts and gunshots and engines. Nothing she could make sense of.

LeeAnne took the front this time, Blessing next, then Coryn, and Day at the rear. They went up fast but quiet, up a flight of stairs, turning to climb another flight, up again.

Just after they turned the second corner, a small camera drone buzzed LeeAnne's head. Blessing—a full head taller than the rest of them—grabbed it with his right hand and smashed it against the outside wall. A trickle of blood dripped from his palm.

"You okay?" she asked.

"So far."

She giggled softly, nervous.

LeeAnne stopped twice to listen at doors. Both times Day waved her forward from below. Coryn decided the two of them could talk to each other telepathically, or with signals or some other tool invisible to everyone else. Either that, or they'd been working together so long that it only took the smallest gestures to give each other paragraphs of information.

They came to the top of the highest flight of stairs, which was bounded by two doors. One had a window in it that looked out on a roof patio, and the other was different from the entrance doors to the other stories . . . metallic and reinforced. It looked thick.

Coryn leaned close to Day and whispered, "Is there a sniper out there?"

"Not anymore." LeeAnne pulled on a leather glove and tugged something small out of her pocket. She aimed it at the door lock, which glowed red and melted. She hit the glowing knob with her fisted leather-clad hand,

and the knob clattered to the floor; her glove sizzled, a trail of chemical-laden smoke puffing from it. LeeAnne ignored the smoke and used the same hand to pull open the door. A scream escaped though the opening, and a raised voice answered.

A drone slipped over the top of the doorway. Blessing slapped this one as well. It bobbled. A second slap sent it careening down the stairs. Pieces broke off and the whine of its engine stuttered and then stopped.

The loud voices came from straight ahead. Day slid past them all and took the lead, walking with his hands fisted. He carried something in each hand, but she couldn't tell what. Now Blessing walked behind her, LeeAnne in front. They sped up, and she nearly stumbled as she worked to keep her place in line.

Day clearly had an objective in mind; he didn't hesitate as they passed the first two doors.

Blood pounded through Coryn's heart and drummed in the tips of her fingers.

The hallway opened up into a huge room with a wall of covered windows. Two people argued with each other, the voices clear now. A tall, broad-shouldered man leaned over a much smaller, older woman, saying, "—can't leave. Orders!"

An equally strong man shifted his head from where he had been watching through curtains. He spotted Coryn and the others and turned toward them.

They were all the way in the room now. Day's hands twitched and both men fell. Exactly like the two outside. Fast and like rag dolls. Day didn't bother to try and catch anyone's head this time, and one made a rather sickening crunch as he hit a table on the way down. The woman turned toward them, looking calm.

"Don't move!" Day demanded.

The woman's fingers twitched and a drone appeared from someplace in the ceiling. It sped toward Day. The machine swooped back upward, almost catching LeeAnne on the chin.

Had it been deflected?

Day stepped forward and grabbed the woman's hands.

The drone turned near the ceiling and dove for her and Blessing. Blessing put up his hands in defense of them both. A sickening, searing smell filled the air as the drone dropped something that smoked and stung on his hands.

Blessing yelped.

Day knocked the woman down, physically this time, forcing her to her back on the carpeted floor.

Coryn jumped up at the drone, slapping at it, unable to get close.

LeeAnne grabbed the drone with her still-gloved hand and squeezed. It bucked and hummed, buzzing loudly. Something inside cracked and she opened her hand to reveal pieces that clattered onto the floor.

Blessing rubbed his injured hand on the walls, desperately trying to get rid of whatever hurt.

The palm of LeeAnne's glove smoked and stank, and she ripped her hand out of it.

Day, leaning over the woman, said, "Sink."

Blessing didn't seem to hear him, but Coryn saw an industrial-style sink and tugged him to it, plunging his hand under a stream of cold water.

LeeAnne watched the way they had come in.

Day spoke softly and insistently to the woman, his voice honey with a cold edge. Coryn heard *keys* and *where* and no answer.

She didn't see any sign of Lou. Coryn left Blessing scrubbing his hands violently at the sink and headed toward the man who had been near the window. He had fallen facedown, and she rolled him over, his body heavy and hard to move. She searched his pockets. Nothing.

"It'll be electronic," Day said. "Look for a device."

There was nothing except a clear plastic band around his wrist. She tried to take it off, but it wouldn't slide over his thumb.

Blessing had left the sink and started searching the other man with his good hand, holding the injured one close.

She pulled harder at the bracelet, afraid it might snap. When she let go, the man's arm thudded back onto the floor. "Help me!" she called.

Blessing came over, leaned down, and squeezed the man's fingers so his thumb rotated in toward his palm. The bracelet slid off, and Coryn landed on her butt with the prize skittering across the floor. She rolled and retrieved it and then came up to help Blessing get a similar device off of the other man. He patted the man's pockets and found a small unexplainable square, which he showed her briefly and then palmed.

She went back and checked the man she had been looking over. Nothing like the little square.

She stood, looking around the room. They had come in a door, and so if there were any captives here they weren't that way. Two other doors led away.

Day treated the woman more carefully than he had the obvious thugs He tied both of her hands behind her back with something plastic and helped her lean against a big, overstuffed chair. He looked up from where he seemed to be in quiet conversation with her and nodded toward the far door. "Down there. She says there's seven captives. Start with our three."

Coryn raced in the direction he pointed, Blessing following. They passed two normal household doors but kept going, since they could see that the door at the far end was metal. There was no obvious latch or handle, just a small glass window in the middle, just above waist high. She held the bracelet she'd secured up to the window.

Nothing.

Blessing's good hand dropped down over her shoulder, doing the same thing.

Nothing.

"Move," he whispered. She stepped behind him and to the side, trying to watch their backs as well as see what he was doing.

Blessing held the small cube up to the window.

Nothing.

She pushed hard on the door, thinking maybe it just didn't make a sound when it unlocked.

A high-pitched alarm screeched in her ears.

Blessing cursed.

She muttered at the sound, "Shut up!" but then moved in on Blessing, feeling around the door for anything unusual. There had to be a way to open it. She ran her hands along the wall outside the door.

It felt smooth and freshly painted.

A picture hung on the wall near the door, a small one that looked pretty amateur. A bird. She ripped it off. "There!"

A square hole.

He slid the square device into the square hole.

The shrieking alarm stopped. The door made a soft and satisfying click.

Blessing leaned into it and pushed it open, spilling himself into the room. She followed.

As Coryn stepped through the door, she realized the woman had lied to Day. There must be close to twenty people in the long, high-ceilinged room, maybe more. She spotted Lou and Matchiko in the far corner with Shuska standing in front of them, staring at the group in the doorway, looking ready to kill something or someone.

Coryn's relief died almost at once. Lou was alive, safe, but what were they supposed to do now? Lead twenty-five people out of the building? Let them loose when they could easily overwhelm Day and LeeAnne if they wished them any harm? They shouldn't hurt the people who freed them—but the look on Shuska's face . . .

Coryn swallowed and walked toward Lou, her head high, hoping Lou would meet her eyes. Shuska blocked her way. Lou and Matchiko, and about twenty other people watched. Lou's face was impossible to read, but it wasn't *I'm proud of you!* Not *thank you* or *pleased to see you*, either.

"Did you come to gloat?" Shuska asked. "Why did you get us captured? How did you do it?"

It took a moment to get any words out at all. "I'm here to rescue you, and I didn't betray you." She took a step closer to Shuska and forced her voice to firm up. "You were the one giving the ecobots orders. Not me. I didn't even know we were separated until the drone fight ended. I *still* don't know what happened to you. But if we don't get out of this building, I'll end up captured with you."

"Where's your pet robot? She might have been calling some of the shots."

"She died protecting me."

That made Lou lean forward and look curious.

Blessing spoke softly to some of the other people in the room.

A few people she didn't recognize started gathering belongings.

"What about Toto?" Shuska asked.

"What?"

"You're little dog. Where's your little dog?"

"*Aspen* is with . . . a friend. Safe. Why are you so hostile?" Indeed, Shuska was so big and broad and so angry that she looked exactly like a pissed-off wall. "I never did anything to you."

"Nothing has gone right since you showed up."

"And that's my fault?" She turned her attention to Lou. "Who do you think betrayed you?"

Lou looked at the ground.

"What about your bosses? Someone let people know you were coming, and they had a plan that jailed you. You and everyone else in here. I heard you and Victor yelling at each other, that day I first met LeeAnne. You were in the trees."

Lou stared at her, eyes wide. She swallowed. "Victor was part of it. But he said something that made us think you were, too."

She stopped, curious. "What'd he say?"

"He said you were conveniently here and from the city."

"Didn't we already establish that in the barn?"

Shuska stared at Coryn, still belligerent.

"Look," Coryn said. "I don't know much. But it looks like you got set up to fail. The city seems to have known you were coming. Everybody got caught. Everybody. All the gates. I didn't do that."

For the first time, a small flicker of doubt ruffled the hard edges of Shuska's face.

Coryn nodded at her. "I get it that you're protecting Lou. Good for you. But I'm here to save her. We can debate details after we manage not to get caught here. Just please . . . *please* believe me."

Shuska turned her massive body—far more slowly that Coryn had seen her move before—and asked her cellmates, "What if it's a trap?"

Coryn wanted to scream. She managed a controlled loud voice directed at Lou and Matchiko. "You were completely captive five minutes ago. Now you have an open door. You can come with me or not. But I'm leaving while I'm still free." She met Lou's eyes, saw she still looked confused, and stepped around Shuska. She expected a heavy hand to come down on her back and crush her to the floor, but Shuska let her pass. She stood nose-to-nose with Lou. "I came out here to find you. You saved me. Now I've saved you—at least if we get out of here. So let's go."

Lou glanced toward Shuska before turning back to Coryn, her voice breaking. "How do we know you're not a spy?"

Shuska's obstinace was bigger than her bulk. She was the decision maker. That hadn't been true before, but something had happened here to change things. Coryn stepped close to Shuska, right inside her personal space. She craned her neck so she could look into Shuska's eyes. "Why would I spy on you? Who would I spy on you *for*?"

Shuska swallowed. "The city."

"Do I look like I work for the city? Any city? I just wanted to find my sister and have a family again."

Lou glanced around the room as if there would be an answer painted on the walls. Whatever had happened to her, she didn't have the confidence she'd had Outside on horseback. She looked lost, younger.

Matchiko watched everyone, clearly letting Lou and Shuska work this out. And Coryn. She mostly looked very curious.

Coryn dropped her voice to a whisper and spoke to Lou. "We have to stick together. You and me."

Lou bit her lip, and then she twisted her hands in her hair, and Coryn knew it would be all right. "You're my only family. Let's go."

Lou nodded.

Coryn turned to lead them out. The room was already half empty. Day was gone, and LeeAnne as well, probably leading this time. After all, they knew the way. So she might as well play sweep. Blessing was nowhere to be seen, but knowing him he was making the people in the middle of the line smile and feel like it was a great day. The thought made her want to giggle, and she had to suppress it and stay serious. This was no time for nerves.

The last few people filed out. Shuska tried to go behind her, but Coryn grinned and gestured her ahead. "After you."

Shuska hesitated, but she walked through the door before Coryn. Well, good.

Blessing stood at the top of the stairs, directing people to go down. They were leaving the way they'd come in, and bringing every single captive. It hardly seemed like a safe choice, but what other exits were there?

From the back of the line she couldn't see anything except a mass of heads and shirts bobbing down the stairs in front of her. They filled the stairway with whispers and shuffling feet.

Partway down the second flight of stairs a clog developed, and people stopped going down. Coryn's heart beat faster. What was happening?

"Up!"

"Up!"

Calls became screams, and Coryn turned, bounding back up the last few steps. She slammed into the door that led outside. She nearly fell through as it flew open.

A long flat roof stretched in front of her, complete with wooden picnic tables and round metal tables with perky red umbrellas. Low lighting threw shadows on the concrete floor. Three people sat at the far end, talking quietly. They barely looked up as Coryn, Shuska, Lou, and Matchiko poured through the door and crossed, making room for others to follow them out. Drones buzzed above them, watching without attacking, probably recording.

Coryn glanced around, frantic for an escape route.

She raced for one edge of the building, Shuska for another. The next roof on her side was too far away to jump to. The big woman called out, "Here."

Coryn dashed to her. She was hoping for a different roof to get onto but there was no such thing, merely a rusted black metal staircase that looked like it had been meant for decoration. She wanted Lou in front of her, but she also wanted to test the slender steps first. She glanced behind her. The escapees were still filing onto the roof, clustered by the door. Blessing squeezed through the crowd like a seed popped from a grape.

She gestured him over and pointed down. "Does that look safe?"

"Safer than here," he said. "I'll test it." He clambered over the side of the roof and took three or four steps. "I think it's okay. One at a time, though. Only one at a time."

A drone buzzed down close to them. A news-bot? "Hurry," Matchiko spoke from behind her. "We can't stay here."

The roof was filling up, and the sky thickening with tiny drones.

Lou leaned over the roof beside Coryn and looked down with her. Clever outdoor lights illuminated a neat lawn below them, and a few smaller lights threw light on the metal stairs. Blessing stood at the bottom, frantically waving them down.

Coryn touched her shoulder. "You next. Go."

Lou's lips thinned. "You're the little sister."

"Go. I'll be right behind you."

Lou stared at her, a look of mild disbelief on her face. She still looked shell-shocked, so Coryn leaned into her and practically shouted. "Don't waste time. Go. I'll be right after Matchiko."

Lou nodded and went, moving fast. She made a small jump at the end to land beside Blessing. Matchiko followed, coming down as fast but more gracefully.

Coryn glanced around. Some of the other escapees were on the other side of the roof, with Day and LeeAnne. Day noticed her and waved at her, gesturing for her to go over the side. Clearly he knew the ladder was there. He probably knew exactly where Blessing stood. She reached for the railing. The metal creaked and shivered under her hands, but it stayed stuck to the brick.

"Come on," Blessing called.

She went, her heart pounding. The narrow stairs shuddered under her feet and the wall felt close and rough. She jumped off at the bottom and stumbled, the ground harder than she had expected. Blessing caught her, folded her in his arms, and whispered, "Good."

She smiled. "What happened? Why did we have to go up?"

He shook his head. "I never got close enough to see. I think Day opened the door and didn't like what he saw. He ordered us all back up but he didn't tell me why. There was no time."

"Are we safe here?"

"Probably not."

She glanced up. Shuska was lowering her right leg carefully over the edge of the roof. "She's too heavy," Coryn whispered.

Blessing hugged her tight, looking up. "Maybe she should wait."

"I've never seen her more than a few inches away from Lou and Matchiko."

Shuska rested with both feet over the edge, most of her weight on the stair, her belly to the wall, and her long dark hair blowing in a slight wind.

Three news-bots swarmed her.

CHAPTER FORTY-SEVEN

Coryn held her breath as Shuska hesitated at the top. In the near dark, it was hard to see her expression. If only she'd step back over, stay up there, and Coryn and Lou could go with Blessing. Now that there were news-bots, surely anyone on the roof would be safe enough. But Shuska pushed the rest of the way free from the roof and started down.

The metal staircase shivered and creaked, but it held.

Two drones flew at Shuska, buzzing her head. She swatted one and the other got away.

A news drone hung out of reach, and Shuska glanced at it from time to time as she minced carefully down, a big woman on a small stair, hugging the brick wall with her side and looking down at Lou with a fixed expression on her flat face.

A loud screech drew Coryn's gaze up to the top. Drones pounded the roof. Two more came whipping down toward Shuska, who had made it to the midway point, partway down the middle story, fifteen or twenty feet above their heads. Shuska slapped at the closest drone, overbalancing. The stairs visibly separated from the wall.

The metal and Shuska both moaned.

One of the drones thudded into the big woman's back and she stepped faster, faster.

The stair began to fall *toward* them. Shuska turned, staring down at them, eyes wide, tensing.

"Run!" Blessing screamed at Coryn.

She ducked her head and ran, Lou beside her, Blessing right behind, with Matchiko on his far side.

They turned as soon as they were clear. Shuska rolled across the grass toward them, clear of the stair. She must have jumped. Her cheek had a bleeding cut on it, but she moved well. "Go!" she called out.

Two drones followed her.

Coryn looked around. No one gave them immediate chase. She couldn't see the street from here. "What about the other people? The ones on the roof?"

"Day and LeeAnne have it." Blessing hissed. "Now we stay safe." He pointed. "That way."

He took off toward a hedge that delineated the property line, and she and Lou and Matchiko followed, Shuska behind them.

The hedge turned out to be juniper, or something equally prickly, the trunks close-set and the thin limbs tangled together. They squeezed through, branches grabbing at Coryn's hair. At least the hedge forced the drones up and over.

They emerged on a narrow, quiet street. Blessing hesitated a moment and then shifted to a fast walk like he had a plan. He led them across the street, still dogged by three drones, then two, then one. "Why did they leave?" Coryn asked.

"Remember, our people are busy convincing them that we're no threat."

Lou interrupted. "Blessing? You convinced news-bots that we're no threat while we're cutting through hedges?"

Coryn had started taking the superpowers of the rich and famous for granted. And Lou didn't know Blessing was more than he had seemed Outside. There hadn't been any time to talk. Since there probably was no good answer to Lou's question, she tapped Blessing's shoulder. "Is Day okay?"

"Almost certainly." He jerked a thumb behind them. It was almost completely dark, but the shapes she saw were intimately familiar from the trip up the PV bridge. Three of Julianna's big drones that had provided cover then now hovered over the house. A hovercraft rose up between them.

"So we didn't need to climb down?"

He shrugged and grinned. "How was I to know? Besides, if they go one way, it will be easier for us to hide as we go another way."

Shuska caught up with them. "Where are you taking us?"

"Back Outside, if we're lucky," Blessing told her.

"What about Aspen?" Coryn asked.

"It will be okay."

She didn't know whether or not to believe him. She dropped back to the end of the line and walked behind Lou. This was what mattered most. She realized she had fallen back into the habit of counting on Shuska to be an effective sweep.

Bright pops of rifle fire still startled her from time to time.

Blessing led them to a thin ribbon of park that ran beside the river. She could see the other side of Portland and, to the north, the graceful curve of the PV bridge. An old double-decker bridge crossed the river close to them. Blessing took a path that led them to the bottom deck, which was less than a full bridge and more like a wide path for walkers and bikes. The water below was inky-black, but low lights illuminated the bridge well enough for them to walk across it.

At the other end of the bridge, they followed Blessing down a thin staircase that descended in tight switchbacks. It ended at an empty dock that rocked quietly in the dark. So much had happened it seemed like it should be dawn, but the sky was still dark above them, the winking lights of drones brighter than the stars. The argument about whether or not Coryn had betrayed Lou still hung thick between them all.

"Now what?" Matchiko asked, her voice thin.

A streetlight let Coryn see the bright sparkle in Blessing's eyes as he pointed. The river began a broad, slow curve, and, coming into view, the bright white lights of a boat slid silently toward them. The craft pulled up beside the dock, sloshing water over their feet as it stopped with a slight jerk.

A woman driver sat in the back, her face obscured by a cloth and a hood pulled up over her head. When she looked at them, Coryn recognized Eloise. Of course she was more than a kitchen servant. If Coryn wasn't very careful, she was going to become something else herself. Or maybe that was already happened. She waved to Eloise and hurried to the side of the boat.

Blessing directed Shuska to the front seat, Coryn and Lou to the back two seats closest to Eloise, and put Matchiko and himself in the middle. He stood, his head almost scraping the low canvas roof. The seating separated her and Lou from Shuska. Shuska sat with her legs straight in front of her, her arms crossed over her chest, and glared at Coryn.

"Is Day all right?" Blessing asked Eloise. "LeeAnne?"

"Yes. One of the women you freed fell and twisted an ankle, and one took a drone shot in the shoulder. She's already getting medical care. Everyone else is fine now. They're sitting in a park, surrounded by news-bots."

"Is anyone likely to follow us?" Matchiko asked.

"Not if we leave. The city rejects what it doesn't want. But it would draw attention if we stayed."

"Why are you helping us?" Shuska narrowed her eyes at Eloise. "Who do you work for?"

Eloise kept her composure in the face of the Shuska's challenge. Her faint smile fit her willowy looks, and would have been natural at a garden party. "Someone who befriended your sister."

Lou turned in her seat to stare at Coryn. "You didn't tell me you had rich friends."

Coryn stared at Lou, searching for words, looking from the boat to the bridge above them, and finally at Eloise. "I don't think I really knew until this happened." She glanced at Shuska. "I really can't talk about it now."

Eloise's eyes narrowed, a sign that perhaps that wasn't the best answer. Coryn glanced at Blessing, who had the same warning in his eyes. But then she'd always known not to talk about Julianna. Instinct like breath.

Maybe it was time for a new subject. They had gotten underway, and the boat rocked gently as it cut a sharp path through the nearly still water. Coryn was still groping for meaning. "What about the hackers? Isn't the city under attack?"

"That's why I'm taking you out of it."

"What about Aspen?"

Eloise looked pained. "You'll see him again."

Maybe rich friends took away choices as well as gave them. She settled into her seat as they turned up the Columbia. The east side of Portland sped by on their right, Vancouver on their left, and in front of them just the wide, slow river.

She no longer had her robot. She might not ever see her dog again. But at least she had her sister.

For right now, it would do.

CHAPTER FORTY-EIGHT

Eloise pulled the boat opposite the Camas gate, stopped at the side of an empty dock, and looped a single line around it to keep them fast. Across the river, the red and blue lights of emergency vehicles filled at least half a mile of road, and Coryn could make out figures darting in and out of the various bobbing and still lights. Ambulances left. Ambulances came. At least one ecobot still rested on its side, completely still.

People screamed from time to time, wails of anguish floating across the river and making Coryn shiver.

Lou leaned toward Eloise. "Can you drop us just on the other side of the dome? We'll want to get our horses."

Eloise ignored her question. "We need to talk."

"We need our horses."

Blessing's position near the middle of the boat let him speak to everyone without raising his voice. "Your old job won't be there anymore. You might not even get to keep your identities, or at least you might not want to."

"You can't hide me," Shuska said. "Once people see me, they remember."

Coryn couldn't take her eyes off of the light show around the gate. "I was afraid it was going to be like this when we came in, that we'd be part of killing people. It almost made me sick. But we didn't do this. I want to know who did."

Shuska looked sad as she said, "Perhaps the city needs some pain. It needs to wake."

Two more ambulances arrived and one more took off, the noise causing a delay in the conversation on the boat. Coryn stared at Shuska until the sound died down. "Do you know who is doing this?"

"Of course not."

Coryn glanced back at Eloise, who seemed to be waiting for them to calm down. "Is it the foundations?"

Eloise whispered, her voice barely audible over the susurration of the waves against the boat and the sirens across the river. "I doubt it's that simple. It appears that many previously disparate forces have chosen to work together."

"Will the city be okay?" Coryn asked.

Eloise stared over all of their heads, watching the activity at the gate. "The city is always okay."

Coryn wasn't at all sure the look in her eyes matched her words. "What did you want to talk about?"

Eloise spoke quietly. "You have to make some choices. I can pull forward, through the dome, and let you all out. You'll be on the wrong side of the river, but the Washington side's not safe for you right now. You can cross back at one of the bridges, maybe near The Dalles, maybe the Bridge of the Gods. You can take your chances on your old jobs, but I agree with Blessing that your chances are not good."

Shuska leaned in toward Eloise, putting physical pressure on Blessing and Matchiko, who sat just in front of her. "Who are you and why should we listen to you?"

Eloise leaned toward Shuska, smiling as if she were speaking to a child. "I'm Eloise, and I'm helping you right now. If you challenge me, I'll make sure we don't get through the dome, and you'll end up back where you were, or someplace worse."

"Where are the others?" Lou asked.

Eloise shrugged. "Other people are helping the ones who were held with you. I expect the distractions—" She nodded toward the Camas Gate "—will allow most of them to get away. But we're wasting time. Either I let you off on the far side of the dome, and you can fend for yourselves, or I can get you to Seacouver, where you can keep working on this and maybe expose the worst of the foundations from inside."

Shuska turned her attention from Eloise to Coryn, glaring at her.

Coryn blinked, surprised. They'd get her back into the city? They could do that? As herself?

Did she want to go?

Blessing leaned down and whispered in her ear. "I'll go with you."

Coryn ignored him, watching Lou closely.

"What could we possibly do in the city?" Lou asked.

Eloise answered her. "We know a lot. There's the analytics of the attack." She pointed toward the Camas Gate. "There's what we found on Coryn's wristlet, and far better computing in the city to study it with. There are other people who might help us."

Blessing grinned, using his usual quiet look that suggested it would all be okay. Then he shrugged. "What can we do Outside, anyway, especially now?"

Lou looked down at the ground, avoiding Shuska's gaze, and Coryn's as well.

This indecisive woman wasn't like the sister Coryn had known in the city, and even less like the sister she had known Outside. Maybe Lou needed a PTSD pill, although it was unlikely they had such a thing handy here. Coryn took her hand, and Lou tilted her face sideways to look at her. "I want you to come with me," Coryn said, realizing that she knew her own choice. "I want to help the wild. I see why you love it. Right now, I can do that from Inside more than Outside."

Matchiko spoke up. "I'm not going Inside. Not ever. I want to go back to the ranch. If they won't take us, one of the other ranches will. We have skills."

Shuska grunted. "That's right. Me, too." She stared at the back of Lou's head, since Lou still refused to look up at her.

Blessing grinned, perhaps having decided yet again that it might be a good day to die. At any rate, he waded right back in. "Look, it's hard to get in. It's not hard to get out. Let's go in and see what we can do."

"Lou." Coryn spoke softly. "You have to choose. None of us can compel you."

Lou lifted her head. "I don't want to go back."

"Good." Shuska looked at Eloise. "Take us all out." She glanced at Blessing. "And you can do whatever you want. I don't care."

Lou stood up and looked Shuska in the eye. "No. It's the ranch I don't want to go back to. Someone there sold us out."

Shuska and Matchiko shared a glance.

Lou took Blessing's hand and Coryn's. She looked resolute and sad. "We'll go together."

"I'm not staying Inside," Shuska declared. "I don't have the manners for the city. But I can't lose you."

Lou simply gazed sadly at Shuska.

Shuska turned to Coryn, a hint of vulnerability in her eyes. "Stay with us."

Matchiko rose to touch Lou's cheek, her eyes pleading. "Do you mean this?"

Lou looked as certain as she had that morning in Sirella's, right before she left. "Yes."

Matchiko's voice nearly broke. "I'm sorry."

Eloise clearly didn't want to waste any more time. She held her small hand out and spoke to Blessing, Lou, and Coryn. "Give me your electronics."

As soon as she had all three wristlets in hand, Eloise dropped them into a thick black bag, zipped it up, and put the bag inside of another bag, and that bag in yet another one.

She didn't offer an explanation, but it had to be some kind of shielding. As soon as the bag of bags had been locked into a cubby, Eloise pulled the boat free of the dock and headed east along the river. Coryn expected her to let the other two off shortly after they passed the dome, but Eloise took them for a cold and awkward half-hour trip, dropping Shuska and Matchiko on the Oregon side near Hood Canal.

The moment the boat stopped, Shuska looked at Lou again. "Please go with us. We need you."

As the big woman stared down at her scrawny but hard-boned and strong sister, Coryn felt sure Shuska was near tears. To her relief she didn't cry, not even when Lou took her hand. "I'll find you again someday." She looked at Matchiko. "You, too."

Matchiko leaned in and brushed her lips across Lou's, a feather of a kiss, and then leapt off the boat. Shuska stepped carefully after her, and they scrambled up the bank, disappearing into the woods.

‡ ‡ ‡

As soon as they slid back inside the dome, Eloise handed Coryn, Lou, and Blessing back their electronics. "Hold on," she said. "We've got a flight to catch." She pulled the throttle toward her and the boat sped up.

Lou glanced at her. "Surely the airport is closed."

Eloise grinned. "Not to private planes."

"Oh."

Blessing whooped so loudly Coryn was sure the city would record him. Then he looked a little sheepish. "I like planes." He looked happier than he'd looked all day.

Coryn had never been on a plane. She tried the same sound he had made, leaning into the cold wind and screaming. She didn't sound nearly as good as he did, so she tried again.

Lou looked at them both as if they were crazy.

"Did you know we were going to fly home?" Coryn asked him.

"How would I learn anything? I've been with you."

"You can't communicate via thin air like Day and LeeAnne?"

He laughed. "That's for people who are done with training."

Lou merely looked confused. Clearly, Coryn was going to have to find a way to introduce Julianna to Lou.

The front of the boat rose as Eloise goosed the throttle. Blessing climbed forward to help keep it more level. It only took about five minutes to get to a fancy private dock just east of the 205.

Eloise helped them off, and they walked up the dark dock through squeaking and rattling boats and crossed a well-lit lawn. They went through a gate and around front. To no one's surprise, a car waited for them on the darkened street.

During the ride, Lou looked a little more energized than she had in the boat. At least she looking around curiously. The car pulled into to a private parking lot at Portland International five minutes later.

Eloise led them through a thicket of tied-down planes, moving at such a fast walk Coryn half expected her to break out into a jog. They made a sudden sharp right, heading for a plane that was already warming up, with light spilling out of an open doorway. It wasn't the biggest plane, but close.

Before she could even start up the steps, Aspen barked. Coryn almost ran over Eloise getting into the cabin, where Aspen jumped into her arms. She buried her face in his fur. "Told you I'd be back," she murmured into his fur. It hadn't been a day, but she had thought she wouldn't see him for a long time, or even forever.

In front of her, Eloise climbed into the pilot's seat. Coryn was only surprised for a moment. Maybe Eloise would be hacking the city next.

One seat was already occupied. Coryn grinned as she slid Aspen into the crook of one arm and extended a hand to help Lou up into the fuselage of the plane. "Lou," she said, "Meet Julianna. She's the reason you're free."

Lou looked a little stunned, but she gamely held her hand out. "Thank you."

Blessing climbed in, closed the door, and elbowed past the three women to go sit right behind Eloise.

"You're welcome," Julianna said.

"Lake." Lou drew the word out. "Lake. You're Julianna Lake."

Julianna watched Lou quietly.

Lou glanced at Coryn. "How?" Then back at Julianna. "Did *you* send her to find me?"

Julianna smiled, softly, as if she were addressing a skittish animal. "I sent her today, to get you free. And Blessing, and a few people you may or may not have met. But only because she asked me to. More importantly, she showed me why I had to do it. Your sister loves you very much."

Lou's mouth clamped shut, and she blinked. She sat down in a chair and stared back and forth between Julianna and Coryn.

Julianna continued, "But I did not send her to find you in the first place. That was her doing."

Lou leaned forward in her seat. "How do you know my sister at all?"

Julianna continued in the same quiet, soft-spoken voice, "Blessing met her on the road. He reported meeting her; not that he knew who she was. But when I saw his pictures, I knew who she was. She and I made friends training to run marathons."

Lou sat back. Coryn hadn't explained her obsession with running or talked about Julianna, and Julianna looked too old for marathons until you saw her run.

"It's all true," Coryn said.

The plane's engines began warming up. "Can I get you something to drink?" Julianna asked.

Coryn realized how thirsty she was as soon as Julianna asked.

Blessing had apparently anticipated the request, as he came in with four glasses of water. "Sit down and hold onto these." He waited until they settled, Lou and Coryn close to each other and opposite Julianna before he handed the water around. "We're about to take off."

Coryn had never been in a plane before. She was sure Lou hadn't either. The lights of Portland and Vancouver rushed past in the window as they sped down the runway, and then shrank as they rose above the city. After that, she watched the long ribbon of light that had to be the Interstate 5 Corridor, and the long blue light that was the hyperloop that ran beside it. The lights of small towns glowed all along the interstate, but on either side it was impossible to see anything. Clearly the coast and the rise up toward the Cascade Mountains were part of the wilding.

Aspen sat in her lap, watching her look out the window. Her sister sat in the seat next to her. She was safe and, for the moment, free.

Oh, and happy. She squeezed Aspen tight, and he licked her face.

‡ ‡ ‡

Julianna gave them about fifteen minutes to stare out the windows before she asked, "Did you wonder why I brought Aspen?"

That got Coryn's attention. "No. But I should have."

"We've been tracking Pablo. For some time. That's why I asked you so many questions about him."

Julianna had asked about a lot. "I liked him. Is he important?"

"Here's what we know: he led the silent army *into* Seacouver. They're camping in a park. We think he's a double agent—that he's working for the good of the people he has with him, but he's also reporting information to the city. We don't know why. But we—my network and I—we don't have any direct linkages to him. Remember, I'm not in power anymore; most of my connections are businesses and NGOs these days. Foundations, although not all of them. I'm on a few Boards of Directors. You've met Pablo, and, perhaps even better, you have a dog he knows. You might be able to get close to him."

The exhaustion came crashing back. Coryn tried not to let her voice waver. "I'm going by myself?"

"Of course not. Blessing will be with you."

She swallowed. "What about Lou?"

"She'll be with me."

Lou and Coryn looked at each other. "We don't want to be separated," Coryn said.

"Lou has a reputation that Pablo will know. In the meantime, she knows a lot about the problems in the foundations. I'm going to assign her to work with one of my accountants to go over books. They'll to try to track where money is going. Money drives power drives everything."

Julianna glanced at Coryn. "She'll be safe. I'll attach her as one of my employees, and she'll register as basic plus one, which shouldn't cause any fuss to the city's systems. Even though they detained her in Portland, they never charged her there. It could catch up to her, but I'm sure we have a few days. Both cities are dealing with a little too much chaos to worry about small things right now."

Blessing leaned forward. "Are you sure? Automated systems can operate no matter what human chaos is out there."

Julianna smiled. "But not on their own." She pointed out a window. "If you look, you can see Mount Rainier coming up. At least a little."

It was quite hard to spot in the dark, but Coryn finally made out a big, dark gray mountain with the tiniest slivers of white dusted across the top. If it weren't for the nearly full moon, she probably wouldn't have been able to see it at all. "It's so different up here. Pretty." She'd grown up with the mountain, but it looked different from this angle.

Julianna got up and walked down the short aisle to a spot where some seats had been taken out. "It also means we'll be landing in about twenty minutes. This is a short flight. Even if systems notice Lou, some person would have to act, and no one will be paying attention to minor alerts. We'll be fine for now, and we'll develop a better long-term solution." She started digging through a pile of bags and packs and coats. "Besides, Lou may not want to stay Inside for long."

"Or at all." Lou had a stubborn look on her face. "I don't know much about accounting."

"But you know what's not getting done Outside," Julianna countered, looking pleased as she held up two small packs. "It's the best help you can be right now."

Coryn watched Lou's face as she absorbed Julianna's words and seemed to accept them. But she wasn't done yet. "What about Coryn? Will she be in any danger? This guy—this Pablo—if he's spying for the city he has to be bad."

Julianna set the packs down on the seat beside her and remained standing, so they had to look up at her. "Nothing is as black and white as that comment suggests. There is much good in the city as well as a thing or two to work on. The foundations are making the wilding work, but they're also stealing money from the project. Your hacker friends helped you get into Portland Metro, but they also helped whoever planned the more violent attack after you. They set you up."

Lou paled.

"You put yourself and Coryn in danger when you left, and you took her into danger in Portland. That's what brave young people do." Julianna tossed one of the packs to Blessing. "She'll be in good company. And it's possible that the city is not that safe anyway."

By now, Coryn was used to Julianna's directness, but Lou looked like she'd just been slapped.

"It will be fine," Coryn told her. "And I think Pablo is good. You know how sometimes you can just tell."

"Where will we find Pablo?" Blessing asked.

"He's inside the dome. Most of the silent army entered on the east border, near Issaquah. That's where we'll send you. You'll take bikes." She handed Coryn the other pack. "This has some food and clean clothes."

Coryn frowned. "Does it have some AR gear?"

"The newest. You'll want to practice with it."

That made her feel better. "It's still dark."

"You two will sleep in the plane, at the airport. Lou and I will leave right away, and you'll wait until morning. Eloise will wake you."

Coryn felt itchy about the separation, but she could get around better than Lou in the city, and Julianna would keep her sister safe. "Is Seacouver still under attack?"

A delicate frown marred Julianna's brow as she glanced at her wristlet. "Yes, although the fighting is almost all at the north and south gates. We'll re-key your wristlets so Seacouver sees you as part of the city before you get off. If there's anything you really need to know, I'll send you a text."

"Is that safe?"

"We made it safe. Let me show you how to text me."

Coryn quickly mastered the method, which started with a series of taps in a particular sequence that would be hard to guess.

"Good." Julianna smiled. "We have a lot of control about what happens to your wristlet by now."

Blessing had taken Coryn's wristlet just yesterday. He'd also promised not to lie to her. Coryn frowned at him, the anger that seemed all too ready to rise inside her these days already simmering to life. "Did you lie to me when you took it?"

He didn't bat an eyelash. "I never said we wouldn't improve it."

Coryn stood up and walked to the back of the plane, fuming.

Crying, screaming, or arguing wouldn't help Lou. *I'm just tired*, she told herself firmly. *If I wasn't so tired, I probably wouldn't even be mad.* She repeated it like a mantra until she felt better. By the time they landed, she was back in her seat again, and calm.

As they got close to the ground, Lou took her hand, clutching it tight. The landing was a reverse of the takeoff, lights growing bigger, rushing by, and then slowing. They were in the air, and then on the ground, and she wasn't even entirely certain of the moment they went from one state to the other. Lou let go of her hand, leaned over, and whispered, "Thanks. Stay safe."

"You, too."

In moments, Julianna had Lou off the plane and whisked into a waiting car. "She'll be safe," Eloise said. "If anyone is safe anywhere, it's with Julianna."

CHAPTER FORTY-NINE

Coryn and Blessing approached Issaquah, riding slightly uphill on the elevated Interstate 90 bike trail just before lunchtime. The midmorning sun sent spears of light down through a sky half full of clouds, bright on a cool day that felt perfect for a long ride. The bike was as responsive as the one she'd left behind in the tunnel in Portland Metro, light and flexible and very fast.

Coryn was in love with both the bike and her AR setup, an even lighter and prettier headset than the one she'd sold for traveling supplies. She kept playing with it, trying out setting after setting to keep track of the other bike traffic around her, the news, and her location relative to Blessing, which at the moment was a full quarter-mile ahead of him. It felt good to be ahead, and to be out—for just a moment—on her own.

The lines defining her side of the trail blinked three times then disappeared. Every other rider disappeared. The news scroll stopped running along the bottom right of her glasses. She ripped the lightweight glasses off her face and turned to look behind her.

The riders closest to her were doing the same thing.

She swerved to avoid being hit by a tall drink of bicycle perfection with legs as long as she was tall; he was looking behind him instead of at her. Aspen yipped. The rider only noticed her as he passed. "I'm sorry!" he called back over his shoulder as he almost hit someone else.

"It's okay." She pulled to the side in a full stop, looking back the way she'd come for Blessing. He was only about thirty seconds behind her. "Is the whole system out?" she called to him.

He looked at his wristlet, shook it. "I just got a text a few minutes ago." He stopped next to her, pulled off his bike glove, and started poking at his wrist. "I think it's just the transportation grid."

A smashing sound made her look over the railing at the roadway below. An older self-driving car had slammed into a newer one. "Apparently, it's not just bikes."

Blessing stood beside her and looked down at the town. The elevated road wasn't very high here, but they were twenty feet above the rooflines of the one-and-two-story buildings that spread out below them. Issaquah had a tall business district full of spiraling bridges, but right now they were above the old city, which was dominated by a park and historic architecture.

Every car below them had stopped. The more expensive self-driving cars had avoided obstacles and ended up parked in odd places. The cheaper ones, controlled partly by the system instead of by the cars themselves, had partly failed. Luckily there weren't any steep hills right nearby. "I wonder how bad it is where there's a higher speed limit?" Coryn asked.

"Or how far this goes."

Bikes, people, robots, and dogs had all stopped moving in an orderly fashion. Some raced one way or another and others stopped and stared like they were doing. Blessing tugged his bike glove back on. "Let's go. We still have to find Pablo."

Before they could pull back into the bike traffic, a text flashed across her wrist. *Trans grid down citywide.* She tapped on it to see if there was anything else, and it disappeared entirely. Probably from Julianna.

"Did you see that?"

"Yes." Blessing's smile had gone grim as he pushed off, struggling for two pedal strokes in order to get started on the uphill slope. They took the exit they'd planned, spiraling down off the elevated roadway in a tight vertical donut with mesh walls. The chaos felt visceral. People blocked the bike paths with dogs and children and companion-bots. A teenager grabbed for Coryn's bike, and she kicked him away. After that they went a little faster, even though it felt unsafe.

"Do you know where you're going?" she asked him after it looked like they had made the same turn twice.

"Sort of. South."

She sighed. "Follow me, then."

He laughed and they ended up side by side for about a mile, heading generally south, on a street that must have been almost empty when the grid went down.

They found the Squak Mountain parking lot halfway full of stuck cars and confused and angry people and far calmer robots. They stayed off the lot itself, walking the bikes, sometimes lifting them over rocks or long-downed trees. She let Aspen out to walk close to them, since that seemed better than spilling him out of her pannier.

"Why don't we leave the bikes?" she asked.

"We will. Look for a hidden place."

The forest was pretty thick. Maybe they could put the bikes into trees. "You don't think it's a glitch, do you?"

Her wristlet lit up again. *Threat: Water is next.*

"That answers my question." She tapped it, again a reflex, and again the message disappeared. She glanced at Blessing to make sure he had seen it. His face had lost all of its ease and invisible laughter. "How are we supposed to find Pablo?" she asked. "Ask anyone we see in the woods?"

"We were supposed to have a day or two to find him. I think we'd better be faster than that."

Her wristlet again. *6 Hours*. You'd think Julianna could overhear them. "That's no time at all. Maybe we should just lock the bikes to a tree."

"And then what?" Blessing seemed to be trying to see in all directions at once. "Wander around with Aspen and hope Pablo sees him?"

Neither of them were usually this snappy. She reached out and touched his hand. "It's a good day."

His return smile looked relieved. "All right, let's put the bikes up. I'm tall."

They found a place where he could balance on a rock and she handed him the bikes, which he hung on a cut limb high enough inside of a cedar tree that they probably couldn't be seen unless you were almost under them, looking up. They took their drinking water and a cup for Aspen, a few snacks, and some dog treats. She marked the bikes' location on her wrist map.

"This could fail completely," she said.

He took her hand. "I know. And we can't separate, especially not with systems going down. So keep my hand."

She blushed. "You're silly." But she didn't take her hand out of his. This was becoming a habit. Holding Blessing's hand. "What do we do now? Walk around and call Pablo?" She called out as if for a dog. "P—ablo!"

Blessing grinned. "Let's take some of the main trails and see what we can learn."

They stayed above the parking lot. Looking down into it, she spotted at least ten parked vehicles, including an RV and a converted school bus that looked like it hadn't gone anywhere in a while. The other cars were the more standard all-wheel-drive squares that could start off in any direction.

The crowd in the lot had grown to more than thirty, people and robots.

Last fall's dried leaves crunched under their feet. Cedars, alders, and vine maple crowded them. They startled two rabbits, who hopped quickly under a bush and froze.

This would be a good spot to hide a small army in. There was public to mingle with, forest to obscure numbers, and bathrooms. The army would probably be on foot, just like when Coryn had first seen them. That matched the intelligence Julianna had passed on.

The edge of the weather dome was a few miles away. Issaquah couldn't have more than about a hundred thousand people in it. It wasn't so small that a few strangers would stand out or so big that a group of people unfamiliar with the city could lose each other. A perfect place. Julianna had shown them drone footage of tents in ravines where camping wasn't allowed, and had suggested the tents belonged to Pablo and his people.

Of course, they *knew* little. Julianna had admitted they were operating on hope and educated guesses about where Pablo might be.

They didn't see anyone until they'd been walking about five minutes. They first passed an older woman, slightly bent over, with a small brown dog and an outsized walking stick. They exchanged polite greetings. After they left her behind, Coryn suggested, "We should have warned her that her car won't start."

He shrugged. "Maybe she deserves her last ten minutes of happiness."

"Do you think it's that bad?"

"Did you want to get hit with that walking stick?"

"You get funnier the more danger we're in."

"Not always."

"Yes, you do. You think this is bad."

He stopped and pulled her close to him. "I don't know. But it could be. Think about it. People are stuck now. Fire and police can't get around— even if *their* systems work, the roads are clogged. They probably have rescue robots they can deploy, but still. Any of those people out there who aren't already hungry will get that way."

"I hope Lou is okay."

"She's with Julianna."

Aspen barked to get their attention. Three more hikers were coming down the trail toward them, two women and a man. One of the women looked like she might be in her fifties, and the other two didn't look much older than twenty. The man wore a beard, which wasn't too common in the city, but their clothes looked like they came from a printer. Coryn looked closely, trying to remember the people she'd seen on the road by the doomed caravan weeks ago. The younger woman *did* look a little familiar, but maybe that was just because Coryn wished it were so.

Blessing pasted on his brightest smile. "Hello!"

The man answered, a cool, "Good day."

"We should warn you, the transportation grid is out."

Apparently Blessing didn't think *they* needed ten more minutes of happiness.

"Thanks," the older woman said.

That didn't seem like enough of a reaction. Coryn added, "That means if you have a car, it won't start."

"Okay. Can we pass?"

Blessing held his ground.

Coryn called Aspen up into her arms.

Usually, people tried to pet him, but these people just looked serious, and like they didn't quite know what to do with the couple blocking their path. "We're looking for someone," Blessing said.

"Not any of us." The man stepped in toward Blessing.

Blessing stiffened and held his ground, but he didn't do anything overtly physical. If anything, he just smiled harder as he blocked their way. Should she ask about Pablo?

Aspen barked again, and Coryn looked where he looked. Three more people, all men. She almost yipped with Aspen as she spotted Pablo on the right. He looked like she remembered, round and brown and jovial. He wore black pants and a black vest over a white shirt, and he walked with purpose, his strides long.

That had been easy. She reached for Blessing and pulled him over next to her. "That's him."

The first three hikers looked from her to the ones behind them. "Who?" the man asked.

Pablo stopped in the trail, apparently noticing the small commotion in front of him for the first time. The two men with him stopped also.

Aspen wriggled in Coryn's arms. She knelt and let him go. He raced up to Pablo, his tail wagging fast.

Pablo knelt, opening his arms wide, his face full of joy.

Aspen leapt into his hands and licked his cheeks.

Pablo held him close. "Hello baby. Hello. How did you get out here?" He glanced up, meeting Coryn's gaze. "Where is Lucien? And the others? They've gone silent."

"It's a bit of a story."

He glanced down toward the parking lot. "Then walk with us. I'm almost out of time."

"We know," Blessing said. He thrust his hand toward Pablo. "I'm Blessing. You remember Coryn. We came here looking for you."

Aspen kept assaulting Pablo, wriggling in his arms, his whole body waving like a flag. "Okay, okay." He was almost giggling. "But I can't be distracted right now, not much."

"I only seem to be able to find the people I need when they're too busy," Coryn commented dryly.

Pablo smiled at her, as friendly as she remembered him being in the caravan. "We are busy. But not too busy to find out about good friends. What happened to Lucien?"

What should she do? Well, they didn't have time for tea. "We need help. We're trying to find the hackers that took down the transportation grid. We think we know at least some of them. And we think they plan to take out the water systems. We think you know that, too. At least that's the rumor."

Only then did she remember that he might be a double agent. She wasn't a very good spy at all. What if he was helping people destroy the city?

Pablo looked at her, hesitation clear in his eyes and stance. He glanced up and down his line of people. "Please excuse us for one minute." He stepped off the trail into the woods, clearly expecting Coryn and Blessing to follow. He stopped a few feet away from the trail near a fallen log. "You have thirty seconds to convince me."

Where to start? Coryn swallowed. "We know people who want to protect the city. And the Outside. They're as mad as you are at the city people who are stealing from the wilding, and at the hackers. We were part of the first wave—the peaceful wave—that went in the gates in Vancouver. At Camas. We think we're on the same side. You and us. Peaceful."

"Who is we?" Pablo looked quite dubious. "It must be more than you two."

She stuttered. "I . . . I . . . I can't say. Not without permission. But they knew enough about you to send us here."

She saw that comment meet its mark. Blessing tapped his wristlet, apparently more capable with it than she was. "Here are our last two texts."

Pablo stared. She couldn't see as well—not on the tiny screen—but they had to be the ones about water being next and there being six hours.

Pablo hesitated, closed his eyes, and his face shifted from disbelief to acceptance. He crossed himself in the manner of a Catholic, opened his eyes, and nodded. "We're on the same team. Even though I was never a formal Listener, I learned a lot from them in my ministry. I'm fighting to get these people inside the city and to get them a life. To get them accepted. They want the city to work for them, to be part of it. This is not so much to ask, is it?" He stared at them so hard it gave weight to the question.

Blessing answered him before she could. "All people should have access to the city. But not everyone can have access to Outside."

She wouldn't have said that, but it appeared to have been the right thing to say. "I agree." He smiled. "We are not trying to destroy the city, but I may know who is. We're going to meet them."

"Why?" Blessing asked. "Are you helping them?"

Pablo shook his head. "I am trying to find my flock a safe place to live. That means helping the city be sure that evil is rooted out and the good prevails." He smiled. "Perhaps God will be sure that we are paid with entrance rights."

It amused her that he seemed to be a priest, and to be setting a trap for the hackers using lies. She also found it heartening. She hoped he'd hand Aspen back to her, but he hung onto the dog, and Aspen stared adoringly up at Pablo without even bothering to glance at her.

When they rejoined the group, Pablo said, "They're with us. Trust them." He made no introductions but merely started back down the hill. She and Blessing walked behind him and the dog.

Where did he plan to go with no transportation network?

Once everyone was walking at a decent clip, he dropped back beside the two of them. "So if you find these hackers, what do you plan to do?"

"Stop them?" Blessing suggested.

"Ah."

"We're not alone," Coryn said.

Pablo grunted. "That's good. You are not enough. Perhaps we can help, but that is still not enough."

She laughed. "No. You don't appear to be very well armed."

"Sneaking into the dome carries a jail penalty. Sneaking in with a weapon makes your jail time much longer. Besides, I'm a peaceful man. Now, please tell me about Lucien."

There was no time to be gentle. "He's dead. So is everyone who was in the caravan that day except you and me. We made it to Cle Elum, and I left them there. Two days later, I found them dead farther east along I-90. Someone smashed Lucien's face. I didn't see Liselle, but Paula did, my robot. She saw Liselle's body, and I saw someone wearing her shoes a few days after that." Her voice shook, but not quite as badly as it had when she told Julianna. Maybe the more often she told the story, the easier it would get. "The caravan was all on its side, and it had been looted. That's where I found Aspen. Wandering outside of the caravan."

Pablo looked immensely sad, but not surprised. "I suspected they were gone after I stopped hearing from them. What about the others?"

"Others?"

"Almost all of the Listeners went quiet. There were a lot of them out there."

"I heard that almost all of them were killed. I didn't see any more, though. I didn't ever meet any except the ones I met when I met you, and some around a campfire in Cle Elum."

Pablo ruffled Aspen's fur. "Thanks for taking care of the little guy." He hesitated, meeting her eyes directly. "Did they die fast? Were they tortured?"

"It looked fast. For Lucien, anyway." She swallowed. "I know who killed them. Lucien and Liselle at least. They couldn't have killed all of the Listeners. I'm certain it was a hacker group run by a man named Bartholomew. He was after the plans and things they had in the trailers."

Pablo raised an eyebrow. "Bartholomew? Are you sure?"

"I'm sure."

"How did you know they had plans in the trailers?"

"I looked. While these people were surrounding the caravan. You were

out with them and everyone left me alone. I was curious. I took pictures."
She wished the data was still on her wristlet. She could show him.

"She's telling the truth," Blessing said.

Three more people jogged up behind them, then a few more. Was the whole silent army here?

"Bartholomew works for money. I may know who he is working for."

"I thought he worked for Lou!" She realized Pablo may not know Lou. "For the NGOs. He helped hack the robots."

"The NGOs have enemies. Sometimes they pay better."

"Who?" Blessing asked.

"Returners. A whole nest of them. Worse, Returners with money and ties to the city. That story will have to wait."

They were close enough to the parking lot to hear the babble of frustrated conversation.

She glanced at her wristlet. It had been half an hour since Julianna intimated they had six hours before water went off. She could hardly imagine. *Everything* always worked in the city. The transportation grid was supposed to have *four* backups. Four. And look what had happened. If the water to the park got turned off, it was going to get worse.

"Who's attacking the city?" she asked.

"Maybe the same people who killed Lucien," Pablo replied.

"Bartholomew?"

"Not alone. I think he's the front man." Pablo let out a bitter laugh. "There was even a time I thought he and I agreed on some things. I should have known better. Any man who treats women like cattle is no good."

"Were you in the caravan?" Pablo asked Blessing.

"No," Coryn said. "He never even saw it. But he's seen the pictures I took. We've been trying to figure out what they mean, but I didn't get everything."

Pablo looked puzzled. "I didn't take you for a spy."

The look on his face made her feel like a five-year-old who had been caught in a bad choice. "Lucien asked me to spy. They had me send them pictures. Mostly they wanted to know about ecobots and people."

"So you spied on the spies. Maybe that's what it's come to." He pulled Aspen close to him. "Where's your robot?"

Paula. Her name was Paula. "She died."

"I'm sorry." He handed Aspen back to her. "I wasn't a Listener. I traveled with them because it was safer, and I could find people who needed help. They liked me because I'm good at getting people's trust."

They were almost to the parking lot. Pablo jogged to the front of the line and turned around, holding a hand up to stop the whole group. Blessing looked around, counting. "Thirty-one," he whispered.

Not the whole army then. Not even close.

"Go quietly," Pablo said. "And not all in a line. Look confused. Look angry. We'll all meet at the bus. The door is around the back." He glanced over at Coryn and Blessing. "Coming?"

Blessing glanced down at her.

"Yes!" Coryn replied. "We need ten minutes." She thrust Aspen into his arms. "To get our bikes."

"We can't wait long," Pablo told her.

She and Blessing raced up the trail. They were breathing too hard to talk by the time they reached the cedar. Blessing pulled her bike down first. "Go! Make him wait."

She glanced at her wristlet. It had already been ten minutes. She mounted, urging breathlessly, "Hurry."

"I'm trying." He tugged on his bike. The front wheel had caught on a branch.

She couldn't see the bus from here, but the passing time beat inside of her. She plunged headlong down a nearly vertical drop. Partway down, the front tire slid on a rock and twisted. She got a foot down, kept the bike up, turned. Again. Again.

Below, ahead of her, the blue bus began to move.

It had her dog in it. And her task, her chance to help Julianna.

She hit the bottom with a jarring pop, kicked off, up and over the curb, and started pedaling for speed. Miraculously, the street tires didn't shred.

The bus had been parked near the exit. It had a clear path. It was an old gasoline thing, illegal but unconstrained by the lack of a transportation control system.

She pedaled harder.

The bus's engine belched and rumbled.

Her breath screamed in her lungs.

Coryn spun her feet faster than the bike could react. She frantically added more gears, standing up, going all out.

The bus lurched forward.

She pulled in front of it.

Brakes screeched.

Pablo's voice poured out of the side window. "Hurry."

She stopped at the front door, but Pablo waved her to the back door. Feet pounded behind her, and Blessing grabbed the doorframe, panting.

No bike.

"What happened?"

"I lost the wheel."

"And you left it?"

"I ran." He paused, panting. "I couldn't let you get away." He reached in front of her and practically threw her bike into the bus. Someone caught it and pulled it in. She leapt in and he followed, his weight slamming her against the far seat.

The door shut behind them.

From the driver's seat, Pablo called out, "Nice ride!"

Everyone on the bus clapped for her.

The noisy, stinking bus pulled out of the parking lot, full of people as illegal as it was, on its way—hopefully—to help save the city.

CHAPTER FIFTY

Inside, people jammed the bus. It must have started life as a school bus; it was bare, with small, rock-hard bench seats. Each row held at least two adults. A few had three or four, close together and hugging or piled up so one sat on the laps of two others. Some stood, in spite of the rocking, lurching movement. A few windows were covered with scraps of multicolored cloth, and a long ugly red-and-gray-spotted rug that had once been a hallway runner ran half the length of the bus, threatening to trip people as they transitioned between the carpet and bare metal floor.

Pablo put three people out in front on foot to test routes visually. They waved the bus forward along side streets big enough for it to pass and empty enough for safety. From time to time, a group in the front of the bus argued over three large paper maps.

Coryn kept glancing at her wristlet, which refused to spring to life and give her the information she craved. Blessing stood braced at an uncovered window, watching the strange combination of bikers, walkers, and people who still seemed to believe they could do something with their cars. "The companion robots look like they're helping to keep things calm," he said.

"Of course they are. They're trying to help."

"They're working together."

"They're machines." Funny; she'd always taken offense when people said that about Paula. Had she started to believe Julianna? She realized that she hadn't missed her in those moments today when she would have been handy, like hiding the bikes and getting them back down to the parking lot. She missed her now since she was thinking about her, and when Pablo had asked about her, but she had been okay about it for a lot of the day.

"I've been thinking," she mused. "Since the hackers gave a specific time frame, there must be something they want. A conversation like 'give me a thousand credits in trade for your transportation grid.'"

Blessing stared out the window. His forehead creased. "It's got to be money or power."

"Or they need more time to get their plan in place. I mean, I don't see an army." Unless they were riding with part of one. But surely these *were* the good guys.

"We should have refilled our water bottles back at the park."

He laughed. "We should have." He pulled her close. "We'll be okay."

People on the streets watched the bus lurch by. Some came up to the doors asking to get on, and they were politely turned away. Pablo deployed more people outside to keep strangers from getting too close.

Everyone, even Pablo, climbed off the bus to clear room on a barely blocked ramp onto the interstate. When they got back on, she and Blessing shared a seat near the front. Pablo sat beside them.

"I thought you were driving," Blessing said.

Pablo smiled. "I have a backup for all things." Once again, he took Aspen, and the little dog curled against his chest.

"If you tell us where you are going, we may be able to get more army than you have there."

"That would be good," he said. "I am worried. I don't want these people to die. Many are fighters—they survived Outside. But the city mystifies them."

"We have some fighters," Blessing assured him. "Do you trust us?"

"I trust God to give me what I need."

Coryn reached across the aisle and gave Pablo a brief hug. She had never had much interest in religion, and, after Bartholomew, she'd become decidedly unhappy about it. But Pablo's belief felt sweet, and it worked in her favor. "Where are we going?"

He gave them a destination in Northeast Bellevue, the biggest local downtown outside of Seattle's downtown. If the bus didn't already stick out just because it was moving, it was going to stick out in Bellevue.

"Why there?" Blessing looked genuinely puzzled.

"Bellevue is where the people we need to meet are."

So he wasn't giving them specifics. Well, she couldn't blame him. "And having more people will help you?"

"Yes."

"Do you expect to fight?"

"Not if it can be avoided."

She looked around the bus and thought of Liselle. "I hope you don't have to fight."

Pablo continued down the bus, talking to others. She and Blessing started sending updates to Julianna, each typing a piece of a sentence at a time in order to force more information through the two small screens. "I wish we could talk to her," Coryn said.

"I know."

"I'm going to ask her about Lou."

"Of course you are. Get her this, first."

"Of course I will."

They sent coordinates and times, and got a rather cryptic message back. "Sending help." When they passed it to Pablo, he smiled. "Bless you."

There was more room for the bus on the interstate, although they had to get off twice and physically move cars. Four to eight people gathered around each dead car and shouldered or lifted it to the side, sweating with effort. At least there weren't as many other people here as on the city streets. The morning clouds had burned away and the mid-afternoon sun made the freeway a hot and boring place. Most people had chosen to get off of it.

A bike trail ran beside the freeway here, and it was clogged with people and families heading both directions on foot and on bicycle. Scooters and some hover boards used the trail, too, and a few policemen in uniform had shown up. They were managing to keep a little order, primarily by shouting, but their hold didn't look very secure.

Halfway between Issaquah and Bellevue, Pablo cursed. "Everyone off the bus!"

Stalled cars packed the road ahead, completely blocking every lane. They scrambled off, yelling at each other to group up. They created teams of six. The teams moved the cars at the edge of the pile-up further out, and then the next cars out, slowly creating a single center aisle big enough for the bus.

While Coryn was helping to force a rather big and fancy round car full of windows and almost no good handholds into a tight spot, her wristlet glowed with an incoming message. *Have plan. More in thirty minutes.*

Coryn checked. They had four and a half hours to save the city, or whatever they were doing.

Thirty minutes seemed like a long time. Way too long. Of course, at this rate, it would be thirty minutes before they moved an inch.

She went back to shoving the gaudy car forward. Vehicles looked a lot better in motion than sitting still.

CHAPTER FIFTY-ONE

Coryn and Blessing obeyed orders from Pablo to set the last car down. The sea of cars had been stacked so close to one another that most of the cars wouldn't be able to open their doors. Still, they hadn't damaged anything, and only fifteen minutes had passed.

Coryn, Blessing, and Pablo were the only three not yet on the bus, and Blessing used the quiet moment with Pablo to pass along that they expected a message in about fifteen minutes. He nodded, glancing up the car-strewn roadway. The closer they got to Bellevue, the less passable the road. Pablo looked almost hopeless.

Coryn sympathized. "Maybe we should just get out and walk."

"We might have to. But we have a lot of gear the bus is carrying for us, and which we might need."

Blessing looked the bus over carefully. "Stored under it?"

"In the back."

At least there was a reason for the ridiculous bus, other than just that it could move at all. Maybe all vintage vehicles would be worth a little extra for a while, even after the transportation system worked again.

Surely it would work again.

The lack of nav systems support made her feel exposed and fearful. And she *knew* what was going on. At least, a little. How did the people in the rest of the city who had no clue feel? Surely they were even more scared? Were there enough police and robots and peacekeepers and emergency people to keep everything calm?

She didn't think so. Despair clawed at her, but there was nothing to do with that. Sitting down on the road and feeling her own fears would do no good whatsoever. She took a deep breath and climbed back into the bus.

Aspen leapt into her arms, forcing a smile from her. Although here she was, taking him into danger again. She buried her face in his fur. "Someday," she whispered. "Someday we'll have a nice little apartment, you and me."

He licked her nose.

The bus let out a great gush of black smoke and slid forward again. They made almost a mile before they had to stop again. This time, only two cars had to be moved. Two minutes. The road trended slightly uphill, and the tops of the myriad colorful towers of Bellevue rose all around them, throwing shadows along the foothills. She realized the time ultimatum and sunset were going to be close to each other and glanced back down at the wristlet.

Blessing whispered in her ear. "The half hour is up."

"I know."

The bus stopped. Pablo stood up from the driver's seat, staring forward. "Be prepared," he called back.

"For what?" someone asked.

"There are people."

Coryn and Blessing pushed far enough up to see out the front window. Four people walked their way, quick and sure, and she thought she saw a few more of them, dodging cars. Late afternoon sun haloed the figures so it was hard to see who they were.

"Day!" Blessing called.

Coryn let out a huge sigh of relief. Day. LeeAnne. A few more faces she remembered from Portland. How had *they* gotten here?

It didn't matter.

She practically screeched at Pablo. "Let me out!"

He took one look at her face and opened the door. She handed him Aspen, and practically rammed through the door. Blessing came out with her.

LeeAnne and Day jogged forward to meet them, everyone hugging. She had never hugged Day before; he felt as solid as stone.

They stepped back, and for a moment it felt almost like a party since she was so happy to see them. "What do you need?" Day asked.

"Are there more of you?"

"Of course. Many more. We're just the advance crew."

She dropped her voice to a whisper. "Is Julianna with you?"

"No. But you're to go meet her. I have instructions. We understand you have one bicycle with you."

"How do you know that?"

"We have sensors on them."

That made sense. "We left one behind. It has a broken wheel."

"It's probably in parts by now." LeeAnne grinned. "The sensor is riding around Issaquah, a little randomly."

Blessing laughed.

LeeAnne turned to Coryn. "Julianna wants you to go to her. You've got to get through Bellevue and up into Kirkland. She's heading toward you. With Lou."

That news dispelled some of her despair. Lou. "Good." Mentally, she reviewed the route to Kirkland. She had been there before. She could do it again. "Can I take the 405?"

"Probably." LeeAnne eyed the bus. "Anything would be easier than this."

"No kidding." Coryn held up her hands, displaying the scrapes and scratches she'd collected lifting cars by whatever parts she could manage to hang onto.

"I need to go with her," Blessing said.

"Well, you shouldn't have wrecked your bike," Day teased him.

"No, really. I want to be there."

"We need you here. Julianna has sent me with more data. We need to cover two places to stop the hackers. You're leading the team with Pablo; I'm leading the other. What we're doing matters more." LeeAnne glanced at Coryn. "Sorry. I didn't mean that."

Coryn shrugged. She had never expected to lead an attack team.

Blessing stared at Day with a look of betrayal that would have been comical under other circumstances. "But we always work together."

"You were going to leave me for Coryn."

"That's different."

Day smacked Blessing on the shoulder and handed a piece of paper to Coryn. "Here's a map. Julianna said you should leave Aspen with us."

She wanted to protest, but Aspen would be safer. Maybe. Maybe no one was safe.

She turned back toward the bus, but Blessing beat her to it. "You tell Pablo. I'll get your bike."

"Thanks."

Inside the bus, she relayed her news while she picked Aspen up and clutched him close. He licked her face but was happy enough to jump back into Pablo's arms. "I want him back after this," she said.

He smiled. "You earned him. He would have died out there."

She leaned down to kiss Aspen one more time, and Pablo touched her forehead. "Go with God and be safe."

"You be safe, too."

"Go," he whispered. "There are only three hours and forty-five minutes left before we all get thirsty."

Outside, she found Blessing standing and waiting for her, her bike leaning against his backside, effectively blocking her from it. He held an arm out, a request for a hug.

She smiled and came in toward him, and then he pulled her closer and this time she did tilt her face up, and he did kiss her.

CHAPTER FIFTY-TWO

Coryn tucked her AR glasses down around her neck and swung her leg over the bike, starting off fast. It took five hard minutes to reach the top of the low hill, panting from the cold, no-warm-up start. Many cars still cluttered the road so she could only periodically glance up at the soaring towers of Bellevue.

One bright side to the broken transportation grid was that apparently no one had figured out how to fly drones safely yet, so her view of the stunning architecture was better than usual. All of Bellevue's buildings looked new and bright, sunlight reflecting in a myriad of windows, patio gardens and green roofs and living walls cutting the glare. Wide bridges provided shade for her in a few spots. A waterfall spilled down one residential building, probably fifty stories of water. The spray created a sunbow.

Realizing the waterfall could dry up soon gave her legs more power, and she made it over twenty-five on the flat, her thighs screaming. It felt glorious. Adrenaline raced through her. She was a machine; she was fast; she was flying; she was doing good.

In fifteen minutes, she made the turn onto the 405, and from there it was only fifteen more minutes before she switched roads again, catching the 520 for just a few hundred feet, and discovering a fabulous peekaboo look at the blue waters of Lake Washington. She quickly found a place to stop and lift her bike over the barrier between the road and bike trail. Before she remounted, she consulted her map.

She hopped back on, merging into bike traffic, and exited the 520 bike trail to ride up a short hill and catch the Cross-Kirkland Corridor. Families with children and dogs, tech workers from nearby businesses, and commuters trying to get home without the train choked the corridor. She shouted at them to make way, and generally they did. One older man rushed her, using his weight to try and push her over, but two young men on foot pulled him away from her. She shouted "Thank you!" over her shoulder and kept going.

She thought, perhaps, she heard the old man call out, "I'm sorry!"

After less than a mile on the corridor, she took a side street and headed down a hill to the address printed on her note. She pulled into the driveway less than an hour after she had left the blue bus, Pablo, Blessing, and her dog behind.

Now they only had three hours left.

She knocked on the door.

No one answered.

She double-checked the address. She had the right place. It was a four-story house with breathtaking views of the northern part of the Seattle skyline on the far side of the lake. Across the water, the Bridge of Stars glittered in the late afternoon sun.

She stashed her bike and followed a groomed gravel path along the side of the house. This put her on a ramp leading down to the water and a long floating dock. She walked almost to the end of the dock and peered out over the water. Instead of being full of boats like usual, the lake was nearly empty. Two ducks shepherded five ducklings away from her.

A few boats appeared to be drifting, and, just two houses up the lake, a loose boat bumped repeatedly into a much larger dock, thumping against it with each small wave. It looked empty.

Sailboats did better. A small catamaran glided by close in front of a house, and, to the north, a couple stood on paddle-boards, moving away from her. There wasn't enough wind for any of them to go very fast, but at least they could decide where to go without the transportation grid.

A canoe slid around the empty boat, keeping a respectful distance. "Coryn!"

"Lou!"

She bounced on her feet as the canoe pulled close. The two-seater canoe had deep scratches in its red paint and looked like it might decide to sink any day. Lou sat in the front and Julianna in the back.

Coryn bent down to help them come alongside the open part of the dock. "Now what?" she teased. "I see we've been in bikes and buses and boats today, and airplanes before that. Did you hide some working hover-boards in there?"

Julianna grinned. "Feet. We don't have far to go. But first, we stop for fifteen minutes. We've been paddling from the north end of the lake. We need a break."

"Is this your house?"

"It's a friend's. I know where the key is. She's moved into old folks' care."

Lou looked happy, maybe even a little triumphant. Coryn offered a hand to help her out of the canoe, pleased when she managed not to drop her in the water.

Julianna levered herself easily out onto the dock. She wore a small backpack, which she kept slung over her back. "Help me with the boat." Together, they awkwardly tugged the canoe out of the water and turned it upside down on the dock, dripping, stowing the paddles under it.

Julianna extracted a key fob from a rock that looked so much like all of the other rocks in the garden Coryn would never had picked it out. She let them into the house and Coryn stopped in the foyer and stared. Wood, glass, and stone filled the house. Light poured in through long, thin skylights, making artful stripes on the gleaming stone floor.

"Come help me," Julianna called, as she rummaged through rich, real wood cupboards for reusable water bottles. She found about a dozen, and Coryn and Lou helped Julianna fill them. "That's more than we need," Coryn said.

"Yes, but someone else may need them."

"Do other people in the city know about this? The water?"

Julianna pursed her lips tight, frowning down at the half-filled bottle she held to the tap. "The warnings only just went out. I have no idea what the Public Information people are thinking. This should have been broadcast as soon as the threat came through."

"Did you learn who is doing this?"

"Drink." She handed Coryn a bottle of water. "Follow me." She led them back out to sit on the dock. Coryn lowered herself to the cool, slightly damp surface beside Lou, wondering what else they could be doing. Sitting here surely wasn't going to help anything. She couldn't keep from swinging her feet in short, restless kicks.

Julianna settled to the dock with practiced grace. "I learned a long time ago that when you're in the middle of a maelstrom, you take a few moments to yourself and get centered. You check your assumptions. And then you do what I've been teaching Day and Blessing and everyone else I've hired in the last fifty years to do: you give it up. You accept that all you can do is your best, and you might win or you might not. You might live or you might die. And then you go right on fighting for whatever you need to fight for, only you've got a cleaner heart to fight with." She took a long drink of water and stared out over the lake.

Lou watched Julianna closely, with what looked a bit like hero worship on her face. Curiosity, at the very least.

After what seemed like entirely too much time, Julianna nodded westward. "That's where we need to go. To Seattle."

Coryn straightened, ready to go. "So you found the people who are funding this?"

Julianna glanced at Lou. "Tell her what we found. You helped." She pulled her pack around and opened it.

Lou looked surprised at the request. She took a deep breath and sat up a little straighter. "We found more than one thing. There are two heads of foundations—one is ours, the Lucken Foundation—who are skimming large amounts of money. Enough that *we* would have had twice as much if they hadn't stolen it." Anger leaked out through her words, and they grew more precise and sharp-edged. "We could have saved a few friends of mine, and maybe at least half the wolf packs. We could have had some security." Her face tightened with anger and pride; a trace of the energy she'd left the city with flickered in her eyes. "I can't tell you how many horses and wolves and buffalo they killed by stealing that money. They're sending it back and forth between here and Portland, and each is reporting that it's being used in ways it's not. Because the two cities have separate tax accounting systems, and the cities are too afraid of each other to share. They've been getting away with it for years."

Julianna picked up the narrative. "We've identified the people whose banks and companies seem to be absorbing the money. The accountant I worked with thought it might take years, but we managed to get it done pretty fast." The end of her mouth curled up in a very slight smile. "I have a few crack data people."

"You found this in a few hours?"

"Some of the background information was in datasets we've been watching for years. It doesn't take long to find things once you know where to look. Lou gave us a few threads to pull." Julianna handed Coryn an energy gel and a handful of nuts. "Eat these. You're going to need protein."

Coryn shoved the food in her mouth without tasting it, while Lou elaborated. "I came in at the end. I didn't help much at all. Only for a few hours, figuring out what we should say about what Wilders need and why. I gave them specifics."

"So we're going after these people? Does that have anything to do with the hackers? Did these people pay the hackers?"

Julianna's smile looked quite placid. "There's more. We've found some bankers who handle the money who have skimmed some of it. I knew that was going on, and I already had people looking into it. But I didn't consider it urgent until you showed up. I've been thinking about the wrong things."

"I still don't see the connection to losing water. Pablo told us he thinks the Returners paid Bartholomew more than the foundations."

Lou narrowed her eyes. "So they double-crossed us?"

"They used you to get the compromised ecobots into the city peacefully."

Lou finished a long drink of water. "I heard Paula shot a policeman."

Coryn's stomach tightened. "She was keeping us from getting arrested. But that's not the issue. The attacks that happened while we were rescuing you were violent."

"They killed at least a hundred and seventy-five people in Portland," Julianna said. "There's still some fighting, and they're still finding people. There were fifteen deaths here. Seacouver's a little more sophisticated than Portland. And the geography is different."

"Don't we need to go?" Lou asked.

"You never stop corruption. You daylight it, and you slow it down, over and over and over." Julianna stretched her legs out in front of her and bounced them on the dock. "You can't be a superhero forever. When you get tired, someone takes your place. I wouldn't be doing this if you hadn't run with me."

Coryn could still feel the time ticking along. "So what can we *do*?"

"We can sit still, right now, right here, and take a long deep breath. Make a circle." She held out her hands, palms upward, in a gesture as commanding as it was inviting.

Julianna's hand felt dry in Coryn's. Lou's was supple and damper and stronger. Coryn squeezed it on impulse and felt a quick return squeeze.

"Close your eyes," ordered Julianna.

Coryn wanted to get up and race to Seattle and do something, but she obediently closed her eyes. There was, after all, nothing else to do. Julianna was the one with a plan.

Julianna's voice captured, commanded. "Take a deep breath."

She did.

"Deeper. Breathe deeper into your belly. Breathe all the way down and feel your belly expand until it's full of breath, and then feel it expand even more." She fell silent for a beat or two. "Now let your breath out slowly."

Coryn took three breaths before she felt full on the last one. And far calmer. A soft breeze she hadn't noticed before caressed her face.

Julianna spoke softly. "Now focus. We are determined to achieve our goals with grace and beauty. We are determined to be protectors of the land and of the city, and all of humanity depends on both."

Coryn tried to repeat what Julianna had said silently. She came close.

"Three more breaths. Think about being fierce protectors of the wild and the human."

Three more breaths. Coryn counted. *I am a fierce protector of the wild and the human. I am determined to achieve our goals with grace and beauty. I am a fierce protector . . .*

Julianna used a quietly compelling tone that Coryn had no resistance to. "And now, take a last deep breath, and, on the exhale, let go of any determination to succeed, of any attachment to success. It simply doesn't matter."

Coryn felt the last breath leave slowly; in its place flowed a sense of ease, of lightness, as if she'd shed a burden she hadn't realized she was carrying. Unburdened, and yet . . . deeply connected to both her sister and to Julianna.

"You may open your eyes."

Lou's voice came out a little husky. "Was that a prayer?"

Julianna smiled. "It's a yoga technique. If there was a God, she would have stopped us from killing everything she made years ago." She stood up and brushed dirt from her legs. She reached into her pack one more time and brought out a pair of bright fuchsia running pants and a pair of shoes like the ones she'd printed for Coryn in Portland. "Time for deadlines. Change into these. We leave in one minute." She handed Lou a pair of bike shorts. "And you, put these on."

"Where are we going?" Coryn asked, hoping that this time she'd get an answer.

"To shine a light. That's what you do with corruption. You light it up. You two are going to help me talk to the city."

"What about the hackers?"

Julianna shook her head, as if dismissing the questions. "I delegated that. Day will get it done. Or not. It's no longer ours to worry over."

At least there was a plan. Now to get . . . wherever they were going.

CHAPTER FIFTY-THREE

"Explain to me again why you think a bicycle is easier to ride than a horse?" Lou asked through gritted teeth, pushing the bicycle up a rise on the 520. Julianna and Coryn were, for the moment, walking beside her.

Coryn smiled sweetly. "You have to ride a while to build your quads."

"I haven't ridden a bicycle since before Mom and Dad died."

Julianna looked back from a few feet ahead of them. "I could leave you two here to wait for me. I want your help, but I can do this alone."

Lou put her head down and dug into walking faster. Good.

In just a few moments they were at the top of the rise, and, as Lou climbed back onto the bike, Coryn whispered, "Downhill is definitely easier. If you start to wobble, use your brakes."

"I'll beat you." Lou took off. The bridge was full of empty cars on the long flat section, but the steep part right below them was empty. Lou quickly picked up speed, becoming a bright streak falling quickly down the sunlit bridge in front of them. Julianna and Coryn raced after her. They faced a bright late-afternoon sun, and Coryn had to keep her eyes down to keep from looking directly at it. In spite of the inconvenience of the glare, it felt oddly freeing to be almost the only people on a bridge that was usually choked with transportation of all types.

Coryn's breath rasped in her throat by the time they caught up to Lou near the top of the far rise into the University District. As they flanked her on either side, Julianna panted, "Get off at the next exit and head for the Arboretum."

"What's at the Arboretum?" Coryn asked.

"Tunnels."

Lou looked confused, but Coryn laughed. "You'll see."

The Arboretum was jammed with people. Most of them were calm, although the tone and tenor of some of the voices they heard sounded either panicky or angry. In the distance, someone screamed at someone else in anger.

When they came up beside a small shed near a water reservoir, Julianna said, "Leave the bike."

"Here?"

"Someone can use it."

Lou's eyes widened, but she obeyed, leaning it against a tree.

The shed held the entrance to a well-lit and compact tunnel. The stone floor was uneven in places, but the ceiling had a string of lights in it and a few red emergency buttons as well. In the short distance between the Arboretum and downtown, they took three turns and passed many other people. Julianna stopped and talked to an elderly Asian man for five long minutes, her voice low.

Just before they turned under the Convention Center, about fifteen people sped up as soon as they spotted Julianna. They clapped her on the back and touched her hands, her shoulders, and one tall woman leaned down and kissed her on the cheek.

Julianna barely even slowed down. The small crowd quickly formed a flying oval around all three of them. Even though the crowd carried them forward, it largely ignored Coryn and Lou as everyone focused on Julianna, talking over one another in their hurry to get information to and from her.

Coryn pulled Lou to the back and spoke quietly. "I'm sorry the revolution didn't work out like you thought."

Lou smiled a trifle sheepishly. "I've learned a lot on this trip."

"Like what?"

"Like I should do a better job of keeping in touch with my little sister."

"That was a surprise?"

Lou looked down, then lifted her head and met Coryn's eyes squarely. "It was selfish to leave."

"You said you had to go."

Lou brushed her hair out of her face, hesitating before answering. "I might have killed myself if I stayed here."

"But you won't do that now?"

"Of course not. The buffalo need me."

Coryn laughed. "Maybe that's what wrong with the city. It doesn't need people. At least not specific ones. I wonder if it would run with only robots?"

Lou laughed. "Probably only for a while. The city may not need people, but the robots do. They still break." She grew quiet and then turned a more serious face to Coryn. "I'm going back out, you know."

"Of course you are. The buffalo need you."

"Don't be flip."

"I learned a lot over the last few years, too."

Lou glanced toward Julianna. "I guess you did. And you're better at making friends than I thought you would be."

"You mean I made a good friend? I think that was sheer luck, or else the city just knew I needed something more than Paula."

"So the city doesn't need individuals but it helps them? Even small and low-value people like us?"

Coryn laughed, this time a little bit at herself. There was no way to tell if the city and its myriad systems wanted anything at all. It felt so good to be home, to be back with Julianna, to have Lou beside her. She let her voice get campy, like Blessing often did. "The city is a strange and mysterious being, many-headed—"

"Are you going back out with me?" Lou interrupted.

That was the crux of the problem. She'd found Lou, and she and Lou had learned a lot about each other, and maybe forgiven each other. But that didn't mean Coryn knew what she wanted. There was Blessing. There was the beauty of Outside, the way the horizons and the wildflowers and the rivers had reduced her to dumbstruck awe. In contrast, Seacouver had soaring skyways, fabulous entertainment, and it had Julianna.

Julianna led them out of the tunnels and into the former parking garage for Seattle City Hall, which had been changed over to cheap hosteling for basic-basic students and older people. Coryn had stayed here once in the summer between junior and senior year, although just overnight. It didn't look like it had gotten any better.

It took two elevators to get to the top floor, which had been redesigned as a news location long ago. By Julianna, if the dedication plaque on the outside was right. So they were going to talk to people?

Outside, lights brightened against the dusk.

They were led into a dressing studio, where people handed all three of them into two minute showers, shoved clothes at them, then styled their hair and brushed on makeup. Such a thing had never happened to Coryn, and she found it a little frightening and a lot strange. Her dresser's name was Susan, a nervous, chatty woman with strong hands and short dark hair.

Somehow they were utterly transformed in under twenty minutes.

When Coryn looked in the mirror Susan held for her, she found her hair in long, red curls. She looked far older than she expected. Her face had been covered with thick makeup to hide the sun damage and a few scratches, and her eyes had been painted so they looked darker blue than usual. She'd never seen her lashes or eyebrows so distinctly.

Susan bit at her lip, watching Coryn's reaction closely. All Coryn could get out was, "I barely recognize myself."

"Do you like it?"

"Yes." She didn't, not really. But the small white lie seemed like a fine thing to offer. Susan looked pleased and began cleaning her things up.

Coryn glanced over at Lou to find she had been equally transformed. Her hair had been braided on her head—very similar to the way she had often done it in high school, only this time not a single hair lay amiss.

"Do you have any idea what Julianna's planning?" Coryn asked.

Lou grimaced. "I suspect it has something to do with being all over the evening news."

Coryn glanced down at her wristlet. A half hour left to go before the water utility deadline. "She'd better hurry."

Julianna came up from behind her. "I heard that. Come along. We're doing this together."

"I don't want to be on video!" Coryn protested. She hesitated a moment. "And you look . . . severe." Julianna's long gray hair had been cropped short and turned the slightest bit under. In truth, she looked older, and also—oddly—more familiar.

"That's the idea. This is my old haircut. People will remember it from when I had actual power." She was grinning ear to ear, clearly enjoying herself.

Coryn couldn't even remember the name of the current mayor. It was a man, and people seemed to like him, but it wasn't an election year. Now that she was old enough to vote, she should pay attention to such things.

"Come on." Julianna led them to a door, and then stopped them right in front of it. "Big breath. All together." She took both Coryn's and Lou's hands and inhaled audibly.

Coryn followed, and they all matched on the exhale. She felt stronger after that, braver.

Inside, the room was a large rectangle, with two windowed offices on the far side. The walls were a flat neon green, and a black curtain had been pulled partway along the longest wall. Movable tables sat at odd angles to the length of the room and comfortable black rolling chairs were scattered among the tables. One long wall held multiple cameras, some fixed and others mounted on moveable arms. Four of the people who had met them in the tunnels sat around the room in relaxed, watchful stances. Bodyguards?

A young woman dressed in dark navy blue and wearing her hair up in a tight black bun greeted them with a disingenuous smile as wide as her face. "Julianna. It's such a pleasure to see you again."

"I've never met you," Julianna said, clearly back in her more severe mood. "What have you been telling people about the transportation system?"

The woman swallowed. "The commercial news is reporting this as a hack or a great failure on the part of the city. Nobody is acting like they know. The conspiracy nuts are out in force as well."

Julianna looked grim. "They might be the closest to the truth."

The woman sounded defensive. "We've been saying we're working to get our systems back under control. We know that's true."

Julianna's voice sounded clipped and dismissive. "Please tell the commercial stations we'll begin streaming in five minutes."

"Very well." She turned and stalked toward one of the offices, which had the words *Control Room* scrawled on it in artsy letters. Her posture radiated displeasure with Julianna. She opened the door and turned around. "I'm Rachel, by the way. If you need me, just ask." The door slammed behind her.

"Why'd you make her mad?" Coryn asked.

"I shouldn't have. I'm nervous as hell."

Coryn bit her lip. She'd never heard Julianna admit to being worried about anything. "Why?"

"I always get nervous before a big speech. I used to be brilliant at this, but I might not be anymore." For just a moment she actually looked vulnerable, and a little shaky.

Coryn put a hand on Julianna's arm. "You'll do great."

Julianna's smile was soft and a little wistful. "I only have a ghost of the power I used to have. I have the power of people's memory, and that's short. Half of the city wasn't born yet when I ran it."

"What do you want *us* to do?" Lou asked her.

Julianna led them to a long table with four seats on one side. She pushed one of the seats out of the way. "The cameras in here are automatic."

"I don't want to be on television," Coryn repeated. What if she said something stupid while the whole city listened?

"What do you want us to say?" Lou asked again.

Julianna gave them a look that seemed to demand they each *take a deep breath*. She fiddled with some controls on the table. "Damn it. They've changed some things. I've got to . . . this one?"

Coryn watched the cameras move, pointing them out to Lou. She almost jumped as she realized one had focused on her.

"There!" Julianna said. "I think I've got it figured out."

Rachel came back into the room, her face ashen and her words clipped. "No one will take our stream of you right now. All the water in the city just went off."

CHAPTER FIFTY-FOUR

They all stopped moving when they heard the water was off. Julianna had one hand on the controls but didn't push any buttons. Lou looked stone-faced. Coryn had no idea what to say. They hadn't beaten the hackers. They hadn't even gotten their message out before the water systems went off. After a few breaths, Lou drummed her fingers on the table and a calm settled over Julianna. "Rachel?"

Rachel stopped in the control room doorway and turned, her face expressionless except for an angry twitch in her jaw. "Turn us on anyway," Julianna said, using a voice Coryn couldn't imagine disobeying. "There are auto-feeds, and when a few people realize we're interesting, more will take us. Some people will want to know what we've got to say."

Rachel turned. "Do you have real news?"

Julianna just stared at her. It took about a minute before Rachel stammered, "Okay. Okay. I'll do it."

Julianna's severe look melted into a brief smile. "Thanks. And please turn on the city dashboard. I'll want to watch it. Feel free to break in with other news if you get any everyone needs to know. Just give me a flashing warning and I'll cut over."

Rachel nodded. She looked a little better since the tone in Julianna's voice had softened, but she still didn't quite smile. "Do you want the dashboard broadcast?"

"Can I toggle to it?"

"Top button. The blue one. The red one will blink on when I'm about to override your feed. That's going to happen. It will only blink for ten seconds, and you can pick your timing within there. Otherwise I'll just break in."

"I know how the room works." Julianna's fingers played on top of the buttons without actually pushing anything. "I expect to be joined soon. I'm not sure if he'll come in person or on a channel. Hopefully in person, but he could have trouble getting here. Please keep a channel open."

Who was coming and why wouldn't Julianna say?

Rachel disappeared behind her door again, this time closing it quietly.

A white light came on, and Julianna stared at the central camera. "Hello,

Seacouver. Some of you will remember me." She smiled, a serious but welcoming smile, and let a single breath of time go by. "Let me introduce my friends. I'll be interviewing them a little later, after I share some news that I know you need to hear. But even before that, I know your water is off. I know who turned your water off. That's what I'm about to tell you. It's the same people who turned off the transportation system and who stranded a lot of you in cars and kept you from getting to work, to events, to your kid's school, and worse. But one thing at a time. Quickly, the two young women with me are Lou and Coryn Williams. They've both taught me things I needed to know, and they have information that you want to know." Again, she paused for a moment.

Rachel came out with three glasses of water and set them down. Julianna didn't even glance at her or the water, just at the camera. "First, what we know. The same systems are down throughout the city, and they may be down in Portland Metro as well. Both cities have been under attack by sophisticated hackers. Ecobots were brutally directed at Portland and caused over two hundred and thirty deaths."

Coryn gasped. So many. She'd stared at some of that death, on the water with Eloise, at the Camas Gate.

Julianna gave her a look that reminded her she had a microphone in front of her.

A sound buzzed and the door opened. Julianna raced to the door and held the thin, bent man who had just entered. It took a moment for Coryn to realize he was the former mayor of Vancouver, Canada, the man who had joined Julianna in creating the country-spanning double city.

Seeing Jake surprised and pleased her, like seeing an icon, and she realized with a startled little jerk that she had become accustomed to being in Julianna's presence.

Jake Erlich looked at least ten years older than Julianna. Maybe more. He had grayed, and his cheeks were wrinkled and stained with dark circles under his eyes. He walked slowly and deliberately as he came over and took the fourth chair.

Both of their smiles were so genuine Coryn felt awed by the depth of feeling between them and surprised they could sit five feet away from each other. It felt like they should be touching, like the two of them were a single, connected organism. It was a clue to how the Jake and Lake Team had created Seacouver in the first place.

Julianna gave Jake a tender kiss on his papery cheek, and then she returned her gaze directly to the lens, so natural in front of the cameras that she seemed to embrace them, to turn them into an extension of herself.

Coryn suspected that if she were watching from home she'd feel like Julianna was talking directly to her.

Julianna spoke clearly, radiating confidence. "Jake and I chose to address you together in this emergency. We no longer run the city. We know that. The people who do are busy working to fix this. In the meantime, Jake and I are going to tell you a story together, and then my friends here will corroborate it. You will be the judge of our truth. While we're at it, we'll bring you information about the unfolding crisis as we get it.

"We will begin with a very brief reminder of the great balance. Humanity is continuing to grow. But we have not outgrown our cradle, and in spite of our active space program, in spite of our string of stations, it's very likely that we will need the earth for all of our future. We share our home with many beautiful beings, from birds to butterflies to insects. We have already killed over a third of these beings—at the species level— driven them extinct. That's genocide."

Lou nodded. Coryn thought the word might be a little strong. But then she thought of the wolves Lou kept losing over and over.

"In order to save our civilization and our souls, we enhanced and beautified our cities and began rewilding to preserve the species we had not yet destroyed, and even to return some we had driven to extinction, using DNA and the great genetic arks."

Jake leaned into the table, and the camera swiveled to him. "This is the only way to save humanity, and it's working."

Julianna glanced at the bank of screens next to her, where one of the buttons had started blinking. "Let's take a moment to bring you up to speed on the current news." She pushed the red button.

Images of the transportation gridlock showed on the screen, while a woman's voice spoke: "Many people remain trapped far from their homes. The city of Seacouver assures you work is being done to restore the grid. In the meantime, for those who can make it home on foot, public safety staff and robotic teams have been dispatched to assist along major roadways. Citizens in distress are advised to find the biggest roads that they can."

A still image of a simple faucet showed on the screen. "The city's water system is compromised. Water is not running in many areas. Restoration of water flows is being given the highest priority possible."

As the news story continued for thirty more seconds, Julianna drank water from one of the containers they'd filled and put it under the table.

Lou said, "Who'd have thought you could make an emergency sound boring?"

Julianna glanced at her wristlet. "City news writers. It's meant to keep people calm. It's—" A bell dinged and Julianna looked briefly apologetic as she sat up straight. The moment the recording stopped, she pushed the blue button again and picked the story back up: "We were reviewing the grand bargain made to save the climate. Greed has harmed that work recently, and hatred. So has unfairness, some of it our own fault."

She and Jake glanced at each other, and he nodded. "When we set this up we did it well, but we did not do it perfectly. That was human of us. Some of our enemies—the enemies of all of us in the city—are attacking our borders. These people would betray the balance we've strived for."

Julianna looked grim. "And some of our own people are part of the problem." She started naming names that Coryn had never heard, and describing crimes of finance. Since she didn't appear on the monitor that showed what was live, Coryn scrolled through her wristlet for news. Fourteen people had been left dry on a water ride down near the seawall, and rescue crews were trying to reach them. Hospitals had cancelled elective surgeries. Not that the transportation systems outage didn't self-cancel them anyway. School children sheltered in place.

She suspected it would get worse fast.

The doorbell dinged again. A scuffling followed by a light thump drew her attention to the doorway. It took a second to parse what she saw. Two men dressed in black had entered. They stood with their feet apart and braced, pointing weapons at Julianna and Jake.

Julianna's bodyguards dived for them.

Julianna seemed to recognize one of them. She looked directly at him and said, "No. Not—" and then he fired. Her body shivered, and she slumped out of her chair and rolled onto the floor. There had been no noise from the weapon.

But Coryn screamed.

CHAPTER FIFTY-FIVE

Everyone in the studio seemed to be moving at once. Two bodyguards had been in mid-leap when the shot hit Julianna. One took part of the shot meant for Jake, but nonetheless fell hard enough on the shooter to knock him to the floor.

Jake slammed the door closed and pressed the locking mechanism so no one else could get in.

A bodyguard pushed Coryn down under the table and shielded her, pinning her to the ground. She lost her ability to see anything except one of Julianna's feet and the bulk of the bodyguard who was on top of Julianna.

"Lou!" she screamed.

"Okay!"

Feet scuffled. People grunted. Various short sentences struck her. "Get her off stage."

"Turn off recording."

"Is Jake hit?"

"No."

Jake's voice. "Leave the recording on."

"Here's this one's gun. It's a stunner."

"She's breathing."

The bodyguard's weight shifted, lifted some. Not enough for Coryn to move, but it became easier to breathe.

"Jake's okay."

"Recording on. Get them off the set."

"Clear the room."

Jake's voice again. "Leave me and the girls. Guard the door. Whatever you do, keep the stream going out."

The bodyguard piled off of her. It turned out to be one of the women, a fairly pretty blonde only a few years older than she was. "Are you all right?"

"Sure. Is Julianna okay?"

One of the bodyguards said, "She's going to sleep for a few hours."

Jake leaned over her. "Are you up for a show?"

What could she say? "How's Lou?"

"Who was that?" Lou said. "I'm all right, but who was that?"

"We'll find out," Jake said flatly, his face grim. "We're still on camera. Can you sit up?"

"Sure."

Lou had managed to scramble to a stand, and Jake bowed and held a chair out to her. When he did the same for Coryn, she got a good look at him. His hands shook, but his face showed only control and determination. He whispered, "Take a deep breath."

She nodded and drew in a breath, looking at Lou. Lou nodded, drawing her own breath.

As she let out her breath, stuttering and too fast, two bodyguards picked Julianna up gently and carried her out, and then came back for the shooters. Everyone acted as if such things were normal.

Who were these people?

Nevertheless, she drew another breath, pulling air down as deep as she could and struggling for the calm to hold onto it. As she regained some control, Jake told the audience, "You've been introduced to Coryn and Lou Williams. You've seen all of us attacked and Julianna stunned. She is safe, but she cannot finish this broadcast, so we will." He glanced at Coryn. "Please share some of your background."

Which, she realized, he didn't know. She finished letting the last bit of her centering breath out and pretended she was merely talking to Jake and not to cameras anywhere. "This is home. I grew up in a good family, with my sister, Lou—" She nodded at Lou, who gave her a shaky smile in return. "—but in spite of that, our parents committed suicide. They never fit in here." She couldn't stop, since she might cry if she did. So she talked faster. "After they died we were sent to an orphanage to finish our education. Lou was already a senior, and as soon as she graduated, she left. Maybe Lou should tell that part of the story."

Lou nodded.

Coryn was sweating from the lights and the excitement, and her hands shook whenever she didn't rest them on the table.

Lou started out with her voice low. "I had always been interested in the wilding. My mother hated the city, so I hated it." She glanced at Coryn. "My sister loved it. Maybe she still does. In some ways, I do too. Caring about the wild is loving the city, although the fewer of us who are out there, the better for the land. Julianna was telling you about what she and I discovered, that people—"

Jake cut her off. "Before you get there, what do you love about the Outside?"

Lou went with the redirection. "Everything. It's wild and dangerous and beautiful. You've never seen flowers until you've seen a field of spring wildflowers after a rain, high up in the hills above the river. At night, the stars spill over the sky and wolves and coyotes howl at the Milky Way, and on a good night they will let you join them, and you can have a sort of conversation." She was smiling. "You can howl, and they will howl back, and you can answer." Her face and voice practically glowed, and Coryn felt jealous.

Jake seemed to feel the same way. "That sounds fabulous. Can you talk about the challenges?"

"We get less than half of the resources that we're promised. That means we can't always be sure all of the animals have enough food or safe places or that new babies are tagged. I found a dead bear cub in the woods last spring. It hadn't been tagged, and neither had its mother. We didn't even know they were there! Some idiot shot them both and left them to bleed out." Her voice shook with anger. "We've worked for years to restore grizzlies far enough to create families. That might have been the first cub born in the wild in the Palouse for a hundred years or two hundred. Someone murdered it."

The red light had started blinking.

Lou hadn't seen it. She kept talking. "The city is supposed to provide protection. It does. It provides us. But there are nowhere near enough of us, and there are outlaws everywhere out there. That's who's coming in—"

"Okay." Jake held up a hand to stop her. "On that note, let's stop for another one minute update. I hear the current mayor has something to say." He wasn't sitting exactly where Julianna had been, and he had to reach across to his right to push the button.

The screen came back to life, showing the mayor of Seacouver, a tall brown-skinned man with slightly Asian features and light hair. His name flowed across the bottom of the screen: Mayor Justin Arroya.

Rachel leaned in. "You've got four millions views. All because of the shooting."

The door to the studio banged open as loudly as it had banged closed just after the strangers stunned Julianna.

Coryn froze.

Bartholomew walked through the door, staring right at her and Lou. He wore a white shirt and black pants, with expensive AR gear lining his shoulders and tiny glasses up on his head. He looked less like a creature of the city here than he had Outside.

Behind him, Milan came though, a fresh scar on one cheek and the other cheek marred by a deep purple bruise.

Two other men she recognized from the camp followed him in. One was the man who had guarded her tent and kicked her in the lip, and the other she'd merely seen there, once near the food table and once near the ecobots. They took formal positions off-camera, with their backs to the short wall, weapons visible in their right hands. She couldn't tell if they were stunners or something worse.

Bartholomew sat in the chair Julianna had used. He stank of sweat and smoke, and she scooted a little away from him. Milan tugged on her arm, forcing her up, back-marching her until she stood against the wall opposite the two men, where they could see her but the cameras could not. The monitors showed only Bartholomew, Lou, and, after he sat back down, Milan.

Coryn's breath threatened to strangle her, and her fists clenched. How had he found them? Or was this just the best place to broadcast from? But that was silly. It was a hub, but there had to be more, and anyone could stream to the whole city if they could just get attention. So had he known where to find them?

He began talking. He wasn't addressing them directly, but the city. "We have turned off your transportation grid and your water. We will turn off your power next. We control all of it. All of it."

He sounded so powerful, and so sure of himself.

Jake's thumb smashed against the red button over and over.

Bartholomew paused long enough to pick up Jake's hand and set it on the table a few inches from the controls. He said nothing, probably because of the cameras, but the threat on his face caused Coryn to paste herself further against the wall.

He turned back toward the cameras, stared a little, and said, "We have a series of demands that we have sent to your leadership. While they are contemplating their response, I will share those demands with you.

"You must open the gates to people who live Outside. You must provide a basic income to those of us on the outside of the dome, and you must allow our cities to grow. Those of us who don't want to come into such crowded and horrid deathtraps must be allowed to rebuild on a saner level. There is plenty of land."

"No!" Lou interrupted, her voice loud. "There isn't."

Bartholomew slammed his hand onto the table, palm flat.

Lou stared at his hand as if she were contemplating smashing it with a rock.

Coryn's brain had started to work. What about Blessing and Day and LeeAnne? Had they failed? Pablo?

Was Aspen okay?

Bartholomew turned in his seat to stare at Lou. "You are my ally. Remember that."

"Not in this!" Lou protested. She didn't look at all frightened. She ought to.

What would Julianna do?

Not only did Lou look entirely calm, but she stood up so she was a little taller than Bartholomew. "You helped us get into Portland for a peaceful protest. That's all. We never . . . never would stand for what you are doing now."

Coryn swallowed. She couldn't let Lou take it all. She stepped forward. Jake waved her back.

She ignored him. She came up beside Lou, on the far side of Bartholomew, so the two of them and Jake took one side of the table and the two hackers had the other side. For some reason, she wasn't afraid. She felt good. Her words came out sounding calm, in spite of Bartholomew right next to her and people in the city watching. "Lou would never harm the city. She only wants to save wild things. We all need that." Events started to click into place in her head. Bartholomew only did things he was paid for. "Someone else is paying you. Someone from Outside. They just paid you more than the NGOs."

The two guards had stepped closer. Coryn glanced at the monitor. They were still invisible to the audience. It would be good if they came closer.

Jake was trying to sneak a hand back toward the controls.

She heard a soft click. At first she thought it was a gun, but then she realized she had heard Rachel slide the control room door shut.

Bartholomew glanced at the control room, then the cameras, then at Lou and Coryn. He had nothing like Julianna's calm presence in the room. His gaze stopped and he looked at Lou and smiled broadly. "You paid me." He glanced at Coryn. "That's why I followed you here. So people would know that."

Lou had the presence of mind to look at a camera. "I did pay you. To get us in peacefully."

"You paid me to hack the ecobots. And then to hack the rest." He sounded proud. "The water system, the utilities, transportation. Even the dome."

They had talked about the hacks in the little cabin. Lou and Bartholomew. But only about security. Lou would never have planned any danger to the city! She stepped even closer to Lou, touching her, staring at a camera that had come quite close to them. "Lou came here now, with Julianna and Jake, to talk about the NGOs. The heads of the NGOs."

Bartholomew crossed his arms over his chest. "Who paid me."

"Who locked me up," Lou said. "They locked up all of us who came in peacefully. They did it so you could come in behind us and cause problems."

Milan stood up and circled around them. He stank, too. Coryn looked right at the cameras. "This man is a liar and a hacker. He may have killed people shutting down systems."

One of the men on the wall raised a gun and pointed it at her.

Milan put a hand on her shoulder, forcing her to sit down.

Lou kicked at Milan.

He caught her foot.

She slid it free and turned into him, inside his reach, and stomped on the top of his foot.

Coryn fisted her hand and powered it toward his face.

He grabbed it.

The door slammed open again, catching one of Bartholomew's men in the arm. Day came through, his hands full of small, round things. He did something with them, a movement so fast she wasn't sure she caught it at all. Both guards fell to the ground.

Behind Day, Blessing, LeeAnne, Pablo, and two others crowded into the room. Blessing immediately slid behind Milan, ripping him away from Coryn and throwing him onto the floor. He made a gesture similar to the one Day had, and Milan crumpled to the floor.

Lou and Coryn still stood, as did Bartholomew. They were surrounded. Bartholomew was looking hate at Lou, who smiled up at him. "You are never in charge when you let others run you," she said.

Jake still sat, the only person in the room with anything like Zen on his face. He turned toward the cameras, a reminder to Coryn that they were probably still live. She felt Blessing come up behind her. He slid an arm around her waist, but she slid free, although she stayed close to him. It didn't feel good to be claimed on-screen. She did whisper, "Thank you."

Bartholomew sat heavily, a fierce look on his face. Day stood right behind him, an equally fierce look on his face. Bartholomew was bigger and scruffier, but Day looked like he could take him easily.

The control room door opened, and Rachel stuck her head out. Her face had gone completely white.

Jake smiled at her and raised an eyebrow. "Are we on?"

"Yes."

Jake turned back to Coryn and Lou. "I take it you know our saviors? Are they from the city?"

"They're not." Coryn was still smiling. "They're—I don't know. They're from here, though. From Julianna. That's why Julianna was attacked. They're heroes."

Jake looked right at the camera. "We apologize for that unscheduled interruption. The forces of good seem to have prevailed. We will have more news for you soon on that front. In the meantime, we're going to resume the interview with Lou and Coryn Williams, which was so rudely interrupted. You in the audience won't know this, but the people you just saw win a fight on screen are reportedly friends of these two young ladies." He turned to Coryn. "Can you verify that you know these people?"

"Yes." But that wasn't enough. People would remember Bartholomew's words about Lou. "We rescued Lou and the other original protesters. They were being held by these people." She was sure of that now. They'd seen Milan down there. Sure, he was tied up, but that was probably how he got into the city.

Blessing stepped forward, drawing the attention of one of the cameras. "I can verify Coryn's story. With video." He glanced toward the control room. "Can you stream something?"

In a moment, Rachel stuck her head out. "Send me the address."

Blessing poked at his wristlet. Coryn filled the empty airtime. "Outside is far more dangerous than the city tells us. But you saw today that it's dangerous enough to hurt the city. That's startling. Frightening. And you should remember it."

The red button blinked.

Jake nodded at her.

She smiled at him, and he pressed the button.

Video footage started playing on the monitor. A fast-forwarded clip of them coming in, the small group of protestors that had included her and Lou and Aspen looking insignificant next to huge robots. She drew in a breath when she saw Paula with her, watching over her closely. Aspen looked like a small, fast-moving white dot with legs.

The scenes had clearly been patched together from multiple news-bots. They jumped in time and resolution, with no transitions between them.

She saw herself, Blessing, Day, Paula, and Aspen carried off in one direction. She saw what she hadn't seen; the other ecobot was swarmed with men and women in uniform who ripped Lou and her friends from the top. Shuska fought so hard it took three people to overwhelm her. Day spoke above that scene. "Those are not police. They don't work for the city." The camera zoomed in on faces and on an insignia on the uniforms that she had never seen, a globe with the words "FREE ME" on the top. One of the zoomed-in shots showed Victor's face. Lou gasped.

The video stopped as Lou and the others were marched into the loft and guards placed around and on top of it. Day narrated again. "Three days passed. Then we rescued them." The monitor showed scenes from the approach they'd made, her and Day and Blessing and LeeAnne, and from the top of the roof right after the rescue.

Lou squeezed Coryn's hand.

Day spoke again. "So you see, Lou and her friends were trying to help, to come in and tell you what we are all collectively telling you now. And behind them—" He pointed at Bartholomew, who sat between two guards now. "—behind them, these people came in to do actual damage and to make demands that have nothing in common with the Wilder's goals."

The video stream came to an end.

The control room door banged open, and Rachel proclaimed, "The water's back on. The whole utility is restarting. They're letting it start slow and beginning with the outer neighborhoods. The next news update is being filmed now. It's the mayor. Three minutes."

Five uniformed police came in, and Bartholomew and the three people he'd brought with him were escorted out of the room.

Coryn leaned into Blessing and whispered, "Is Aspen okay?"

"He's with Pablo."

A knot in her middle let go. "Thank you."

Even after it was empty of bad guys, it felt full with Day, Blessing, and LeeAnne in it as well Lou, Coryn, and Jake. Jake turned to the cameras. "I don't know if you could hear Rachel without a microphone, but the water is reportedly back on everywhere. The transportation grid is becoming responsive but it will take a little more patience." He smiled broadly, his voice relaxing into a cadence he seemed to know instinctively. "As you know, transportation is a little bit more complex than water. But the city will restore those systems. While I can't verify it for sure, I would say that the city is out of immediate danger. I'll shortly be turning this broadcast over to the people in current charge of the city, as they will have the most up-to-date news for you. In the meantime, Coryn, Lou, do you have any final words?"

Coryn swallowed. She stared at the camera, her heart racing. "I've now been Inside and Outside. I've seen the view from the Bridge of Stars, and I've seen the first restored herd of buffalo. We need both, and we need to pay attention." Her hands still shook. She closed her fingers into fists to steady them, pressing them against the table. "Attention. Resources. The city is a vibrant, happy place for many. But not for everyone. I talked earlier about my parents' suicide." She reached for Lou's hand, and Lou gave it. "That almost destroyed my family. But we could have been paying attention to each other. We can help each other Inside. And even more important, we can send resources Outside. In here, I was in danger from myself. That's what killed my parents. Lack of self. But out there?" She stood, leaning toward the camera, which zoomed in on her. "I almost died three ways. We live inside a weather dome, and we don't know what the wind howling through a barn and ripping the roof off sounds like. We don't know what starving, angry people do to each other. We don't allow starvation or anger. Not Inside. But we allow it Outside."

Jake stood as well, putting an arm around her. He whispered in her ear, "Enough now." Then he spoke out loud, "Lou?"

Lou stood also, so they all stood together. She held her head up. "Outside is dangerous beyond belief. Friends have died. I have almost died. I have hurt others in order to live. My sister almost died. Coryn is right; you cannot ignore the Outside. If the buffalo herds die again, if the grasses die, if the wolves stop howling, then we all die."

Jake simply said, "Thank you," and pushed the red button to take them off the air.

The three of them hugged, a spontaneous and warm hug that filled Coryn with relief.

CHAPTER FIFTY-SIX

Coryn leaned over the rail on the Bridge of Stars, looking out toward the Olympic Mountains, green and gray this morning and completely bare of the snow. Mount Rainier was also visible, mostly a gray rounded rock, with the barest slivers of glaciers slashing the top. The last of the permanent ice in Washington State was expected to melt in the next few summers.

Her mother's earrings dangled in her ears. Lou stood beside her, her face brightened by the wonder of the view. "I'm so glad you talked me into coming up here."

"Well, you showed me buffalo."

Lou grinned, looking lighter and less worried than Coryn could remember seeing her since before their parents died. "You still haven't answered me," she said. "Are you coming with me? You're still on my books as a wrangler."

Coryn threw her head back and laughed. "I think I'm better on a bicycle than a horse. But I'll be going back and forth. I'm to be part of Julianna's and Jake's Outside-N Foundation."

"Do we really need a new foundation?"

"The Lucken Foundation filed for bankruptcy."

"I kind of figured I'd go somewhere else."

"You can go whoever you want. But now I know that I'd better come see you from time to time. I'll be basic plus three, so I'll have enough money to do it."

"Will you be a little more careful about how you get out to wherever I am?"

Coryn smiled. "I suspect I'll have more company."

"Blessing?"

Coryn shrugged. "I have no idea what will happen between him and me. He's keeping his job as a—competence man, I guess—for Julianna. You might be more likely to see him than I am. I didn't want that work. So I don't even know if I'll see him."

Lou's smile held a bit of mischief. "I bet you will."

"We'll see. I'm not at all sure I want a boyfriend. Ever." Better to just get Lou off the topic entirely. "What about Matchiko? What is that for you?"

Lou grinned. "Like you and Blessing. I don't know."

"I'll race you down the hill."

Lou stopped her with an outstretched hand. "Not yet. Let's stay up here for a while. I might not get back for a few years. Or ever."

Coryn was content with that. A perfect blue sky arched above them. Sailboats plied the Sound, ferries ran on two distinct routes, and maybe if they watched long enough they'd see a pod of orcas.

ACKNOWLEDGMENTS

The first people to thank are family. A writer's family has to put up with a spaced-out person who is often lost in another world entirely, who barely notices anything around them. Thanks to Toni and Katie, and even to the dogs (Nixie, Cricket, and Gryffin), all of whom lose some of me so that I can do this.

Thanks to my editor, Rene Sears, for acquiring and believing in this book. Thanks to my agent, Eleanor Wood. Special thanks to Sheila Stewart for a hard copyedit. This book is better because of Rene and Sheila, and any remaining awkward sentences or wrong words are mine.

Thanks also to all of my first readers. That includes my father, my friend Darragh Metzger, my friend John Pitts, and one of my oldest friends, Gisele Peterson.

Thanks also to people whose ideas contributed in small ways to the story and world I built here. I don't think the end result came out anything like their original ideas, but thanks to Karl Schroeder and Kim Stanley Robinson for making me think of wilding, and to futurist Gray Scott for the idea of the ecobots (I'm sure his ecobots are much sleeker). Thanks also to a number of authors whose nonfiction informed this book. The most influential of these was E. O. Wilson's *Half-Earth*, which I read shortly after I started this book, and which gave me a good framework in which to place ideas.

This book was written during my first three semesters at the Stonecoast MFA in Creative Writing. It wasn't workshopped there (I was busy writing poetry), but I hope being there infused it with some of the creative energy and community of that program. Thanks to all of the faculty and administration—there are too many of you to name, but some of your advice about writing social justice work and writing good sentences stuck in my head. Hopefully some of that also came through onto the page.

Thanks most of all to people who read my work, review my work, talk about it, and who send me messages. All of those things matter greatly to me and convince me I may be writing into a conversation and not into a void.

ABOUT THE AUTHOR

Brenda Cooper is the author of the Glittering Edge duology, *Edge of Dark* and *Spear of Light*, the Ruby's Song duology, *The Creative Fire* and *The Diamond Deep*, and the Silver Ship series. *The Silver Ship and the Sea* was selected by *Booklist* as one of the top ten 2007 adult books for youth to read and won an Endeavour award. The other books in the series are *Reading the Wind* and *Wings of Creation*. *Edge of Dark* was a finalist for the P. K. Dick Award and won the Endeavour Award. She is the author of *Mayan December* and has collaborated with Larry Niven (*Building Harlequin's Moon*).

Photo by Toni Cramer

Brenda is a working futurist and a technology professional with a passionate interest in the environment.